ALSO BY K. M. WARFIELD

Scales and Stingers (Heroes of Avoch Book 1)

Shield and Scepter (Heroes of Avoch Book 2)

SWORD AND SOUL

SWORD AND SOUL

K. M. WARFIELD

Published in the United States by Creative James Media.

www.creativejamesmedia.com

978-1-956183-66-5 (trade paperback)

First U.S. Edition 2024

For my chosen family.
You know who you are.

ONE

Thia reached up and pulled the hood of her coat over her head. The cold rain had picked up, switching from a simple mist to something far more annoying. "How much farther to Solace?" she asked.

"We'll be there tonight," Jinaari said.

Thia nodded, shifting in her saddle. Three weeks since they left Cirrain and her muscles were almost okay with riding. Almost. A few still protested, like now. Peering up into the clouds, she sighed. The sun was up there . . . somewhere . . . but they hadn't seen it for days. Just varying shades of gray.

"At least it's not snowing," Caelynn said as she rode next to her.

"There is that," she said. "I wonder if we'll go past Tanisal. We're heading south, after all."

"We'll ride past," Jinaari said, "but I don't plan to go into the ruins. It's east of Solace, about a day's ride."

"Gnat not live in Ghost City," the cobalus said from his seat in front of Adam.

"No reason to go, then. Not unless you think of one." Jinaari looked over his shoulder at her.

Thia glanced at Adam and kept her voice light. "Not unless we want to hunt some spiders."

The warlock's head snapped around, and he looked at her in surprise. "Thia, I'm sorry for that. It's just that I had to know."

"I'm teasing you, Adam. I'm good with leaving them alone unless we have to do something about them. The city is theirs."

"Someone will have to deal with the nest eventually, Thia," Jinaari looked back at the road. "It was larger than most, and that attack was coordinated. With a colony that size, food will run scarce and they'll move to farms. Cows, sheep, and people would die needlessly."

Thia urged her horse forward and pulled up next to Jinaari. "If it's going to be a problem later, why not take care of it now? We'll be close enough." She kept her voice low. "Why leave it for others? Aren't we supposed to be killing monsters, defeating evil?"

"Because Gnat makes my teeth itch," he said, glancing her way. "I know there's a reason he's here. I have no idea what he's like during a fight, though."

Her tone turned serious. "You don't trust him yet. Is that it?"

He nodded. "I have to watch him instead of knowing he'll do what he needs to do."

"Taking out the nest would do that, and it would be an easy task for us. Why not deal with it now, when they're dormant?"

He glanced at her, a puzzled expression on his face. "When did you learn the habits of giant spiders?"

"I got restless waiting for Samil to bring you to us, so I found the library. Adam had told me everything, and my stubborn nature wanted to know what could've happened if things had gone bad."

"Thia . . ." he began to say.

"Don't." She held up her hand, cutting off what he was going to tell her. "I needed to know, Jinaari. You weren't there. It took my mind off of where you were, what you were going through. Those thoughts were far worse." She smiled at him, changing her tone to something lighthearted. "Did I make your teeth itch when you found out you'd be babysitting me?"

"No," he said, "but I did wonder how long it would be before you complained about something. A blister on your foot, the weather, or that you broke a nail. That was before I learned how stubborn you are."

"It's your arrogance. I was determined to make you see I wasn't what you expected."

"You proved that to me on the docks, when Alesso grabbed you. And then when you healed me on the ship. By the time we were put ashore, any ideas about you I'd formed when we first met were gone."

"That I was Fallen, and therefore unworthy of your trust?"

He shrugged. "To a small degree, yes. I was surprised when I saw your eyes. But Garret and Keroys both said you were to come, so I wasn't going to argue." He smiled at her. "Dare I ask what your first impression of me was?"

"I was confused. I didn't know why I was summoned to begin with. When I saw the other paladins outside the office, I thought I was needed to bless a journey in some way. When Father Philip said I was leaving with you," she paused, "I didn't know what to think. I saw your reaction when you looked at my eyes, Jinaari. I wasn't sure I'd be safe, to be honest."

"What changed your mind?"

"You did, when you told me that my actions showed you what you needed to know. After I said I was raised on the surface, that Papa was human, you stopped focusing on my Fallen heritage. Outside of Father Philip, no one had ever done that." Her mind searched for the memory. "I think," she said, "you'd asked me how I came to worship Keroys when Lolc Aon never allowed that in Byd Cudd. I explained I'd never lived there and there was a shift in you. You were still insufferably arrogant, but that's when I started to realize you weren't going to intentionally harm me.

"Later, when we found Adam and Caelynn, I heard him ask about me. You didn't tell him anything I'd told you, just said he needed to ask me himself. I think that was the first time I'd met someone who wasn't willing to talk about me behind my back since Papa died." She felt a tickle at the back of her throat and began to cough.

"You okay?"

"Just some dust from the road," she replied. Reaching down, she unhooked the waterskin and uncorked it.

"It's raining, Thia. There's no dust."

Swallowing the water, she resealed it. "Good point. Must've been something else, then."

He looked at her, his dark eyes concerned. "Let's pick up the pace," he said, raising his voice. "A warm, dry inn will do us all some good."

"I'm fine," she said. "You don't need to babysit me."

"Maybe my socks are wet," he said, teasing her.

Thia snorted. "You're more likely to rust in that suit of armor."

"I'm just glad Samil wasn't wearing my helm when you dented his skull. That would've taken weeks to get hammered out."

His suit had been returned by Agrana before the army went back to Dragonspire. *One more step in repairing the relationship between him and his mother*, she thought. *Small to some, but it meant something to him.*

An hour later, the town came into view. The rain had turned into a steady downpour, and Thia was glad to see the small collection of buildings. Jinaari led them down a wide, muddy street. A few residents, shopkeepers for the most part, stood on covered walkways and watched them. "Are strangers so odd here?" Thia asked.

"They shouldn't be. It's on the main road," Adam said.

"Then why are they staring at us?"

He smiled. "Probably because we've done some amazing stuff and word's gotten around."

Jinaari held up his hand and she stopped her horse. "Thia, come up here."

She urged her mount forward. "What is it?"

He pointed to a small group of well-dressed people standing in the road. "The council wants to meet us."

"Why us?" she asked, puzzled.

He looked at her, pointing toward her waist. "Because it's not often the Shield and Scepter show up in areas like this."

"Oh," she said. "I forgot. Do you think word has reached them already?"

"Elizabeth sent out messages, with Mother's help, to make sure everyone knew there'd been a change. It's possible some people from either army came from here and witnessed what you did first hand. I don't know of any other reason why they'd be out in this downpour. Come on," he said, "we need to say hello."

Thia sat up straighter in her saddle and kept her horse even with his. The two men and one woman began to bow when they approached. "Please, don't," Thia told them. "It's miserable out here, and the Shield and I don't require such gestures."

"Welcome to Solace," one of the men said. Rainwater dripped from the wide brim of his hat. "What do the Shield and Scepter require of our small village?"

"We're only looking for an inn for tonight. Someplace where our horses will be tended to, the beds are comfortable, and the food hot. Can you recommend one?" Jinaari asked.

"Of course," the other man stammered. "The Black Cat is just there," he turned, pointing to a well-built two-story building. "The stables are in the back. Mistress Jala here runs the kitchen. I'm certain you'll find the food satisfactory." he gestured to the woman at his side. Her round face beaming beneath the colorful shawl she wore to try and keep the rain off her head. Judging by the way it dripped down the front of her brown dress, it wasn't helping.

"We would be honored if you'd join us at our meal," Jinaari said.

Thia started, darting a quick glance at him. *I'll ask later.*

"Of course. Once you're settled, Shield, just let us know. We'll await your summons." Mistress Jala said.

"Until then," Jinaari said as his heels clicked on the flanks of his horse, urging it forward. Thia followed suit, knowing the others would be right behind them. The sooner she got out of the rain and into a warm room, the better she'd feel.

The gate to the stables came into view and several young men came running out to take the reins of their horses. Thia waited until they were under shelter before she dismounted. Her legs ached. Reaching up, she untied her pack. A hand grabbed it before she could sling it over her shoulder. "Pardon, Scepter. I didn't mean to startle you." The young girl had wide, green eyes and red hair pinned up in braids. "Mistress Jala has others taking up water for the baths. I'm to get your things inside."

Thia went to protest as the girl ran off. "Don't," Jinaari said.

"Rule number one?"

He nodded. "We're likely the closest thing to nobility, or royalty, they've ever seen. Don't be surprised if any number of grievances are brought to our attention during dinner."

"Is that why you invited them to eat with us?" She followed him down a narrow, covered walkway that led into the inn. Water ran over the side of the roof, splashing into puddles in the mud.

"Yes," Jinaari said. "I'd rather get them out now, take care of anything they think we need to decide for them, than have to stay here for days while they put together a list. Though," he looked at the torrent of rain that fell, "we may be here for more than one night. Riding in this could injure the horses."

Thia didn't argue with him. While her coat kept her warm and dry, she was tired. They'd been riding for three weeks, camping on the side of the road. "A few days with something thicker than my sleeping pad between me and the ground would be nice."

"What's wrong? You've never complained about camping before," he said, his face unreadable.

"I'm fine," she said. "Just tired. The weather's not exactly cheerful."

He opened the door to the inn, and a blast of warm air welcomed her. "After you," he said, gesturing her forward. As she passed, he muttered, "I'm still your protector, Thia. If I say we stay, we stay. Don't fight me."

Thia walked through the opening. The interior was well kept. A large fireplace, with a roaring fire, dominated a wall at one end. The light bounced off a half dozen circular tables of polished wood. Most had a few people sitting in chairs, eating or drinking. As she entered, their heads turned toward her. Chairs were scraped against the wood floor as two men rose. They stared at her, and she shifted her stance. She'd seen the hatred before. "We're going to have a problem," she murmured to Adam as he walked up to her.

The larger of the men spat in her direction. "Solace is a good town," he said. "We don't want no Godsforsaken Fallen scum here!"

"Hush, Bryant!" Mistress Jala strode toward the pair. "That's the Scepter you're talking about! The Daughter of Keroys!"

Bryant turned toward her. "You seen that 'Mark' she says she has? The Scepter's been lost for centuries. Ain't no way Silas or any of the other Gods would let some Fallen witch carry it. It's fake, I'm tellin' you."

"The letter came from the Queen— both of them—and had the royal seal." She stared him down. "And my own boy was there when the Scepter took down the warlock! I don't need to see more proof! I know! Either you behave yourself or you and your friends can eat elsewhere until you can!"

Thia stepped forward and felt Jinaari's hand on her arm. "I don't recommend that," he said.

Reaching down, she raised his hand and moved it away. "I'm supposed to change minds like theirs," she said. "We won't do that with a sword." She looked at the two men as she walked toward them. "What grievance would you put toward the Shield and Scepter?"

Both started, visibly surprised at her words. "I ain't talking to no Fallen witch!" Bryant growled.

Thia shrugged but didn't look away. "It's probably a good thing I'm part human, then." She stopped within arm's reach of them. Both were taller than she was and could knock her out cold with a single blow. *Don't show them any fear. Stay calm!* Carefully, she removed her gloves while she stared at Bryant. "You want proof I'm Marked? Later on, the Shield," she gestured back toward Jinaari, "and I will be down here, ready to hear what problems Solace and its citizens have. If there's any we can help with, we will. I will make it so any who want to see the Mark at that time can. Until then," she finished pulling off her gloves and let the sparks be seen, "will this do?" Holding up both hands, she watched his face.

"Blimey, Bryant," the other man said, awestruck. "I reckon none but the Gods or one they Marked can do stuff like that."

"I ask again; What grievance would you put before the Shield and Scepter?" She stared at him, refusing to back down. *There's got to be a reason behind his anger.*

He snorted, then turned away. "Any grievance I have, witch, will be told to the Shield. No woman, Fallen or otherwise, is going to make anything right." Without another word, he shoved open the door to the inn and left. His friend quickly followed.

"I'm sorry about them, Scepter," Mistress Jala said, her words coming out in a rushed tumble. "Bryant's not been himself for several years. Used to be all nice and now he's full of hate."

"What happened?"

"He was in love with a young woman, but she spurned him. A week later, she disappeared. I went to Cirrain a year ago and saw her. She'd married herself a blacksmith, was raising a family. Bryant never accepted that she'd refused him, so he tells people that she was taken by your people." Jala said.

"They're not 'my people,' Jala. Not really." Thia glanced back at her friends. Caelynn and Adam stood on the staircase, waiting for her. Jinaari leaned against the newel post, his face impassive. "We're going upstairs, get cleaned up. Will you and the other Council members be ready to talk with us when we're done?"

"Of course! Soon as you're ready, Scepter." The older woman curtsied.

Turning around, she walked to the staircase. "All done?" Jinaari asked as she passed him.

"For now, I think." She saw him turn and start following her up the stairs.

"Good," he said behind her. "We'll talk up there."

Nodding, she followed Caelynn and Adam up to the

second story. A young woman stood in the hallway. "Mistress Jala said to give you the best rooms," she said as she gestured to doors on each side of her. "These will each sleep two. We don't have any that are larger." She glanced at Gnat. "I'll see if we can find a cot or something for him."

Adam glanced over his shoulder past Thia, then turned back toward the woman. "I'm sure they're fine," he said, holding out his hand. "I'll take the keys."

She handed them over, then curtsied before running to a second staircase at the end of the hallway. *It probably leads to the kitchen,* Thia thought. *Less than a year ago, I wouldn't have noticed it or cared where it went. Now, I want to know the exits we might need to use. Or where others might come at us from.*

"Thia," Jinaari's voice brought her attention back to where they were. "You and Caelynn are in here," he pointed to an open door. "Adam, Gnat, and I will take the one across the hall. Get cleaned up. Soon as everyone's ready, we'll go down and eat."

Nodding, Thia followed Caelynn into the room. It wasn't large, but it was comfortable. Two small beds, piled high with blankets, sat against one wall. In front of the hearth were a pair of copper bathtubs, filled with steaming water. Caelynn moved her pack on the bed closest to the door. "I don't know about you," she said as she stretched, "but that bath is one of the best things I've seen in weeks."

Thia began to unbutton her coat. "I'd love to stay in there until the water got cold, but we can't. Jinaari invited the council to talk with us during dinner. He wants to find out what they need from us, officially. That way we can plan when we leave."

"The storm's not going to go away overnight," Caelynn said as she pulled her tunic over her head. "And we're dry here. I'd rather stay a few days than ride for a week in the rain."

"I think that's what'll happen," Thia replied as she began

to pull the chain mail shirt up her body. "I've seen that look on Jinaari's face before. He's worried about something."

"Any idea what?" Caelynn asked as she lowered herself into one of the tubs.

Thia finished undressing, folding the clothes neatly on a chair. "I don't think it's anything here in town," she said.

"Then what?"

Walking across the room, she got into the other tub. The warm water chased the chill from her skin, seeping into her tired muscles. Picking up a bar of soap, she said, "Me, probably. Though I don't know why. If I was getting sick, I'd know it and just heal myself."

"You can do that?"

"Yes, it's one of the first lessons we were taught at the cloister." She grinned at her friend. "I've kept watch on all of us. Adam's been fine, but Jinaari picked up a virus. I healed him while we rode. He never knew he was sick."

Caelynn laughed. "That was sneaky of you."

Thia slid down, submerging her hair, and came back up. Working the soap through her scalp, she said, "Yes, but it was better in my mind than waiting for him to admit he was sick. Or argue with me about doing the healing."

"He does tend to say he's fine, even when he's bleeding." The other woman looked at her, "What happened with the locals?"

She briskly scrubbed her arm with a rough sponge. "Nothing that hasn't happened to me before. People see my eyes and instantly think I'm something evil. Changing their minds will take time. I'm not sure the Thahion can integrate in the outlying areas as easily as they'll be able to in Almair. Even there, the prejudices run deep." Thia sighed. "No one knows what drove Lolc Aon underground, taking her people with her. If they'd stayed on the surface, would things have been different? There are so many similarities between your people and the Thahion, Caelynn. Both have distinctive features. You have your hair; I have my eyes. Yet your people are accepted, welcomed. No one's ever reached for a weapon simply because you walked into a tavern and started to play." She tried to keep her voice neutral but failed. The bitterness came out.

"Thia," Caelynn's voice was insistent, "you're not responsible for what other people think. I've never met anyone like you, and that has nothing to do with the wench who birthed you. You're my sister, and I'll shove my fist into the throat of anyone who dares question that!"

"Thank you," she said, smiling, "but that really won't make a difference and we both know it." She sighed. "I'm so tired of fighting just to prove I'm not what they assume I am." Pressing her fingertips to her forehead, she closed her eyes. *Why am I so tired?* "I'm getting ready. The sooner we eat, meet with the council, the faster we can make a plan." Thia stood, trying to keep the water from splashing onto the floor. Grabbing a towel, she wrapped it around her body before stepping out of the tub.

As she rubbed the rough cloth over herself, she heard Caelynn get out of the second bath. The fire added warmth to the room, but it wasn't much. Diving for her pack, Thia brought out the gray dress with the cut out back and began to put it on.

"You sure you want something that formal tonight?"

"I have to," Thia said as she pulled the fabric over her hips. "We must be the Shield and Scepter down there. Plus, I promised the pair who didn't like me I'd make sure anyone who wanted to see the Mark could. This is the easiest way."

"The sparks weren't enough for them?"

Thia shrugged, then dug back into her bag. The boots she rode in were covered with mud. Pulling out a pair made of soft leather, she said, "I think it did for one of them. The bigger one will need something more concrete he can't dispute. Or Jinaari's word. He said something about any grievance he had would be for the Shield's ears or such." Once her feet were in the clean shoes, she picked up the other pair and placed them closer to the fire.

"Where do you want this?"

Turning around, she saw Caelynn holding up her riding tunic. "I'll take care of it," she said.

Caelynn pulled the fabric back and shook her head. "No. This was what we agreed to, remember? That I was your attendant, and Adam was Jinaari's. At least, in places like this."

"Caelynn," Thia said, exasperated, "I'm perfectly capable of taking care of my own laundry! No one else is here to know!"

"Put it on the chair, over by the fire," Jinaari said from the doorway.

Thia crossed her arms, throwing him a dirty look, while Caelynn giggled. "We're not in public," she growled.

He entered the room, followed by Gnat and Adam. "No," he said once the door was closed, "but it's a new location. Adam?"

The crystal in the warlock's staff flared briefly. "We're good."

"We go down, eat dinner. Let the council and locals tell us if there's any problems they need us to deal with. I doubt there will be many, but we need to hear them if there are. Caelynn," Jinaari continued, "you and Adam watch the room for anyone who seems hostile. And keep an eye on Gnat. We've already had issues with a couple of men. They've had time to complain to friends now, so there may be more in the room. Thia," he looked at her, "I'll leave the healing requests to you. Let me field any other questions."

"Why?" she asked.

"Why what?"

"Why can't I help with anything else?"

"Until the man you stared down earlier airs his grievances, I'm going to be cautious. I don't trust him farther than I could throw him, though I'd like to see how far that is."

"Jinaari," she said, "we can't strong arm the entire world into accepting the Thahion. That's going to make things worse, not better."

He nodded. "I understand that. However, the Shield is supposed to protect the Scepter. Which means, yes, I will throw someone across the room if they come after you."

Thia sighed, giving up her argument. *I'm too tired, hungry, and ready to sleep in a real bed. The sooner we do this, the faster I'll be able to sleep.* "Then let's go meet the locals, hear what problems they have."

CHAPTER

TWO

Thia pushed her plate away from her. There was still some food left, but her hunger was sated. Wiping at the corner of her mouth with the cloth napkin, she tried to listen to the councilman as he droned on. He hadn't said what he needed yet, just kept talking about circumstances and yields.

She folded the cloth neatly, laying it on the table, and tried to look interested in what was being said.

"So, you see, it's hard for us to constantly pay taxes to the Crown. We think we're current, and then another collector shows up with a new book." The councilman looked at her and Jinaari. "We don't want to avoid paying our share, Shield, but we don't even know what that is anymore."

Thia glanced at Jinaari, then back to the man. "What did you mean by another collector shows up with a new book?"

"New taxes sometimes require new people to collect," Jinaari said under his breath. Shifting in his seat, his voice carried across the entire room. "Queen Agrana used an antiquated system set up by King Christos. The Scepter and I are certain that Queen Elizabeth would hear your concerns.

She wants to make sure everyone pays what is due but doesn't think levying new taxes every six months is in the best interest of anyone in Avoch. Harvest yields cannot be guaranteed each year, and we'd rather you feed your families here—have everything you need to care for each other—over having grain to the rafters in Cirrain."

"While that's great to hear, Shield, you must understand our hesitation." The man played with the wide brimmed hat in his hands. "What assurance can you give us beyond your word?"

Thia scanned the room. Standing against a wall across from them were three people. The plain brown uniform, orange sash, and quarterstaffs they each carried told her who they were. "You there, in the back. You're monks dedicated to Silas, are you not?"

Everyone turned in their seats to stare at the three. The one in the middle met Thia's gaze, "We are, Daughter." Her voice was even.

"How far is your monastery?"

"Not far from Tanisal. We're tasked with keeping watch over the ruins." The woman shifted. "We were unaware of the passage you and your companions used to enter. It has been sealed now."

Thia nodded. "A worthy task, and I'm glad to hear that way is closed. You know the people of Solace, and the farms around it?"

"Yes."

"The honesty of your Order is well known. If I gave you a task, would you do it?

The woman inclined her head. "Silas has commanded us to aid all, to make up for the corruption that once spread through his faithful. As long as it is not one that will cause these good people harm, we would do so. Know that, should you ask us to do them harm, we will refuse your request."

Thia rose. "I would ask that you take a census. Write down how many shopkeepers, how many tradesmen, reside within Solace. Include all farmers who come in to do trade. I'm not interested in what their profits are. I have no doubt that the blacksmith has repaired a plow in exchange for bread, or a weaver traded cloth for milk. I want an accurate count of the people, including children, that rely on each other to live. How many merchants versus the farmers and ranchers. Make this list and bring it to us. The Shield," she gestured to Jinaari, "and I will write a letter to the Crown. We will explain what has happened in the past, and recommend that only a single collector come, once a year, and any taxes levied be based on what the town can afford. Will you do this task?"

The monk nodded. "Aye, Scepter. We would see that as just and fair."

Thia looked at the three council members sitting at the front of the assembled crowd. "Will the council abide by such an accounting and agree that we have treated this matter as best we can? The final decision will, of course, rest with the Crown. But we will encourage her to accept our solution."

"Aye, Scepter, we can live with that." Mistress Jala nodded her head.

"Good." Thia glanced at Jinaari, trying to read his face. Was that pride in his eyes? Looking back at the crowd, she continued. "Anything else? It's been a long day for us, and we'd like to rest if there's not."

"If you're the Daughter of Keroys and not Lolc Aon, why'd I find this in my east pasture last night!" Bryant stormed through the crowd carrying a cloth wrapped bundle. Stopping in front of the table, he stared at her before looking at Jinaari. "She's a fraud, Shield. I got proof." He let go of the bottom of the bundle, letting the contents fall onto the remains of her meal.

The pale-yellow egg was translucent and larger than the

plate. The soft shell reflected the light of the room, illuminating the inside. Thia stared at the shadowy form that moved within, trying to figure out what sort of creature it was. Bile rose in her throat as she made out the eight legs and segmented body. It was everything she could do not to try and swat at the ghostly touch above her head.

"I heard you went into Tanisal, Scepter," Bryant's voice dripped with disdain. "If you weren't a follower of Lolc Aon, those things wouldn't still be alive. Let alone coming out this far to infect our livestock." He turned and looked at the people in the inn. "I had to burn ten cows today. Each one had at least two of these damn eggs inside it. The monks are watching, but they aren't stopping them. Giant spiders are creatures of evil. No true follower of Keroys would've left a nest alive! Yet this Fallen witch let them be! And they're coming after us, at her bidding! It's not a coincidence she shows up and they wake up!"

"Stand back," Jinaari muttered.

Thia took a step back while he stood. Drawing his sword, he plunged it into the spider embryo. The creature stopped moving. "That the nest is still there is not on the Scepter, Bryant. It was my decision to retreat." His voice was low but carried across the suddenly silent room. "She wasn't aware of her Mark. None of us were. If we'd tried to fight them, we'd have been killed. And so would've every other person in this town. However," he continued, pulling the blade out, "we've already discussed taking care of the problem." Picking up a napkin, he cleaned the blood and ichor off the weapon before sheathing it. "I invite you to come with us. That way, you can see what Thia's capable of first hand, know that the problem's resolved."

Thia noticed the shift in Jinaari's stance as he leaned forward and put his fists on the table in front of him. "That is," he continued, "unless you're willing to accept her authority here and now."

Bryant's eyes darted between her and Jinaari. She could see his emotions play across his face. Jinaari had trapped him and he knew it. If he didn't go with them, he'd lose all credibility with the townsfolk. If he went, he'd have to fight something he'd always run from. "When do we leave?"

"First light. We won't wait for you."

"I'll be here."

Jinaari nodded, "Good. The Scepter, myself, and our companions are going to get our rest. Tomorrow will be a long one."

Thia walked past him, threading her way through the crowd toward the staircase. Caelynn, Gnat, and Adam waited at the bottom. Gathering the front of her skirt, she ascended the steps to their rooms.

"Which one do you want to talk in," she muttered under her breath.

"Yours," Jinaari replied. "Adam's spell is still in place there."

She reached the floor and walked to the door on the right. Caelynn slid up next to her, the key in her hand. As soon as her friend opened the door, Thia walked into the room.

The tubs had been removed, but the fire had kept the room warm. Thia sat on her bed, crossing her legs in front of her beneath the folds of her skirt. Caelynn stayed by the door until the other three joined them.

Gnat looked at her, worried. "Why did Mean Man call Friend Thia names?"

"Because he doesn't know me, Gnat," she said, keeping her voice even. "Sometimes, people only see the color of my eyes and think they know who and what I am because of them. Bryant is one of those people."

"Gnat keep Friend Thia safe from Mean Man!"

"I know you will," she said with a smile. "So will Jinaari, Adam, and Caelynn."

"Gnat, I've got a job for you." Jinaari sat in a chair near her.

"How can Gnat help Nice Brother?"

"You get to hurt the mean man if he does anything to Thia you don't like from now until we come back to this inn."

Thia shot him a look. "That's rather broad, isn't it?"

"Maybe, but it'll make it so they're both occupied while we're taking care of the nest." He stretched his legs out in front of him. "We'll need to have Bryant lead us to where he found the egg, make sure that colony's dealt with first. I don't want to kill one nest only to find another one's snuck up behind us. It should be easy. Don't show off, Thia, but don't hold back either. Bryant needs to see what you're capable of to believe it, but I don't know that he should see the full range of your magic."

"What about us?" Adam asked.

"You already know what to do, and when to do it. This time, though, don't worry about getting Thia out." Jinaari looked at her, "I don't think you'll run when you see them. Not now."

She shook her head. "You know I won't."

"Good. You and I have a letter to write tonight, too."

"Why tonight?"

"The monks won't take more than a day to do the survey. That was brilliant, by the way. They're known for their honesty. The citizens trust them or they'd never have come into town to begin with. Adding our letter to their census will make Elizabeth realize what's been going on here. I doubt they'll have the same issue again."

Thia looked down for a moment. "I, ah, somewhat tuned out what he was saying for most of it. His voice was putting me to sleep."

"That doesn't matter. The solution was perfect and one they'll abide by here. None of us want to find out later that we taxed a town into starvation."

Thia rose and grabbed her pack. "I've got a kit Elizabeth gave me in here."

"Don't forget your signet."

Pulling out the box, she nodded. "I put it in with the rest so I wouldn't lose it." She walked over to a small table next to Jinaari and put the box down before settling into the chair. Opening the lid, she removed a quill, ink jar, sealing wax, parchment, and the carved metal stamp.

"We'll take Gnat over to the other room," Adam said, "get him settled for the night. Normal watch rotation?"

Jinaari nodded. "Yes. Caelynn, I'll have you start yours once we finish the letter."

Thia turned in her seat and watched as the others left the room. "Do you think we need one here? Outside of Bryant, everyone's been welcoming."

"I'd rather set one and not need it over be surprised in the night." He picked up a small chunk of golden yellow wax and placed it in the metal spoon. "Let me know when you're done writing it and I'll melt the wax."

"I have to write it?" she stared at him. "Why not you?"

"It's your idea. You'll explain it better than I could."

Uncapping the ink bottle, she dipped the pen into it as he rose. "Where are you going?"

"Rule number two. We already know the inn's staff has been in since we last were, even with us locking the door." He walked to the door.

Thia heard the bolt slide home. Turning around, she focused on the task he'd given her and began to write. The sharp quill scratched against the parchment. Jinaari sat back down in the chair opposite her. Signing her name, she looked up and held out the pen. "Your turn."

Taking it, he scrawled his name next to hers.

"You're not reading it first?"

"I trust you, Thia." He put the quill down and held the spoon near enough to a candle for the wax to begin to melt. "We'll use the signets on the outside."

She sealed the ink before placing it back into the box, followed by the quill. Pulling out the shaker, she dusted the letter with sand before finding a length of blue ribbon. She took out her signet and placed it near the parchment. "Ready?"

"Almost."

Thia folded the letter, wrapping the ribbon around the open edges. Using her fingers, she kept it in place while Jinaari poured the melted wax in the center. Quickly, they each stamped their seal into the rapidly cooling mass.

He leaned back, looking at her. "How are things with you?"

"They're good," she said as she put the last pieces of the kit back into the box. She secured the lid and picked it up as she rose. As she put it back into her pack, she gave him a sidelong look, "Why wouldn't they be?"

"You'll have to be around a jerk, for one. And I'm concerned you're getting sick."

Thia shook her head. "I've dealt with people like him my entire life, Jinaari. Changing his mind is part of what Keroys wants me to do. And," she leveled a direct look at him, "I'm not getting sick. I'm a healer. I'd know it if I was and take the appropriate steps."

He rose and walked toward her. "You've been tired and had a cough. I know what you're capable of, Thia, but don't ever think I won't get concerned. I can't keep them alive nearly as well as you can. If we need to stay somewhere for a few days, let you catch your breath, we will. None of us will see you as weak."

"I'm fine," she assured him. "But, if it makes you feel better, we can stay here for a few days once we deal with the spiders. Gnat's home won't disappear if we do."

"I'll hold you to that," he said. Pointing to her bed, he walked toward the door. "Get some sleep. I'm going to push hard tomorrow so we can get this done and be back here before nightfall."

"Are we that close to Tanisal?"

"No, but I don't think where he found the egg is that far out. We'd get there, eradicate the nest, and rest up before heading back to the city. Deal with the nest we know about once we're done with Bryant."

"Why split it up? Why not go into Tanisal right away? We'd be closer than we are here."

"We've got two unknowns with us. I've never seen Gnat fight, and I have even less confidence in the local we're taking with us. He absolutely hates you for all the wrong reasons, Thia. I'm not letting him near you." He unlatched the door and opened it. "I'm sending Caelynn over. Get some sleep." He left, closing the door behind him.

She sat on the bed and rested her head in her hands for a moment. *He's right about one thing. I have been tired lately. That doesn't mean anything's wrong with me, though.* Reaching for her bag, she pulled out a clean tunic that was big enough to sleep in and began to change.

The door opened and she turned her head as Caelynn walked in. "Good," she said as she locked the door behind her.

"What's good?" Thia asked as she folded her dress.

"You listened to Jinaari and are going to bed. He told me you were being stubborn about things."

Thia snorted, "I'm not sick. I'm fine. I'd know it if anything was wrong. He's worrying about nothing." She finished packing away the dress and shoes. Placing her bag on the ground, she walked to the head of the bed. "I think we've all been tired. Sleeping on the side of the road for three weeks will do that." Getting into the bed, she adjusted the blankets over her body.

"I know him, Thia. Jinaari anticipates every possible outcome. He always has. If he's concerned about someone or something, it's with reason." Her voice was calm, but Thia heard the catch. "I've seen it, too. Something's not right with you." She sat on the other bed and looked at Thia.

"I'm not going to run off again, Caelynn," she reassured the woman. "Yes, I'm tired. We've had a lot happen. I'm still adjusting to what it all means, the additional weight of the responsibilities. That's all. I'm fine, really. I've got a better idea of who I am, who I want to be, than I did when I pulled the stunt back in Almair." She sighed, feeling the weariness begin to overtake her. "You need sleep, too," she said through a yawn.

Closing her eyes, Thia gave in to sleep.

THREE

"Gnat, are you sure you don't need a jacket or hood?" Thia asked him as they rode in the downpour. The storm had strengthened during the night, and Jinaari wasn't letting the horses run in the muck.

"Gnat is fine," the cobalus replied. "Is Friend Thia okay?"

She looked at the small creature that rode in front of her. "I'm fine, Gnat. I'm just anxious to be done with this." Jinaari kept a slow pace. The idea he'd had the night before about returning to Solace was now a certainty. There was no way they'd reach Tanisal in this weather.

Bryant rode up front, next to Jinaari. *I was surprised to see him this morning,* she thought. *Maybe there's more to him than his hatred of the Thahion.* Spurring her horse forward, she moved on the other side of Jinaari.

"How close are we, Bryant?" she asked, keeping her voice even.

"Why?" he growled. "Are you eager to see the plague you've brought to Solace?"

"I warned you, Bryant." Jinaari's voice was low but held the note of command she'd heard so many times before.

"Not far," the man grumbled. Pointing out to the horizon, he said, "Just on the other side of that hill's where I burned my cattle. Couldn't save any of them, and at least the eggs died that way too."

Jinaari looked at her and said, "Get ready." Turning in his saddle, he gestured to Adam and Caelynn. The two turned aside, taking a path that would bring them around the hill ahead.

"Gnat, stay with me. Okay?" she said.

He looked up at her, his ears drooping. "Gnat can fight."

"I'm sure of it. But," she said, "I don't want you to get trampled if the horses get spooked." She scanned the terrain ahead of them. Grassland for the most part, with a few hills. In the distance, she saw the forest that separated them from Tanisal. The land dipped ahead of them, and the ribbon of a road led into the trees. *If he burned his cows yesterday, we should still see some smoke. Even in this rain. It'd be smoldering. Something's not right.* She swung her leg behind her, dismounting her horse.

"Thia?" Jinaari said, his voice barely registering in her ears.

"This isn't right." The words came out as a breath. She glanced to her left. Bryant's horse was riderless. "Where'd he go?"

A blast of red light exploded on the bottom of the hill, shaking the earth beneath them. "That came from Adam's staff!" Jinaari dismounted, drawing his sword as his feet hit the ground. "Take Gnat, head to the right!" he screamed at her before running to his left.

"Come on, Gnat," she said as she reached up for him. "Stay with me, okay?"

"Gnat keep Friend Thia safe. Gnat promised Nice Brother!"

The ground beneath her was soaked from the storm. Her feet sank into the mud, slowing her down as she chose her path around the hill carefully. Rounding the corner, her eyes bulged in terror.

Adam was pulling Caelynn back, his staff shooting out beams of light toward a cave in the hill. Jinaari stood where the light stopped; his shield was raised as his sword slashed at something in the darkness.

Movement within the blackness caught her eye. The spider was easily the size of a barn! The head filled most of the opening; thousands of glassy eyes stared at Jinaari as mandibles snapped at him. A single leg, the tip dripping ichor, slashed at him. As he parried the blow, the creature reared up and a thick rope of webbing surrounded his legs. The spider jerked, pulling him off his feet and dragging him closer.

Thia stared at the creature, thinking of the sigil she used against Drogon, and let loose a blast of flame toward the strand dragging Jinaari. It caught fire, spreading toward the beast. "Get him free!" she screamed at Adam. Stepping in front of the cave, she made hailstones the size of small boulders rain down on its head.

"Kill it!" Jinaari ordered.

Turning her head, she saw one of the legs catch the webbing still attached to him. With a sudden jerk, he flew toward the razor-sharp mandibles.

"No hurt Nice Brother!"

Thia looked up as Gnat screamed. The cobalus launched himself from the crest of the hill, landing on top of the spider's head. With his short sword in both hands, he began to furiously stab at the creature's eyes. "Gnat make it so you can't see Nice Brother! No hurt Nice Brother!"

"Adam! Aim for the eyes he's damaged!" Thia began to throw energy into the bleeding holes as Gnat continued his rampage. Adam ran up to her, adding blasts of his own. "Caelynn!"

"I've got Jinaari! Kill it!"

Thia thought of a new sigil and created a ball of pure light. "Can you guide it?" she asked Adam. "I need it to be in the spider before I make it explode."

"Absolutely," the blonde man said.

She made it fly toward the spider, then waited for Adam to guide it into one of the larger wounds. Once inside, Thia changed the sigil. The energy detonated. Blood and ichor covered them as the beast exploded.

Gnat landed hard at Thia's feet. Kneeling, she released healing magic over his prone body. "Gnat?"

"Gnat didn't think he could fly. Flying is fun but landing hurt!"

"Stay still. I healed you, but it's going to hurt a while longer." Thia rose, looking around for the rest of her friends. Adam knelt next to Jinaari. The two men watched as Caelynn cut through the webbing that bound his legs.

Walking over to them, she forced her voice to stay calm. "Anyone else hurt?"

"Bryant will be, when I find him," Jinaari said. Caelynn sawed through the final strand and he jumped to his feet. "How's Gnat?" he asked as he wiped his sword clean with a cloth.

"He'll live. Had the wind knocked out of him, broke a couple ribs when he hit the ground. I've healed him."

Jinaari nodded. "Good." He sheathed his sword and looked at what remained of the spider. "We were led here. There was never any nest of eggs. Just one that it handed over," he pointed at the corpse, "so Bryant could convince us to come."

"Why?" Thia asked. "I mean, what would be the point?"

"Test your power maybe. Or to try and kill one of us." He turned around and looked at Caelynn. "Track Bryant. Find out where he went. He left as soon as we got here. I'd like to discuss his actions. At length."

Caelynn grinned. "Can I make him fall down a few times if he doesn't want to come quietly?"

"I won't argue if you do."

She grinned, then headed up the hill where they'd left the horses. "I'll go with her," Adam said.

"We'll get the horses and follow once Gnat's able to walk. Make sure we know which way you go."

Thia stepped back and began to look at the cave opening. "This isn't normal," she said.

"Not much about giant spiders are," Jinaari said.

"No, but look at the way the earth curves at the top." She pointed as she spoke, "You can make out spots where it was enlarged. Also," she continued, looking behind her toward where Tanisal would be, "we're still hours from the city walls. The monastery is between here and there. This one couldn't have made it out here unseen. It's too big. So," she looked at Jinaari, "how'd it get here? That was huge, even by the standards of the species. It doesn't make sense."

"You're right. It doesn't," Jinaari said. Walking forward, he said, "I wonder how far back this cave actually goes. It's too big to have moved underground. That means either it came on its own or something else."

"What do you mean by 'something else'?"

"Gnat," he said, glancing at where the cobalus sat on the ground, "how are you feeling now?"

"Friend Thia made Gnat feel better. Is Nice Brother okay? Gnat didn't like that Big Spider wanted to eat Nice Brother."

"I'm fine, Gnat. Thanks for asking. You're smaller than we are. Can you get behind the corpse? See what else is back there? Thia and I can't get in there, and we need to know if there's another way out of that area."

His face lit up, "Gnat glad to help Nice Brother!" He scampered off, disappearing between the legs of the spider.

"Does he still make your teeth itch?" Thia asked, looking

at Jinaari. "He did really well in that fight. Distracted it so you didn't die, made it so Adam and I could do some real damage."

"Only when he calls me 'nice brother.' But," he sighed, "you're right. He did better than I thought."

"The nickname's easy to fix. Just tell him that your name is Jinaari and you'd prefer he used that. He'll ask if that means you're his friend, probably get excited. He can't call someone by their name unless they say they're his friend. Something tells me his life has been full of rules we don't understand."

"He likes you and Adam well enough. Can't the two of you figure out these rules of his so we know what he's going to do? Pan talked all the time, but he knew when it was time to get to work. I don't want to go into a fight only to find out he won't because the wind is blowing from the south instead of the east."

"He saved your life, Jinaari. Can't you trust him a little? What happened to someone's actions determine who they are?"

He turned and looked at her. "Something's not right and I don't know what it is. I've had the feeling ever since he led us through that tunnel."

"It was the crystal he has," Thia said, "that's all. It was affecting all of us until Adam figured it out."

He shook his head. "I know, but I can't shake the feeling. It should've left me when I was Samil's prisoner, because Gnat wasn't anywhere near me. By the time I was back with the rest of you, Adam had dealt with Spoone's problem. I know there's something going on, a missing piece to a puzzle, that's right in front of me but I can't see it."

"Jinaari," she took a deep breath before continuing, "could it be something that Samil planted in you while you were his prisoner? He was manipulative on a level I can barely comprehend and played a very long game. And was host to

Lolc Aon's spirit." He turned away from her and she reached out, putting her hand on his arm. "Think about it, anyway. Talk to Adam. He's the one that saw it in Spoone. If he can find something, then we can get rid of it. If you let us look."

He nodded, and she saw his jaw relax slightly. "Later, when we're back in Solace. Right now, we need to find answers out here."

"Gnat have answers!"

Thia turned at the sound of his voice and saw Gnat scampering out from the cave. "What'd you find, Gnat?"

"It's one big hole. Lots of bones and sticky balls, but no tunnel that Gnat could find. Gnat knows how to find tunnels, too."

"I know you do, Gnat," Jinaari said. "Did the sticky balls look like the one at dinner last night?"

Gnat nodded enthusiastically. "They were smaller sticky balls. Couldn't see things inside them, but same type of sticky balls."

"What are you thinking, Jinaari?" Thia asked.

"I'm thinking we torch the inside, burn both the corpse and the eggs all at once." Jinaari said.

"Nice Brother believes Gnat?"

"Yes, Gnat," he said with a sigh. "My name's Jinaari, not nice brother. I'm not always as nice as Amara thinks I am."

"Gnat has two friends now!" Cackling with glee, he began to jump around in circles.

Jinaari threw Thia a look of exasperation that caused her to giggle. "You didn't tell me he'd do that," he muttered under his breath.

"It's actually more contained than the one he did when I said he could use my name. He must like me more than he does you. That arrogance of yours can be off-putting," she said, smiling.

"It's not nearly as bad as your stubborn streak."

"Hey!" Thia and Jinaari both looked up at the sound of Adam's voice. "We found him."

"Take Gnat and go," Thia said. "I'll ignite the nest. The fire will be hot enough to keep going even in this rain, but stay contained. We'll want to move the horses back, though. That roof may collapse in."

"Come on, Gnat. We need to move the horses."

Thia waited until they were at the top of the incline before starting to form the sigil. *A tweak or two beyond the fire. There's still life in the eggs; I don't want them to feel pain.* When she knew she had everything right, she positioned the fire at regular intervals beneath the legs of the creature. The flames appeared and grew together, forming a wall of white-hot flame burning every inch of the space.

Carefully, she walked up the hill. She saw Jinaari and Adam standing over Bryant. Caelynn held the reins of the horses. Gnat was already sitting on one. Jinaari looked up at her as she came closer. "Are we good?"

"Yes," she said. "It's all taken care of." She nodded at Bryant. "Where'd you find the coward?"

"He wasn't far," Adam said. "He was watching from a safe distance."

"Bryant was in Tanisal when we were, Thia." Jinaari's voice was even, and she recognized the tone. "He took an egg, hoping to sell it. When he couldn't find a buyer, he let it hatch and gave it a home in that hill. The more it grew, the more he dug it out."

"Why?" she asked.

"We haven't gotten to that part yet." Jinaari said. He turned back to Bryant. "Answer her question."

The man took a deep breath. "I met someone when I was trying to sell it. He said that someone was going to be Marked, and that the scepter would answer to them, but that you'd end up being worse than Lolc Aon. He said you'd come this way again one day. If I raised the spider, it could be trained to attack you. He said you'd be a curse on the world if you weren't killed before it was too late."

"Nannan has Lolc Aon's spirit now. If the mother of the Gods doesn't want her to return, she won't." Thia said. "And I have no aspirations to take her place." She kept her voice even. *Why would someone think I'd be worse than Lolc Aon? The Goddess was nothing but hatred and malevolence incarnate!*

Adam interrupted her. "Who was the man who told you this?"

Bryant shook his head. "Didn't get a name. He had a southerner's accent, like you hear from the merchant caravans that come up from Tavisholm. Tall, lean fellow with strange eyes."

"How were they strange?" Thia asked. *Was he Thahion?*

"They weren't like yours. They were blue where they should be white, then white where the color should be."

Adam's head snapped toward her and she drew back from the fear on his face. "Later," she whispered. *He knows something, but we need to get back to the inn. Be some place we can speak without being overheard.*

"Mount up," Jinaari ordered. "Bryant, give your reins over to Adam. He'll lead you. When we get back, you're to surrender to the council. Tell them everything. It's up to them to determine your fate."

Thia mounted her horse behind Gnat. Picking up the reins, she waited until the rest of her friends were ready. It would take time to get back, and that gave her the chance to think of questions to ask.

Adam knew something, but what? And would they still need to go into Tanisal and deal with the other spiders?

FOUR

Jinaari hung back as the rest of the group dismounted in the covered area. "Adam," he said, keeping his voice low, "take everyone upstairs. Make sure Caelynn gets Thia into something dry, then take Gnat into their room. I'll join you shortly."

"What are you going to do?" Adam asked.

He swung off the horse and glanced at Bryant. "I'm going to do what I do best. Be a menacing presence while he confesses to the council. I want to make sure he tells them everything and hear anything new. They may ask him questions we didn't think of." He pulled off his helm and handed it to the stable boy. "Take this and my shield to my room, please."

Adam nodded. "I'll tell Caelynn," he said as he glanced over his shoulder. The two women were walking toward the inn, Gnat trailing behind them. "But you know Thia. She'll probably tell her she's fine."

"She's not. That's the problem."

The blonde man looked at him, concern in his voice. "What makes you say that?"

Jinaari shrugged. "A feeling I have, that's all." He shook his head, clearing his thoughts. "It's probably nothing. The weather's bad and none of us want to be stuck here for a month." Walking over to Bryant, he pointed to the door leading to the inn. "You and I are going to sit down and wait for the council to arrive. You'll tell them everything you told us and answer any question they ask you. Got it?"

The other man nodded. "I understand, Shield. I'll accept any punishment given to me." The bravado he'd shown before had left.

Jinaari waited until Adam and the rest disappeared through the door before pushing Bryant forward. *I don't need Thia hearing this. What happened in Byd Cudd still haunts her, and finding out someone is out there, spreading lies, shook her. I saw it in her face. Adam knows something about this stranger, too. I need to know what.*

He followed Bryant into the inn, glad for the warmth of the common room. Mistress Jala stood behind the bar, watching them. "Would you ask the rest of the council to join us?" he asked, keeping his tone neutral. "We'll wait over there," he said as he pointed to a small table near the fireplace.

Jinaari sat in a chair where he could see the staircase. Bryant sat across from him; his shoulders slumped in defeat. *Whatever happens is up to the council. He brought a monster into their midst. Eventually, it would've outgrown the hill and gotten so big he couldn't keep it fed. Solace would've been under a web at that point; its citizens cocooned for meals. And for what? Revenge because some woman didn't want him?*

"Shield, please tell her I'm sorry."

He glanced at the other man. "Who?" *Say her name. Use one of her titles. Something to acknowledge who and what she is.*

Bryant pointed over his shoulder to the stairs. "The Scepter," he said in a tired voice. "I didn't think she was real, even with what the man told me. I don't think she's what he thought she'd be. Not now."

A barmaid brought over a couple of mugs of ale, placing them in the center of the table. "Mistress Jala sent Robert out to fetch Masters Pipyr and Cormac," she said, stepping back. "Let me know if you needed anything to eat. They'll be here soon, but we've got some stew if you're hungry."

"That would be good. Thank you," Jinaari said. Deliberately, he removed the steel gauntlets he wore and placed them in front of him. The table was close enough to the fire that he felt the warmth. "How long do storms like this one last around here?"

Bryant coughed. Briefly, he met Jinaari's gaze before looking down again. "A day or two, usually. It should be clear tomorrow. Will you still go into Tanisal?"

"We can't leave the nest there. The monks will keep them contained, yes, but they should be taken care of. The city needs to be cleansed of several things."

"Like what?"

Jinaari leaned back, studying the man across from him. "You should know. You were there about the same time we were."

Bryant played with the mug in front of him, turning it in his hands. "You took care of the Forsaken, though. The cloud left."

"Yes, it did," Jinaari said. "But there were more than giant spiders in the ruins." *I'm not volunteering the graveyard of undead Thia blasted apart, or the pit of scorpions. If he didn't see it, he wouldn't believe it. Knowing Caelynn, there's probably songs out in Avoch already about those things.*

"Shield," a man's voice said.

Rising, Jinaari saw the three council members approach them. "Thank you for coming. Please," he gestured to the empty chairs, "Bryant has something to tell you." Sitting back down, he stared at the man. "Go. All of it."

A bowl of stew appeared in front of him. Dipping his spoon into it, he listened as Bryant confessed his involvement to the other three.

"How did you feed it?" the dark-haired man, Cormac, asked.

"Sick cows I had, ones that wouldn't give milk. At first, anyway. It kept growing so I had to get creative."

Jinaari put his spoon down. "Creative?"

Bryant swallowed. "A family of Fallen showed up at my home one night. They claimed they were escaping Byd Cudd, that they now were some other race. I took them in, waited until they were asleep, then I tied them up. There were five of them, if you count the children."

"You fed it Thahion? You lied to them, offered them hospitality, then let that monster eat them?" Jinaari couldn't keep the disgust out of his voice.

"They were Fallen!" Bryant insisted. "I don't know what you called them—"

"Thahion."

"Whatever. Nobody was going to miss them."

"You're wrong," Jinaari said, his voice deathly quiet. "The Thahion are coming to the surface to rejoin Avoch. They're not inherently evil. They're trying to find their way in this world, and the Crown backs this effort. As does Almair and anyone with a sense of decency." He rose, slamming his palms down on the table. Bryant jumped at the force, but Jinaari kept his gaze locked on him. "You committed murder, Bryant. I said your fate was up to the council, and I'm a man of my word. But I won't hesitate if they ask me to be your executioner."

"We're a peaceful town, Shield," Cormac coughed. "I

don't know that we'd be entirely comfortable sleeping at night if we did that."

"Aye," Mistress Jala said. "In the past, lands and property would be forfeit and the person banished from Solace."

Jinaari straightened. "Then you leave him to his fate. I'll abide by your decision, no matter what it is, in regards to Solace. Know this, Bryant," he said as he picked up his gauntlets. "If I hear of you doing anything malicious to another Thahion, harming one in anything but verifiable self-defense, I will come for you. Avoch isn't big enough for you to hide from me forever." Without another word, he walked across the room and began to ascend the stairs.

I'll have to tell them what he did. They've already got questions, and it'll save time if I do have to kill him later. He wasn't sure how Thia would take it, though. *I don't know what's wrong. It could be stress from all the pressure she's under. She barely accepted being Marked, and then the Scepter landed in her lap. She's handling it well, but something's not right with her.*

As he turned down the hallway, he caught sight of Adam's red cloak disappearing into Thia and Caelynn's room. Good. He wouldn't have to get everyone together. He reached the door, knocking lightly on the wood. "It's me," he said.

The door swung open. Adam stepped aside, giving him room to enter. Gnat sat on the floor, near the fire. Caelynn and Thia were on the beds. All of them looked at him expectantly.

"What happened?" Thia asked.

Placing his gauntlets down on a small table, he walked across the room and sat in a chair with a sigh. "I'm not sure. The council was debating his punishment when I left. Normal for them is seizing property and throwing them out of town. Bryant, though . . ." he paused, "I may need to carry out their decision tomorrow."

"They'd have him executed? Why?" Caelynn asked.

Jinaari glanced at Thia. "He'd been feeding it some of his cattle. Not long ago, however, a family of Thahion came by his home. He took them in, offered them a place to sleep." He paused, choosing his words carefully. "While they slept, he tied them up. They were taken to the spider after that."

"A family?" Thia stared at him, horrified. "He fed the spider a family?"

He nodded. "Yes. Including the children."

"Shit," Adam said, his voice barely above a whisper.

"Exactly. I gave my word that I'd abide by the council's decision. And I will. But I also promised him that I'd hunt him down if I ever heard of him harming another Thahion in anything but verifiable self-defense."

Thia shook her head slowly; he could see the shock on her face. "I know you think we can change the way they're seen without violence, Thia, but not everyone will be that easy. Elizabeth, Tomil, and I all know there's going to have to be some messy examples made."

"I know," she said. Sitting up straighter, she let out a breath. "In cases like this, I'd agree. His arrogance evaporated once we defeated the spider, but I wonder if it was more because he knew he'd be banished over executed."

"It's possible," Jinaari shrugged. "He certainly got a shock when I told him I'd hunt him down."

"You're still in your armor," Adam said. "That leaves an impression. So does your reputation."

"Adam?" Thia asked.

"Yes?"

"What do you know about the stranger Bryant mentioned? The one with the odd colored eyes?" Jinaari looked at his friend, waiting.

The warlock shifted in his seat, leaning forward. "There's a sect of warlocks, ones that choose to pursue a path of dark knowledge. It leaves a mark on them. Not like yours, Thia," he leaned back, "but it changes their eyes because they see the world so differently than the rest of us."

"What sort of knowledge?" Jinaari asked.

"No learning is forbidden in Helmshouse. Primarily because so few of us leave once we're fully trained. Those who study death; how to prolong life, prevent death, or even steal the essence of life from another can be great to debate with, learn from."

"You're talking about death mages, aren't you?"

"Yes." The blonde man let out a sigh. "Back before the insurrection, there were more of them that moved in the world. They began to charge a high price for their services, one that most couldn't afford to pay. Those that could, eventually, turned against them. Instead of being celebrated, the mages were hunted. Few study death now; even fewer leave Helmshouse. The last one I know of left about the same time I began my studies."

"When was that?" Thia asked.

Jinaari caught a quick look between Adam and Caelynn. "Some time ago, Thia," Adam said. "I'm older than I look. If I told you I remember what Tanisal looked like before Nannan destroyed it, would you believe me?"

Thia's eyes grew wide and she glanced at Jinaari in shock. He nodded once. "It's true. Is that a problem for you?"

Recovering, she shook her head. "No," she said. "You're still family." A small smile appeared on her face. "Is this one of those skeletons you warned me about before I confronted Samil?"

Adam grinned. "Yes. You'll hear them all, I promise. But I need to spread them out so you don't get bored." He rested his hands on his knees. "Dealing with death, siphoning off the memories and knowledge of those who have just died, changes a person. Notably, their eyes. The coloring shifts, bleeds out from the iris. Most will be mistaken for being blind. A mage that's lived long enough for the color to appear in what is the whites of the eyes for you and me is extremely rare. They've been around for more centuries than I'd like to contemplate, gained knowledge that most everyone in the world would kill for. If that's who this was, he's been in hiding for a very long time."

"Why would he have any knowledge about me, though?" Thia asked. "Bryant was in Tanisal around the time we were, then encountered this mage. I didn't know I was Marked yet, let alone it becoming common knowledge in Avoch."

"He didn't know it was you, Thia," Jinaari pointed out. "All Bryant said is that someone would be Marked. As far as he knew, it could've been Samil the death mage was referring to."

Caelynn looked at him. "Did Bryant give you a name, Jinaari?"

"No. Even if the mage said it, I don't think Bryant would remember. He's been raising a spider, nursing a hatred. He had no idea we'd even come this way." His mind drew back from what would've happened if they'd chosen a different road south. "Rain or not, we leave tomorrow. We'll go to the monastery, spend the night. Take care of the nest in Tanisal once and for all."

"Gnat not go home?" Gnat asked, his voice breaking.

Jinaari looked at him. "We'll get you home, Gnat. I promise. This won't take long."

The cobalus's face lit up. "Gnat go home!"

Rising, he looked at each of them. "Caelynn, can you see if we can get some food brought up here? I'd like us to stay in our rooms over being seen downstairs. We eat, get some sleep. Tomorrow isn't the problem, but I'm not sure what all has moved into the ruins. We need to be rested and ready for whatever's there."

The bard rose. "I'll go back down later and play a few

songs. I can listen in on conversations, see if there's a rumor we need to know."

"Good idea. Thia," he looked at her, "give her the letter for Elizabeth. That way, the monks can get on the road to Cirrain faster."

She rose and picked it up. Handing it to Caelynn, she looked at him. "What about what you and I talked about earlier?"

"Is something wrong?" Adam asked.

"Caelynn, take Gnat to help with the trays." Jinaari waited as the pink-haired woman led Gnat from the room. When the door was closed, he looked at Adam. "I've had a feeling that something's not right for a while now."

He nodded. "You said so downstairs."

"Thia thought it might've been the influence from Gnat's crystal, but I don't think so. If it was, the feeling would've left me as soon as you transported him and Amara away. Samil had my armor for a while, and Alesso gave me my sword back. Or, at least, I think it was him. It could've been another illusion. Her theory is that Samil placed the same sort of spell on my gear as he did to Spoone."

Adam looked at him, his brow creased in thought. "It's possible. I can look, but I want your word on something first."

"What?"

"Gnat clawed the hell out of me because of the influence he was under. I know your strength, old man. I won't be able to do this if you throw me across the room."

Jinaari nodded once. "I understand. Thia?" He turned and looked at her. "Is there any way you can restrain me?"

"Yes," she said. "It'll work better if you're sitting. You're too tall for me to do it otherwise." She pulled a chair into the center of the room. "Adam? What do you need from him or me?"

"Sit and put your sword across your lap." Jinaari did as Adam instructed. "Where's your gauntlets and helm?"

"Helm is probably in our room, with my other gear. Gauntlets are on the table over there," he pointed to where he'd placed them earlier.

"I'll get the helm," Adam said as he walked to the door. "I'd hate to not have it if it's where the spell is centered." He left, closing the door behind him.

Thia walked over and got his gauntlets. "Here," she said, holding them out to him as she came back.

"How are things with you?" Jinaari asked.

"I can't believe he'd do that," she said. "To feed them to that spider . . . do you think any were still alive when I burned the nest?"

"Don't go there," he said. "I've seen what the venom does to people, Thia. Even if they were alive, you couldn't have saved them. No amount of healing could purge that much poison." She opened her mouth to protest, and he grabbed her hand. "I know what you're capable of. Even if they were breathing, their souls were gone. I'm not even sure Garret or Keroys could've saved them."

"Did you really threaten to hunt him down?"

He met her gaze. "I don't threaten people, Thia. I make promises I intend to keep. You know this."

The door opened again, and Jinaari looked past her. Adam came in, closing it behind him. "Found it," he said as he held up the helm.

"Good. Want me to wear it?" Jinaari asked.

"No," the other man said as he walked closer. "I'll put it down here, between your feet. It'll be close enough for me to work into the spell."

"Where do you want me?" Thia asked.

"Someplace close enough to do what you need to do. Just .

. . don't move once I get started. It may take a few minutes if you want to grab a chair and sit down."

Jinaari pulled on his gauntlets, then drew his sword and laid the blade across his lap as Thia moved a chair closer to him. "Is this okay?" she asked from beside him. "I'll sit as soon as I'm done."

Adam said, "It's fine. Oh, one more thing," he smiled. "You just need to keep him from standing up, swinging his arms, that sort of thing. I'd like him to be able to respond if I have a question. Breathing is good, too."

A strange sensation came over Jinaari's body. Every muscle and tendon felt weighed down. "Try moving something," Thia said.

Jinaari tried to shift his hands and feet, but they wouldn't respond. "I can't."

"Are you in pain at all?"

"No," he said. "I just can't move."

Adam walked in front of him. "Good. I'm going to start now." A red glow came from his staff and settled over Jinaari's body.

His skin warmed considerably, and he resisted the urge to pant. His heart began to race. "Am I supposed to get this hot?"

"I'm not sure," Adam replied. "I've done this on inanimate objects before. If it gets too much, let me know and I'll stop."

Jinaari felt a bead of sweat begin to trickle down his face. "I can handle it. Keep going."

"And you say I'm stubborn," Thia said.

"You are," he said, teasing her.

"Don't talk," Adam said, his voice insistent. "I may have found something."

A wave of disgust rose in Jinaari. All the feelings of betrayal and anger he'd felt when Adam confessed he'd been sent to kill Thia crashed over him in waves. He clenched his jaw, biting back the words he knew he'd regret saying. "Hurry up," he growled.

"What's wrong?" Thia asked.

Jinaari squeezed his eyes shut and concentrated on his breathing. The anger within him was irrational; he knew that. *I can't answer her. I have to keep this under control. It's not me.* "Hurry up," he repeated.

"I found it. I've almost got it. There!" Adam said, a note of triumph in his voice.

The corrosive anger disappeared. Jinaari opened his eyes. His heart was beating normally, and his breathing was even. "All good?"

"Yes. Thia, you can release him now." Adam said.

Jinaari felt his muscles relax as she dropped the spell. "Where was it?" he asked. Someone knocked at the door, and they all turned toward the sound.

"I'll get it," Thia said as she rose.

"It wasn't one place, not like it was with Spoone." Adam explained as they watched Caelynn and Gnat come in with trays of food. "Think of it as a bunch of threads woven into the joints and straps of the armor."

"Is that why I got so warm?"

"I believe so. I had to find each one, and they didn't want me to play with them." The blonde man looked at him, a frown on his face. "What did you feel when I got started?"

"Anger, for the most part. I remembered when you told me your orders regarding Thia, and the betrayal I felt. It's a good thing she had me locked down. I was tempted to say or do things I would've regretted."

"Would've regretted? If you're not sure I told you everything . . ." Adam's voice trailed off.

Jinaari looked at his friend. "I trust you. Not because I have to, but because you've earned it a hundred times over." He glanced over where Thia was helping Caelynn and Gnat move the food off the trays. "Standard rotation tonight, with whoever's on watch in here with her."

"You're still feeling like something's wrong, aren't you?"

He shook his head. "It's not that. Bryant knows where we sleep, and I don't trust him."

FIVE

Jinaari watched the light in the room grow steadily brighter. Dawn was coming. He stood and walked to the fireplace. Pulling the poker off the rack, he prodded the remnants of wood that hadn't turned to ash. *No reason to throw on another log,* he thought. *Room's not cold, and we'll be on the road soon.*

Thia stirred and said something too low for him to make out. Glancing back, he saw her hand adjust the blanket as she slept. Her sleep had been restless since he'd started his watch. Adam hadn't mentioned anything amiss, but he couldn't shake the feeling.

I know he found the spell Samil used, and the feeling is less now. But I still think something's wrong with Thia. What is it I'm seeing that none of the rest are? Including her?

"Are you going to sit in front of the fire all morning, blocking the heat?" Thia said, her voice barely above a whisper.

He rose, chuckling. "It's not cold in here and you know it." Walking over, he sat on the other bed and looked at her. "The sun's coming up. Caelynn said one of the monks would be waiting to lead us to the monastery. We'll rest there, take on the problem tomorrow."

"I know the plan, Jinaari," she said. "I'm tired, not stupid."

"No, stupid is not a word I'd use to describe you."

She rose, propping herself up by an elbow. "I have a good idea what words you would use," she said. The smile on her face reached her pale lilac eyes and he grinned back at her.

"Probably not. I'd have to have a discussion with anyone who called you stubborn. Beyond me, Adam, or Caelynn that is. The world doesn't need to know that the Scepter, the Daughter of Keroys, has faults."

"Oh? I know the world is aware that the Shield is an arrogant prick. What's different with me?"

"For one, my reputation was well established before I met you. Second, it's expected of me. I'm supposed to be that menacing presence in full armor, scaring away anyone who would think about harming those I'm sworn to protect." He tilted his head. "How are things with you?"

She flopped back, her blonde hair fanning out across the pillow. "I'm fine," she said with an exasperated sigh. "I thought Adam took care of your problem."

"It's lessened, but the feeling's still there. Just . . ." he paused, "promise me you'll tell me if something isn't right."

"You know I will." She yawned and looked at him. "When do we leave?"

"Soon as we're all up and ready." Rising, he said, "I'll go wake the others. Mistress Jala said something last night to Caelynn about sending some food with us. When you're ready, head to the stables. I want to be on the road within the hour." He walked across the room and opened the door. Crossing the threshold, he closed it before walking the few feet over to the other room and knocking.

"We're up, Jinaari," Adam called out.

He twisted the knob and walked in. Caelynn smiled as she brushed past him. "Is Thia awake?"

Jinaari nodded. "Yeah. She's getting ready."

"I'll stay with her, don't worry," she said as she rested her hand on the door to Thia's room. Before he could say anything, she disappeared through the opening and closed it behind her.

"Need help with the armor?" Adam asked.

Turning, he saw the warlock pull a clean tunic down past his chest. "No. I'm not wearing all of it today. With the monk leading us, we shouldn't have problems until we get to Tanisal tomorrow. There's not much between here and the monastery that would've survived that spider, either."

The blonde man sat on the edge of one bed, pulling on his boots. "Gnat's taking my gear down to the stables now. I didn't let him touch yours." Adam paused, giving him a direct look. "How are you feeling today?"

"Better," Jinaari said as he straightened the padded gambeson over his hips.

"But not all the way? Don't hide it, old man," Adam continued. "If you think there's a problem with Thia, it concerns all of us. She's family."

Focusing on his armor, he kept his voice neutral. "It's not that something's wrong. More like I'm missing a piece to a puzzle that no one but me can see or solve." He jerked at the strap, tightening it to the correct hole. "I'm a tactician and I don't think I'm seeing the entire field."

"How's Thia this morning?"

"She says she's good, just tired. She was pretty restless last night. Did Caelynn say anything to you when you started your watch?"

"No," he said, shaking his head, "she didn't. Thia slept fine during my turn. Maybe she's sensing your nerves."

"I'm not nervous, Adam," Jinaari said. "I've got a job to

do. That means staying vigilant." He put his gauntlets into his pack, then closed the top flap. "I'm good. If you or Gnat can take that down to the horses, I'll take our leave with our host. Find the monk, meet you and the rest in the stables." Turning around, he walked to the door. Twisting the knob, he left and headed downstairs.

The common room was cool, with few people in it. Staff moved around wiping down tables and sweeping the floor. One young man knelt before the fireplace, cleaning the ashes from the night before. Jinaari looked around for either Mistress Jala or their guide. As the youth stood and picked up some fresh logs, he recognized the wide orange sash that circled his waist. Making his way across the room, he said, "Good morning."

The brown-haired man focused on arranging the logs. "Good morning, Shield. Are your companions ready?"

"They're meeting us in the stable. I'll give our gratitude to Mistress Jala, then we'll be ready."

"She's not here," he replied. He struck a piece of steel against the flint stone resting at the base of the andiron. Sparks flew into the straw stuffed between the logs, igniting them. "She went with the others to confirm that Bryant has left what was his home." Rising, he looked at Jinaari with orange eyes. "My name is Mishar."

"You're part Thahion?" Jinaari kept his voice even, hiding his surprise.

"Yes," Mishar said. "The Grandmaster felt it would make the Daughter more at ease if I were to lead you to Temple. She has encountered too many in her young life that cannot see beyond her eyes."

"Your Grandmaster is wise. Shall we?" He gestured toward the back door.

The monk nodded and walked past him. Jinaari followed. *Thia's going to have questions, but will she want to hear his story? She didn't have an easy childhood, but her father made her feel loved. Wanted. The chance that Mishar had the same is slim. I'm curious, as well. Mishar's the first half-Thahion beyond Thia I've ever met. He follows Silas, and not Lolc Aon. How much of his life parallels hers?*

The cool morning air mixed with the damp earth, making Jinaari wish he'd put his gauntlets on. There were gloves in his pack; he'd have to find them before they set out. Thia and the others waited in the open area. Grooms stood with the horses. Curiosity was on her face as they approached. Caelynn whispered something in her ear. Adam was getting Gnat up on his horse.

Mishar stopped in front of her, bowing ceremoniously with his arms folded across his chest. "Daughter, I am Mishar. I have been tasked to escort you to Temple."

Jinaari walked closer, keeping an eye on Thia's reaction. For a moment, she glanced at him and he saw her shock. "We're glad to have you lead us, Mishar. Please, call me Thia. The road is no place to be caught up in ceremony or titles."

"She's right," Jinaari said as he reached her side. "Mount up. Any questions can be asked as we ride." He reached into his pack and pulled out his riding gloves as the others climbed on their horses. Taking the reins from the groom, he swung up onto his. Thia looked at him.

"Did you know he was part Thahion?" she whispered.

Shaking his head, he said, "No. The Grandmaster sent him specifically to put you at ease. Let's put him between us, so I can hear any answers he gives you. I know you have questions. I do, too." Raising his voice, he looked at the monk. "We'll follow you, Mishar. Once we're out of town, Thia and I will join you. Lead us to your monastery, please."

Mishar nodded once before turning his horse toward the gate. Jinaari followed, confident that the others would do the same.

The street was deserted. A few shop owners could be seen through their windows, getting ready for the day. Water splashed up as his horse walked. The road was still muddy, but the puddles weren't deep. Thia rode up next to him. "Did he say anything to you about his family?"

"No, and I didn't ask," he said. "I know you're curious, Thia. So am I. Let's respect his privacy and wait until we're where no one else will overhear. He may not trust us any more than you did at first."

She nodded, saying, "I can relate to that."

"I do not mean to eavesdrop. Sound carries far in the silence of morning. To answer your question; trust is not easy for either of us, Daughter," Mishar said. "It is hard to do so when those around us are more likely to kill us instead of offer kindness. The Shield is correct in that I would not want my answers to be overheard. I will tell you my story, as I believe you will understand it. The citizens of Solace, however, are not as trustworthy."

"We can wait," Jinaari said.

Mishar urged his horse to trot and Jinaari followed suit. *He wants out of town, and quickly. Thia's reception wasn't completely welcoming. I wonder if Mishar's had bad experiences here, especially given the prejudices we've seen. If I hadn't been with her, would they have even let Thia stay?*

Ten minutes later, they passed the last building that could be considered part of town. The road widened. Jinaari nodded once to Thia before urging his horse forward and drawing up alongside their guide. He knew Adam would keep Caelynn back far enough to give them some privacy as they talked. As Thia came up on the other side, Mishar said, "You both have questions. I will attempt to answer them. Know that I may not tell you the complete story, as I may not know all you wish to know."

"That's an odd way of saying you won't tell us everything," Thia said.

"Perhaps," their guide replied, "but it is an honest one. For example, I do not know the motivations of others. As I do not know them, I cannot tell you information I do not have. Especially if they are dead."

"We respect that," Jinaari said. "Thia, why don't you start?" *It's more important she starts, if he was truly sent to put her at ease. I'm sure her questions are the same as mine. Most of them, anyway.*

"Were you raised in Byd Cudd or on the surface?"

Mishar kept his eyes on the road. "On the surface. I was abandoned as an infant, and the monks raised me." He turned his head toward her, and said, "Before you ask, I do not know who my parents were. Or which one was human and which one was Thahion."

"You know that's what they're calling themselves now, though. Instead of Fallen," Jinaari said. "Has word spread that quickly?"

"Silas made it known to the Grandmaster, who told us. After the corruption was weeded out from his followers, Silas commanded his faithful to tell no lie. If the Grandmaster says they are now Thahion, then that is who they are. The other name is not for us to speak."

"You've erased it from your history?" Thia asked.

"No. Our records stay true to what was, and no names or events are struck out. Ever. To modify the texts is seen as being untruthful. An entry was made to explain that they chose the name for themselves. From that point onward, all our writings will call them Thahion. We would do this for any race."

Jinaari watched Thia absorb the monk's words. She wouldn't want history to be erased. "You said you didn't know who your parents were," she said.

"That is correct."

"Do you know how you came to live with the monks?"

Mishar nodded. "The compound has two main areas. There's the area where the Temple is, and one where we welcome those who need shelter for a time. A troupe of performers were caught in a bad storm and took shelter within the walls. One was great with child. I was born that night. The woman disappeared from the healer's room and left me behind. By first light, they had all left."

"Were the monks kind to you?"

"Of course," Mishar said. "Silas teaches us to be kind to everyone. The corruption led to so much division within his church. People were hated for being who they were, instead of having their character be the determining factor. The abuse that was rampant among the paladins was, I'm sorry to say, brutal." He glanced at Jinaari. "You are a credit to your Order, Shield. You and most of your brothers have reclaimed the honor that befits your skill and training."

"Most of my brothers?" Jinaari asked.

"Recent events made us concerned that the same corruption that had happened within our history had begun to take hold within yours. As that person was Foresworn by Garret, we are hopeful that the seed did not take root within your Order."

"My brothers held to our vows when Samil marched on Cirrain. None sided with his cause. I don't presume to know Garret's will, but I cannot believe he'd allow any such seed to grow. Alesso Potiri was one man, whose motives were understandable. His means, however, were the problem."

"That is good to know," Mishar said.

"You said the monastery has two areas. Will we be housed in the outer area tonight?"

"No, Daughter. The Grandmaster has asked that rooms within the Temple be prepared for all of you. You are to be honored guests." He turned his head and Jinaari caught the flash of a smile. "None will disturb you while you're visiting us, but any will answer questions." Mishar's head swiveled toward him. "There are several of the *curaidh*, our fighting corps, who are keenly interested in sparring with you, Shield. It is not often we can train with one of your skill. If you are interested in doing so, that is."

Jinaari nodded. "To fight with a quarterstaff is a skill I don't know well. I'd be honored to learn from those who would teach me."

"The healers," he looked back at Thia, "are hoping you would speak with them, as well. There are sigils or spells you know and they are eager to learn them."

Jinaari caught her startled jump. "You have healers that can use magic? I thought Silas banned that, after what happened."

"To ban something, forbid knowledge of a kind, is to invite disaster. Rather, those who have any stores are trained. Not just in how to heal, but the ethical responsibility behind it. The training is rigorous, and some choose to have their stores nullified before they finish. Silas is not complacent with those to whom he grants magic. I don't know what training your warlock friend has experienced," he gestured back to where Adam and the others rode, "but my understanding is that Silas is as stern as the Solar."

"You have no stores, then?" Jinaari asked.

"None to speak of. I'm apprenticed to one of the historians. Most of my day is spent making parchment, binding the sheets into books, or grinding pigment for ink."

A comfortable silence fell over the group. Jinaari's mind started to wander, and he was certain Thia was trying to take stock of what their guide had said. *They were both raised on the surface. While Thia knew her father, a God stepped into their lives in some way. Keroys may have Marked her at birth, but he also was there when she took her vows. Something tells me Silas has kept a close watch on Mishar.*

"Will we be at your home before nightfall?" Thia asked.

Mishar stopped his horse, raising a hand to the horizon. "Well before then, Daughter."

Jinaari looked where their guide pointed. The road ahead cut a wide berth through the forest that bordered the farmland. In the distance, a tall gate stood. The doors were open, and figures lined the road leading to it.

"The Grandmaster does not often welcome visitors in this manner," Mishar said. "I know you asked me to call you Thia, but we cannot. To us, you are the Daughter of Keroys. The Scepter and the Shield. We will honor you. To do otherwise is to defy our faith."

Thia smiled, and Jinaari recognized the flash of resignation that played across her face. "Then the Daughter, the Scepter, I shall be. Please, Mishar, lead us to the Grandmaster. I would not wish to keep them waiting."

Their guide spurred his horse to a canter. Thia threw Jinaari a look, and he nodded. He moved his horse closer to hers as they moved toward the monastery's entrance.

Thia took a deep breath and forced herself to sit straighter in her saddle. Mishar rode ahead of them. "I understand now," she whispered to Jinaari.

"Understand what?"

"Why you always avoided court. Tomil and Elizabeth make it look so easy. The scrutiny . . . it makes me wonder what people are finding wrong with me."

Jinaari nodded. "There's that, yes. Court of any kind will attract people who want to find fault with those in charge. They look for some sort of weakness they can exploit, or even a new type of fabric. Your gray dress, for example."

She started and looked at him. "What about it?"

His head moved, eyes looking into the forest that all but surrounded them. "The design is something no one's seen before. I have no doubt you'll see versions of it all over Almair when we go back home."

"That's ridiculous. Keroys gave it to me, so the world can see my Mark. Why would anyone want to copy it?"

He smiled at her. "Because it's different, unique. And worn by one of the most powerful and influential women in

Avoch. What you, Elizabeth, and Amara wear will decide what the rest of the nobility will want from dressmakers."

"But not you or Tomil? You both have as much influence and power as we do."

"We're not nearly as good looking, though," he said. "Fashion is the world of women, not men. We're supposed to stand there, look good, but not outshine the woman we're escorting. Tomil's got his military uniform, I've got this," he tapped his fist against his breastplate, "and that blasted circlet buried in my bag. I could wear almost anything, as long as it was clean and not ripped to shreds."

Thia sighed, glancing at the monks that lined the road. As they passed, each one snapped to attention; the ends of their quarterstaffs came up and formed a solid line. The precision left her in awe. The sash circling their waists varied in intensity. Some were bright orange, while others were a darker, more subdued shade. "Do you know why the sashes are different?" she asked Jinaari. "They're all orange, but different shades."

"It's our way of showing where we are in the training, and which discipline Silas has assigned us," Mishar said from in front of them. "The Grandmaster is the only one allowed to tell outsiders of the designations, though I would not be surprised if you learned some of it on your own. You and your friends are known to puzzle things out, Daughter."

"We do our best," she said. Looking ahead, she saw a single figure standing in the center of the massive gate. "Is that the Grandmaster?"

Mishar stopped his horse, and she followed suit. As their guide dismounted, Thia glanced at Jinaari. He nodded once before doing the same. She got down and held onto the saddle horn while her legs found their footing. Five children ran up and took the reins of their horses, leading them away. Moving closer to Jinaari, she saw he'd buckled his shield onto his arm.

"Do I need to have the scepter in my arms?" she asked, her voice low.

"No. It's visible where it's at. Mine's harder to see when it's on my back. Besides," he threw her a quick grin, "I doubt there's anyone left in Avoch who would see your face and not know who you were. Your reputation's grown."

They fell into step behind Mishar as he walked toward the Grandmaster. Raising her head, she looked at their host. Their head was shaved, and the face was serene. Their hands were hidden within the arms of the pristine white robe. A wide sash in varying shades of orange wrapped around their waist, secured with a single band of deep amber. They bowed as she approached.

"Welcome, Daughter and Scepter. Welcome, Shield," the Grandmaster's voice was lyrical, washing over Thia and encouraging her to relax. "Silas stands with his siblings and bid me to welcome you to his Temple."

"We thank him for the shelter and company given to us this day. May he continue to bless you and all who answer his call," Thia said. "How may we address you?"

"I am the Grandmaster. No other name is necessary." They stepped forward and held out their hands. Thia took one, and Jinaari the other. "Silas sees our soul, not the physical form. I am not male or female as you would know the terms. Rather, a union of both. This confuses some, but I hope your own experiences will allow you to see past such limitations."

"Of course, Grandmaster." Thia let go of their hand.

"Come." Grandmaster clapped their hands together once. Around them, the monks snapped to attention in a single motion. "Rooms are prepared for you all, including the cobalus. Your gear will be delivered once your horses are tended to. On the way, I will show you around our Temple. It's not nearly as grand as the palaces you're used to, but it is home for us."

"We've slept on the ground more than in a palace," Thia said as she fell into step with their host. "Our home in Almair is above an inn."

"Thia's right," Jinaari added. "We have tasks we're commanded to do, and that usually involves a fair amount of travel."

"Where do you head now?" Grandmaster asked.

"Tanisal, first. We need to take care of the spiders, and anything else within the city that may cause trouble if it gets loose."

"Ah," Thia caught a sadness to the Grandmaster's voice. "I wish it was not so. All creatures should be allowed to live their lives in peace and not to be hunted."

"The nest is going to overtake the city if we don't do something," Jinaari said. "When that happens, even your *curaidh* cannot contain them fast enough. There were other things within the city that woke when Drogon had his lair beneath it. Things no one wants to see set free."

"This is true, Shield. Silas has warned me of what is within the city walls. I understand the need but shall still mourn the loss."

A cough rose in her throat and Thia forced it down, but part still escaped. Jinaari and the Grandmaster both looked her way. "Are you ill, Daughter?'

She smiled. "No, it's just some road dust. I feel perfectly fine." She knew the look Jinaari shot at her. *He doesn't believe me.* "Mishar told me the healers would like me to teach them some sigils?"

"Only if you're willing, Daughter. The sigils we use are basic. While we understand your magic works differently than ours, Silas has said that we could learn much that could be adapted to how ours flows. There is concern that, should a war come, we would be ill prepared to aid those who need it. That you were able to settle the last one so decisively and without bloodshed is something we appreciate. The future, however, may not be as kind."

"I like avoiding bloodshed when I can, especially on a mass scale," Thia replied. "It can't be helped sometimes, though." She pushed the image of Jinaari's blood spilling out onto the ground from her mind. *It wasn't him, not that time. What happens if I don't have a week to prepare, though?*

The Grandmaster nodded once. "I can understand that." They walked through another gate, and Thia caught her breath.

The interior building surrounded a well-manicured garden. Seven paths, each one paved in different colors, spiraled inward. At the center, a pristine white pool stood. The stones were cut to resemble dragon scales. Thia walked closer, awestruck. Stopping in front of the yellow path, she asked, "The stones you used, they're meant to represent the Gods?" She whispered the words, afraid that anything louder would disturb the overwhelming sense of peace and belonging she felt emanating from the image before her. Something pulled at her soul. *Whatever's in there, it wants something from me.* For a moment, the blood in her veins felt ice cold. Whatever it was, Thia feared finding out.

"They are, Daughter. Nannan is eternal, the center of all creation that we know of. Each path, like the Gods, leads from her will into Avoch."

"Lolc Aon is no more," Jinaari said from behind her, and she jumped slightly.

"True," the Grandmaster said, "and we grieve along with Silas. Losing a sibling, no matter how misguided they've become, is still a loss. Silas has assured me that another, eventually, will take his sister's place. Nannan wants all races in Avoch to have representation at her table." They smiled and stretched out a hand. "The garden is open to all who wish to walk to the fountain. I recommend you allow me to show you to your rooms first, though. Your companions may wish to rest while you seek answers from within the garden."

"Of course," Thia said, smiling. She felt Jinaari's hand on the small of her back. "Please, I didn't mean to interrupt your tour."

They began to walk toward a ramp. "The temple is meant to be accessible to all, and some have difficulty traversing stairs. Each level is accessed by these inclines." Thia listened distractedly to what their host was saying. The building that surrounded the garden was a series of open-air corridors, with doors leading to separate areas. "Daughter?'

Thia stopped, blinking. The Grandmaster had stopped in front of a set of doors. "I'm sorry, Grandmaster. My mind must've wandered."

They smiled. "It happens often. The garden wants you to visit as much as you wish to do so. It is no more patient than you."

"You speak as if it's alive."

"To us, it is. Those who are fortunate are able to speak with Silas. A handful have heard the will of other Gods, or even Nannan herself. But, here," the door stood open, revealing a room, "this room is for you. There is a common area in the center, beyond the interior door. Your friends will be close at hand."

"Thank you," Thia said as she stepped into the room. She glanced back at Jinaari and the others as the Grandmaster closed the paneled wood door.

Braziers filled with glowing coals sat in regular intervals, heating the room. Oil lamps hung from chains to illuminate the plain wood furniture. A thick rug, in reds and golds, kept the chill of the floor at bay. Opaque orange curtains surrounded the bed. Thia looked back at the closed door. The urge the Grandmaster spoke of was stronger than she wanted to admit. *All I want to do is walk to the center*, she thought, *but I'm scared I won't want to come back out.*

"Thia?"

She jumped at the sound of Jinaari's voice. Turning around, she saw him closing a door she hadn't seen. "That goes to the common area?" she asked.

"Yeah," he said. He walked over to her; his face serious. "How are things with you?"

Letting out a sigh, she sank into a chair and cradled her face in her hands for a moment. Raising her head to meet his gaze, she said, "There's something about that garden. As soon as I saw it, I..." she paused, "I can't describe it. I need to walk to the center. More than I've needed to do anything else in my life. But I don't know if I can come back out if I do."

"What do you mean?" he asked. Thia bit her lip, trying to make sense of the jumbled emotions and thoughts racing through her mind as he pulled a chair closer to her. "Talk to me, Thia. It doesn't have to make sense. I'll understand."

She took several deep breaths to steady her heartbeat. "I must go in there. I'd follow the path for Keroys, that's certain. And," she felt her body shake slightly, "I'm wondering if Nannan will speak to me when I got to the center."

"Would that be bad? She spoke to you when you were fighting Samil. You told me she said Keroys had chosen well when he Marked you or something like that. Surely that means she'd be open to speaking to you."

"That's the thing," the words rushed out of Thia's mouth, tumbling over each other, "I don't know what she wants of me. I don't even know if that's who will be talking to me! I know what Keroys expects. I've accepted that. I'm mostly comfortable with it, and I'm adjusting to the role of the Scepter. But what if that's not all? What if Nannan's got something else in mind? Or if it's not her but someone else?" Tears fell in large drops down her cheeks but she kept going.

"What if the task is something that takes me away from you? Or kills Adam or Caelynn? You three are my family, Jinaari. I don't want to lose any of you, not now that I have the one thing I've wanted more than anything since Papa died. I'm scared that's what'll happen if I go in, but I know I must."

"Hey," he reached out and gently wiped away her tears. "We aren't going anywhere, Thia. We want you with us as much as you want to be here. All of us do. I didn't feel the same pull you did, but nothing the Grandmaster said indicated that only one person could enter at a time. Garret's path was next to Keroys. I'll walk that one, keep an eye on you. There weren't enough plants, or distance, that would prevent me getting to you if something attacked." She felt the pressure of his hand on her chin and raised her head, looking into his dark eyes. "The Shield protects the Scepter. And I've been your sworn Protector even longer than you've had that," his head inclined toward her hip. "I'm not letting anything happen to you. Trust me."

A calm resolve washed over her at his words. "I know. I trust you."

"Good. There's some food in there," he pointed at the door he'd entered through. "Caelynn and Adam are waiting on us, though Gnat probably ate half a chicken already. You've hardly eaten since yesterday." Thia started to protest but he silenced it with a look. "Don't start. Some of what you're feeling could be related to that. Let's eat, then we'll go see what Nannan wants with you."

Thia nodded. *He's right. Some hot food will help.* "That sounds like a good plan."

"All my plans are good ones," Jinaari said. "You just argue because it's your stubborn nature."

She laughed. "Arrogant prick."

"It keeps us alive."

She laughed, rising from her chair, and forced a smile on

her face. The fear was still present, but it was less. One look at Jinaari's face told her she hadn't fooled him, though.

"They won't see it, Thia. But I know you better than they do. We'll do this, together, like we have everything else."

"After we eat," she said.

"Yes. And you will eat more than five bites."

Staring at him, she said, "Are you threatening me?"

Jinaari shook his head. "No. I don't threaten people. I make promises. Our friends are in there," he pointed at the door, "and they're going to hound you as much as I will if you don't. Adam and Caelynn have noticed it, too. Something's not right with you, Thia. I know you're going to tell me you're fine, that you'd know if you were sick. My concern, and theirs, is that it's something you can't see until it's too late."

"Will you stop nagging me if I eat? I appreciate the concern. I do," she paused, "but I really do feel fine. There's nothing wrong with me."

"I'm going to need proof of that. My instincts are better than yours. As much as you know that you have to go into that garden, I know that something's wrong with you." He moved closer and grabbed one of her hands. "We're going to watch you like we did before. Every stumble, yawn, cough, or ache will be noted, even if you don't tell us. And it's not about you being Marked, or that the scepter chose you. It's because you're family. It won't be any different than when we went beneath Tanisal."

"It is different," she insisted.

"How?"

"I know you're doing it this time." Thia sighed, giving up on the argument. *He's right. They've always watched over me, even when I didn't know.* Her stomach growled and she giggled. "Let's eat. I'd rather not meet any of the Gods when my stomach sounds like that."

She let go of his hand and walked to the door. Opening it,

her stomach grumbled again as the aromas within wafted under her nose.

Adam, Caelynn, and Gnat sat at a round table. The cobalus barely looked up from the whole chicken he held between his hands. She met Caelynn's gaze and smiled. "Did you save any for me?"

"There's plenty," Adam said.

Thia walked to an empty chair and sat down. Adam handed her a bowl full of steaming vegetables. "Smells wonderful," she said as she scooped some onto her plate.

"Not to say Elian's a bad cook," Caelynn said as more dishes were passed to Thia, "but whoever cooks here could give her some great recipes."

"If the esteemed bard would like, I will introduce her to our kitchen staff. I am certain they would allow this. We want the Shield and Scepter to remain healthy so that they may continue to protect all of Avoch."

Thia snapped her head around at the sound of Mishar's voice. He stood in a recessed section of the room. "I hate that you're there, Mishar. Please, join us." She pointed to an empty chair at the table.

He smiled. "I am honored, Daughter. I ate some of each dish, to ensure they were unspoiled, before your companions entered. I remain only so that I may guide you to the healers when you're finished." She saw his gaze shift to Jinaari. "Shield, the *curaidh* train near the infirmary. You expressed interest in our methods, and many are anticipating the chance to see how they fare against you."

Thia dove into her meal, surprised at how hungry she really was. "Give us time to eat," she heard Jinaari say, "then we'll follow you. Thia and I both wish to visit the central garden, as well."

"I am not surprised," Mishar replied. "The Grandmaster requested that any who wish to walk a Path to the center do so in this hour, so that it may be clear for the two of you. All should be done by the time you're ready." Thia heard a door open and she glanced over to see Mishar standing in the opening. "I'll remain outside, so that you may speak freely. When you're ready, I'll escort you," he said as he closed the door.

"Gnat ate too much," he groaned.

Thia looked across the table. Gnat leaned back in his chair, the chicken on his plate nothing more than a pile of bones, as he closed his eyes.

"Gnat," Caelynn giggled, "why don't you go take a nap? We'll be okay."

"Friend Thia does not need Gnat to help her?"

She smiled. "I'm sure Jinaari and the others can keep me safe while you sleep."

The cobalus slid from his chair, shuffling through an open door. Within minutes, snoring rumbled from the room.

Adam leaned back, placing his napkin on the plate in front of him. "Do you want us to come with you?"

Jinaari shook his head. "I don't think so. The likelihood of anyone trying to come after either of us here is low."

"We didn't think anyone would come after me at the cloister either," Thia reminded him, "but an attempt was made."

"You didn't have your stores unlocked then," Jinaari said.

"Plus, you've grown up a lot," Caelynn added. "Any attempt made on your life won't come from someone with a sleeping draught, Thia. They'll plan it out for months. We didn't decide to come this way until yesterday." She looked at Jinaari, then back to Thia. "If what The Grandmaster and Mishar have said is all true, and I think it is, Silas would retaliate swiftly against anyone who made any move against the two of you while we're here. He's still trying to make up for what happened a century ago."

"Ancient history," Jinaari said. "His monks have more than made up for the acts of the Corrupted."

"It's not ancient to them, old man. Or to Silas. He's watching his followers closely if he's nullifying stores over ethical concerns." Adam's voice was stern. "I agree, though. The likelihood of anything attacking us here is slim." Thia caught Adam's hand caressing Caelynn's for a moment. "The two of you have things you need to do here. Caelynn can get her recipes; I'll keep an eye on Gnat. I think we can afford a night without a watch. Do you agree?"

"Yeah. A full nights' sleep for all of us would be good. I'm not certain what we'll face once we reach Tanisal. I want us all rested and our stores replenished," Jinaari said as he rose. Looking Thia's way, he continued, "Ready to teach a class?"

She pushed her chair back and rose. "On one condition."

"What?" he asked, crossing his arms.

"You don't get so beat up sparring with them that I have to demonstrate anything on you."

Thia rose, and the dozen or so healers followed suit. "I think that's about it," she said. "The sigils are similar enough that you should be able to adapt them to something Silas will grant."

"Thank you, Daughter," the eldest said. "We have learned much today and will endeavor to perfect the designs before they are needed."

"I'm glad I could help, though I hope you never find yourselves using them." *Some of those sigils were ones I used to keep Jinaari alive after he drowned, or when Alesso was poisoned. For any of these people to use them, the situation would be dire indeed.* A movement caught her attention and she saw Jinaari enter the room through a door on the opposite side of where she was. "If you'll excuse me, my companions have need of me."

The monks bowed in unison, then parted so that she could walk through them. As she got closer, she saw the deep red mark that started at the corner of his eye and disappeared into his beard. "What happened?"

"Later," he said.

"Do you need me to heal that?"

He looked at her, and she saw the certainty in his eyes. "No. At least, not until we know we won't be back here."

"You can at least tell me why," she muttered as she walked through the doorway. Night had fallen, and hundreds of lanterns hung from the covered walkways.

"It's a matter of honor," Jinaari's voice was low. "It took me fifteen minutes to convince them that I wouldn't be offended if they didn't pull their blows, that we couldn't learn from each other if we weren't trying our best. The last opponent I faced was smaller than the rest, but damn fast. She got a blow past me. I saw the reactions of the others. They'd seen her as a lesser warrior for some reason, but now they respect her. She's the only one among them to actually leave a mark on me. As such, I won't diminish her accomplishment by hiding, or healing, the bruise."

"The minute we know we won't be back for a while, I'm healing it. You know that, right?"

He chuckled. "I've dealt with bruises my entire life. I'm fine."

Thia snapped her head up and glared at him. In the yellow glow from the lanterns, she saw the faintest hint of a smile cross his face. "You're horrible," she laughed.

"If I'm not, the wrong people die."

He stopped, and she looked up. They were in front of the garden. Two paths, yellow for Keroys and silver for Garret, waited silently. Each one was flanked with lanterns hanging from tall, hooked poles, giving off enough light to illuminate the way. There were shadows between the paths; dark, deep ones that made the hair on her arms stand up. "I can do this," Thia whispered. "I have to do this."

"Thia?"

She snapped her head toward Jinaari. "What?"

"How are things with you?"

Closing her eyes, she let out a long breath, letting the anxiety go as she exhaled. "I'm good," she said as she opened her eyes and looked at him. "I've faced worse, right?"

"You have. I'll stay even with you. If you need me, I'll be there."

Standing up straight, she drew in another deep breath. "I know you will," she said. Moving before she lost her nerve, she stepped onto the yellow stones before her. Out of the corner of her eye, she saw him do the same.

The first change she noticed was it was warmer. The winter chill was gone, and the air was fragrant. A memory rose in her mind. *Papa built a swing on the tree by the barn one spring day. The first time he pushed me on it...the grass had been cut short and I could smell the promise of new life rise from the earth. The higher he pushed me, the more I laughed. I felt his love at my joy.*

"Not all memories should be forgotten, Daughter."

Thia turned her head at the sound of Keroys's voice. He walked beside her, a small smile on his face. "I am honored," she stammered. "I didn't expect you would come see me."

He laughed. "I placed my Mark on you. When you have need of me, I will be there." She drew breath but held her thoughts as he raised his hand. "You did not need me when you faced the Forsaken, Daughter. Nor when you faced Lolc Aon or her Son. The strength to do what needed to be done was within you, and you found it."

"So, why are you here now?"

"Because you doubt yourself, Thia. Your faith in your friends is considerable, and well placed." She glanced to her left, making out Jinaari as he walked Garret's path. "He cannot see me. Garret had need to speak with him and is probably doing that now."

Turning her attention back to her God, she asked, "Is everything okay with him?"

"Oh, I imagine it is. Jinaari isn't Marked as you are, but Garret has always seen a purpose to his life." The path curved as they walked. "I didn't come to discuss my brother's will with you, Daughter."

She nodded. "Jinaari and the others are sure something's wrong with me. That I'm sick in some way. But I don't feel ill, and I can't get through to them that I'm fine." Thia looked up at Keroys, surprised at the concern on his face.

"I see nothing that is worrisome. Perhaps a cold is developing. It is winter, after all." He paused, "I don't believe it's anything you, or your friends, should lose sleep over. A small cough won't interfere with what you do best."

"What is that, exactly?" She sighed. "I'm sure you're tired of my whining and questions, but I'm not at all sure about what I'm good at."

"You take care of others, Thia. Sometimes it's your companions, other times it's old women who wish to see their loved ones before they die. You give of yourself, sometimes to your detriment, but always with the hope that a small gesture will change one mind. And that, my Daughter, is something that cannot be taught. I saw it in your soul when you rested in Herasta's womb. It is why I Marked you. And it is why we are here tonight."

"What does Nannan want from me?" The words came out as a whisper, and it was all she could do to hold back the tears.

"Nannan? She's not who summoned you."

"Then why am I here?"

Keroys smiled. "My brothers and sister wanted to meet you; let you know that they are not angry for what happened with Lolc Aon."

Thia blinked. *I never thought how the other Gods would respond! I didn't think about anything beyond wanting to be free of her!* "I'm not the one that killed her, though. Jinaari did."

"He's walking with Garret, isn't he? He killed her physical form in Byd Cudd, but you forced what was left of her spirit out of her Son and gave Nannan the chance to cleanse Avoch of Lolc Aon's evil forever. For us, who mourned the sister we once had, you both need to know that we hold your acts as just."

"All of them will be here?" Awe crept into Thia's voice.

"Yep! We're all here," a young man's voice came from the back side of the fountain that now stood in front of her.

Blinking, Thia watched as four figures—three men and a woman—came around the centerpiece. Jinaari stood at her side as Garret and Keroys joined the others. Her heart raced at the sight of the six Gods. Silas's face appeared sad, while Ash wore an infectious smile. One that reminded her so much of her cousin that she was filled with happiness. Hauk, the oldest of them, stood in the rear. One hand rested on Lexi's shoulder, highlighting the unstrung bow that rested across her back.

"Between the two of you, our sister is gone from this world. She left many scars, in both the people and the land, that will take lifetimes to heal. Let it be known, here and now, that none of us hold malice or hatred to either of you for Lolc Aon's death." Hauk's deep voice, tinged with sorrow, washed over Thia. As he spoke, she felt stress she didn't know she carried begin to wash away.

Lexi raised her chin. "What she did to you, Thia, was abhorrent. Men have done enough harm to women. We should not do worse to each other."

"Lexi," Ash interrupted, "we're not all drunken fools. Most of us are honorable sots!"

"We cannot stay longer. Taking the cobalus home is a noble task, and one that will test the bonds you have with your friends.

Remember what we have said, your training, and hold onto the trust you have in each other. In the end, trust and friendship are the strongest bonds we have." Keroys smiled at her.

"Keep your oath, paladin." Garret said, and Thia heard an edge of irritation in it. Glancing at Jinaari, she saw his head barely move.

She looked back at the fountain, and the Gods were gone. A wave of dizziness hit her and she sat down on a bench.

"Thia?"

She looked up at Jinaari. "I'm good. Just . . . that was overwhelming. To be in the presence of one deity is one thing . . . but all six at once?" She shook her head. "And all to make sure we knew they weren't upset that we killed Lolc Aon?"

"I didn't think we were in the wrong, but to hear them agree . . . You're right. That's not something that we can ever really describe." He sat down next to her. "We'll stay here until you're ready to head back to the rooms. There's no rush. I'm sure Gnat's still asleep, and I doubt Adam and Caelynn will be waiting up for us."

"Is it that late?" Thia raised her head, trying to determine the time. The lanterns were bright enough to make seeing the stars difficult.

Jinaari coughed. "I doubt they're sleeping, Thia. The only time Adam's asked for a night where we all got to sleep when we were on the road was if he and Caelynn were planning on sharing a bed."

She felt her cheeks flush, and she buried her head in her hands. "I don't need to know the details."

"Neither do I."

They sat for a few moments, and Thia was happy with the silence. It felt right, after what they'd just seen. "How long have you known Adam?"

Jinaari sighed. "Over a decade. I was barely fourteen when I was sent with others to escort him from Helmshouse."

She giggled, imagining him being that young, his hair and whatever shadow of a beard he had, tinged white from the avalanche.

"What's funny?"

"Caelynn told me the reason he calls you 'old man' is because you got caught in an avalanche and your hair and beard were so white with frost it made you look old. I was imagining it."

"Is that what you were told?"

"Is that not the truth?"

Laughing, he leaned back against the bench. "Not even close. There was an avalanche, yes. Several of us were sick with frostbite and spent time in the infirmary at Helmshouse. Lukas was one of them. This was his first command mission, and he felt horrible about what had happened. I think it was part of the reason he went to the chapterhouse in Almair." He sighed, then kept talking. "Once we were recovered enough to travel, we headed back to Dragonspire. Adam was supposed to be evaluating the initiates, including myself, for their magical aptitude. This may come as a shock to you, but I was arrogant before I joined the Order."

"You? Arrogant? I'm shocked," Thia giggled.

"In the palace, I was raised to believe I would excel at any task I put my mind to. My skill was praised, no matter how good or bad I really was. The goal was to groom me for the throne, of course. Nobody wants their ruler to hesitate or have large gaps in their education. Initially, I was to be an officer within the palace contingent. We'd gone out to the chapterhouse on a visit when I was seven, and I saw some of the training they went through. It appealed to me on a level I had never felt before. It took four years to convince my parents that formal training within Garret's Paladins would make the army respect me as a leader more than some ceremonial position.

"The day after we got back, I was summoned to Drakkus's office. Adam was there. He got right to the point; I was going to be removed from magic training immediately. My stores, he said, would never be at a level where advanced magic would answer my sigil. I can do basic healing, enough to keep someone alive or walking, light a fire to stay warm, but not much beyond that." He turned his hands over and Thia's gaze went to them. They were calloused, with small scars crisscrossing across both the palms and backs. "These hands are meant for swords, not sigils. I protested, of course. I intended to be the best the Order ever trained. How could I do that with such meager stores? Surely Garret would change that at some time.

"Adam stared at me, and said, 'You've got what you've got, nothing more. There's no capacity within you to hold more. It doesn't matter if you trained until you were an old man, Your Highness. You will need to rely on others if magic is needed'."

"Did you listen to him?"

Jinaari shook his head. "Not at first. I'd sneak into the upper-level classes, try a sigil when I was alone. Every time I tried, it backfired. And Adam would be there, shaking his head and calling me 'old man'." Thia saw his face relax as the memories played in his mind. "I grew to hate the sight of him, to be honest. After six months, though, I realized he was right. I limited my sigils to the ones that wouldn't use much, so I could manage my stores better."

"It took you six months to realize that? And you call me stubborn!"

He glanced at her, and she caught the mirth in his eyes. "That's because you are. Anyway, I kept training, took my vows, and became a full brother within the Order shortly after my sixteenth birthday. Two weeks later, Drakkus called me to his office again. Adam was needed in Almair, and I was to escort him so he'd arrive safely. I saw this as the perfect chance to show him I wasn't the 'old man' he constantly said I was. We got to Cirrain, rested up in the house and were feasted that night. I had too much to drink, but I was so certain he didn't think I was worthy of being a paladin because I didn't have much in the way of stores. He is a warlock, after all. Their entire society revolves around using magic.

"I went out on the battlements, trying to appear in complete control, and caught a whiff of something foul. Before I knew it, I was on my knees purging my meal."

"Wait," Thia interrupted. She tried to hide her amusement, but the giggle escaped. "You're telling me that you got sick and threw up on the battlements? I've seen you drink before, Jinaari, but I've never seen you drunk. Let alone that drunk!"

"The ale was stronger than I realized. And it taught me that moderation was a good thing, especially if I might be needed to draw my sword." He laughed, and she joined in. "It was something I definitely needed to learn. The next thing I knew, Adam was there. He helped me up and said it was good to know that I was human after all. The next day, once we were on the road, he took care of my hangover. The nickname, however, comes out any time he feels he has to remind me there's things I'm never going to be the best at."

Thia couldn't hold back the laughter anymore. She threw her head back and howled.

"It's not that funny," he chided her.

"Oh, no," she replied, tears streaming down her cheeks as she tried to breathe through the laughter. "The idea of you being that drunk is perfect. You're human, after all."

Glancing at him, she saw his shoulders start to shake as he got caught up in her amusement. "I suppose it is. What he told Caelynn sounds far more heroic, though."

"I don't think this counts as a secret we need to share with her," Thia said as she wiped at the tears on her face. "It's not something that can be used against you."

"What do you mean?"

"It's something we talked about, when you were Samil's prisoner. When we're back in The Green Frog, the four of us will have a long conversation. There's always going to be people who try to use things from our pasts to get us to do what they want, make us distrust each other. If we're honest with each other and share them, that takes away any advantage they'd have over us."

"Good idea. Who thought of it?"

She smiled. "I did."

He looked at her and said, "I should be surprised, but I'm not. Come on," he rose and held out his hand, "it's getting cold out here. I want to be on the road at dawn. We still have an hour's ride before we're at Tanisal, and I want everyone to have full stores."

Taking his hand, she rose. "I'm fine, even if you don't think so."

"Maybe I'm worried about mine."

She laughed again as he led her from the garden.

EIGHT

Thia slowed her horse to a walk, following Jinaari's example, and stared at the main gate into Tanisal. The brass fittings showed their age; green and black dulled the once-bright metal. Gaps between the planks were large enough in places to put her arm through. *I know what lives in there*, she thought. *Is anything small enough to come out into the world?*

"Have no fear, Daughter," Mishar said as he came up next to her. "Silas himself warded the main gate. Nothing evil may escape through the cracks. Or over the walls," he pointed to the top of the stone battlements. "The shield was meant to contain what was within."

"Yet your Order is tasked to make sure nothing comes out," she said. "If it's so well shielded, why do you keep vigil?"

"It was meant to keep the evil within, not prevent others from entering. Though we've monitored, and sealed, the entrances of which we knew. The barrier will not prevent anyone from the outside from entering, nor will it keep them from bringing things out. Like the man from Solace who stole the spider egg." He sighed. "I trust Silas. He has shown me kindness and given me a home when many would've killed me as an infant. He did what he felt was best when Tanisal fell. At that time, it was necessary. Time has passed, however, and I wonder if the shield is nothing more but a reminder that keeps the wound from healing."

She looked back at the city in front of them. The mortar between the bricks was crumbling away. *Maybe he's right. Maybe we need to put the ghosts of long ago to rest as much as we need to kill the evil that lives within the ruins.*

"Hey."

Someone tapped her leg and she looked down. Jinaari stood there, his hand on the bridle of her horse.

"How are things with you?"

Swinging her leg around the back of her horse, she dismounted. "They're good," she said as her feet hit the ground. "Just wondering if I should bless the ruins when we're done. Maybe it's time the site began to heal instead of reminding the world of what went wrong."

He put his hand on her elbow, urging her forward. "It's an idea. We'll discuss it once we know we're not about to be attacked."

Mishar took the reins of her horse. "We will stay here," he said, "and wait for you to return." Turning around, he led her horse toward the small group that had ridden with them from the monastery.

"Come on," Jinaari said.

Together, they walked to where Adam, Caelynn, and Gnat waited. "What's the plan?" Adam asked as they approached.

"I'd like to avoid a building-by-building search if we can," Jinaari replied as he began to buckle his shield across his arm. "That'd take too long."

"Get me to the center fountain," Thia said. "I'll take care of things from there."

He glanced at her. "How?"

Using the toe of her boot, she started to draw in the dirt in front of her. "I can do a series of waves, centered on me and going outward, and target specific creatures. The one drawback is that each wave may wake up anything dormant. We may get other things coming at us once I get started."

"What are you talking about?" Caelynn asked. "You think there's stuff asleep in there?"

Thia looked at her. "The bodies in the graveyard were at rest until we entered the mausoleum. Drogon may have known of the entrance and set a rune to awaken the dead. He must've had multiple layers of security, and there may be spells still in place from the time the Corrupted held sway here. I can take care of everything, but it has to be in stages. The sigil that would affect the spiders is different than one against scorpions."

Jinaari nodded. "I understand. How long will you need between casts?"

"Not long," Thia replied. "The longer it takes, the more things show up, the higher the chance I'll have to catch my breath. I have the stores to do this. You four need to keep anything that moves faster than I can cast from interrupting me. That's all."

"Gnat, you watch Thia's back. Adam—"

"I won't be out of arms reach of her. If I have to, I grab and transport."

Jinaari nodded. "Caelynn, go see if you can borrow a bow and some arrows from one of the monks. We may need you to pick off some to keep them from getting too close."

"Gnat can shoot rocks!"

Thia glanced down at the cobalus. He held a leather sling in one hand. "The fountain was in ruins, so there's probably a lot of rubble small enough for you to use, Gnat."

"I'll clear us a path to the fountain, if we need it. Once we're there, we let her do her job."

"Sounds good, old man."

Thia lowered her head, trying not to giggle at Adam's words. *Maybe I shouldn't have asked about the story.*

Caelynn came back, with a young woman following behind. "I got us more than just a bow."

"Sayge," Jinaari said, nodding his head. "Why are you here?"

She raised her head and met his gaze without blinking. "The bard said you needed a bow, Shield, in case the creatures came quicker than the Daughter can cast."

"I anticipated the loan of equipment, not someone to operate it." Thia watched as he sized up the young woman in front of them. "I make this decision, not you. I know well how skilled you are with your staff, but not a bow."

Sayge raised her chin slightly. "The bow is my best weapon. I do not miss my target. By comparison, my skill with a quarterstaff is that of a novice."

He raised one hand to his face, a single steel-clad finger touching the bruise on his cheek. "This was not given to me by a novice."

"Then you should have no reason to question my skill with a bow." Sayge bowed at Thia. "Daughter, it is my honor to be allowed to aid you. Rest assured; no evil shall come within reach of you while I draw breath."

"I need you to watch over someone else," Jinaari said, and Thia recognized the tone of his voice. It was the one he used when he wasn't going to be open to other ideas.

"Is not the Daughter of Keroys, the Bearer of the Scepter, the one most likely to be targeted?"

He nodded. "She is, and the rest of us will make sure she is safe. That is our job. What I want you to do is watch Adam's back," he pointed at the warlock. "If things go wrong, he's tasked with transporting Thia to safety. He can't do that if there's an axe in his spine."

Sayge turned toward Adam, nodding slowly. "To protect the one who will guarantee her safety is a solemn task." She looked back at Jinaari. "I shall not fail in this."

"Stay with us until I tell you differently," he instructed, "then find the place you feel is best for you to see your targets. Don't waste your arrows."

Thia saw a small smile creep across the young woman's face. "I never do." Bowing again, she stepped back and walked toward Adam.

"She's the one, then?" Thia asked, her voice low.

Jinaari looked at her, confusion on his face. "The one what?"

"That gave you the bruise."

He nodded. "Yes. And you are not—"

"Don't worry," she interrupted him, "I can see what it means to her, both personally and within the *curaidh* itself. I won't touch that until we're well away from here."

"I've been bruised before, Thia," he said. "It'll heal just fine on its own."

"You may decide our tactics, Jinaari, but I'm a much better healer than you are. If I decide to make it go away, it's going to." Threading her arms through the straps of her pack, a chill ran down her spine. She looked at the gates as the cold settled in her veins. *Something's about to happen, something big.*

"Hey, you okay?"

Thia nodded. "Yeah. Let's do this before it gets any colder." She pulled at the cuff of each of her gloves, making sure they were snug. "We may be further south, but it can still snow. I'd rather be done and back at the monastery before it does."

"I was hoping we'd keep heading south, but you're right. Those clouds make the monastery sound better." He nodded at the pack on her back. "If we're going back, take what you need and leave the rest with the horses."

Quickly, she shrugged off the pack. "I should've thought of that," she muttered. Digging into one of the side pockets, she pulled out a hard leather case.

"I'll take it over," Caelynn offered, scooping it off the ground before Thia could respond.

Thia nodded. Straightening up, she opened the pouch around her waist and put the other one inside.

"What's in there?" Jinaari asked.

She looked up at him. "Three vials of codal potion."

"Codal?" She heard the puzzlement in his voice. "Why would you need that?"

"I can't heal myself if I'm distracted by pain. Even forming the sigil in my mind will be problematic. It numbs me enough to let me do the rest." His face grew concerned, and she continued, "I know what else it can cause, Jinaari. I only use it when I absolutely need to, like when I broke my arm during the cave-in. That was the only time I've ever used it. I'm in no danger of becoming addicted. I sat with a few who fell under its spell, back at the cloister. There's no recovery, only death. Still, it's the only thing powerful enough to make the pain go away so I can do what I need to do if I'm injured.

"You planning to get hurt in there?"

"Not at all. But, if I do, I'll need it. I've been around you enough to know that being prepared for possible outcomes, no matter how slim, is usually a wise thing." She looked back at the gates. "Shall we knock or just go in?"

"I'm not going to ask permission." He walked toward the city, gesturing at the others to follow. It was time.

Whatever's in there, I'll get rid of it. It's time for the city to be reclaimed. It's been a tomb long enough. Thia paused; *Will anyone think the same about Byd Cudd? But it's not abandoned, not yet. Eventually, though, it will be.* Shaking her head, she quickened her step to draw up next to Jinaari. *Focus on the here and now, not what was. I can't change the past.*

The six of them stopped before the gates. "How do we get in," Adam asked. "I don't think knocking will work."

"The gates weren't locked when Silas sealed the city," Sayge said. "A good shove should move them enough for us to go through."

"If the hinges aren't rusted shut, you mean."

"Only one way to find out," Jinaari put his shoulder to one side of the center and leaned onto the gate.

The metal ground against itself, breaking the silence of the morning. Thia looked toward the side. Large flecks of red fell from the hinges; a shower of rust staining the ground. For a brief moment, it looked like blood. *But whose?*

"Move it, Thia," Jinaari's command interrupted her thoughts. She caught sight of Adam's red cloak as the warlock dashed through the small opening, followed by Gnat. "I can't hold it open forever."

She ran through the opening. Turning around, she grabbed the edge of the door. "Help me," she said. The others joined her, straining to hold it until Jinaari joined them. As soon as he was through, they let go. The gate swung shut with a shudder; rust, dust, and slivers of wood rained down on them.

"Think it'll be that hard to get out?" Thia asked.

"No," Sayge said. Thia watched her jog over to a section near the hinges. "There's another door here," she called out. "All I have to do is unbar it." Lifting the thick, wood plank off the iron brackets, she tossed it to one side. "Mishar told me of this, after studying old documents about the city. My brothers know I would make it available to them, should we need their aid." Sayge jerked at the door, making sure it would swing open, and closed it again. "It will make our exit easier."

"Good," Jinaari said as the young woman rejoined them. "Thia, you and the rest are with me. Sayge, you know where to go. Keep an eye on us, let us know if you need our aid."

She nodded once before running toward an arched opening and disappearing.

Thia turned and looked down the wide street that would lead them to the center of Tanisal. Rubble was strewn across the blackened cobblestones; bits of grass and weeds sought to reclaim the path. In the distance, she saw the broken spire that marked the fountain. The toppled remains of a building blocked the way. "So much for an easy walk," she muttered.

"Let's get closer," Jinaari said. "If there's a way around it, that's better than taking side streets."

Adam moved up alongside her, and she caught Caelynn walking on Jinaari's right. "Where's Gnat?"

"Gnat can find way!" the cobalus said, scampering ahead of them.

"Be careful, Gnat. We don't want you to find out the hard way there's anything bad in that rubble."

"Gnat be careful, Friend Jinaari!"

Thia watched him run toward the ruins. "We came in on the other side of the city, didn't we?"

"Yes," Jinaari said. "Why?"

"I'm trying to figure out where we are in relation to where we were, that's all."

"We should be close to where we went down into the tunnels," Adam said. "Though I don't recall any buildings that were burned like that one."

"I set fire to the place before I went down the pipe. Given how old the wood was, it would've spread rapidly," Jinaari said.

Thia looked at him. "You could've turned the entire city to ash!"

He shrugged. "Too much stone, so I knew that wouldn't happen. If it had, we wouldn't be here now. Besides," he continued, "there was a bunch of spiders coming after us. Too many. I had to buy us time to get away."

Turning her attention back to the road, she focused on her breathing. Her mind began to form the sigils she might need. *It's a different sort of fight than I've been in before. This time, I'm taking the lead. They won't need to do anything if I do this right. And that means not holding anything back.* The restraint she normally had on her hands fell away. Her fingers tingled as the magic danced; the gloves making it painful. Resolutely, she pulled them off as they marched through the ruined city.

"Thia?"

She didn't look at Adam. Rather, she started to send out tendrils of magic to find what rested within the city that she needed to take care of. "What?"

"You're showing the sparks."

"This is the only warning the residents will get, Adam. I am their doom, a reckoning for walking the path they have. I know they'll come after me. They should know who they're dealing with." Out of the corner of her eye, she saw Jinaari's head snap toward her. Ignoring him, she kept walking. *I need to focus right now, not answer questions. There'll be time for that later.* The wind picked up, lashing against her face with cold precision. A sense of urgency made her quicken her pace. "Let's get this done," she said. "I'd like to get back to the monastery before the snow gets too deep."

"It's not snow . . ." Caelynn started to say, then stopped as large, white flakes began to fall.

"We still need to get around the building, Thia," Jinaari said.

Something about his voice nagged at her mind. *Does he think I'll let that stop me?* "We're close enough," she announced as she came to a halt. "I'm strong enough that the blasts will reach the edges of the city from here."

"No, we go to the center."

She turned to him, her jaw clenched, "Don't you believe me?"

"I do," Jinaari replied. His voice was calm, even. "That courtyard's more open than this street. We'll be able to see what's coming and prepare for it better."

"Nothing's going to come close enough to do any harm!"

He tilted his head to one side, giving her an odd look. "You said it yourself, Thia. One wave might wake up something else. You've also said I'm the tactician. We go to the center, wait for everyone to be ready, then you start the spell work. I know you'll do what you've said you can do. I don't doubt it for a minute. But my job is to make sure the risk isn't higher for any of us because you don't want to be in a snowstorm."

Thia blinked, stammering, "You're right. I . . . I don't know what I was thinking just now."

His expression changed. "Clear your mind. We'll talk later. Right now, we have a job to do."

She nodded, tucking her gloves into her belt. "I'm keeping them off for now. It feels right for the sparks to be loose. Don't worry, they're keeping my hands warm enough."

"It's not the sparks that worry me," he muttered. "Gnat!" he called out.

"Gnat here!" His small form popped up from behind some of the charred wood. "Gnat find path for Friend Jinaari and Friend Thia and their friends!" He began waving at them. "Follow Gnat!"

"Single file," Jinaari said.

"We know the drill," Thia replied, surprised at the annoyed tone her voice had. "Sorry," she stammered. "Guess I'm tired or something."

"It's the something that worries me," he said, soft enough that only she heard him.

Thia watched him climb over the debris; cautiously testing each step he took before moving forward. *He's the heaviest of us, with the armor. He's in the lead to make sure we don't fall.*

The irritation left her as quickly as it'd arrived. *Maybe he's right. Maybe there is something wrong with me.* He stopped, looking back at her. "I'm coming," she said as she began to climb after him.

The path down was easier. As her feet hit the cobblestones, she said, "We'd better not be chased out of here. That'll make it harder for us to get clear fast enough."

"It'll delay any pursuit just as much."

"Only if they're not spiders that can climb over it," she forced her tone to be light, trying to put him at ease. The concern didn't leave his face, though.

"Then we make sure they're not alive to chase us." He nodded toward the ruined fountain. "That where you need to be?"

A center obelisk stood, surrounded by a rubble-strewn platform. "Yes. There's enough room for me to move around, change the direction of the spell if I need to."

"Go. Gnat, fill your pockets with rocks for your sling then follow Thia. Stay up on the platform, but on the opposite side. I don't want you accidentally hitting her."

Adam came up next to her. "You won't be so high that I can't reach you if I need to. I'll stay near your feet."

"Caelynn?" Jinaari asked.

"I'll move fast, stay low, and go where I'm needed. Same as always."

As she got closer, Thia began to figure out the best way to get up to the raised area. Larger bits of carved stone—a head here, a torso there—gave enough elevation for her to climb up. Once she was set, she glanced at the burned down building. "Which way did we come from, Adam?"

"Over there," the blonde man pointed.

Thia placed her hand on the obelisk and walked to the side where he pointed. "When you're ready," she called out.

Jinaari stood in front of the fountain's base, watching her.

Nodding his head once, he lowered the visor on his helm. The hiss of his sword leaving the scabbard was muted by the falling snow.

It was time.

Taking a deep breath, she imagined the first sigil she'd designed. The one meant to kill not just the live spiders, but the eggs as well. The magic flowed out of her, radiating in a massive wave that pushed through walls until it reached the fortifications that surrounded the city. A few high-pitched screams echoed through the city, dying off as fast as they began. Without hesitating, she moved to the next sigil. Fifteen sigils, fifteen waves of magic, and she never faltered. Something within her clicked every time she let loose with a new blast; an audible movement of tumblers in a lock, lining up in perfect sequence to keep her friends safe.

She lowered her arms after the last one, smiling as adrenaline surged through her veins. The final piece fell into place, and she saw it in her mind. The cage unlocked, and a pair of hands cloaked in black feathers pulled the door back.

Scrambling down from the fountain, her eyes wide with terror, she looked to her right. One street over, the spire of a church that had once been dedicated to Hauk rose above the other buildings. The bell in the tower began to peal as the ground heaved.

"Keroys," she breathed as she sunk to her knees in despair. "What have I done?"

NINE

"Thia, stand up."

Jinaari's voice cut through the blind terror she felt. "I didn't know," she stammered as she looked at him.

"I know you didn't. Adam!" he shouted, "get the others and find Sayge. If one of us falls, get them out."

"What about you and Thia?" Adam said as Thia stood. Her legs shook with fear.

"We're the only two that can fight this. Your magic won't touch it. If you're too close, you'll die. It can't leave here, and I won't waste your lives."

Caelynn looked at her, then Jinaari. "What's coming?"

"Corse," Thia choked out the word.

"I'll keep us close enough to heal one of you if you're hurt," Adam said. Thia turned to the warlock; his face was somber. "I won't leave unless I have to."

Jinaari nodded. Thia stood, watching her three friends run away from them. "I didn't know I'd unlock his cage." Her voice was soft as dread took over.

"I did, Thia."

She turned to him in shock. "You knew? Why didn't you stop me?"

"Because this is what Garret told me to do." His words were clipped, angry. "I couldn't get to the cage myself. Silas buried it within the bedrock. I needed you to unlock it, set him free to come find me." He turned toward the noise, sword at the ready.

"You could've told me! Jinaari, Corse is a demon!"

"I know what he is, Thia. And he's going to be pissed after a century in his prison. We're the only two with the ability to finally kill him. Isn't that what you wanted to do? Purge Tanisal of everything evil that lived here?"

She nodded, swallowing her fear. "How can I help? I've never fought anything like this!"

"You've fought worse and survived. We all did." He glanced at her, and she could barely make out his dark eyes through the face guard of his helm. "I know you're pissed at me for not telling you. Let's take care of this, and I promise you can yell at me as much as you want. Right now, I'm trusting you to have my back."

"I'm going to hold you to that, you know."

"I do. You're too stubborn to let it go."

The street in front of them began to buckle; paving stones cracked sharply, rising at an angle as something underneath them struggled to come out. A single arm, cloaked in black, emerged.

"One condition," she whispered.

"What?"

The earth shook, and Thia lost her footing. Falling to the ground, she covered her head with her arms as rubble flew toward her. Something screamed; an inhuman bellow that echoed within her soul. She stood, staring at the creature.

The demon was a head taller than Jinaari. His body was covered with black feathers; blood red eyes stood out against the pale skin of his face. A cacophony rose from the buildings; hundreds of crows stood at the edges of rooflines, crying out to their master.

Corse turned his gaze to them; a smile forming on his face. "You have come, like you promised. I held true, Lolc Aon! I waited, and prayed, and now you know I am worthy of you!" He began to walk toward them.

"Lolc Aon is dead," Thia said. "And you will join her soon enough."

"No," the demon said, shaking his head. "She stands before me."

Thia felt something grasp her and she rose from the ground. Staring at Corse, she struggled against the unseen bonds.

"I know the smell of my Beloved," the demon said. "She is within you. I will find her, lure her out. You will embrace her and then you will remember me."

Jinaari screamed, and Thia watched him charge toward Corse. The demon shifted his focus, but she remained in the air. *Concentrate! He needs my help!* Pushing down the fear, she formed a sigil and sent a wave of healing to Jinaari as he was thrown into a wall. Timing her spell perfectly, she caused the snow around them to become thousands of small daggers of ice. Spinning them around, she threw them at Corse to distract him as Jinaari regained his footing. The demon screamed in pain, turning toward her. The bands tightened around her, crushing her arms and ribs, making it difficult to breathe. Without warning, they evaporated and she plummeted to the ground. Her leg made a sickening sound as she landed. Pain wracked her body. The crows began to scream again, followed by the earth shaking. Thia forced her eyes open and saw Jinaari standing on Corse's back, the pommel of his sword buried deep in the demon's skull.

Another wave of pain hit, making her scream as her body arched.

"Thia!"

She barely heard his voice; all she knew was agony. He was asking her something, but she couldn't hear him.

Something warm washed over her, chasing away the sharpest edges. "Codal," she gasped.

He took off his helm as he said, "I'll find it. Just one vial?"

She slammed her eyes closed against the pain, nodding slightly. *One should be enough.* If it wasn't, she'd wait until she was alone. "Water after."

"I'll have it ready. Keep your eyes closed for now." His voice was steady, reassuring. "I have to raise your head. It's going to hurt."

It can't get much worse, she thought as she nodded. She felt his arm slide under her shoulders and raise her slightly. Something touched her lips and she opened her mouth. The bitter liquid went down quickly, and she gratefully drank the water that followed. "Thank you," she said as he lowered her back to the ground.

"How long?"

"Not long," she said. The drug moved through her system, numbing her enough that she could breathe without cringing. Opening her eyes, she looked at him. "The others?"

"On the way. We'll wait for you to get where you can heal yourself enough to ride, then head back. There's nothing in the city left for us to do."

"Do you know what he meant?"

"About what?"

"About Lolc Aon being alive in me?"

He pushed her hair back from her face, "It's garbage, Thia. He was a demon. They lie. It's what they do. There's nothing about you that is even close to what she was. Not even the color of your eyes."

She relaxed at his words. The codal began to dive deeper into her body, and she raised her arms. "That's a good sign," she said. "I was worried they were broken."

"Your arms aren't." Jinaari's voice was calm, but she heard the concern.

Pushing herself up on her elbows, she glanced at her legs. The left one was twisted in three directions. "Oh, that's not good."

"You're the best healer I know, Thia. And you're stubborn. I have no doubt you'll be fine."

She laid back down. "You're going to have to put my leg straight before I can fix it."

"That's going to hurt like hell."

"I'm as numb as I can be and still get the sigil right. Don't tell me, just do it."

She bit her lip to keep from screaming as he straightened her leg out. Tears fell from her eyes, but she kept her breathing steady. Forming the sigil in her mind, she released the spell and waited for the bones to mend. The magic dissipated, but the pain remained. She recast the spell, panic overcoming the pain as her body refused to accept the healing. "Jinaari," she whispered, "something's wrong."

"What?"

She stared at him. "I can't heal myself."

"Adam!" he screamed, "I need you!" Turning his head back to Thia, he said, "Did you feel me do something earlier?"

"Yes." Reaching out, she touched his cheek while visualizing the sigil. The bruise on his cheek faded. "I can still heal you. Why isn't it working on me?" Panic flooded through her body and her breath came in short gasps.

"I don't know, but we'll figure it out. Gnat, go find some pieces of wood. We're going to need to splint her leg."

"Gnat find what Friend Thia needs!"

Caelynn's face came into focus, and the other woman grabbed one of her hands. "What's wrong?"

"We don't know yet," Jinaari said, "but she can't heal herself. I've given her a dose of codal, done as much as I can, but she'll need more. Enough to get her back to the monastery and let their healers work on her."

"Splint it first, please," Adam said from near her head. "I'll have to restrain you, Thia. Not much, but enough so you don't move. I don't want to heal bones that aren't straight."

"I understand," she said. The codal was deep in her muscles now, and she was feeling sleepy. "Do what you need to do. I'm not feeling much pain." One question screamed through her mind. *Why can't I heal myself?*

Too many questions. What had Corse meant about how he could smell Lolc Aon in her? Why could she heal Jinaari but not herself? *Is part of Lolc Aon still living in me? Is that why? Keroys, you said you'd answer if I needed you. Where are you?*

A ghostly finger of pain made her open her eyes. Jinaari and Caelynn were securing the splint around her broken leg. "Do we make a litter? She's half asleep from the codal," Caelynn said. "She can't walk unaided, and you can't carry her the entire way."

"Sayge left when we saw Corse fall," Adam said. "She was going to tell the monks what happened. They'll come in if we don't come out, eventually."

"I don't want to leave her out in this weather while we wait." Jinaari looked at her, then at Adam. "Can you transport us outside to the horses? Or back to the monastery?"

"Not with the codal in her system. It could cause too many other reactions."

"There," he pointed behind her, but she didn't have the energy to see what he was talking about. "We get her in there, keep her warm. Then one of us can get the monks while the others build a litter."

"I can walk," Thia said, trying to push herself up.

Jinaari put his hand on her shoulder, gently pushing her back down. "I know you think you can."

She closed her eyes again, too tired to argue with him. Someone picked her up, but it wasn't Jinaari. "I've got her," Adam said. "It's not far and you need your sword arm free."

"There's nothing left in here for me to fight."

"No, but I've seen that face before, old man. You're ready to break something, and Thia's already hurt."

Thia's body began to tremble. *Why? I don't feel cold.* "I'm fine," she muttered.

"You will be, Thia. We're family. That means we're going to take care of you."

She rested her head against his chest and gave up.

Her body ached, but it wasn't the sharp, stabbing pain that she'd felt in Tanisal. She was warm and laying on something soft. Opening her eyes, she saw the opaque orange curtains that hung from the ceiling, surrounding her bed. The Temple? How? She sat up, trying to remember how she'd gotten there. The last thing she recalled was Adam carrying her.

"Are you awake?" Jinaari's voice called out softly.

"Yeah. How'd I get here?" Thia saw his outline rise from a chair and walk toward her. *My leg!* She moved aside the blanket and looked. The splint was gone.

"We got you into a house, then Caelynn led the monks into the city. We built a litter, hung it between two horses, and put you on it. It was slow, but we got you here." He pushed aside the curtain and sat next to her. "The healers spent hours working on you before they were happy. I think every single one had to heal something, as a matter of honor. It's not often they'd get the opportunity to help the most powerful healer in Avoch."

She looked at him, swallowing the lump in her throat. "If I'm so powerful, why did my body reject my attempts?"

"Try now. Something small. There's bound to be at least one bruise on you somewhere that they missed."

Thia closed her eyes. She could see the sigil clearly in her mind. Releasing the spell, she felt it touch her skin, then dissipate. Opening her eyes, she looked at him. "It just goes away."

He took one of her hands in his. "The sparks are still here. And you healed me, after you got hurt. This could be temporary."

"What if it's not?" Panic tinged her voice.

Brushing her hair back from her face, he looked at her. "Then we'll adjust, deal with it. You don't get into direct combat anyway. Adam and I will make sure you get healed, if you need it. We can take our time heading south; Gnat's home will be there." He shifted. "We can't leave until Adam comes back, so you can go walk the garden again. Maybe Keroys will visit you and give you answers."

"Where'd he go?"

"Back to Almair. He transported himself once he'd rested and knew you'd be okay. He said he needed to check something in one of the books back in his room. I didn't argue, because I knew you needed the rest. Even if you don't want to admit it. Are you hungry?"

"Are you trying to change the subject?"

"Some, yes," he admitted. "But I also know you need food to get your strength back." His face grew serious. "Something's wrong with you, Thia. It's not a simple cold, either. Your personality shifted when we were in Tanisal. You said things that surprised all of us. Just as quickly, you were your normal self again. Then, your magic won't work on you. It doesn't make sense."

"But I feel fine!"

"I believe you, but that doesn't change what we've all seen. You can't deny it, Thia. Not anymore. Whatever's wrong didn't start with that cough, and I fear it's going to get worse if we can't figure this out."

"Worse how? Are you keeping more secrets from me?" Her tone was bitter, and she saw him flinch at her words. "You say you want me to have your back, but you don't tell me what I'm walking into so I can!"

"Garret told me not to. I can't defy him any more than you can defy Keroys."

She tilted her head to one side. "Really? You're going to fall back onto that excuse? I bought it when you said that's why you didn't tell me I was Marked, but I thought you trusted me enough now that you could tell me the truth!"

Jinaari rose. "There's food on the table. Caelynn will be outside if you need something. I trust you, Thia. Garret said you were the only one that could unlock Corse's cage, but that knowing it would make you hesitate. That you'd balk at casting the last spell because you didn't want to face him. I argued that you were smarter than that." He walked to the door, glancing back at her. "Maybe it's you that doesn't trust me enough to realize I won't lie to you. I may not tell you everything you want to know, when you think you should know it, but I've never lied to you." He left, closing the door behind him.

Thia fell back on the pillows, tears stinging in her eyes. *Jinaari's right. Something is wrong with me. But how can I find out what if I can't heal myself? And why am I blaming him for things that are completely out of his hands? If Garret told him not to tell me, he can't. He swore an oath!*

Sighing, she pushed aside the blankets and swung her feet

onto the floor. A tray with small bowls sat on a low table between two chairs. *Maybe if I eat something, my head will clear up. I'm not thinking straight.*

She tested her left leg, making sure it would hold. It felt weak but supported her. Halfway to the table, the room spun violently and she fell, blacking out before she hit the ground.

CHAPTER

TEN

J inaari placed a hand against the smooth wood as he released the handle. *I don't know what's wrong, but we'll figure it out, fix it. Somehow.*

"Is she awake?" Caelynn said.

Turning, he nodded. "Yes."

Caelynn crossed her arms and stared at him. "But she's not better, is she?"

Jinaari opened his mouth when he heard a muffled thud come from Thia's room. Spinning around, he jerked the door open.

Thia lay on the ground, one hand outstretched toward the food he'd left on the table. "Thia!" he screamed as he ran into the room. Dropping to his knees, he checked for a pulse. "She's alive," he said.

Caelynn knelt opposite him. Her face mirrored his concern. "What's wrong with her?"

"I don't know, but we'll figure it out. See if there's any blankets or furs in that chest," he said as he eased his arms under Thia's body. "I'll get her back in bed. The room's gotten

101

cool, and she needs to stay warm." Slowly, he stood with her in his arms. Her face was pale and scrunched up in pain.

"Found something."

He carried her over to the bed, easing her onto it. As soon as he drew the covers up to her chin, Caelynn was throwing another one on top. She looked at him, expectantly.

"Stay with her. I don't care what she says, one of us is with her at all times until we know more. I'm going to ask about getting fresh coals in the braziers." Jinaari took one more look at Thia's face. "For now, we keep this between you and me. I'll bring Adam up to speed when he gets back."

"Okay," Caelynn said as she sat on the bed and took one of Thia's hands in hers. "He knows what he's looking for, so he'll be back as soon as he has the stores for the transport. I already told the Grandmaster to expect him outside the main gate at some point. He shouldn't be kept waiting in the cold."

"Keep the doors closed except for me and the monks bringing the coal," he said as he crossed the room. Opening the door, he left, closing it behind him.

Garret, if you can hear me, Thia's sick. She needs Keroys. Please . . . talk to your brother and ask him to come. As he stepped out onto the walkway, he saw Mishar to his right. "Mishar," he said, trying to get the man's attention.

He turned around, bowing as Jinaari approached. "Greetings, Shield. How is the Daughter feeling?"

"She's still asleep, but I'm certain she'll be fine. Her room has grown cool, though. Would it be possible to get some fresh coals brought in?"

"Of course. I'll see to it personally."

Out of the corner of his eye, Jinaari caught a movement below them. Someone was in the garden, on Garret's path. "I appreciate it. Caelynn's in the room with Thia to let you in. If you'll excuse me," he said in parting. Darting around Mishar, he began to walk down the ramp. The pull to the garden grew with each step.

He didn't hesitate when he reached the path. As soon as he crossed the threshold, time stopped. The monastery melted away, becoming a small room within a cabin. Two chairs sat in front of a fireplace; the logs within crackling as they burned.

"Put your feet up, Althir," Garret said from one of the tall chairs.

Jinaari walked slowly toward the other chair, glancing back at where he'd been. The wall was solid wood; no window or door where he would've entered through.

I can't leave unless he lets me. "My Lord Garret," he said, lowering his head respectfully, "You honor me."

"Stop the formalities, Althir. I told you to sit down."

Jinaari sunk into the other chair and stared at the fire, waiting for his God to speak.

"You did it. And Avoch is safer for it. Corse was the last of his kind. Had he lived, even Nannan wouldn't have been able to stop him."

"I was surprised he fell so easily," Jinaari admitted.

Garret shrugged. "He was distracted. It's one reason Silas chose to lock him away over killing him."

"Is that why Thia had to be there without knowing what she would do?"

"I knew you would kill him, Althir. I haven't invested in your training without reason. She was there to unlock his cage, make him think he'd won, and give you the opportunity to do your job."

Jinaari shied away from the matter-of-fact tone in Garret's voice. Part of him wasn't surprised at the tactics, but his soul wasn't as ready to accept Thia as nothing but bait. "Corse said that Thia had part of Lolc Aon in her. Is that true?"

"He was a demon, Althir. They lie just by breathing. Anything he said shouldn't be believed."

The nagging thought resisted Garret's reassurance. "Thia's been acting strangely lately. If she is, in fact, somehow carrying part of Lolc Aon within her . . ." he started to say, stopping as Garret waved his hand dismissively.

"Keroys's favorite is flawed, Althir. He likes picking damaged souls to do his work, unlike me." He turned and stared at Jinaari. "You made promises, vows, to *me*. Not my brother. I've told you before that you can't have two masters. You are who you are, what you are, by my grace. Don't think for a heartbeat that I won't find something else for you to do, with other people, if it suits my need."

Garret's rebuke hit him hard, and Jinaari sat straighter in his chair. "Is that why you summoned me here? To tell me I need to leave my companions?"

"No," Garret sat back and picked up a goblet. "I had planned to tell you that you could take some time off. Your entire purpose since birth was to do what you did in Tanisal. This whole Shield nonsense, trying to protect Keroys's pet, is annoying but you got the job done. That's what matters."

"Why am I here, then?" Jinaari kept his voice even.

"You seemed rather desperate when you called out to me."

"Thia's sick. I didn't think Keroys would respond if I appealed to him, so I hoped you would intervene on her behalf."

Garret sputtered. "I'm a God, Althir," he sneered, "not some damn messenger boy! What makes you think his brat deserves my help in any way?"

"She can't heal herself, My Lord."

"So? As long as she keeps you alive, who cares if she can heal herself?"

"It's not just that. Her personality is shifting. She's snapping at people, making unfounded accusations. When we were heading into the city, she called herself 'their doom, a reckoning for the path they chose to walk'. The spiders were large, yes. They're carnivores and would be a problem if they hadn't been contained within the city. But they don't think like we do. They don't choose evil or good, they just follow their instincts."

"She said what? Her exact words, Althir."

Jinaari cringed at the tone. "We'd entered the city. She took her gloves off, and the sparks were showing. Adam questioned her about it; it's not something she normally does, show off her power like that. Her reply was, 'This is the only warning the residents will get, Adam. I am their doom, a reckoning for walking the path they have. I know they'll come after me. They should know who they're dealing with.' I asked her if she was okay, and she returned to her normal self."

"Shit." Garret's voice was low, almost too soft for Jinaari to hear. The God leapt to his feet, and Jinaari followed suit. "Stay with her, Althir. If there are other changes, anything that makes you question her, tell me in your heart. I will hear you."

The room disappeared, and he found himself standing on the path in the garden. A sense of dread washed over him. Something about what Thia had said scared Garret. But what?

He left the garden but didn't rush back to their rooms. *How much do I tell her, and how much should I keep quiet? Whatever's wrong has her questioning her trust in me as it is. If I tell her Garret's worried, will that make her worse? If I don't, and she finds out, she could stop talking to me entirely. Garret didn't specifically tell me not to tell her, just to stay with her. Why? Because she needs me or because he wants to watch her closely? I didn't know he had such a low opinion of her. She's not Keroys's pet any more than she is broken or flawed. No more than the rest of us, anyway.*

"Jinaari?"

Adam's voice broke through his thoughts. His friend stood next to him, concern on his face. "You're back."

"Just now. What's wrong? Hasn't Thia woken up?"

"She did, then passed out again after arguing with me. Caelynn's with her now." He started walking toward the ramp, "Did you find what you needed?"

Adam fell in step next to him. "Unfortunately, yes."

"What do you mean?"

The blonde man sighed. "The demon wasn't lying, Jinaari. Part of Lolc Aon does live in Thia. It's several generations removed, but she's a direct descendant of one of the female children the Goddess had."

"Shit," Jinaari breathed. "She's not going to take that well."

"Do you think we should tell her? She's not herself, Jinaari. Finding out you're related to someone that was everything you've ever fought against in your life would send anybody over the edge. I'd rather not have her lose control and create a crater where we stood."

"We have to trust that she won't, Adam. She deserves to know, and it's better if it comes from us than someone else. If you were able to discover it, someone else can." Adam started to speak but Jinaari cut him off. "I don't care if the books are under wards that only you can unlock. You didn't write them. Which means someone, either in Helmshouse or someplace else, discovered it." He paused, then said, "Did the book actually list her name?"

"No," Adam admitted. "The genealogy ended with Herasta's birth."

"That's bad enough. Herasta let all Byd Cudd know Thia was her daughter. There's the chance that a copy of the book is somewhere in that city. Someone besides you and I know. It's got to come from us."

Adam nodded, "You're right."

They stopped at the door to the common area. Opening the door, Jinaari said, "Get settled, grab some food if you need it. I'll wait here. We'll go in there together." Closing the door behind him, he turned and saw Caelynn sitting at the table. "Why aren't you with Thia?" he asked. "I told you to stay with her."

Caelynn stared at him. "Keroys came and told me to wait out here. I'm not arguing with a God. If he can't help her, no one can." Turning her head, she watched Adam disappear into his room. "Did he find out anything?"

"Ask him," Jinaari replied. He pressed his ear against Thia's door. He heard a male voice muttering but couldn't understand what was being said.

"Come in," a man said, his voice loud enough for Jinaari to hear. "Thia is deep asleep and we can talk freely. There is much for you and I to discuss, Shield, so that you can best protect my Daughter."

He twisted the handle, opening the door enough to slide inside. Closing it behind him, he glanced toward the bed. The curtains were drawn; he could see her lying still beneath the blankets.

"Sit with me, please."

Turning his head, he saw Keroys gesture toward a chair as he sat. Jinaari walked closer, trying to keep his step light. "Is she going to be all right?" he asked.

"In time, I believe so." Keroys looked at him. "You can check if you like."

"No, My Lord. I do not doubt your word."

"Please, sit. There's no reason to stand on ceremony with me. Unlike my brother, I take little comfort in formalities." He paused. "Do you mind if I use your given name? We both wish to keep Thia safe, and alive. Tripping over names and titles will deflect from that goal."

Jinaari sat, surprised at Keroys's words. "I would be honored."

"Good. I am impressed by you, Jinaari. You saw this illness in her when I did not. She mentioned it when we met in the garden yesterday, but I couldn't see then what is so obvious now."

"What's wrong with her?"

"I'm not certain of the source, but something is trying to control her from within. There's a part of her—something that's always been there, dormant—that's awoken. Her will is strong. You know this."

"She's the most stubborn person I've ever met," Jinaari said with a chuckle.

"Indeed, she is. I strengthened my Mark on her. It won't give her any additional stores. Rather, it will help her fight against that which seeks to overtake her."

"What do you mean? Is she possessed?" Jinaari asked, concerned.

"Not in the sense that you're thinking of. Thia has always been of two worlds. You know this. Even with her rejecting one, part of that is still within her. I fear it has awoken." Keroys paused. "Garret told me what you said. I would hear all your concerns. Of her companions, she trusts you the most. I believe you know her better than she knows herself. Unless it was something she said in confidence, I want to know."

Jinaari rested his arms on the chair. "The first thing I noticed was about a month ago. She had a cough that didn't sound right. She'd blame road dust, but it didn't make sense. She's healed me after a single sneeze. It's not in her to allow something like a cold fester in any of us. By the time we reached Solace, she wasn't eating much. I thought a hot meal in town would help, but it didn't. I talked to her about it, but she said she was fine.

"When we got here, she fell apart. She knew she had to go into the garden but was terrified about doing it."

"Why? When I sent out the summons, it was not meant to frighten her."

"She thought she'd see Nannan at the center, that she'd be

told to do something that would take her away from us." Jinaari sighed. "She sees us as family, something she hasn't had since her father died. I reassured her that we felt the same way and that, should she be told to go somewhere, we would go with her. After we met with you and the other Gods, we stayed in the garden. I told her a story that made her laugh. To be honest, it was the first time she'd laughed that much in months. I thought whatever was bothering her was gone.

"We developed a plan; get her to the center fountain in the city, let her do waves of magic to take care of the creatures within the city who needed to go. The giant spiders, scorpions, undead...anything she felt was evil or a threat if it left Tanisal."

Keroys leaned his head to one side. "Did you tell her that it would unlock Corse's cage?"

Jinaari shook his head. "No. Garret told me not to. He feared she'd hesitate, refuse to finish the process once she knew." He glanced over to where she slept. "Thia has every right to be angry at me for that."

"My brother's arrogant belief that he knows best in all situations is not one I agree with. I trust my Daughter; she would have argued with you out of stubbornness and her own fear but would've seen it needed to happen. Her sense of what is right has never wavered, even when her courage has."

"I tried to explain that, but he insisted. I cannot break my oaths to him any more than she can break those she made to you."

"Nor would I expect you to. Thia understands this, as well." The God paused. "Once you were in Tanisal, though, something changed?"

Jinaari nodded. "She normally hides the sparks that fly from her hands, either through magic or wearing gloves. She took them off, let them be seen. Adam questioned her, and her answer sent a chill down my spine."

"That's when she announced she was their doom?"

"Yes."

"Was that the only thing she said that alarmed you?"

"No. At one point, she stopped and announced she was close enough, strong enough to do what she needed to do. I told her we needed to get to the fountain, and she accused me of doubting her ability to kill everything before it could reach us. I reminded her of the advantage we'd have if we were in the center, and we kept moving."

"Did Garret tell you she had to be at the fountain?"

"Yes," Jinaari admitted, "he did. She argued with me, as I said. After that, everything went smoothly until she realized she'd unlocked Corse's cage. She was rather angry when I told her I knew it would happen."

"She's not likely to forget that."

"I know." Jinaari smiled briefly. "At this point, I welcome her yelling at me about that. It'd be a sign she's back to normal." He paused, taking a deep breath. "Corse said he could smell Lolc Aon in Thia before I killed him. I told her it was a lie, gave her some codal. That's when she discovered she couldn't heal herself. I tried to heal her the best I could." He leaned back in his chair, glancing at the bed. She hadn't moved. "We brought her back here, got her injuries healed. Adam and the others heard what Corse said, and he went to check on it. I was here when she woke up. I encouraged her to try to heal herself again, but it didn't work. Her personality shifted, and she accused me of not trusting her because I didn't tell her about my mission. I left, heard her fall. Caelynn and I got her back in bed. I went to the garden, talked with Garret. When I was coming back here, Adam found me. He'd investigated Herasta's lineage. It led straight back to Lolc Aon."

"My sister did not have the . . . restraint . . . the rest of us do regarding children. Where the rest of our family chose to restrict it to figurative offspring, like Thia, Lolc Aon wanted to have a personal connection with the few worshippers who followed her into the darkness." Keroys's voice was tinged with sadness. "And, despite what my brother thinks, Thia is not damaged. She's flawed, but then we all are. Garret is a fighter, a tactician. He believes in strength in arms more than he does magic. You are what he believes the rest of Avoch should strive to become: arrogant, confident, honorable, and ready to defend the land and its people at a moment's notice. Thia is strong-willed and stubborn, but she lacks your confidence. Her compassion is great because she knows what it's like to be shunned and hated for no reason other than the color of her eyes. The incidents you mention are bothersome because they are not the words of someone who has these traits."

"Is it possible that the connection to Lolc Aon is behind this illness?"

"I don't believe so. My sister was forceful, manipulative, and could match Garret in arrogance. However, the relationship is generations removed. Her power comes from me. Thia rejected everything that was Lolc Aon when she fought back down in Byd Cudd. Even if she comes from that bloodline, she is her own person. Her choices, decisions, are all hers."

Keroys looked toward the bed, and Jinaari did the same. Glancing back at the God, he asked, "I need to know the truth, My Lord. Is she going to get better?"

"Eventually, I hope so. But only if we can determine what is causing this." He paused, "Continue to head south as you planned. Don't change your route without reason. Thia will do better where it's warmer." He leveled a direct look at Jinaari. "You and your companions will need to keep her healthy. I took care of what I could, but her soul is fighting something I cannot see. Any magic she can use on herself is holding whatever this is at bay, preventing it from getting worse. How long that will last I cannot say." His voice dropped to a whisper before he locked eyes with Jinaari. "If we cannot find the cause, she will grow weaker, drawing on her magic to live. Her stores are considerable, but they are not bottomless."

He saw the concern and sadness in the God's eyes. "How can I help her?"

"You can start by not talking about me behind my back," Thia said.

ELEVEN

Keroys rose, and Jinaari followed suit. Thia sat on the edge of the bed, partially hidden by the curtains. "There is nothing said between us I would keep from you, Daughter. Nor do I restrict your friend from divulging it. I trust you to do what is right, as I always have."

Jinaari stayed near the chairs as Keroys walked to her. The God placed his hands on her shoulders. "How are you feeling?"

"Tired," Thia replied. "Annoyed, scared, and not sure why you took away my ability to heal myself." Her voice was soft and made Jinaari's chest hurt from the despair he heard.

"If you heard our conversation, you know that was not my doing. Your body is waging a war, and I cannot determine the foe. If I cannot find a cure, I'm certain your companions will. This will not be forever your fate. You have a long road to travel, Daughter. Your trust in your companions is well-placed, no matter how many questions you have about their motives. Not every truth comes to us when we want it. Remember that and stay strong. I know your soul, Thia, and I am proud of who you are." Within a blink of an eye, Keroys disappeared.

An uncomfortable silence descended on the room. *She's waiting for me to say something.* "How much did you hear?"

"How long have you known I was a descendant of Lolc Aon?" Her voice was tired, but strong.

"Less than an hour. Adam came back and told me shortly before Keroys invited me in here." He walked closer and leaned against the wall across from her. "I wasn't going to keep it from you, Thia. I told Adam we needed to tell you. It was going to be easier coming from us than it would from someone else. The lineage was written down, a straight line between her and your mother. If Adam could find it, make the connection, others could too. And would, eventually."

She nodded, saying, "Who else knows?"

"Me, Adam, probably Caelynn by now. Keroys." He looked at her. "Garret knows you're sick, but I don't know if Keroys will tell him about the connection with Lolc Aon."

Her head snapped up and she stared at him, her lilac eyes angry. "You told Garret about me being sick?"

"Yes. He's my God, Thia. I don't have any reason to think yours would respond to a prayer from me. I knew Garret might, and he did. I asked him if what Corse said was true, but he didn't give me a straight answer. He only reminded me that demons always lied."

She looked away and sighed. "What did Keroys say before I let you know I was awake? His voice was too low for me to hear." Her head snapped up and she stared at him. "He said he didn't put any restrictions on what you could and couldn't tell me, so don't even think about lying to me."

He took a deep breath, trying not to react to her words. "He told me that, if we don't find out what's wrong with you and get rid of it, your magic will be the only thing that sustains you. That you'll get to a point where you'll have to draw on it simply to live. Then he reminded me that your stores aren't bottomless." Jinaari kept his focus on her face, watching her expression shift as the reality settled into her mind.

"I'm going to die?" The anger had left her voice, replaced with fear.

Pushing away from the wall, he knelt in front of her. Taking her hands in his, he looked into her eyes. "I swear to you, Thia Bransdottir, I will not let you leave this world without a fight. This is my vow. Whatever it takes to find a cure, rid you of whatever this is, I will do it. I will see it happen. Tomorrow, we'll head south. Keroys thinks the warmer climate will help, and we promised to get Gnat home. As we travel, we'll track down every library, healer, mage, or wise woman we can find. Someone will know what's wrong, and how to cure this."

"Thank you," she muttered.

"Can I ask you a question? There's something I'm wondering about and I'd like to get an answer before we let Adam and Caelynn join us."

Her eyes grew wide. "What is it?"

He smiled slightly. "Before the fight, I promised you I'd let you yell at me as much as you wanted to for not telling you that you'd unlock Corse's cell."

"Do I get to do it now?" Her voice was playful, giving him hope the flash of anger she'd shown minutes ago was gone.

"No, because you said, 'one condition.' You never told me what that was." She lowered her head and chuckled. *Good*, he thought, *she's herself again.*

Raising her head, she met his gaze and smiled. "I think the condition was that you'd tell me everything Garret said about me. I had some strange thought that he didn't explicitly tell you to keep me in the dark, that you said that to cover your ass."

Rising, he let go of her hands. "Do you still need to know?"

"No," she said, shaking her head. "I know I've said things lately that make it sound like I don't trust you, Jinaari. I do." She sighed, leaning forward. The sparks danced around her fingertips. "I don't know why I said those things. It was as if part of me went to sleep and another part woke up. It keeps happening, and I can't control it. I don't even know it's happening until the words are out of my mouth." He saw a single tear fall onto her arm, forming a small, damp patch on the fabric of her tunic.

Jinaari closed his eyes briefly at the fear in her voice. "Thia," he said quietly, "there is nothing you could say to me that would make me break the vow I just made. Or any that I've made before now. I know who you are, the woman that the rest of the world doesn't get to see. I can tell when it's you speaking, and when it's . . . whatever this is. Caelynn and Adam will learn fast enough. I'll have one of them talk to Gnat, tell him you're sick. He does need to guide us to his home. I don't need him thinking you're mad at him."

Thia flopped back onto the bed, her pale blonde hair fanning out beneath her. "Gnat . . . I haven't said anything bad to him, have I?"

"Not that I'm aware of." Someone knocked softly on the door, and he turned his head to the sound. "Who is it?"

"It's me," Adam said. "Caelynn and I found something you should see."

Jinaari glanced at Thia. She stood at the end of the bed, hanging onto a bed post. "She's awake. Bring some food in with you." Walking over, he placed one arm around her waist. "Don't," he said, "I'm going to help you sit down before they come in." As he led her toward a chair, he kept his voice low. "How much they see will be up to you. I know you're stubborn and don't want to look weak. They won't care anymore than I do, but what they know is up to you." Easing her into a chair close to a brazier, he glanced at her hands. "Do you need your gloves?"

"No, I think I'll leave the sparks dancing for a while. Who knows? Maybe they'll give us a clue before my mind switches so you're ready for it."

"Good idea." The door opened and he watched as Caelynn stepped inside. Adam followed, carrying a small tray with food on it. Gnat trailed behind him, carrying a long tube.

"Friend Thia is better now?" Gnat stopped, looking at her.

"I'm feeling fine right now, Gnat. Thank you for asking."

"We're going to need more chairs," Adam said as he put the tray down on the low table. "Gnat, can you keep the door open while Caelynn and I get them?"

"Friend Jinaari hold this!" He thrust the tube at him. "Gnat help Magic Friend and Pretty Lady!"

Taking the item, Jinaari looked at Thia, shrugging his shoulders. He leaned it against the leg of the other chair, then picked up a bowl from the tray. Handing it to her, he said, "Eat. I'm not asking you; I'm telling you."

She took it from him, looking at the contents. "Do I have to eat all of it?"

"No," he said as he moved the chair and tube closer to hers. Sitting down, he continued, "Take your time, eat as much as you can. But make sure they see you eating."

"You're certainly looking better than the last time I saw you, Thia," Adam said as he placed a chair down. Caelynn put hers down next to his. "How's the leg?"

"It's good," Thia said. "Keroys healed what the monks couldn't. I'll be able to ride in the morning."

"Speaking of that," Adam looked around, pointing at the tube near Jinaari's feet, "Hand that to me."

Jinaari gave it to him. "What is it?"

"Mishar overheard something about us heading south and gave us a map. Gnat was able to show us where he lives." The warlock opened one end and pulled out a large parchment. Unrolling it, he said, "Move the tray, Caelynn." Once she cleared the table, he put the map down.

Jinaari looked it over, finding areas he knew well. "We're here," Adam pointed to a small symbol for Silas not far from Tanisal. "And Gnat . . ."

"Gnat live here!" the cobalus jabbed his finger enthusiastically at an area to the bottom of the map.

"In Taigh Forest? At the foot of Mathaireil?" Thia asked.

Gnat smiled, nodding vigorously. "Gnat has nice cave! Gnat show Friend Thia!"

"Okay," Jinaari said, studying the map closer. "We know where. Gnat, where does your friend live? The one with Nyfe?"

"Furry Man not Gnat's friend. Not like Friend Jinaari. Furry Man lives here." He pointed to another part of the forest.

"It'll take us half a day on a good day to get between the two," Thia said.

"That doesn't bother me. What does," Jinaari said, "is getting from here to there. That's going to take us a month, possibly two. Adam," he looked up from the map, "have you ever been here?" He pointed to a town called Tavisholm.

Adam hesitated and looked at Caelynn. "I have," he said after a pause. "So has Caelynn. Why?"

"If you transport us there, it's going to save us time."

"No," Thia said.

He looked at her. "Why not? I'd rather not spend two months in a saddle if I can avoid it. You don't need to be sleeping on the ground, either."

She met his gaze. "But what if the one person who knows what's wrong with me lives between here and Tavisholm? There's plenty of small villages," she waved her hand over the map, "along the way. If the map's accurate, lots of farmland.

Which means barns we could pay to sleep in, out of the weather, if there's no town with an inn. Plus, given what Keroys told me, we're going to need Adam's stores. I don't want him wasting them by transporting us."

"What did Keroys tell you?" Caelynn's voice shook.

Thia looked at him, nodding her head. Her hands trembled slightly. "Her magic is keeping whatever this illness is from getting worse, and that's why she can't heal herself. If we don't figure out what's wrong, and how to cure it, eventually all her stores will be used to keep her alive. As strong as she is, though, they're not bottomless."

Caelynn leapt from her chair and hugged Thia. "I won't let that happen! We must find a way to keep you alive!"

"We're going to. No one wants that to happen." Jinaari waited as the bard sat back down, wiping tears off her face. "Thia's right. We should start by going overland. But we need to say we're on a quest for someone else, not her."

"Why lie?" Thia asked. "If this gets as bad as Keroys thinks, people will know I'm sick."

He turned to her. "We must hide it as long as we can. It's one thing for our friend to be sick. Avoch would be thrown into chaos if they knew the Scepter was deathly ill."

"Amara?" Adam suggested. "We could send some carefully worded messages to Elizabeth and Tomil, so they can keep up the illusion that Thia's okay."

Jinaari nodded. "A runner would take too long. They need to know before we leave here. I trust the monks; they won't say a word about this, even amongst themselves." He looked at Adam. "How are your stores?"

"I'm not full, but I can make a few more trips if it's just me."

"I'll write the messages; we'll both sign and seal them. You're known in both Almair and Cirrain, no one would deny you access to either of them. Make sure you're alone, give them the letters. If they have questions, answer them but leave out details of where this might go. No reason worrying them over something that won't come to pass."

"What if it does, Jinaari? My aunt should know . . ." Thia began to protest. He put one hand on hers, reassuring her.

"If Keroys wants to fill her in, he will. Elizabeth's a politician, which is why you and I agreed she should wear the crown. Killing demons, defeating monsters, isn't without risk. She knows this. The less we tell her, the easier it will be for her to show the world that she's not worried."

"What can I do?" Caelynn asked.

"Gnat help, too!"

"You two stay here. One of us needs to stay with Thia at all times."

"I've had a few moments when I've said things I didn't mean," Thia said, her voice quiet. "Please don't hate me if it happens when you're around. It's not me, it's whatever this sickness is. My mind goes to sleep and something takes over."

"Her injuries were severe enough that her staying in her room shouldn't raise questions. Once Adam delivers the messages and comes back, we'll head south," Jinaari said.

"What about the records?" Thia asked.

"What records?"

"Mishar told me that they write down everything that happens, keep a record for history. There's an entire library here. That we came, what we did in Tanisal will be written down. They'll likely mention I couldn't heal myself."

"Caelynn, I want you on this," Jinaari said. "Have Mishar take you down there. Don't argue about anything they write; Silas commanded them to be honest and I'm not expecting them to defy him. See if there's anything in their archives that talk about a healer who can't care for their own wounds . . . a Marked individual whose magic changed suddenly. There may be a clue here that we need."

"I'll start as soon as Adam's on his way," she promised.

"What can Gnat do?" the cobalus asked.

"I need to sleep," Jinaari said. "Can you stay here and watch Thia while I do that?"

Gnat nodded his head enthusiastically. "Gnat talk with Spoone and Forkke! They keep Friend Thia safe with Gnat!" Without warning, he climbed into Thia's lap. "Friend Thia not do anything without Gnat knowing!"

Thia rolled her eyes and Jinaari held back the laughter. "Great idea, Gnat." He looked at the other two. "I'll get the letters written while you get ready, Adam. Gnat, I need Thia to sign it and use her signet, so you'll have to let her move enough to do that. Caelynn?"

"I'll stay with Adam until he's gone, then head to the archives." She rose, following the warlock out of the room.

Jinaari stood and looked at Thia. "I'll be back in a few. I'll keep things vague, let Adam fill them in if they have questions. If you need something, ask Gnat to get it for you." Ignoring the annoyed look she wore, he left.

It didn't take long to write the two letters. They were practically identical, letting each recipient know they were heading south toward Tavisholm, that any message they sent there would be received in a few months.

As the wax melted, he looked back at the words. *Adam and Caelynn both reacted oddly when I asked if he'd ever been there. I wonder why?* Pouring some wax onto each letter, he pressed his signet ring into the puddles. He picked both up and took them to Thia.

Gnat was still sitting in her lap when he walked into the room. "Gnat," she asked, "do you see my pack?"

"Gnat see pack!"

"Inside is a small box with some wax and a ring inside. Can you bring those to me while I read the letters and sign my name?"

"Gnat get box!" He jumped off of her and ran toward her pack.

"I hope you don't plan on taking a long nap," she muttered.

"As long as I need. The bed is comfortable, and I'm not as concerned about your safety while we're here." He brought over a candle. "You're the one who said he's harmless."

"He is. He's also absolutely devoted to you. I'll be lucky if I can get him to turn around so I can use a chamber pot!"

"Gnat find box!" He came scampering back over to them, holding it out to Jinaari.

"It's Thia's, Gnat. You should give it to her," he said.

Gnat looked at her, then back at him. "Friend Jinaari said Gnat should not let Friend Thia do anything."

"Oh, bloody hell," Thia muttered under her breath, barely loud enough for Jinaari to hear her.

"Gnat, Thia is perfectly capable of doing some things for herself. Opening a box is not hard. What you need to do is stand watch, not let anyone besides one of us in here, and let me know if she falls or something like that. If she wants to bathe, I don't expect you to stay in the room while she does. Understand?"

Gnat's eyes darted around as several thoughts played across his face. Suddenly, his skin grew pink as he realized what Jinaari was saying. "Oh."

"Thank you," Thia said as she pushed her signet into the second letter.

Folding them, he wound the ribbon around one while she did the same with the other. "I'll get these to Adam, see him on his way," he said as they finished sealing the letters shut. "I can come back here, let Gnat rest, if you'd prefer."

"I'll be fine with him," she replied. "You worry about me too much. If you were here, and I was awake, you wouldn't get any sleep. You need it as much as I do."

"I'll come back when I wake up. I promise." Rising, he looked at Gnat. "Keep her safe." Without another word, he walked to the door and left.

Crossing the main room to Adam's room, he paused when he heard Caelynn's voice. "We can't get all the way there without telling them, Adam."

Jinaari put his ear against the door, picking up Adam's reply through the wood. "We won't. I'll know when the time's right to tell them. So will you."

Jerking the door open, he stared at both of them. "What's wrong with now?"

They looked at each other, guilt written on their faces. "Would you believe me if I said there were too many ears? It's something neither of us want the monks to record, Jinaari. It's nothing even close to why I left Helmshouse in nature. Ancient history that bears little if any relevance to the situation at hand."

"If it's ancient history, as you say, then the monks already know." Jinaari kept his voice even as he stared at Adam. "You can make it so we're not overheard. I thought you and I agreed; no more secrets."

"You weren't exactly forthcoming with the knowledge that you were planning on facing a demon in Tanisal, you know!" Adam spat the words at him. "Even if you didn't tell us, you should've told Thia! She had every right to know what she would do when she cleared the city!"

"Garret forbade me from doing so. You don't have an allegiance to a God, Adam. I can't go against that vow! Ever! Or I'll be worthless trying to keep her safe!"

Adam stared at him, slowly shaking his head. "You have no clue who I have allegiances to, Jinaari. You've never asked."

Caelynn stepped between them, throwing her arms out. "Stop this, both of you!" She glared at Jinaari. "We're all scared for Thia right now, but we're not helping her by screaming at each other. Jinaari," she stared at him, "I know you feel hurt because we won't tell you this story right now. We have reasons, valid ones. Including being afraid that she'd level the entire compound when she hears our truth. There will be a time, between here and Tavisholm, where Adam and I will tell both of you everything. This is a story of our past, at the very start of our lives. It has little if any relevance to Thia's problem. I promise you that. Please," she lowered her arm, "I don't know everything of your life before I met you. Or of Thia's. That doesn't mean I don't love and trust both of you."

"Here," Jinaari said, holding the letters out to Adam. "I'm going to go lie down. We'll be ready to go when you return." Without waiting for a reply, he left.

A wave of exhaustion hit as he crossed the threshold into his room. *I'm not going to do her any good if I'm too tired to fight. Caelynn's right. We're all scared for Thia right now. I'll have a clear head after I sleep.* He unbuckled his belt, leaning the scabbard and sword against the head of the bed where he could reach it easily. Sitting down, he pulled off his boots. Laying down, he fell asleep within seconds.

TWELVE

Gradually, the dreamless sleep she'd fallen into faded away. As Thia woke, she heard someone shift in a chair. She stayed still, waiting for something to clue her in on who it was. *Gnat insisted on sitting on the floor, near the bed. Caelynn? Jinaari was exhausted. He should still be asleep.*

"Good morning," Jinaari said softly.

Sitting up, she saw him rise. The curtains and shadows in the dimly lit room hid his face. "How late is it? Is Adam back?"

He walked toward her. "It's not quite mid-morning. Caelynn sat in here, studying, until I woke up. I've been here less than an hour. She's resting. And, no, Adam's not back yet. I don't anticipate him until this afternoon. We'll have a lazy day, head out tomorrow. I want him to have full stores before we get on the road." He sat on the side of the bed. "How are things with you?"

"Okay, I guess. No headaches, I'm not tired, I'm just . . ." She sighed and looked at him. "I guess I'm waiting for something to happen that tells me it's getting worse." She looked at her hands; the sparks still danced as if nothing had changed. "I'm sorry," she said.

"Thia, you've done nothing wrong."

She raised her head and looked at him. "I promised you I wouldn't heal the bruise Sayge gave you until we were away from here. I know what it meant to her, and for you to have it show, but I healed it anyway."

His hand closed over her, reassuring her that he wasn't mad. "You needed proof that you could still heal others. It was visible, easy, and you saw it disappear. Your confidence needed the boost. I am not upset that you did it. It was necessary."

"I gave you my word, Jinaari," the words tumbled out of her mouth in a rush. "People already think the worst of me because of my eyes. If people start thinking I can't keep a simple promise, it'll—"

His finger touched her lips, and she fell silent. "If anyone asks, which no one here will, I'll tell them I did it. That the healing I can do also works on myself."

She shook her head. "I don't want you lying for me."

He smiled. "I won't be. The largest healing spell I can cast, the one I used on you, does help me at the same time. I'm a warrior, Thia. I get injured, as do my brothers. That sigil is designed to keep one person alive while healing the caster enough that they can continue to fight. It's also unique to Garret's Paladins, so I can't teach it to anyone. Not even you."

She cocked her head to one side. "Are you so sure about that?" Stretching, she continued. "A lazy day, you said? Does that mean you plan to get another bruise from sparring? I've never known you to simply lounge around."

Her heart skipped a beat at the look in his eyes. "Maybe I'm thinking of a different kind of sparring." His voice was low as he moved to kiss her.

Someone knocked softly on the door. "Jinaari?" Caelynn said as she peeked her head into the room.

"Later," Thia whispered as he drew back.

"What is it, Caelynn?" Jinaari asked. He walked closer to the bard. Thia pushed aside the blankets and searched for the socks she'd kicked off as she slept.

"Thia?"

"I'm awake."

"I may have found something. I don't know if it is, but it's the closest to what you're experiencing." Caelynn sat in a chair.

Walking toward the others, Thia threw a shawl over her shoulders. The bard held a large book in her hands, fingers marking a page. The leather binding was cracked with age; faded gold lettering decorated the spine in a language she didn't know. "What's that?"

"It's an alchemist's journal. He lived centuries ago in Tavisholm. Most of it is pretty dull reading; notations about potions requested, ailments they were good against. The local healer was a snob, apparently. They only healed those whose injuries they felt were 'worthy' of their magic. The rest of the city went to this guy. Here," she opened the book and sat it on the table, "is where it gets interesting."

Thia leaned in, trying to read the area Caelynn pointed to. "What language is it? I can't read it."

"That's the Old Tongue," Jinaari said. "It fell out of use after the kingdoms were united by the relics. Few know it now."

She looked at Caelynn in amazement. "You know this?"

"I'm a bard, Thia," she replied. "Some of the best tales are the oldest ones. I had to learn if I wanted to use them in songs or stories."

"What does it say?"

"A client came in, worried about their friend. They had an illness that was causing them to speak differently, show a different personality. At first, it was nothing but a cough. By the time the client came to the apothecary, it was much worse. Their family had shunned them because of the things he'd say, so this person took them in. Over time, however, the symptoms got more severe. The patient was tired, but unable to sleep. His speech patterns would change mid-sentence. When they tried to go to the local healer, they turned them aside in horror. And I quote, 'the priest declared before those waiting that the curse was divine in nature and that he would not undo the will of the Gods'."

"Cursed?" Thia looked at Jinaari. "Who would've cursed me? And when? I'd have known if this happened!"

Jinaari looked at her. "The symptoms aren't identical to yours, Thia. It's possible it's not a curse." He turned back to Caelynn. "What else does it say?"

"The apothecary gave them some potions, and instructions on how and when to use them." She looked up, and Thia drew back from the sadness in her friend's eyes. "I know the combination. It's used to induce a deep sleep. In the amounts specified, the patient wouldn't have woken up."

Thia sat back, stunned. "The apothecary helped this person kill their friend?"

"That's not the important part, Thia," Jinaari said. "If it's a curse, that explains why neither you nor Keroys could find anything wrong."

"But who could've cursed me?" she asked.

"Samil," Adam said.

Thia looked toward the door. Adam closed it then walked toward them. "When? How?" she asked.

"I don't know," he said as he settled into a chair. His face was tired. "When I confronted him in the Green Frog, he said something about you not being able to trust those around you, or appearing mad. This could be what he was talking about. If he did this, it happened between when he showed up and then."

Thia buried her head in her hands. "I was careful, though," she said. She felt Jinaari's hand on her shoulder, reassuring her. Raising her head, she looked at Caelynn. "You were there, almost every time I saw him. I refused the gift he wanted to give me. The one time he touched me, when I fell, he didn't say anything even close to a curse. He laughed about my elbow being sharp."

"It is," Jinaari said. "You've jabbed me in the ribs with it enough."

Thia glared at him. "That's not the point. How can he put a curse on me when I've never taken anything he's offered? I know how they work, Jinaari. It's either attached to an item, or the words are said to the recipient. Nothing he ever said to me could be considered a curse. He needed me alive, wanted me aware of what he was making me do."

"Where's the arrowhead?" Adam asked.

She blinked, trying to remember. "I'm not sure."

Jinaari looked at her. "What arrowhead?"

"When Samil pretended to be you, he wore a necklace—an arrowhead on a leather strap—around his neck. He said it was the one that he—you—were shot with and it was a reminder that he wasn't immortal. It proved my suspicion that it wasn't really you. You've never taken off your medallion that I know of. I got him close enough to break it off his neck. That's when the illusion shattered. It was the real thing he used to make my mind believe." She looked at Adam. "I remember showing it to you, when Samil disappeared. But I don't know what happened to it after that. As far as I know, it's back in your room in Cirrain. That, or I put it in my pocket and took it back to my room."

"Check your pack. Make sure it's not hiding in there," Jinaari ordered.

Thia rose and picked up her bag. Tossing it on the bed, she

began to rifle through everything. "Why can't I remember what happened to it?"

Adam coughed. "You had a fair amount of mead that night."

"Not so much I can't remember what happened." She threw the last bit of clothing aside. Picking up the bag, her hands searched every pocket. "If it's a curse, shouldn't it have died with Samil?"

"He's not dead," Jinaari said, "unless the Solar's decided otherwise."

"No. There's not been word about that from Helmshouse. I do, however, have these." Adam said.

Thia dropped the pack. "It's not in there." Walking back over, she took a letter from his hand. "What's this?"

"It's from Elizabeth and Pan. Jinaari's comes from Tomil and Amara."

Thia sat. The gold ribbon was accented by a blue border. The seal was her aunt's private one, not the one of the Queen of Avoch. Glancing at Jinaari, she saw him slide the other one between his leg and the arm of the chair. *Neither of us want to read them in front of Adam and Caelynn. Why? I have to tell them what it says. I trust them. Or, I should.* Shaking her head, she slid a finger under the seal and broke it.

"Thia?" Jinaari asked, "how are things with you?"

She looked at him. "No secrets, right? If there's something in here that we all need to know, that keeps me alive, then why wait?"

Adam coughed. "Tomil and Elizabeth both asked some questions before they wrote those letters. I tried to keep my answers positive, especially when it came to the seriousness of Thia's illness. That's what was asked of me."

Thia nodded, then began to read the letter.

My dear niece,

Your friend says you are well, all things considered, and I hope he is right. You are missed, and I look forward to seeing you ride back through the gates of Cirrain before midsummer. I've asked Pan to do some research, without telling him why as it would only worry him. If anything is found, I will send a message to Tavisholm. I have an old friend there who will watch for you.

Elizabeth

Shuffling the pages, she saw Pan's name at the bottom of the second one.

"Any news?" Jinaari asked.

"None yet," she replied, glancing at him. "Only that I'm missed, that she hopes we can return to Cirrain by midsummer. And that she put Pan in charge of research without telling him why. There's a note from him, as well." She noticed his letter was unsealed. "What news from Almair?"

"That I need to be back before my niece or nephew is born or my sister will have my head on a stake."

Thia smiled. "Amara's pregnant! That's great news!"

"Tomil said he'd send word to us in Tavisholm if he found anything."

"So did Elizabeth." Thia focused on the letter again, reading the second page.

Cousin!

Are you sick? Did Caelynn get hurt? Mother told me to look for something that might cause some strange symptoms but not why. I hope you're not sick. That wouldn't be good. But you're the strongest person I know, so it can't be you. You don't have to tell Jinaari I said this, but you're stronger than he is. Not with a sword or in a fight, but you've faced some pretty terrible people and came out on top. I mean, we kinda helped. I think. Eli says hello and that I have to stop writing or Adam will leave without my letter. It was nice to see him. I miss you all soooo much! Stay safe!

Pan

"If the arrowhead isn't with her, then it can't be the source of the curse," Caelynn said.

"Maybe it's not a curse?" Thia looked at Jinaari, hoping he'd agree. His face was blank, though. *That's odd.*

"Anything else happen we need to know about?" Jinaari's tone was flat.

What was in that letter?

Adam shook his head. "No. I went to Cirrain first, then over to Almair. Took a short rest while Tomil wrote the letter, enough to recharge my stores, and came back here. Where's Gnat?"

"Sleeping. You need to as well. I'm on watch. I want everyone ready to leave at first light." His voice was firm.

The other two rose. "I'll take this with me, see if I can find anything else," Caelynn said as she picked up the book.

As soon as they left, Jinaari said, "Thia, go lock the door. Put the key someplace, then bring me the pitcher and bowl over there."

She glanced to where he pointed. "What's wrong?"

"Do it."

"Okay," she said, rising from her chair. She locked the door, then walked over to where the items he wanted were. Leaving the key on top of the cabinet, she brought them over. "What's going on?"

He looked up at her, his face serious. "They're lying."

"Who?"

"Adam and Caelynn." He poured water from the pitcher into the basin. "I caught them arguing before he left. There's something they're not planning to tell us until somewhere between here and Tavisholm. Caelynn said it was about their past, had nothing to do with your illness, but she didn't translate the book correctly."

"You can read Old Tongue?"

Jinaari nodded. "Our spells use it. It's Garret's native language." Pulling a dagger out of his belt, he carefully pried up the wax seal on the outside of the letter he was given.

Thia blinked. "What did she get wrong?"

"The curse was put on the man by a death mage and could only be undone by either the caster or a God. At the time, death mages worked for anyone rich—or desperate—enough to afford their services." Jinaari sighed. "The man hired the mage, desperate to save his daughter from a disease. The priest had refused to, because the family wasn't well-connected. When his daughter got better, the mage asked for payment. Only the harvest had been lean and the man hadn't been able to earn enough from his crops. That's when the mage cursed him. Garret cured the man and gave his daughter to the mage as payment. He then turned on the priest, furious for his refusal to help. He disbanded the clerical part of his followers there and then, saying only those who knew the meaning of honor, would fight for justice, would ever be allowed to earn a place among his warriors. It's the day my Order came into existence. The story is taught to us as initiates as an example of why we must hold to our word."

Thia sat back; her chest tight. "I . . ." she stammered, "I don't understand. Why would she not tell us that?"

"I'm not sure. Garret can be an arrogant prick, and the story does paint him in a bad light to anyone who doesn't understand why he is the way he is."

"Is that where you get it from?" Thia tried to lighten the mood, but her mind reeled from what he was telling her.

"It certainly didn't lessen it."

"Did Amara say anything in the letter beyond being pregnant? You didn't share much."

"She did, but not in writing." He picked up the seal, "Back when I first went into training, Amara found a way to send me messages that couldn't be read. It was her way of keeping me informed of some of the more interesting things going on at court, since I wasn't there." He traced a sigil, then put his hands on each side of the bowl and whispered, "Calidus."

Steam rose from the water as Jinaari released his spell. "She could put a small drop or two of her blood into the molten wax of a seal. Until that letter got over twenty feet away from her, the seal would record everything she saw or heard, through her eyes. Any message with the words, 'blood strengthens us,' meant she'd done this. All I had to do was put it into hot water and let it melt." He glanced at her as he dropped the wax into the bowl.

Thia leaned forward, not sure what to expect. The water turned a dark red, then the color spread away from the center. She saw Tomil's face.

"I don't know, Amara," the duke said.

"Trust me," Amara's voice drifted up from the water. "He barely answered our questions and wanted unlimited access to the archives. Adam's traveled with Jinaari for years. I've never seen him so anxious."

Tomil handed her something, "You're sure this will work?"

"It will."

The background changed, and Thia watched as Amara headed down a hall and then a spiral staircase. "Adam?" she called out. "Are you down here?" She rounded a corner.

Adam stood in front of a wood table. Three books sat open in front of him. His eyes were wide. "I didn't think you'd be done with the letter this soon." Thia caught the catch in his voice.

"Tomil didn't want to say much. He trusts Jinaari to take care of Thia. Are those the early texts?" Amara asked as she walked closer.

The warlock slammed the books closed. "Yes, well, I was

hoping to find a clue as to the person Gnat spoke of. Helix." He took the letter Amara offered, tucking it between the pages of one book. "I've got to get to Cirrain yet, and we can't stay at the monastery that long. I know your brother's itching to get back on the road." He slid the book into his satchel. "I'll make sure to return this one. Don't worry." Colors swirled around him, and the water in the bowl became clear.

Thia looked at Jinaari, her eyes wide. "He told us he went to Cirrain first. Never talked about the book. Why?"

"I don't know. And that's the problem." Jinaari gestured at the letters she had. "We should burn those."

Handing it over to him, her mind reeled. "They worked so hard to gain my trust," she said, her voice quiet. "Both have saved my life. Adam helped me save yours. He told me there were some skeletons in his closet, but what could be so bad that he'd lie to you like that?"

Jinaari stood and walked over to one of the braziers. Thia saw him trace a sigil. The papers ignited, and he dropped them onto the glowing coals. "I don't know, but I intend to find out. They weren't willing to tell me earlier, so I'll give them a few days. Until then, I'll set up any room we stay in where I'm between you and them. They won't get past me."

Thia stared at him, horrified at his suggestion. "You don't think they'd do anything to me, do you? Jinaari, they're my family!"

"So was Herasta. Right now, I trust them as much as I did her."

THIRTEEN

Rain poured in sheets, chilling Thia to the bone. The road wound through featureless plains; outside of occasional herds of wild horses, they hadn't seen any evidence of other life for a week.

The air sizzled as lightning chased across the dark sky. "We need to find something," she said to Jinaari. "You're going to get hit if we don't."

"Over there!" Adam shouted.

Thia looked to where he pointed. In the distance, barely visible through the torrential rain, was a house. A barn sat off to one side, and smoke rose from the chimney. "Do we ask if they'll let us stay?"

Another bolt of lightning struck nearby. Thia cringed as the thunder roared in her ears. The smell of scorched earth rose from the ground. "We don't have a choice," Jinaari said. "Stay close, but ride hard."

"Hold on," she whispered to Gnat. The cobalus sat in front of her, shivering in the weather. She urged her horse into a gallop, chasing after Jinaari.

As they got closer, she saw three people trying to get some

sheep into the barn. The taller one turned as they approached. A father and his children? Jinaari slowed his horse to a trot, and she did the same.

"You picked a bad time to be traveling, friend," the man shouted over the storm.

"It wasn't by choice, but necessity," Jinaari replied. "Can we weather the storm in your barn? We can pay for the trouble."

"Nonsense. It's our duty to shelter those who need it. My wife's inside. Supper's almost done, and there's plenty. She always makes more than we need. Let the ladies go inside, dry off. Deion and I will help with your horses. Maide?" He glanced at a young girl, maybe ten, standing near him. "Run inside and let Mama know we have guests."

Jinaari grabbed Thia's reins. "Go," he told her. "Take Gnat and Caelynn. Adam and I will bring the packs."

Thia nodded, swinging her leg around the back of her horse. The mud was slick, and she grabbed the saddle to keep from falling. "Come on, Gnat," she said as she reached up.

"Gnat like mud!" As soon as his feet hit the ground, Gnat began to splash in the puddles.

"Please, Gnat," she said, "we're going into someone's home. It's considered rude to track a bunch of mud in with us."

His ears drooped. "Gnat sorry. Gnat forgot not everyone love mud like Gnat does."

Thia watched as Jinaari and Adam followed their host toward the barn. "Come on," Caelynn said. "Let's get out of the weather. They'll join us soon enough."

A pair of windows flanked a door. Firelight bathed the interior in a welcoming light. A large wood awning protected the entry. The door was open, beckoning Thia to go inside and get warm. Keeping her head down, she rushed across the muddy yard and up to the house.

Standing at the door, she called, "Hello? We were told to come inside."

"Please!" A woman called out. "Find a seat by the fire. I'm getting a few blankets to help warm you up."

Thia kept her hood up. As she walked toward the fire, she willed the sparks to hide before she pulled off her gloves. Gnat stood near the hearth, as did Caelynn. Steam began to curl up from their clothing as the heat evaporated the water. *I don't want them to treat us special because of who I am, who Jinaari is,* she thought. *Best to keep things quiet as long as we can.*

"Maide," Thia turned at the sound of the voice, "please take the bard and cobalus up to the guest room with these." A woman with pale blonde hair handed several folded blankets to the youth.

"Yes, Mama," Maide said.

Someone touched Thia's arm. Caelynn said, "The men will be in shortly. I'll go see how much room we'll have." She glanced at their hostess, and back to Thia. "I think she needs to tell you something without us hearing it. Come on, Gnat."

Thia watched the other two disappear up a staircase, a sense of unease growing within her. "We don't want to be a bother," she said. "We could easily stay here, on the floor. Or in the barn. We'll be out of your way as soon as the storm clears."

The woman turned toward her, and Thia took a step back. Pale blonde hair curled around her face. Except for the red eyes, she could've been Thia's twin. "Nonsense. After all, we're family."

Thia glanced toward the door. It stood open; the storm raging outside made it impossible to know where Jinaari and Adam were. "Who are you?"

"Please, make yourself comfortable. My name is Valtikka. And, yes, Herasta was my mother." She walked closer, gesturing to one of the chairs. "You look tired, Thia. I have no plans to harm you, though I understand your hesitation."

Thia swallowed her fear, pushing it down. "You startled me, that's all," she said as she sat. "Your husband and children didn't appear to be Thahion, so I didn't expect . . ." she paused, "family to be here."

Valtikka took a seat opposite of her. "I can see why that would be a shock. Mycchal isn't my husband. He says we're married to make things easier when we have visitors. He took me in during a storm similar to this one. His wife had died a year earlier, and he needed help teaching the children, keeping up the house."

"How long have you lived with them?"

"Not that long," she said. "I was near the surface, hunting for you, when word came that you were found. And what happened hours later. I decided to keep going forward instead of back to Byd Cudd." Valtikka leaned back, folding her hands across her lap. "I wasn't there, Thia, but I know what you did to Herasta."

"I was drugged," Thia said, keeping her voice even. "Lolc Aon coerced me into killing her, thinking it would be a step closer to me changing my affiliation to her."

"It doesn't matter. Garret's puppet did what really needed to be done, clearing the path for the one that we should've followed this whole time."

Something in the woman's voice unsettled Thia. "The Thahion have a choice of Gods to follow, if they choose." Rising, she said, "I'm going to go check on Caelynn and Gnat."

A small smile crept on Valtikka's face. "If you must. It won't change your fate but go ahead."

With measured steps, Thia walked toward the staircase. Valtikka remained in her seat, hands neatly folded on her lap.

She focused on the tread of each step, listening for something telling her which room Caelynn was in.

Reaching the landing, she stopped. Behind a closed door to her right, she heard something. Her heart raced; she knew the sound far too well. Thousands of feet skittering across the wood floor beneath her. Readying the sigil in her mind, she threw open the door.

Gnat and Caelynn lay on the floor; hundreds of scorpions swarmed away from their bloated bodies. They crawled out from under their clothing and their mouths. Her friends stared at her with lifeless eyes. Thia watched the scorpions as they scrambled toward a shadowy recess. The young girl sat on a chair, mouth open, as they went inside her.

"No," she muttered in terror, stepping back. Turning quickly, she ran downstairs.

Valtikka still sat in the chair. Mycchal stood near the fire, warming his hands. Neither looked at her as she ran into the room. "Knew the one was going to put up a fight, but didn't anticipate him cutting down Deion, given his age."

Thia stared at two large stones near the front door. They hadn't been there earlier. A bolt of lightning illuminated the room, and she screamed. Jinaari and Adam's severed heads stared at her.

"There," Valtikka said, clapping her hands, "you're free. No more ties to bind you to the life you had before. You can become who you were meant to be, who Lolc Aon herself feared. Welcome home."

"They were my family . . . you offered us shelter . . . how could you?" Thia stammered in terror.

"Sister, they weren't family. You had no blood ties to them. They were a means to an end, a way to keep you safe until you found me. I'm the only one you can trust to keep you safe."

Thia shook her head, "No." Tears ran down her cheeks

and she didn't care. The pain of grief was second to her anger. "They were family in a way you will never understand. I am no kin to you, or any other Thahion. I am the Daughter of Keroys." The sparks on her hands began to shift; becoming small flames.

Valtikka rose, "You may be Marked by that pretender, but Lolc Aon's blood runs through your veins. Her power, her glory, is your destiny. What trust does Keroys even have in you when he didn't give you the power to save your friends? They failed their Gods, and you. That is not family."

Thia roared, fire erupting from her hands. She sent it toward the two people near the hearth, bathing them in bright yellow flames. They screamed in agony; the smell of burning flesh made Thia want to retch. Her mind and soul numb, she ran out of the house and back into the storm.

The rage subsided, and the grief hit her like a tidal wave. Her feet kept moving; she didn't know where she was going, just away from that house. From their bodies. Images of their eyes floated in front of her. "I failed you," she screamed. "I said I'd keep you alive and then you died! For what? I can't do this without you!'

"Thia!" A deep voice, calm and reassuring, called out from behind her. "Stop!"

"No!" she screamed as she ran faster. "I won't do it! I won't become what she was!" Through the darkness, she caught sight of a rock formation. Her breath came out in ragged gasps as she sprinted for it. The footsteps of the person chasing her grew closer. *I need to hide!*

"Thia!"

She closed her eyes for a moment at the sound of Jinaari's voice. "You're dead!" she screamed. "You're not real!" A sob escaped her throat.

A pair of arms grabbed her, pulling her to a stop. Twisting

her body, she clawed at them. She lost her footing in the muddy ground and fell, taking her captor with her.

"Thia, I'm not dead. I'm right here. I don't know what you're seeing, but it's not real." His breath was warm against her cheek. "Please, come back to me," he pleaded in a whispered voice full of pain.

Her entire body shook as she twisted, trying to break free, but they wouldn't let go. "Let go of me!" she cried, the words coming out between sobs.

"No. I promised you I would keep you safe. I'm not leaving you."

"You're dead!" she sobbed. "You're all dead and it's my fault! I wasn't strong enough to save any of you!"

"I believe in you, Thia. I know what you're capable of. I've seen it, down in Byd Cudd. You broke free of the illusions then; you can do it again."

"I can't!" The pain was too much; she stopped fighting and bent forward. "I can't," she whispered. "I'm too tired to fight any more. I killed the only family I had."

"I'm right here, behind you. Adam and the others are on the way. We're not dead, Thia."

"I saw your bodies," she whispered.

"It wasn't real. Whatever you saw was a dream, an illusion. You have to fight back to break it, like you did when you defied Lolc Aon. I'm not letting you go until you're free of whatever this is."

Her captor shifted how he held her, and she felt wet fabric bump against her ankle. She opened her eyes and saw a sock-clad foot near hers. The fabric was soaked with mud. Her eyes grew wide as hope rose within her. *He was in his armor earlier. It's why we had to get out of the storm. If it's really Jinaari*, she thought, *then he's right. I can break free. If it's not, I'd rather die fighting.* Reaching back, her left hand closed around the hilt of a sword. Her fingers caressed the carved pommel, feeling the design that was unique to his blade. "Close your eyes," she said.

Methodically, she shoved all the pain and grief within her into a single sigil in her mind. She threw her head back and screamed as it dispersed, bursting out in a brilliant flash of light. She kept screaming; throwing in every single moment of doubt and pain she'd kept inside since her father's death.

The rain stopped. Her breath came out in ragged gasps, causing her to cringe in pain from her raw throat. Glancing back at his foot, she asked, "Why aren't you wearing your boots?"

"Because you needed my help more than I needed to have dry socks," Jinaari said. She felt his head touch the back of hers. "How are things with you?"

She took a deep breath. "Better, now. I think. What happened?"

His arms urged her to turn around, so she shifted her position. "You woke up and ran out of our camp. I chased you down." He reached up and pushed her hair back from her face. "What happened, Thia? I can't protect you if I don't know."

"I . . .," she paused, looking into his eyes, "I don't know. I thought we were traveling in a storm. We found a house, asked for shelter. One person led you and Adam to the barn, while the rest of us went inside. The woman, she was Thahion. She was one of Herasta's daughters. Caelynn and Gnat went upstairs. I found them, later, dead from scorpions. There were thousands of them. I ran downstairs and the man was inside. Near the door," she closed her eyes at the memory, "were two heads; it was you and Adam."

"Hey," he said, "look at me."

She opened her eyes and stared at him.

"It wasn't real. I'm right here, alive and well. Though I might have a cold if I don't change my socks soon."

Thia laughed. "That's your fault. You grabbed your sword but not your boots."

"I didn't know what made you run; I needed it. Plus, I can buckle my belt when I'm sprinting. I can't put boots on." He smiled, and she saw his body relax. "The others are coming. I told them to break camp and come find us when they were done." He looked up, and she followed his gaze. The rocky terrain offered little shelter from the wind that blew around them. "Let's find a place to wait out of the weather. You're soaked to the bone." He rose, pulling her up with him.

The wind cut through her shirt, making her shiver. Thia looked at the sky; the dark clouds were coming together. "At least you're not in armor. The lightning won't be attracted to you this time."

He looked at her, confused.

"In whatever that was I was stuck in; you were in your armor. There was a lightning storm. It's what drove us to take shelter where we did." Her voice trailed off. *It felt so real!*

Without warning, he pulled her close to him. She rested her head against his chest, listening to his heart beat. "I don't know what you saw, Thia. I only know what I saw. And that was someone I care a great deal for setting fire to a tent and running into the night, screaming. I haven't been that scared since we came back from Byd Cudd and you were in a coma. I didn't know if you'd hear me, but I had to try."

Thia raised her head and looked at him. His dark eyes were full of tears. "You look at me," he continued, "and see strength. I see that same trait in you. If I'm not sure, have any doubts, you remind me that it's okay. I survived what Samil did to me because I thought of you. I'm your sworn protector, but I didn't anticipate this. I don't know how to keep you safe from whatever it is that attacks your mind, Thia. And that terrifies me." He pressed her head against his chest, and she felt his head rest on top of hers. "I can't lose you."

"I can't lose you, either," she replied. Several large raindrops fell onto her shoulders, sending a chill through her.

"We need to get you warm," he said as he shifted his arms. "I can get a fire going if we find a place dry enough."

She followed him, one hand on the rock wall, as he searched for some sort of shelter. The rain came faster, and her teeth began to chatter as the cold seeped into her bones. "There," he said. He grabbed her hand and led her toward the small cave.

It didn't go back far, and the entrance wasn't wide. But it was dry, as long as the wind didn't shift.

"Stay over there," Jinaari said. As she walked to where he pointed, he said, "Looks like someone else used it for shelter. They left a stone ring and kindling. I'll have a fire going soon."

Thia rubbed her hands across her arms briskly, trying to chase off the chill. "Will it be hard for them to find us here?"

"I doubt it," he said. His back was to her as he worked. "Caelynn's one of the best trackers I've ever known. I know I left footprints big enough for her to follow." A small wisp of smoke curled up past his head, and a soft glow from the growing flames provided some light. He rose and waved her closer. "Come here. You need to warm up."

Gratefully, she walked closer. There wasn't enough room for both to be near the fire and stay out of the rain. "What about you?"

"You first," he said. He stood behind her. "You're soaked."

"So are you."

"I'm taller than you. I'll be fine."

For a moment, she thought about using magic to increase the size of the fire. As she dismissed it, she thought of something else. *Keroys, I hope this works!* Forming the sigil in her mind, she drew the moisture out of their clothing. In a matter of seconds, they were both dry.

"What did you do?" Jinaari asked her.

"Sped up the process with magic." Outside, the rain was coming down in sheets again. "You said I burned down one of the tents?"

He wrapped his arms around her, pulling her into his embrace, as he replied, "The smoke was what woke me up. I grabbed my sword, screamed at Adam to put out the fire, and sprinted after you."

"I could've killed someone," she whispered.

"Yes, but you didn't. You'll see for yourself when they get here." He paused. "The people in your dream. Did they talk to you?"

"Valtikka, that was the woman's name, did all the talking. She looked exactly like me, except her eyes were red. She said her mother was Herasta, that I was finally free to join my 'real' family and take Lolc Aon's place." She sighed. "At least, I think that's what I remember. I was scared, angry. It hurt so much to see the four of you dead, when I could've kept you alive."

"We aren't dead, Thia. It was a nightmare, nothing more."

She shook her head. "But what if it was something more? Jinaari, what if this is part of what's wrong with me? What if I'm going mad, like Samil told Adam I would?"

She felt his lips on the top of her head. "Not going to happen, so don't worry that it will."

She turned around and faced him. "That's not being realistic and you know it. There's something wrong with me. I don't know if it's a curse or what, but there is. I can't heal myself; I'm having nightmares that seem real. Eventually, I'll mess up when we're around other people and word will get out. How will they accept Elizabeth's rule if the Scepter can't even take care of herself?"

"Whatever's wrong, Thia, we'll figure it out. Together. I'm not leaving your side." His fingers caressed her cheek as he leaned toward her.

"Neither are we," Adam said from behind her.

Thia leaned her head against his chest. Glancing back up at him, she sighed before turning around.

Adam and Caelynn sat on their horses, leading the other mounts. Gnat looked at Thia from in front of the warlock. His eyes were sad. "We'd invite you inside, out of the rain, but there's not enough room," she said.

The blonde man looked at Caelynn, then back at her and Jinaari. "There's another place, not far from here. It'll hold all of us, easily." He tossed something at Jinaari. The boots landed with a thud near his feet. "You probably need these."

Thia took the coat Caelynn offered, grateful for the warmth. Jinaari was shoving his feet into the boots. "Where are you thinking of? There's nothing but thieving dens in the canyon. We won't reach safety until we're in Tavisholm."

"It's hard to explain," the warlock started to say.

"Try harder."

Thia watched as Adam and Caelynn exchanged a look. A nod of resignation passed between them. "It's not a den, but a refuge," Adam said with a sigh. "It's where Lexi took us, after the attack."

Thia's eyes grew wide as she looked at them, stunned. She heard Jinaari come up behind her. "When was this?" he asked.

Adam locked his gaze on Thia. "After the caravan our families were in was raided by Lolc Aon and the scepter our parents made was stolen."

FOURTEEN

Thia stared at them. "What scepter?"

Caelynn raised a hand, pointing to her waist, but didn't meet Thia's gaze. "That one."

Her hand reached for the weapon at her side as she stared at the two of them. "Your parents made this? And you didn't tell me?"

Adam coughed. "You've got questions. We knew you would. Here is not the right place to ask them. We can lead you to the refuge, make sure everyone's warm and dry. Feed the horses, let them rest. This storm's not going away, and bandits will have our trail soon if we don't move." His shoulders slumped as his focus shifted to Jinaari. "I know you don't trust either of us right now. I wouldn't either, if I was in your shoes. And maybe you won't after we tell you everything. But this is not the place for that discussion. Ours is a story not meant for many ears."

"Get on your horse," Jinaari whispered in her ear, "and stay close."

She walked toward her mount and saw him extinguish the small fire. As she settled into her saddle, she saw him pause at

Adam's side. "We'll do it your way. For now. The minute I think you're still lying to me, though, Thia and I leave. Don't even think about following us."

"She's our family, too. We never wanted to hurt either of you."

"I meant what I said, warlock."

Thia watched Jinaari mount his horse. Caelynn looked at her, tears in her eyes, but didn't speak. *Their parents made the scepter? And they didn't say anything until now? Why? What could they know about it that is so bad they kept it hidden this long?*

Adam turned in his saddle. "Caelynn, make sure we're not followed." The bard spun her horse around, giving them room to pass her. The warlock looked at her and Jinaari. Gnat sat in front of him, confusion on his face. "It's not far." Facing the road, he urged his horse to a walk.

"Stay alert," Jinaari whispered as he rode next to her.

Thia nodded, keeping her gaze on Adam's back. The red cloak he wore seemed faded somehow. His shoulders were slumped, as if defeated. *There's more to this. A lot more. If there wasn't, they would've said something before now. If not to me, then to Jinaari. The scepter was lost for centuries! He told me he was old enough to remember when Tanisal was a thriving city, and I accepted that. Why not tell me the whole story?*

"When we get where he's leading us," Jinaari said, his voice barely above a whisper, "I need you to listen. Things are likely to get heated between us. You might pick up something I miss. Watch Caelynn's body language closely. She thinks she can hide how she's feeling, but she does have her tells."

Thia nodded. "I've got questions, too. Especially about the scepter."

"Ask them. We won't let them rest until we know everything. If I think they're hiding anything, you and I will take Gnat and leave. Understood?"

"Yes." *I don't want to leave them behind, but his reasoning makes sense,* she thought. *First, it was that Adam was sent to kill me. Now, his parents helped make the scepter? Is this why he lied about going to Cirrain first? Or why he didn't tell us about the book he borrowed from the archives in Almair? What else are they hiding? And why didn't they trust us enough to say something before now?*

Adam stopped in front of a smooth part of the canyon wall. Dismounting, he looked at her and Jinaari. "We have to lead the horses. Keep a tight grip on them; they might get spooked at first." He reached up and helped Gnat down.

Thia glanced at Jinaari, waiting for him to agree before she dismounted. He looked at her, nodding once. She swung her leg over the back of her horse, easing herself onto the ground. Walking toward the horse's head, she grabbed his bridle as she looked ahead.

Adam stood next to a nondescript rock wall. The moon, obscured by the storm clouds, provided no details beyond it being wet. "It's solid stone," she said.

"Not as solid as you might think," Adam said, turning his head to look at them. "Keep a tight hold on your horse." With one hand on the bridle and the other leading Gnat, the warlock walked forward and disappeared.

Thia glanced at Jinaari; his face was a mask. "Go," he told her, "I'll follow."

Taking a deep breath, she tugged at her horse and walked toward the stone. *Don't think, just go.* As she got closer, she raised one hand, expecting it to hit solid rock.

It didn't.

As soon as she went past the illusion, the rain stopped. The air was warm and dry. A forest surrounded a wide path. Adam stood several yards away, still holding his horse's reins. Gnat was on the saddle, watching her.

"Friend Thia made it!" he said.

She walked closer to them, "Yes, Gnat. I made it." Mounting her horse, she glanced back. Jinaari emerged from the wall, followed by Caelynn. Turning toward Adam, she said, "Where are we?"

"We're not there yet," he said as he swung up into his saddle behind Gnat. "The refuge isn't far. The entry is keyed. No one can follow us, and there's nothing in here that will cause us harm."

Jinaari moved alongside her. "You didn't answer her question."

"This is a sacred space, one that Lexi made. It mirrors where she grew up, before she was raised up by Nannan. It's used now as a place of rest, solace, for those she thinks need it." Adam turned his horse and started to head down the path.

Thia breathed in the fresh pine of the forest. "At least it's not raining," she said.

"No, it's not," Jinaari replied. "Dawn's coming. That'll help us see."

"What do you think this refuge will be?"

He shrugged. "Whatever it is doesn't matter unless we get the truth out of them."

Looking back to the road, she saw a field about a hundred yards ahead of them. In the center sat a house; the front door flanked by large windows. As they got closer, she saw a barn to the right. A tall man, with two youths, stood on the path. For a moment, her heart stopped.

"What's wrong?" Jinaari asked.

"It's," she struggled to find the words, "it's almost identical to the house from my nightmare."

His head snapped toward her. "How close?"

She shook her head. "It's a common enough design to put a barn to one side, have the door in the middle of the house. The people waiting where they are." She took a deep breath and exhaled, "Lexi and Keroys have always been on good terms. If this is truly her refuge, I don't anticipate an ambush."

"That's the problem," he replied. "We don't know yet if it *is* her refuge."

The forest retreated, revealing a well-tended meadow filled with wildflowers. To Thia's left, a line of archery targets stretched out in the distance. Turning her attention forward, she took a closer look at the people waiting for them. The tall man, with gray hair and beard, stood with his hands folded in front of him. The other two imitated his stance.

Adam stopped, dismounting, and Thia brought her horse to a halt. The man pulled a small axe from his belt and laid it on the ground; the blade handle pointed toward Adam.

"Get down," Jinaari said. "It's safe."

"How do you know?" Thia asked.

He looked at her, pointing at the axe. "He put it down so Adam could use it against him, if necessary. It's a sign of trust."

Thia dismounted, grabbing the reins as she moved to the horse's head. Adam had helped Gnat down, then approached their host. Picking up the axe, he said, "We would not seek hospitality if it was not sorely needed."

"Lexi would not have sent me to welcome you, if she did not wish to have you here." The man looked up, watching as Thia and Jinaari walked closer. "I am Volk, First Arrow of Lexi Stormbow. In her name, I offer you refuge within her home."

"We are glad for the refuge offered," Jinaari said.

Volk looked at them. "The Shield and Scepter are welcome always. Lexi knows of your recent trials, Daughter of Keroys, and is most distressed over what happened. It is why she could not be here to greet you herself. She meets with her brothers, in an effort to find the source of your night terror."

"Purr-purr?" Gnat asked, tugging on Volk's pant leg.

He smiled. "Lexi did send him, knowing you would want to see him. He's inside."

"Purr-purr!" Gnat exclaimed, running toward the house.

Volk looked at Thia, smiling. "Lexi is fond of cats. There's one in particular, a white and gray one, that Gnat has a connection with. He's normally a cantankerous cat, but he'll stay still and let him pet him for hours. Don't be surprised if you see little of Gnat during your visit. But, come," he nodded, "your night was long, and your bodies are as weary as your souls. I shall show you to your rooms." He pushed the two youths forward, and they came to collect their horses. "Micha and Cinna will care for your mounts, make sure your gear is brought to you, while I escort you inside." His face went stern as he turned to Adam. "Lexi has instructed me to tell you and the bard to tend to your own mounts and gear. Once you are done, go to the chapel. She has much to say to you before you rejoin your companions."

"Please, Daughter?" One of the youths nodded toward Thia's hands that gripped the reins.

"Oh, yes. I'm sorry," she stammered as she handed them over. Jinaari moved closer to her as their horses were led away. Adam and Caelynn didn't look at either of them as they followed behind the stable hands.

"We have questions for them, as well," Jinaari said. "Will they be gone long?"

Volk gestured at the house, and they walked toward it. Their host joined them as he spoke. "Lexi takes as long as she must. Surely, you've encountered the same with Garret and Keroys? The Gods don't bow to our timelines but create their own." He paused, then continued, "I am sure you will both have plenty of time to rest, recover from the recent events. Lexi was beyond displeased at the night terror you were subjected to, Daughter. To be frank, she was cursing worse than I've ever heard when Keroys contacted her."

"Keroys knew, then?" Thia asked.

"Only that he couldn't find you, sense your presence. Had the Shield not been able to reach you, the Gods themselves would've intervened. When he gave chase, Garret alerted his family that he knew where you were physically. But none could find your soul, it was so well hidden from them."

Thia glanced at Jinaari. "The Shield is likely the only one who could've reached me, Volk. I'm beyond grateful for his intervention."

They reached the house. She sighed inwardly; the structure was stone, not wood. Up close, there was nothing outside of the position of the windows and door that reminded her of what happened earlier. "If you'll follow me," Volk said as he opened the door, "I'll show you to your room. I have to apologize, however. Lexi has never been one for grand homes, and this refuge isn't meant for many guests."

"I'm Thia's protector, Volk. I'm not leaving her alone."

Volk nodded, "I anticipated as much. There are two beds in each room." He stopped after walking down a short hallway. "The keys are inside. I'll let you choose which one is most to your liking." On either side of the corridor were two heavy doors. "If you'll excuse me, I need to make sure Gnat has found Purr-purr." He bowed once, then walked between them and left.

Thia looked at Jinaari. "Well? Which one?"

He opened the door to one, then closed it. "That one," he said, pointing to the other door.

Twisting the knob, she opened the door and walked in. The room wasn't large. Two beds, with a small table between them, sat against a wall. Across from them, logs burned in the hearth, warming the room. A pair of sturdy chairs and a table were close enough to keep the occupants warm.

"Get some sleep," Jinaari said. "I'll keep watch."

Thia sat on one of the beds. "I'm more hungry than tired."

He turned the key in the lock, then looked at her. "What did you say?"

"I'm hungry, not tired. Do you think they'll take long with our packs? I could really use something to eat."

"Thia," he said, "you've barely eaten for a month." He walked over and sat on the other bed. "How are you feeling?"

She blinked. "Fine, I think. I'm still mad at Adam and Caelynn, anxious about what else they've been keeping from us. And my stomach feels as if it's hollow." *I wonder*, she thought. She looked at him, hope rising. "Do you have a dagger?"

"Yes. Why?"

"Give it to me."

Reaching behind him, he pulled out a small knife. The blade was smaller than the palm of her hand, but it would be sharp enough. "What are you thinking, Thia?"

She smiled, unable to contain her excitement. "I'm hungry for the first time in a month, Jinaari. I'm not coughing. What if," she paused, "what if the way I broke free of the nightmare purged whatever was making me sick?"

"It's possible," he said, his voice even. "I've only seen you do that one other time."

"Exactly." The words came out in an excited rush. "When I was Lolc Aon's prisoner. It purged all the drugs she'd forced me to take out of my body. Doesn't it make sense that it would do it again?"

"But that doesn't explain why you want this," he held up the blade.

"If I couldn't heal myself because my body was using my stores to fight the illness... and if it's gone . . ." she started to say.

"Then you should be able to heal yourself again," Jinaari finished the thought. "You want to use this to find out."

Thia reached for the knife, but he pulled it back. "It won't be a big cut," she said, "nothing you can't heal if I can't. But I need to know."

"I understand your logic, Thia. I'll do it, after you've eaten something." The hand he had the knife in disappeared behind his back. "Your body's shaking right now. Lack of food, sleep, the nightmare . . . any of those would throw someone off balance. I don't want you to cut yourself in such a way that you do damage I can't fix."

Someone knocked on the door, and Thia looked up. "Wait here," Jinaari said as he rose. Walking to the door, she saw him pull the key out of a pocket. "Yes?"

A muffled voice said, "Pardon, Shield. We have your bags, and food if you're hungry."

Jinaari's body blocked her view, but the door opened. The two youths from earlier came inside. One carried their packs, while the other took a tray over to the table near the fireplace. "Where would you like these, Scepter?" Cinna asked, raising the bags.

"Over there, please" Thia replied, pointing to the end of the other bed. "Thank you."

Both of them bowed and left without another word. Jinaari closed the door, and she saw him pocket the key. "Eat," he said, pointing at the table.

Rising, she stared at him. "Only if I have your word that we'll try my idea when I'm finished."

He tilted his head, giving her an exasperated look. "You really need me to give my word?"

Crossing her arms across her chest, she nodded. "Yes. You've said, multiple times, that you're my sworn protector. You're supposed to keep me from getting hurt. We're going to do just that and I don't want you trying to weasel out on a technicality." She relaxed slightly. "I need to know, Jinaari. Especially since there's a chance we won't have the others with us when we leave here."

He walked over to her, putting both his hands on her arms. "If it sets your mind at ease, then you have my word. But not until after you've eaten." He turned her around and pushed her toward the table. "Start slow. Your body needs the food, but eating too fast will make you sick."

Thia laughed, finding her way into a chair. The tray held goblets and two covered dishes. Lifting one, she saw a steaming pile of meat smothered in a rich gravy, and vegetables. "It smells wonderful," she said.

He sat opposite her, picking up the other plate. "Eat, Thia. Then we'll do your experiment."

She stabbed at a piece of the meat, reminding herself to take it slow. It smelled so good, and her stomach growled in anticipation. *Has it really been a month since I wanted to eat?* She thought back as she chewed. *Pan's wedding feast, the night we left Cirrain. That's the last time I really felt hungry. Was I sick before then?* "Even if this illness – curse – whatever – is gone, I want to figure out what it was. If there's a way to prevent it from coming back, or cure it in others, it's worth tracking down."

"It is," he said. "There's a chapterhouse in the city. If they don't have a library, they'll know where one is. We can spare a day or two searching. Go visit Gnat's friend, get his property back, take him home."

"After that, what will we do?" Thia asked. She put her plate back on the tray. It was practically empty.

"Go back to Cirrain or Almair, see if there's any problems we need to take care of." He looked at her, a sadness in his eyes. "If things aren't cleared up with Adam, you and I should find other another place to stay besides the Green Frog. Did you leave anything important in your room?"

Thia shook her head. "No. Just some clothes, nothing I can't replace easily." She leaned back in her chair. "Do you really think it's that bad? Whatever else they need to tell us?"

"It's not what they're going to tell us, Thia. It's what they don't, and their reasons why they kept this quiet for so long." He pointed to her hip. "I was angry when Adam told me about his mission, how he led you into the spider nest. That he was ready to kill you if they came after him, trying to protect you. If it comes out that there's something either of them knew about the scepter that is behind what you've gone through," he shook his head, "I can't trust them to keep you safe when my back's turned."

"I can't think about that, not right now," she said. "I trust you, know you'll make the right decision. If you say we leave them behind, that's what we do." She felt a tear trickle down her face and she wiped it away. "They're still family, though. We need to hear them out."

"We will. I promise."

She held out her hand, palm up. "Where do you want to make the cut?"

"Not on your palm," he said as he rose, pulling the chair closer. "There's too many important parts. You won't want to hold anything if you've got a bandage across your hand." He took her hand and turned it over. "I'll make the cut here," he traced a small spot on her forearm. Looking up, Thia was taken aback by the severity in his eyes. "You get two tries at this, no more. If it doesn't work, I'm healing you and we move on. Understood?"

"I understand," she said. Taking a deep breath, she watched him bring his blade back out. Without hesitating, he drew it swiftly across her skin. A thin, red line formed; blood seeped out in a slow trickle.

She formed the sigil in her mind and released it. Her heart sank as nothing happened immediately, then she noticed the skin begin to fuse together at one end of the cut. Seconds later, all that remained was a drying trickle of blood. She looked at Jinaari, a small smile working its way to her face. "It worked."

Her voice cracked as she began to cry from relief. "It's gone. Whatever made me sick is gone."

Jinaari pulled her to her feet, and she folded herself into his embrace. "That's one less thing we need to worry about," he said.

FIFTEEN

Stretching, Thia waited for the last of the sleepy fog to lift from her mind. *I didn't realize I was that tired*, she thought. Opening her eyes, she saw Jinaari sitting in a chair near the fireplace; the stiff brush in his hand moved rapidly across something.

"What time is it?" she asked.

He didn't look up. "Late afternoon, by my reckoning."

Thia pushed herself up on the bed, "Did you get any sleep?"

"Some," he replied. "How are you feeling?" He raised his head and looked at her.

"Better than I have in weeks. I'm glad Adam brought us here. I needed a place where I felt safe after what happened."

He nodded and set the brush aside. Thia saw him pick a sock up off the table, dropping it into a small bucket of water. "Have you remembered anything else about the dream? It's possible that there was something that happened before you were pulled in. If we can pinpoint that, I can keep an eye out for it, pull you out of the dream before it starts."

"No. I remember making camp that night, having you and

Caelynn both try and convince me to eat something, going to bed and listening to the rain hit the canvas of the tent. The next thing, I was on my horse, riding in the storm with the rest of you. I suppose I should've known then that it wasn't real; I don't remember waking up, breaking camp, or the rest."

"Don't worry about that," he said as he wrung the sock out. "We've done those things so often that they can blur together. What concerns me is that it happened after you were asleep. Watch has always been about making sure we're not surprised by an attack from outside the camp. Now we need to watch you sleep, too."

She fell back, her pale blonde hair fanning out against the pillow. "Don't. Please. It's bad enough that the four of you watch me when I'm awake. I'm not going to sleep well if I know that's going on, too."

"I've watched you sleep for months, Thia."

"That's different," she said. "With the other three, it'd be creepy." She heard him start to scrub the brush against the sock again. "What are you doing?"

"My laundry," he replied. "My socks were caked with mud. When you dried us off, it solidified into stuff that's harder than rocks."

"You wanted us to get dry. My way was faster."

He looked at her, a small smile on his face. "Faster isn't always better."

Someone knocked on the door, leaving her response unspoken. Jinaari rose, motioning her to stay where she was, and walked to the door. "Yes?"

"It's Volk. I've brought you and the Scepter some dinner."

Thia threw off the blanket and grabbed her clothes off the floor. Throwing on the tunic, she reached for the pants as he said, "Just a moment." When she was done, he unlocked the door and opened it.

Volk walked in, carrying a tray with dishes on it. "I hate to interrupt," he said, "but I didn't want your food to get cold." He placed the tray on the table.

"We appreciate that," Thia said.

The man bowed, then walked back toward the door. He stopped in the opening and looked back at them. "Your companions have rested. When you're ready, they will meet you in the main room. It's my understanding there are things they need to speak of that I don't need to hear. When you enter, a barrier will go around that room. No one else will know what is said." He turned and left, closing the door behind him.

Jinaari locked it, then pointed at the table. "Let's eat," he said, "then we'll go see what they have to say."

Anxiety tied her stomach into knots, but she nodded in agreement. She walked barefoot across the smooth wood floor and sat in a chair. "I am hungry," she said.

"That's good," he said, sitting opposite of her. He moved the brush and sock, placing them on the floor. "If that changes, though, I need you to say something."

"I will," she promised. "I know I push back sometimes, but I know you have a job to do. It's just," she paused, "I spent so much of my life hiding. I'm not used to being the center of attention, not like you are. It's hard enough when it's necessary, when I've got to be the Daughter of Keroys or the Scepter. When it's just the four of us, I want to relax. I want to be who I really am, the person you all know. If I know you're watching, I start thinking I'm doing something wrong."

"I'll make sure you don't notice, then." Grabbing one of the plates, he pointed at the other one. "Eat. I'm not entirely convinced that whatever it was that made you sick is gone. You can heal yourself again, and your appetite is back. Those are encouraging signs, Thia. You're right in that we need to figure out what it was, though. If we don't, it could come back.

Given Keroys's warning, I'm concerned about what a second bout would do to you."

"I am, too. It didn't bother me when it was mild. When I couldn't heal myself," she paused, then continued, "I was terrified. I haven't been that scared since I found myself face to face with Lolc Aon. Magic's been the one constant in my life; the one thing I knew would always be there when I needed it."

"You have me."

She smiled. "I do now. I didn't when I was ten and Papa died. Or when I was sixteen and hated by every other acolyte because Keroys personally blessed my rites to become his priestess. I've only had my magic to rely on up until I met you. I trust you, more than I've ever trusted another soul, and that took work. You know this. I can't unlearn almost twenty years of behavior in less than one."

"You're doing better than you think, Thia." He reached for a goblet and drank before continuing. "But I do hear what you're saying. The goal is to keep you safe; it always has been."

She sighed. "That's part of the problem right now. I learned to trust Adam and Caelynn, grew to love them as family. I was angry when he told me about the spiders, same as I was at you for not telling me I was Marked to begin with. You both had reasons for staying silent. Ones that are understandable. This bit with the scepter, though . . . one of them should've said something after it was given to me."

"We'll hear what they have to say, decide what our next steps are. I don't want to leave them behind any more than you do. He's my brother, too. The trust has to be reforged, for both you and I, before we leave."

She tore apart a roll, swirling it into some gravy on her plate. "How did you two meet Caelynn? She said that you and Adam had been running together for a time, but she'd only been with the two of you for a year or so before I showed up.

If their parents made the scepter, they've known each other for centuries."

He leaned back in his chair. "Honestly, I can't remember many details. We were in an inn, in Dragonspire. Kathra and Flink had joined us, and we'd stopped on the way to a cave. I think there was a troll bothering a caravan route or something. Caelynn was playing at the tavern, I remember that. During one song, Adam got quiet. When she was done, he went to talk to her. The next morning, she rode out with us. I asked him, and he said he thought she'd be useful. I trusted his judgement."

"What happened to them?"

"Who?"

"Kathra and Flink. I remember you saying something about Flink's death, and that Kathra felt responsible."

Jinaari nodded. "It was a year later. We'd heard rumors of monsters near a village, so we found the caves they were said to hide in. It was far more elaborate than we expected. A local mage had gone mad, created a dungeon full of monsters and traps. Luring locals into it with the promise of gold was his idea of amusement. We opened the wrong door, and a swarm of Dangreth came after us. More than we could handle. I called a retreat, got Adam and Caelynn out. Flink was keeping the door open, giving us time to leave, but Kathra refused. He grabbed her by the arm and threw her out, then moved so the door closed between him and us. There's no way he could've survived." He took a drink, then said, "We found another route, took care of the mage. On the way out, we found a second entrance to that room. Caelynn mixed up a powder. We filled a bottle with it, threw it into the room. Kathra hit it with a spell. When it exploded, it sent out a gas that choked the Dangreth to death. We found Flink's body near the door. He'd taken out two dozen or more of them before they killed him. As soon as we left,

Kathra went back to her church. She blamed herself for his death. Which is wrong. Had she stayed in the room, she would've been killed like he was." He looked at her, a small smile on his lips. "What is it with you healers and being stubborn?"

Thia smiled. "I could say the same about paladins and arrogance. We take our vows seriously, too. It's one thing if it's a natural death. We all face that at one point. If it's natural, we are charged to ease their passing, give them peace. But if it's one we could've prevented and didn't, that's different."

Jinaari nodded, "I can see that." He rose and held out his hand. "We've stalled long enough. The food's gone. We may not like what they're going to tell us, but we need to hear them out. We gave our word."

Taking his hand, she rose. "Let me get my shoes on," she said, her voice quiet. *He's right. We may not like what they tell us, but we'll know more if we listen. Sitting here isn't going to solve anything.*

She grabbed her pack off the floor and tossed it onto her bed. Pulling out some clean socks, she sat and began to put them on. Jinaari sat across from her, doing the same. His belt lay nearby. "You're not taking that?"

"No. Make sure to leave the scepter here, too. I'm not spilling their blood in a Goddess's home. Not unless I break a nose, that is." He looked at her. "I'm not planning on doing any fighting, Thia. They're my family, too, and I care about them. If I have to, to keep you safe, I will."

She took a deep breath and let it out slowly. "I'm ready. For what, I'm not sure. But sitting here, blindly guessing, isn't going to give us answers." She rose, and he did the same.

"Wear your mask, if it helps. Watch their body language, see if anything indicates they're not telling us everything. And don't be afraid to ask questions. You're likely to think of some I don't. You're smarter than Adam. You proved that in the scheme that freed me. The more questions we ask, the more answers we get. I hope."

"I understand," she said. "I'll follow you. You've got the room key."

Jinaari turned, and she followed him out the door. Once in the hallway, he stopped long enough to lock the door. "You good?" he asked.

"Yeah, I'm good."

Thia followed him down the hallway. The sun had set, but they could see perfectly. Looking up, she tried to pinpoint the source of the light. "Don't," Jinaari said. "We're in the home of a God. Rules don't apply here. If Lexi wanted light, she'd get it."

Ahead of them, the light changed. It flickered, causing shadows to dance in the hallway. Jinaari stopped, and she came alongside him. The room was well lit beyond the fire burning in the fireplace. A table, with four chairs, sat in the center of the room. Goblets and small plates filled with sliced meats and cheese, along with some fruit, were within easy reach for anyone who sat.

Across the room, Caelynn and Adam stood behind two of the chairs. The bard's face was tear stained; Adam's hand rested on her shoulder. "Are you two ready to talk?" Jinaari asked.

"We are," Adam replied, glancing at Caelynn. Her head nodded, but she stayed silent. "Are you ready to listen? Without judgement until we're done?"

"We always have been," Jinaari said. Thia felt his hand on her back, urging her forward. She walked into the room, heading for the chairs closest to the hallway. "The two of you chose to keep secrets."

Pulling out one of the chairs, Thia sat. Jinaari sat at her right, while the other two sat opposite of them. "I didn't always trust the two of you," Thia said, "because I didn't know you. My experience taught me that there were few people in Avoch who would see beyond my lineage. But I've never kept something from you intentionally. A few things," she glanced at Jinaari, "I kept between the two of us at first. You've learned them all by now."

"Not why you ran from the camp," Caelynn said, her voice barely a whisper.

Thia looked at her. "I had someone play with my mind while I slept, and I was certain what I saw was real. Including the three of you and Gnat being killed. I was fighting back, running in terror and grief, when I left. I don't know who it was, or how they did what they did. When Jinaari found me, I thought he was the illusion. I didn't believe he was alive. He reminded me of how I broke free from the drugs Lolc Aon gave me, shattered her hold on me." She smiled. "That's when I realized he didn't have his boots or armor on. The Jinaari in the dream did. I broke free."

"That must've been the bright light we saw," Adam said.

"You're caught up," Jinaari said. Thia was startled at how direct his tone was. "Thia and I will stay quiet, unless we have a question, until you say you're done. I meant what I said before. If I don't feel we can trust you any longer, we will leave you behind."

"We understand," Adam said. Taking a deep breath, he folded his hands on the table and looked at the two of them. "I'm sure you've figured out by now we're both a lot older than we look.

"We grew up in Tavisholm, when it was about an eighth the size it is now. My father was a gem cutter; he had a gift that let him see the perfect shape of a stone before it was polished. Caelynn's mother," he glanced at her, "was a blacksmith. Not an ordinary one, though. She could work with any metal."

"Silver and gold require different skills than steel or iron," Caelynn said, her voice soft. "Mother was smaller than her brothers, who ran the smithy, and excelled at softer metals. Ones that required a gentler touch."

Adam cleared his throat and continued, "One day, two people came to both shops. They stayed hooded and cloaked, so we never saw who they were. Our parents, though, met with them behind closed doors. As soon as they left, her mother and my father started working on a special commission.

"We didn't know each other, not yet. I had been given notice that I was to study at Helmshouse. Caelynn had gotten her acceptance to a bardic college in Tanisal, the best in all the kingdoms. When my father had cut the crystal, I went with him to the smithy. Caelynn was there, with her mother. We watched as they joined the shaft to the head, and the scepter came to life."

"What do you mean, 'came to life'?" Thia asked. *I've felt something from it, but it didn't feel alive. Or did it?*

Caelynn looked at her. "When the two pieces came together, it glowed. I remember hearing a 'click,' and the entire scepter was bathed in light. When it faded, it was a single object. I don't think it had any sentience to it. Not then, anyway. I know you've said you've gotten impressions—feelings—from it, Thia. It wasn't meant to have that ability."

"Our parents told us that two of the Gods had come and commissioned the scepter. It would be one of three symbols, and that we would unite under a single kingdom instead of endless warfare. The crown was made in Almair; the shield in Dragonspire. Made by craftsmen and women from those cities. Once all three were in Tanisal, people would be selected by the Gods and the symbols themselves. And from that moment onward we would be Avoch.

"The next day, we prepared to leave. Everyone from our families would go, both to see the scepter handed over to its wielder, and to see Caelynn and myself off. Few left

Tavisholm, let alone to go to such prestigious schools, and the entire city came out to wish us well. Cappen, our king, rode at the head of the caravan. He went with us, to either accept a symbol or swear allegiance to those who were chosen. He told his soldiers to stay home; confident in the truce that had been hammered out. No one would attack him or try to steal the scepter. Or so he said.

"We made it into the canyon, and one of the wagons became stuck. By the time we got it free, it was twilight. Cappen ordered us to make camp."

"Everyone was so happy that night. I was asked to perform, and I chose a song few outside of Tavisholm knew. It was the one that the representative of Óran Sgoil heard me sing that made him speak with my parents. I saw Adam," Caelynn looked at him, and put a hand over his, "but that wasn't his name at the time, as he wasn't a warlock." She looked at Thia. "It's been so long, and he's made vows that I will respect, so I can't tell you what it was. He was watching me, and that's when I knew my soul was never going to rest unless he was with me."

"I felt it, too," Adam said, and Thia's chest tightened at the sadness he put into the words. "She finished the song and left the firelight. I followed her. We found each other on an outcropping of rock about thirty feet above the canyon floor. We just sat with each other, not speaking. We didn't dare. We were both to go to places so far apart that we knew it'd be years before we'd see each other again. If we ever did." He grabbed a goblet, swallowing the contents, and continued. "It was then that Lolc Aon led her forces into the canyon, attacking the encampment. We watched, unable to do anything, as our families were herded before her. She stood there, waiting, while the wagons were searched. They found the scepter, brought the box to her. After she opened it, she asked to meet the artisans. Our parents were the first two to die.

"I tried to gather up the small bit of magic I could at the time, ready to do something—anything— to stop the slaughter. To keep the scepter from Lolc Aon's grasp. A voice behind us told me to stop."

Caelynn said, "It was Lexi. She told us now was not the time, to follow her or we'd be found. Be killed like our families were. She led us here, gave us time to grieve. I don't know how long we stayed. It could've been a week; it could've been months. We were both so tied up with guilt that it took time for us to do more than try to comfort each other.

"After a while, though, Lexi came back. She said we needed to go to Tanisal and Helmshouse, as planned. That only by study, honing our skills, would we honor their memories. She also promised us that we wouldn't be parted forever. One day, Adam would come out of Helmshouse with someone he called a brother. Someone else would come later. One that not only I saw as a sister, but who would call me the same. That we'd find our family, because those we choose to love as family are as dear or more so than the ones we had blood ties with. Only after we found them would the scepter come back to the surface." She looked at Thia, tears in her eyes. "That's why I was so happy when you asked if you could say you were my sister. Because I knew I'd finally found my family, and it was complete again."

"The other thing Lexi told us about the scepter coming back was that it would bring about a change. One that would reverberate not just on Avoch but among the Gods themselves." Adam looked at Thia and Jinaari, his face intense. "She did not, however, tell us what it would be, or that Thia would wield it."

"When you pulled it out of the box in court, Thia, my heart stopped," Caelynn said. "I finally had my family again, one that I knew loved me as much as I loved them. I had Adam. I've spent every minute of every day since then trying to figure out what this change Lexi mentioned would be. When you started to get sick, I prayed that it wasn't the thing we were told was coming."

"When we got here, Lexi berated us for not telling you everything earlier," Adam said. "She said, and I quote, 'You must trust them as much as they trust you. If you honestly think they're going to turn their backs on you because you're centuries older than they are, or because you were prevented by me from dying with your families, then you don't know them like you should. You don't trust them. And, yes, I prevented you from dying. Neither of you were skilled enough to take on that many trained warriors, let alone Lolc Aon herself. If you want to say they're family, you must be honest. Even if it hurts like hell.' I asked her about Thia's illness. She's as unsure as Keroys is."

"Why lie about going to Cirrain first, Adam? And what was in the book you borrowed from the archives in Almair?" Jinaari asked.

Thia watched the blonde man's face closely. Amazement crossed his features. "How did you know about that?"

"I have my ways, you have yours."

Thia cleared her throat. "What he's saying is that he and Amara have a way to communicate where he can see things she has seen. I don't understand the magic behind it, but it works. We saw her give you the letter in the archives, put a book into your bag. You then told her you still had to go to Cirrain. Yet you told us you went there first. So, were you lying to her or to us?"

"Her. I'd been to Cirrain. It's closer to the monastery than Almair, and I knew I had the stores to make that jump and still get to Tomil's palace. When I left, I went to our suite at the Green Frog. As to the book I borrowed, I left it with Wilim, with instructions to send it back in a week." He paused, then kept going. "When Gnat mentioned Helix, I was suspicious. The description given to us by Bryant made me even more certain. The book confirmed it. Helix was a teacher at Helmshouse when it first began. His tower was destroyed two weeks after I arrived. I thought it meant he'd died. He didn't. He can't."

"He's a death mage," Jinaari said, leaning back in the chair. "The same one that cursed the farmer in the story you found, Caelynn. I'm right, aren't I?" He looked at the bard, and Thia watched her closely. "Either you need to study up on Old Tongue, or you didn't want to tell us the real story in the journal. Why?"

She shifted in her seat but didn't look away. "I know how devoted you are to Garret, Jinaari. He was an absolute ass to give that girl to Helix as payment of the father's debt. Women aren't chattel to be traded away. I don't care if he is a God; that was wrong. I see you as my brother. I know you'd never do that normally, but you've always done everything Garret demanded of you, so I hesitated. Thia's had enough problems. She needs to trust you the most out of all of us. If I said that out loud, I was afraid it would shake that trust."

"Caelynn," Thia said, "how did you find Adam again?" *I know what Jinaari said*, she thought, *but I want to hear her version.*

Adam cleared his throat. "We weren't completely out of touch. At first, we were. She had her training to do, as did I. When it was discovered a warlock – one well known in Helmshouse – was behind the Corrupted gaining a foothold in the Paladins of Silas, a team was dispatched to bring him back. The Solar knew I wouldn't return if I found Caelynn again, so she kept me behind. I managed to send her a gift, with a trusted friend."

"The other half of the emerald from your tower." Jinaari said.

The warlock nodded. "Yes."

"I don't understand, what are you two talking about?" Thia asked.

"Adam had an emerald in his tower. Caelynn had the other half in her room in the Green Frog. I don't understand the magic behind it, but that's how we were able to let you both know about Alesso. And how she told us about Samil." Jinaari glanced at Adam. "It's gone now, isn't it?"

"Yes."

Caelynn cleared her throat. "I got the gift, and the note. It let me know he was Adam now and gave me hope. I followed the instructions he gave me. Only used it that night to let him know I got it, that I was safe, and I'd try to leave before the city was attacked. After Tanisal fell, I started wandering Avoch. I'd take up residency in a city, stay for a year or ten, then move on. I'd play in any inn that would let me, constantly scanning the crowd. I was at one, in Cirrain, when I overheard someone mention a warlock who'd left Helmshouse and attached himself to Garret's Paladins somehow. The guy was drunk, but he described Adam perfectly. I spent the rest of my time there, listening closely, then decided to move on to Dragonspire. I'd picked up that was the location of the chapterhouse he'd been staying at. One night, in a fairly seedy tavern, four people came in. They couldn't have been more different, but they had a sense of familiarity with each other. I caught a glimpse of Adam's face before he sat. I wasn't certain, but I thought it could be him. So, I played the last song I'd ever sung for my family. The song I'd sworn never to sing again until I found him. About halfway through, he turned around and smiled."

"Is that it?" Jinaari asked.

They both nodded. "Unless you're interested in the details of our reunion that night at the tavern, yes. That's it."

Jinaari looked at Thia, and she laughed a little. Turning her head, she grabbed a goblet and said, "You're older than dirt. Your parents made the scepter. And you've not told us this before because . . .?"

"We didn't know how to," Caelynn said. "Adam and I have spent centuries thinking about that night, how we lost the scepter—"

"Stop that," Thia interrupted her. "You weren't at fault any more than I was with my father's death. You were young, untrained, and wouldn't have stood a chance against Lolc Aon. The only reason I did was because I've got Keroys's Mark on my back. And I'm a fully trained priestess of his."

"Thia's right," Jinaari said. "While it would've been good to know about the scepter's history before now," he looked at both of them, "nothing you've said tonight would've changed how I saw you. Or how Thia does. The secrecy, the hiding information . . . that's why I wasn't sure about you. This stuff? We've all seen stranger things in the last year."

Adam took another drink. Placing the goblet down, he said, "You're right. I shouldn't have hidden the information about Helix. Honestly, it wasn't out of any strange need other than I was concerned about Thia." He looked at her. "That sickness you've had is like nothing I've ever seen. I wanted to confirm it was Helix because, honestly, he's been alive so long he's the best shot we have at finding out what it is. Or curing it."

"That's not a problem any more, Adam," she said. "When Jinaari caught up to me, when I used the one spell, it purged whatever it was out of my system. I was hungry when we got here, haven't been coughing. I even had Jinaari cut me so I could try healing myself."

"Did it work?" Caelynn asked. The hope in her voice warmed Thia's soul.

Holding up her arm, she said, "See for yourself."

Adam and Caelynn leaned back in their chairs, letting out

sighs of relief. "That's some of the best news I've heard in weeks," Caelynn said.

"There's only one thing that would be better," Adam said, looking at Jinaari.

"What's that?" Jinaari stared at him.

"If I'm leaving here with my family or being told to stay behind."

Thia glanced at Jinaari. *I trust them, but does he? Does he believe what they've said?*

"One condition," Jinaari said as he picked up his goblet.

"Name it," Adam said.

"From now on, I get to call you old man."

CHAPTER

SIXTEEN

J inaari leaned against the fence rail, watching the light change. Dawn was here; a mist rose from the field as the warm rays evaporated the dew from the night before. Even this far south, it was cool.

Taking a deep breath, he released some of the tension in his body. Adam was right about this being a refuge. For the first time in months, he woke without worrying if someone was going to come after them, after Thia. *I needed this as much as she did*, he thought.

"We all did."

He didn't turn around at the sound of Adam's voice. "Did you plan to bring us here the whole time?"

The warlock came up next to him. "It was a possibility, yes." He paused. "Jinaari, I need you to understand the reason why we didn't say anything earlier. We've wandered the world a long time. It took a toll on Caelynn. I was sequestered in Helmshouse; the years passed by and I scarcely noticed. She was out, traveling. Singing every night in hopes that she'd find me or hear something about me. She's had her trust abused by people she thought cared. But she kept looking, hoping. When she found us, she was terrified of you. It took a lot of talking for me to convince her that you were trustworthy."

"Why?" Jinaari asked, looking at him in amazement.

Adam shrugged. "You're rather imposing. You've perfected a scowl that sends people running before you even reach for your sword. Add the armor and I'm surprised anyone's still stupid enough to think they can best you." He paused. "I've told her, many times, we needed to say something. Her reason was that our family wasn't complete yet. I had my brother, but she didn't have her sister. She was hopeful with Kathra, but something wasn't right."

"Kathra is a good person. She's not Thia, though."

"No. Kathra was too ready to join a fight. Caelynn's like Thia in that they both would rather find non-violent means to get what they want."

"True enough." Jinaari fell silent, watching the mist rise. "What do you know about Helix that you haven't told me yet?"

"Death mages are strange, Jinaari. They move through time in a way that most people can't comprehend. I never met him, only heard stories. He's always had a reason for what he does, something that benefits him in some way. It's possible that he set the woman in the story free; it's also possible she's still at his house, working off a debt that can never be repaid."

"If you think of anything, let me know. I'll decide what to tell Thia. I don't want to walk into a trap if I can help it."

"You don't want secrets between us, yet you keep them from her. Why?"

"I'll tell her, eventually. I'm in charge of her safety, Adam. That means deciding if she's able to handle knowing all the information at once."

Out of the corner of his eye, he saw Adam turn and look at him. "She's still sick, isn't she?"

"I hope not," he said with a sigh. "I want to believe that

she's good and the symptoms won't reappear as soon as we leave here. This is a sacred place. The energy here, Lexi's presence, may be what's keeping it at bay. If I'm right, she'll start showing symptoms again before we reach Helix. Given what Keroys said about how it would progress, I'm not sure what condition she'll be in when we get there."

"I don't like that scenario."

"Neither do I." He paused, then said, "You said Helix never did anything without something being in it for him. What sort of debt are we looking at incurring for his help? This is your world, Adam. Not mine. What does a death mage that's lived for centuries possibly need?"

"Our memories," Adam said. Jinaari turned, watching him as he spoke. "They fuel their lifespan off the memories of others. He can't be part of normal society, can't live like you and I can. He experiences life from the memories of others. The only way to do so is to take some hair from the person. The mage bottles it, waiting until they need the energy stored in the strands. Unless the person is near death, it must be willingly given. The gold, gems, or other gifts as payment aren't as important. Those are to make it seem normal. The real price that is paid is in the strands of hair. The more you want from him, the more he takes from you."

"With someone like Thia, that's got access to the power she does, would he then gain the stores she has?"

"The stores? No. We're born with what we have. No more, no less. But," he said, "he would know all the sigils she knows, could modify them to his purpose."

Jinaari looked back at the house. The windows in her room remained dark. "That would be bad."

"It would. I'm going to be the one that negotiates with him. If a price must be paid, either Caelynn or I will pay it." Adam held up his hand, stopping Jinaari's protest. "We've lived for centuries, which will intrigue Helix. Thia's also family, a sister to us both. We've talked about it at length. This is how we will repay the debt we feel we owe."

Jinaari nodded, knowing he wouldn't be able to get Adam to change his mind. "When we stop for the night, I want one of us in the tent with her at all times. The nightmare she had . . . she believed every part of it. One of us has to be there, ready to pull her back out if it happens again. I don't want to chase her through the forest."

Adam looked at him, raising an eyebrow. "What you're saying is that you're going to be staying with her. She knows you best, Jinaari. Trusts you the most. The likelihood of Caelynn or myself doing anything beyond holding her down while we scream for help is slim. Even then, she could blast us into a thousand pieces." He paused. "You're constantly worried about her, her nerves are strung about as tight as they were when we were on the way to Byd Cudd. Both of you will sleep better."

"What's that supposed to mean?"

"Nothing more than what I said. You take her safety personally. I remember how you were, when we realized Alesso betrayed us. It's been more than a job to you for months, Jinaari. Caelynn knows it, too. Neither of us care if you two ever admit anything to us. Just don't lie to yourself or her."

Jinaari walked back toward the front door. Adam fell into step beside him. "Do you know the area around where Gnat said Helix lived well enough to transport us if necessary?"

"The forest has changed over the centuries, but there was a clearing not far away on the map. It's one I remember. Why?"

"If Thia shows any sign the sickness has returned, I want you to take us as close as you can. There's no use riding for a week if we can get her there faster."

"Agreed. What about Gnat?"

"We retrieve his item, find out what we can about Thia's

illness. Even if it's not back, she and I both want to know what it was. It stole her ability to heal herself, and that terrified her. The more we learn about it, and where it came from, the more likely we can prevent her from being infected again. We leave, take Gnat home. I'm not interested in spending three months getting back to Almair, if you can help with that."

"It'll take a few days. The distance is too far for me to transport us in one trip. I can get us there in stages, though."

"Good," Jinaari reached the door and opened it. "Let's go wake them up, find Gnat, and get on the road." He walked into the house and headed toward the room he shared with Thia.

Pulling out the key, he unlocked it and went inside. "You could've said something when you left," she said from the chair near the fireplace.

"You were asleep. I thought it best to let you rest over watching the sun come up." Placing the key in his pocket, he walked over and sat.

"I saw you and Adam talking. Everything good between you two?"

He nodded. "I think so. He gave me some information on Helix; stuff about how death mages make deals, etc. It's good to know before we get there. I'm hoping Gnat already paid him for fixing whatever it is Helix has."

"Nyfe," Thia said, smiling.

"Whatever 'Nyfe' is." He watched her, choosing his next words carefully. "I asked him to be ready to transport us close to Helix's location from the map. If your illness comes back when we leave here, I'm not wasting a week or more wandering through Taigh Forest. We go straight there, or as close as Adam can get us."

Her shoulders slumped as she looked at him. The worry that hadn't been there moments ago came back in her face. "Do you really think it will?" she asked.

"I don't know, which is why I'm being cautious. This is a sacred place, Thia. Lexi's home. It could be the spell actually purged the illness; it could also be her influence." He leaned forward, taking her hands in his. "If it does, you're not facing it alone. Your family's got your back. Remember that."

She smiled, but it didn't reach her eyes. "I'm glad they're coming with us, though I still don't know why they thought we'd be mad at them."

Jinaari let go of her hands and leaned back in the chair. "Adam said something just now that made sense. They've had centuries to think about what happened, Thia. Caelynn acts like she's in control all the time, but she's got some of the same insecurities you do. It's one reason you two get along, I think. You carried guilt for your father's death for over a decade and it changed how you saw other people. Imagine carrying that weight for thirty times as long."

He watched her, emotions playing across her face. "That makes sense," she said.

"Good. It's time we left here, headed into Tavisholm. I don't want our host to think we've overstayed our welcome." He rose, walking over to where his pack sat on the floor. "If we leave the same way we came in, we should get into the city before sundown." Tossing his bag onto the bed, he picked up some discarded clothing and stuffed it inside.

"Are we making this an official visit or trying to sneak in?" she asked as she placed her bag on the bed near his. "I'd rather wear the gray dress now over changing on the way."

"Let's try and sneak in. The last thing you and I need is to spend a week feasting with anyone who thinks they have influence within the city. Or want to get on our good side for some reason."

"You have a good side?" she said, laughter in her voice.

He smiled. It was good to hear her laugh again. *Maybe she's really okay now.* "Don't tell anyone. It's a secret that few ever get to know." He walked over and slid his arms around her, drawing her close. "When we're done with this trip, I want to rest for a while. Slow down and figure out what this is between you and I."

Her head rested against his chest. "That sounds like a dream that I won't want to wake up from."

Kissing the top of her head, he stepped back. "It's a goal we can't reach until we see Helix and get Gnat home. Pack up." Reaching into the neck of his tunic, he pulled his medallion out.

"You rarely wear that openly. Why today? I thought you didn't want to be recognized."

"Not as the Shield, no. There's a chapterhouse in the city."

"You said that earlier. What about it?"

"If I wear this, identify myself as part of the Order, we'll be given admittance without question. We can rest there, have access to their library, and remain out of the public eye. It wouldn't surprise me if they knew a secret way out of the city." He folded the flap over the top, securing the buckle. "I'll find someone who knows the way, make sure we can get the horses out. Chapterhouse or not, word will spread that we're in town. The sooner we get out, the less likely we have to do any official business."

He watched her slip her arms into her coat. As she buttoned it, she said, "What about any messages from Elizabeth or Tomil? Both said they'd have letters sent there. Wouldn't those be with the Baron? Or is he a Duke? Who's in charge here?" She looked at him, her brow creased with confusion. "Did they even send forces to help defend Cirrain? No representative came to court the night we crowned Elizabeth. Or any other ceremony we held before Pan's wedding."

He looked at her, stunned. *How did I miss all of that?* "You're right. Damn, I wanted things to be quiet but we can't avoid it. I'll ask the commander, request a private meeting with whoever's in charge with you and I. We'll make it as brief as possible, but we have to figure out if Tavisholm is still part of Avoch or if we've got another war brewing." He paused. "It's a principality. Though I don't know who we'd be dealing with. I heard there was a death, that the coronet was handed to another, but I've never heard who took over."

Someone knocked on the door, and Jinaari turned toward the sound. "We're packed and ready," Adam's voice called through the door. "Caelynn's taking Gnat to the stables now. You two ready or should we wait for you there?"

"We're ready," he replied. Looking back at Thia, he saw her thread her arms through the straps of her pack. "When we get back to the canyon, put your hood up."

"Does it matter?" she replied. "You've got the shield in full view when you ride. The scepter hangs from my belt. People already know who we are before they see my face."

Chuckling, he said, "I always knew you were smarter than you let on. You were too stubborn not to be."

She smiled, humor dancing in her lilac eyes. "Maybe if you weren't such an arrogant prick, I would've let you know sooner."

He laughed. "After you, Scepter," holding out the key.

She snorted but grabbed the key and walked to the door. When she opened it, he could see Adam standing in the hall. "What took you two so long?"

"I had to correct someone's thinking about me hiding," Thia replied as she glanced back at him.

Adam stared at him. "I'm confused."

"I'm not surprised, old man," Jinaari said. "There's finally someone in this family with some real intelligence." He pointed at Thia's back, retreating down the hallway. "Best watch her closely and see if you can learn a few things. Otherwise, she'll end up leaving you in the dust."

Walking outside, he saw Caelynn, Gnat, and Thia already mounted and ready to ride. Volk stood nearby. The two youths stood holding the reins to their horses. Stopping in front of their host, Jinaari said, "Thank you, for everything. Please tell Lexi we are grateful for her refuge."

"She knows already, Shield. And is most pleased that trust has been regained." He paused, glancing slightly toward Thia. His voice dropped to a whisper. "Lexi suggests you keep a close eye on the Scepter. The Gods are not convinced she is fully recovered."

"Already planned to," Jinaari replied. Taking the reins from the youth, he pulled himself up into the saddle. "Will we be able to leave the same way we came in?"

"Yes," Volk said. "There is but one way in and out of the refuge. Be well, my friends. Take care of each other."

Wheeling his horse to face the path, he motioned to Adam for him to take the lead. Thia rode next to him. "What did Volk say about me?" she asked.

"That I should keep an eye on you. Even the Gods aren't certain you're cured." Turning his head, he looked at her. "If they're worried, there's a reason."

She sighed. "Pressing business to the south?"

"What are you talking about?"

"Our excuse," she said. "We meet with whoever's in charge once, and as soon as possible. If they question it, we say we have pressing business to the south. It's not a lie. We were told to talk to Helix. According to the map, he lives to the south."

"I like it. Something that concerns the well-being of all Avoch, but not go into details."

She laughed, but he didn't hear any joy in the sound. "I don't know that me staying sane is something that meets that level of urgency."

"You're the Scepter, Thia. One of the three rulers of Avoch. And you're the Daughter of Keroys, making you the most powerful magic user the world has right now. Keeping you healthy, and sane, definitely meets the criteria."

"It never stops, does it?"

"What?"

"Being watched, every movement and word scrutinized. I thought we wouldn't have it as bad, that we could just live our lives and not worry about meeting with officials or holding court."

"Only when you're with me, or the other two. I'll make sure we keep the official stuff short while we're in town. You won't have to wear your mask long." Adam had stopped in front of a rock wall. They'd reached the exit. Dismounting, he waited as Thia did the same.

"Is that a promise?"

"Absolutely."

SEVENTEEN

Word spread faster than he wanted. They'd barely gotten past the city gates, heading to the chapterhouse, when he saw the amazed faces begin to appear. The elevated walkways, meant to allow the citizens to move about out of the mud-filled streets, became lined with people. Jinaari shifted in his saddle, sitting up tall. Out of the corner of his eye, he saw Thia do the same.

"Should've worn the dress," she muttered.

"You'll need to, later. For now, I think they're too stunned we're here." Glancing at a few shop signs, he noticed a similarity. Above the name, each one had an image of the scepter at Thia's side. "They're proud of the connection to the scepter," he said.

"Is that supposed to make me feel better about being gawked at? Or worse?"

"Neither, actually. More to make you aware of who you're dealing with." He twisted in the saddle, glancing back at the others. Adam's face was a mask, whereas Caelynn was conflicted. Joy at being home, but shame at the same time. Guilt. Turning back around, he said, "Try and talk to Caelynn once we're settled. I'll take Adam and Gnat, talk to the commander, so you can be alone with her. She's taking this homecoming hard."

"You won't need me at that meeting?"

"No," he said, "not the first one. I'll probably send Adam and Gnat to the library, then talk to him alone about who's in charge, setting up the audience." He glanced up. "We got here faster than I thought. It's possible they haven't eaten the evening meal yet. We'd be honored guests, seated at the high table, if they haven't. If they have, then expect it tomorrow." Looking ahead, he caught sight of a line of thirty armored men marching toward them. Banners with the sword and shield of his Order moved as they walked. "The welcoming committee has arrived."

He pulled his horse to a stop, raising his hand to signal the others to do the same. The group came closer. An armored man rode at the front of the procession. He didn't wear a helmet and had a sash across his chest indicating he was the commander. Jinaari watched him closely; something about how he sat on the horse made him look nervous. The creature danced as it walked, picking up on the energy of the rider.

"Welcome to Tavisholm," the man said when he got close enough. "I had word from afar that you may honor us with a visit, Shield. I wasn't made aware of the ladies, though. Or that you would be bringing the scepter to us. It does my soul good to see it return to where it came from."

"Who sent word?"

"The commander in Almair, Ransom. I'm Paul del Prine, Commander of the Tavisholm chapterhouse. Let's see the ladies safely inside where they can rest, then we shall talk business." He wheeled his horse around and headed down the center of the armed force.

"Ransom died," Thia whispered. "Lukas became Commander before we rescued you at Cirrain."

"I know," Jinaari replied. "Something's not right here. Keep your eyes open, make sure one of us is with you at all times. That he thinks you're returning the scepter troubles me." Urging his horse forward, he followed the commander down the middle of the paladins. There was room for one horse, forcing them to ride single file. *This is wrong*, he thought. *Lukas would've notified him of Ransom's death. How does he know I'm the Shield, but not that Thia's the Scepter?* He sat up straighter in his saddle. *He was dismissive of her and Caelynn. Garret's Laws say that all must be treated the same. Tavisholm is isolated, and so much has been happening to the north. Have they ignored his Laws?*

Ahead of him, the gates to the chapterhouse were open. Trash and refuse lay scattered at the base of the walls; rats scurried for cover as they approached. Passing through, he was shocked; the central courtyard was uneven. Broken pieces of slate, half covered with mud, made some areas marginally passable. A small, partially fenced sparring arena was wedged between the open stable and a blacksmith's forge. The dim glow of coals was the only show of activity as the smith's tools lay untended on an anvil.

Youths clad in basic tunics came running up to grab the reins of their horses. "Follow me," the commander said, looking directly at Jinaari. "Bring your man and the cobalus if you like. The ladies will be taken to their chamber. I'll have your horses tended to and gear stowed in another room while we talk."

"We'll share a room. I'm honor bound to protect them both. I cannot do that from down the hall."

Paul looked at him, a haunted touch to his features. "We are all brothers here. No harm would come to them while in our chapterhouse. You have my word." He paused. "If it helps ease your mind, Shield, I'll have extra cots brought in."

"It would. Thank you." Jinaari glanced behind him,

making eye contact with Adam. A single nod toward the warlock was enough to tell him to stay with Thia and Caelynn, make sure things went as the commander promised.

"If you'll follow me," Paul said, "we can speak in my office. I'm certain there's a fair amount of news you have to share."

Jinaari and the rest followed the commander into the main hall. Without glancing his way, Thia went with the others down a separate hallway. Having Adam and Caelynn with her made him feel slightly better.

Glancing back to his guide, he saw Paul turn a corner. Quickly, he caught up to the commander as he climbed a stone staircase. Three flights up, plus a few turns, but Jinaari knew he could find his way out. Finding his friends would be the trick.

"Please," Paul said, gesturing into a room.

Entering, Jinaari looked around. The room reminded him of Drakkus's office back in Dragonspire. A small fireplace, flanked by two windows. The desk was covered with papers. A thick wool rug sat in the center, with a chair waiting. Walking over, he sat as the commander moved behind the desk.

Paul looked at him and began to draw a sigil. It was one Jinaari was familiar with, but never tried to cast. The dome of silence moved outward, surrounding them in secrecy. "My apologies, Shield, for deceiving you earlier. We were not in a place where we could talk openly. Please let the Scepter and your other companions know I meant no insult."

"I will. But why the secrecy?"

The commander sat back, sighing. "Princess Jynth originally sent troops to aid your mother's march on Cirrain. Garret told us to join the rest of our brothers when we got there, siding with Thia's claim. We never got that far. A message arrived before we'd gotten halfway to the city, telling us that Agrana had abdicated. Jynth didn't take the news well. She hates Tavisholm, has tried since she came to the throne to find a way to either Dragonspire or Almair. Emissaries were sent at one point to suggest a marriage between you or your brother. Agrana's reply said you were already betrothed, but left open the idea of Stijyn. It wasn't fast enough for Jynth, so she started writing Tomil. Her first letter back was the announcement of his engagement to your sister." He paused. "To say it upset her would be an understatement. When she heard rumors of a woman that bore Keroys's Mark being in Almair, she started insisting Amara's life was in danger. Another emissary was sent, offering your sister sanctuary here. By the time it reached Dragonspire, she'd bolted for Helmshouse."

Jinaari began to put a few pieces together. "Who delivered the message?"

Paul shook his head. "I never met him, but he had Jynth's complete trust. Which surprised me, as she's always hated the Fallen." He coughed. "Excuse me, Thahion. Old habits die hard. Which brings up another problem."

"What's that?"

"The Scepter. Jynth's not going to accept her heritage. Ever since the raid that stole the scepter away, the people of Tavisholm have had...difficulties...with Lolc Aon's followers."

"Thia is the Daughter of Keroys, Paul. She was raised on the surface by her human father. She's no more Thahion, or a follower of Lolc Aon, than you or I."

Paul blinked, obviously startled. "She's both the Daughter and the Scepter? We thought they were two different people. Most here would believe the other woman with you bore Keroys's Mark."

Jinaari shook his head. "Caelynn? No. She is family, same as Adam, but not in the way you might think."

"How can I help you?" he said, with a sigh.

"Information. Give Adam access to your archive vault. He knows what to look for. Thia and I need an audience with Her

Royal Highness. She didn't come to swear fealty in Cirrain. It needs to happen. You know it does. If she doesn't accept the authority of the Crown, through us, then things could get ugly." *But not until we've seen Helix*, he thought. *Get Gnat home safe, then we fight a war. If it can't be avoided.*

"I know word has reached the palace by now. She's likely expecting you to come to her."

Jinaari shook his head. "No. We do it in the square, where all can see. She has to come to us, you know that. Any semblance that we're here at her bidding won't work. The Shield and Scepter are equal with the Crown, in both symbolism and power. The princess knows this."

Paul nodded. "I'll write a message, send it over. Tomorrow morning?"

"That would be best. We've got business to the south and can't stay long." Jinaari rose, asking, "Has the night meal been served? It would be our honor to join my brothers if it's possible."

"I'll make it happen. You're a legend among us, Shield. The honor would be ours. Come," he said, rising from his seat, "I'll make sure you're escorted to your companions. You'll be notified when the meal is ready." He stopped and rifled through the pile of papers on his desk. "These came for you and the Scepter. They came here, while other messages went to the palace. I've kept them sealed." He handed him two letters.

Taking them, he glanced at the seals. Amara and Elizabeth's private signets. "Thank you," he said, tucking both into a pouch on his belt.

"Let's get you to your friends," Paul said, dismissing the silence spell.

Following him from the room, Jinaari made mental notes about the path the commander was taking. Several other paladins stopped, letting them pass, and the welcoming camaraderie on their faces reassured him. *No matter what, this is still a chapterhouse of Garret's Paladins. We're safe here.*

It wasn't a long walk. Rounding a final corner, he saw two armed paladins standing outside a door. They snapped to attention at their approach. "Give him the key," Paul said, pointing back to Jinaari.

"You locked them in?" he asked.

The commander turned to face him as one of the guards held out a key. "Precautionary, I assure you. I knew you were nervous about being separated from them. I thought it would make the ladies feel safer."

Jinaari laughed, but not with any joviality. "You don't know them, Paul. You're lucky the door's still standing. We'll see you at dinner." Walking forward, he put the key in the lock and turned it. Grabbing the knob, he said, "It's me," before twisting it and opening the door. He sidestepped into the room and closed it behind him.

Thia and the others looked at him, a mixture of relief and anger on their faces. Two beds, plus three cots, filled the room. Chairs and a table had been pushed off to one side so the beds could be closer to the fireplace. Gnat was curled up on one near the hearth, sleeping. "They locked us in here," Thia said.

Jinaari held up the key. "Not anymore. The commander said it was for your protection, but I'm not sure why he felt it necessary." He placed the key on top of the packs near the door. He pulled off his gauntlets. "He sends his apologies for any insult his greeting conveyed. He knew you were the Scepter, but not that you were the Daughter of Keroys as well. He thought Caelynn was." Pulling out one of the chairs, he sat and started to unbuckle his armor.

"Why," Thia started to say, her voice hesitant, "would he think she was Marked and not me?"

He sighed, raising his head and looking at her. "The scepter came from here, Thia. It was this city's ruler, along with their families," he pointed at Adam and Caelynn, "who died trying to protect it from Lolc Aon. They've had a long time to nurse the wound." He watched her closely; the hurt played across her face and vanished, but he could still see it in her lilac eyes.

"They haven't met me but I'm the representation of everything they've lost," she said as she sat on the edge of one of the cots. "That's why they locked the door." She faced him, and he recognized the strength behind her eyes. "What happens now? I can't hide in here forever."

"No," he said as he unbuckled the last piece of armor and put it aside. "Tonight, we'll eat with my brothers. Honored guests, to be certain, but it's not as formal as tomorrow will be."

"What's tomorrow?" Adam asked.

"Her Royal Highness, Princess Jynth, is being summoned to have an audience with the Shield and Scepter. We accept her oath of fealty, or we give her warning that her refusal is not going to sit well with us or Elizabeth. Adam, one of my brothers will take you down to the vault. Check the archives, see if you find out anything more about what made Thia sick. Or who Helix is beyond what we already know."

"Why wouldn't she swear fealty? Isn't Tavisholm part of Avoch still?" Caelynn asked.

"It is, but apparently Jynth has bigger aspirations. According to Paul, she tried to negotiate a betrothal to either me or my brother. When that didn't happen, she went after Tomil." He looked at Thia again. "That's where the rumor that Tomil heard came from. She was trying to get him to break it off with Amara." Reaching into the pouch, he pulled out the letters. "These came for us," he said as he handed one out to Thia.

She rose, walking over to take it from him. "Who are they from?" she asked, turning it over. "Oh, I see."

Adam coughed, and Jinaari looked at him. "When is dinner?"

"Less than an hour, I expect."

The warlock looked at Caelynn. "Time for us to clean up a little. There's a small bath chamber off this room. We can go wash some of the road grime off while you two read your letters."

Thia tugged on the other chair, trying to dislodge it. Jinaari reached out and helped. "Thanks," she said as she sat. Her finger broke the seal and she began to read.

He did the same, though he kept the seal intact.

Brother,

There you are, out saving the world, while I'm stuck in a cold, drafty palace. Why didn't you tell me it snowed more here than back in Dragonspire?!

I wish there was news to give you beyond me complaining about the weather, but there isn't. Give Thia my best. I really like her, you know.

Amara

He folded it back up. Nothing in her note alerted him that she'd added something to the seal. But it also said they didn't find anything that might help Thia.

Raising his head, he watched her as she read her note. "Everything good in Cirrain?"

Nodding, she folded it and looked at him. "I guess. There wasn't anything beyond general wishes to stay healthy and come visit when I can."

Cocking his head to one side, he asked, "How are things with you?"

She smiled. "Still playing your paladin mind games?"

"What makes you think I'll ever stop?" He watched her steady her breathing.

"I don't know why, but hearing that this city hates me

because of my lineage hurt. I thought I'd proven myself enough. I guess not."

"I'm wondering how much of what they've been told was true," Jinaari replied. "I think Jynth believes you're going to return the scepter, give it to her."

"Why don't I?" She looked at him intently. "You and I both know I didn't want to carry it. I don't want to rule. I have days where I still think Keroys made a mistake in placing his Mark on me, let alone this."

Jinaari shook his head. "You and I both know it's not that easy. The way Caelynn told the story, the scepter chose you. Tomil dropped to his knee, in his court. I know it's not a burden you wanted, Thia, but you can't simply give it away. Plus," he paused, "you don't know Jynth at all. Neither do I. But what I heard today tells me she is not someone who would put Avoch ahead of her own desires." He watched her pull the scepter off her belt and cradle it in her hands.

"But what if the only way to prove that to her is to surrender it and let her feel the rejection?" Her voice was barely above a whisper, and there was something in her tone that alarmed him.

"Let's sleep on it," he said, keeping his voice even while watching her face. "I'm not ruling it out, Thia. It's possible that she'll do what she should and simply accept we are who we are. For now, we have a dinner to attend with my brothers." A shadow of frustration played across her face, disappearing so fast he wasn't sure it was there.

"The dress?" she asked, looking at him.

"It's not a bad idea. Showing your Mark would solidify my brothers behind us if things go bad tomorrow."

She rose, walking to the pile of packs. Grabbing hers, she tossed it onto one of the beds before opening the top. Jinaari watched her shoulders drop. Rising, he walked over and put his arms around her. "I know how hard it is for you to have people watch you, Thia. I'll be there. So will Caelynn. We can let Gnat go with Adam if he needs help. We go, eat, be seen. Come back here and find out what Adam found, get some sleep. That's it."

"For tonight," she said as she pulled the gray dress out and tossed it onto the bed.

"I don't like it any more than you do, Thia, but it's who we are. What we agreed to." She leaned back into his chest and he rested his cheek against the top of her head. "It's not going to last forever. An hour, two at the most, of being seen tonight. Tomorrow could be longer, depending on Her Highness and if she's even a quarter as stubborn as you are. After that, we put them away for a while."

"But for how long?"

He gently turned her around to face him. "Until they're needed again. I daresay a death mage that's lived as long as Helix has probably doesn't care for titles. If we're lucky, we won't have to wear them again for months."

"Good," she said, leaning into him, "because I much prefer being me."

Wrapping his arms around her, he held her close. "That makes two of us," he whispered.

CHAPTER
EIGHTEEN

Jinaari reached for his goblet, trying to pinpoint the reason behind his restlessness. It was random, without cause or reason. Yet it settled into his soul the moment he escorted Thia into the hall for dinner with his brothers.

Glancing to his left, he looked past the commander at Thia. She'd stopped eating; placing her silverware across the top of the plate. There was still food on it, but less than half what she'd been served. *Good*, he thought, *she's still eating.*

The large wood doors at the end of the hall were pushed open violently, and Jinaari shifted his focus. A man strode in; one hand resting on the pommel of the sword at his waist. His brown hair was pulled back. The medallion he wore was the same as Jinaari's. Leaning back, he watched the newcomer approach.

Paul cleared his throat, and the conversation within the room stopped. "You're late, Vadim."

The newcomer stopped in front of the table. "My apologies, Commander." He turned to Jinaari. "You are welcome, brother."

"Jinaari Althir is more than your brother, Vadim. He is the Shield, the Protector of Avoch."

Vadim raised an eyebrow, "Is he? Truly, then," he bowed at Jinaari, "are we blessed by more than Garret's grace to have him visit us."

"I appreciate the welcome, brother," Jinaari said, inclining his head. "I didn't come alone, though. Allow me to introduce you to the Daughter of Keroys, and wielder of the Scepter of Avoch." Pushing his chair back, he began to rise.

Vadim looked around, shocked. "I see no one else of note, brother. Are you sure she's here? If so, I would gladly make her acquaintance."

Walking around the table, Jinaari stared at Vadim. "She sits to the left of your commander, *brother*," he emphasized the last word. "Does your eyesight fail you in your youth?"

Turning, Vadim threw up his hands and spoke toward the assembled paladins. "I see only a Fallen witch. One who stole the scepter, slayed our kin, and has no honor." He glared at Jinaari; his face twisted in hatred and contempt. "Or have you brought her to us to atone for her sins? A whore for us all to take generations of pain and loathing out on?"

A stunned silence descended on the room at his words. Paul pushed his chair back, placing his fists on the table in front of him, "Have you lost your mind?!" he roared. "No paladin of Garret would dare say such words about a guest!"

Holding up his hand, Jinaari kept his focus on the man in front of him. "I would rethink your words, friend," he growled. "She is not who you think she is. Garret himself tasked me with her safety. Against any who would do her harm."

Vadim stared back at him. "No brother of mine would associate with a Fallen witch. If you truly believe our God told you to protect this mongrel, then you're a fool. Garret would never help a follower of Lolc Aon!" He swiveled, spitting in Thia's direction.

Glancing up, Jinaari saw Caelynn urging Thia to get up and leave. Her face was a mask, but he could see the pain in her eyes. "You need to apologize."

The other man stepped closer, his face within inches of Jinaari's. "Make me."

"I will. Tomorrow morning, in the arena."

"Bring your whore," Vadim growled. "It will do her good to watch me cut you."

Jinaari stared at him, resisting the urge to start the fight immediately. Paul appeared between them, pushing them apart. "This is still Garret's chapterhouse. Respect will be given!" He stared at Vadim.

"The challenge has been accepted," Jinaari said, making sure his voice carried throughout the room. "I say, here and now, that this man is no brother paladin of mine. Tomorrow, I shall prove it when our blades meet in the arena. I invoke the law of hospitality. As long as my companions remain within this keep, they shall have peace. Regardless of the outcome in the morning."

"Such is the law," Paul said, his voice laden with the command as it rang through the hall. "If any here present," he shot a look at Vadim, "think they are above the law, or can violate it, let him leave this keep now."

Five men stood and walked single file toward the exit. The remaining stayed. Jinaari studied their faces. A few were curious, others cautious. The majority held a steadfast resolve. They would be safe within these walls, or his brothers would die while they escaped.

"Get out of here with your friends," Paul said, jerking Jinaari's thoughts back to Vadim. "You are not allowed through the gates again until tomorrow morning."

Vadim sneered, "This is my home more than any whore's refuge."

"Get out," the commander said from between clenched teeth. "Go find an inn or see if the Princess will let you warm her bed. Garret's Law on this is clear. May the Gods help you tomorrow. You're going to need it."

Vadim stared at Jinaari, but he didn't back down. Inside, he seethed but knew he couldn't show it. "The only one who needs help is you, Althir. You've sold your sword to evil." Turning, Vadim strode from the room.

"Go," Paul said, his voice low, "your friends will need you. And you need to prepare for tomorrow. I'll set extra guards on the hall you're in. None will disturb your rest."

"Thank you, Commander," Jinaari said. Walking quickly, he headed up the stairs and toward their room. Behind him, he heard the steps of ten men. Glancing over his shoulder, he caught the gaze of the closest one.

"Vadim's an ass," the man said, "and I look forward to watching you teach him some lessons tomorrow. The Scepter is more than she appears, yes?"

"Much more," Jinaari said over his shoulder.

"Then fear not for her safety, brother. None of us will allow so much as a flea to come near her."

Nodding his thanks, he looked forward and focused on the door at the end. He'd given Caelynn the key earlier. *They should be in the room with Gnat and Adam. Caelynn was staying there until they returned. She'd come into the hall about halfway through the meal. Garret, I hope Adam found something helpful.*

Knocking on the door, he said, "It's me." It opened, and Adam stepped aside. As soon as he was through, the blonde man closed and locked it. "Find anything?"

"No," Adam said. "I hear you're fighting in the morning."

"It's necessary."

"It's stupid. That's what it is," Thia snapped at him.

Looking at her, he shook his head. "He insulted you, your position, and all you stand for, Thia. He needs to learn to think before he speaks."

"How? By you breaking his legs? I've been insulted before, Jinaari. It's going to happen again. We're not going to change minds about me, the Thahion, by sheer brutality." She sat cross-legged at the end of one of the beds. The gray dress had been replaced by the long, linen tunic she normally slept in.

"And I've told you," he said, keeping his voice light, "that sometimes that's what will need to happen." Grabbing a chair, he dragged it across the floor and placed it near her. Sitting down, he stared at her. Anger and hurt danced in her lilac eyes. "This is what I do, Thia. I'm a fighter, and a man of honor. I cannot let the insult stand. If I do, it diminishes you and I both. It emboldens our enemies. I won't kill him. But he will learn, painfully, that he needs to apologize."

"I can do that myself. I don't need you to do it for me."

He sat back in the chair. "No. It has to be me. The Shield protects the Scepter, remember? You'll be there, watching, but stay out of it." He stared at her, his voice firm. "You don't heal me. You don't help me in any way. Or hinder him. If I thought it would help, I'd tell Gnat to sit in your lap."

Shock and disbelief warred with each other on her face. "You honestly think I'll sit there and watch this?" Her voice bordered on incredulousness.

"You have to, Thia. If you're not there, it gives him the advantage. It would look like you don't see me as your champion."

She stood, staring at him. "Maybe I don't," she said before running toward the bath chamber, slamming the door behind her.

Jinaari started to stand up but sank back down as Caelynn held up a hand. "Don't," she told him. "She's not going to hear you. Not right now. I'll talk to her." The pink-haired woman walked toward the door. Opening it quietly, she disappeared through it.

His chest felt tight. How could she not see him as her champion? Everything he'd ever done was meant to keep her safe, protect her. Was it not enough somehow? "Maybe you don't trust me as much as I thought," he whispered.

"Trust isn't the problem," Adam said.

Jinaari turned his head toward him. "What are you talking about?"

The blonde man sat on a bed. "I'm saying some things you already know. Thia's stubborn, almost obstinate—."

"I know that."

"But so are you. You're expecting her to know about how your Order views honor, all the intricacies of it. I've been your brother, fought at your side, for over a decade and even I don't know it all. The only thing she knows is what you've told her, or she's learned by watching you. There might be a few books she's read, but I doubt it. Jinaari, she doesn't know what all of this *means*. To you, to the other paladins, or to us. All she knows is that someone she cares about is planning on fighting someone who insulted her. Which, to her point, has happened numerous times and likely will again." He paused. "Thia trusts you. You know this. What's got her spooked is that she doesn't understand why this is happening. You've told her to sit and watch you get hurt." Jinaari drew in a breath, ready to protest, but Adam held up his hand. "I know. You're the better swordsman, and this won't be much of a fight. There's always the chance he'll get in a lucky shot. Alesso did, more than once. You're not invincible, no matter how much you pretend you are."

"I would've explained it, if she'd asked. Instead, she stormed off."

"Let Caelynn do that. A lot of songs are based on exploits

of your brothers. She understands better than most outside the Order and can explain it in a way that Thia will understand. You need to get your rest."

Jinaari shook his head. "I can't leave it like this, Adam. She said she didn't see me as her champion. I need to know she'll be there tomorrow. It's going to undermine so much of what we discussed with Elizabeth if she's not."

Adam gave him a direct look. "She'll be there. Talking to her now won't work, though. She's not going to hear you. I know her tells, almost as well as you do. She's scared, possibly as terrified as she was when we were heading down to Lolc Aon. Pressing her to explain what she's feeling before she's ready isn't going to work."

"What's she scared of? I'm not losing tomorrow."

"She's scared of the things she can't control. Just like the rest of us. I know she said in the refuge that she's cured. I'm not so sure. There was something else to how she reacted when they came back to the room."

Concern rose in him. "What happened?"

Adam shrugged. "It's hard to explain without seeming crazy. She stormed in, Caelynn following, and pulled her shift out of her pack while I was told what happened. I watched Thia's face. I swear, at one point she smiled. It was when Caelynn told me the insult Vadim used. There was a second when I thought her eyes shifted color."

"What?"

"It was probably a reflection of the fire, honestly. Her eyes are so pale to begin with. For a moment, though, they appeared red."

"Shit," he cursed. Adam gave him a questioning look, and he said, "In the dream she had when she ran, she said there was someone who looked exactly like her, except their eyes were red. It was the only person she said talked to her."

"What'd they say?"

"That they were Herasta's daughter, same as Thia. That it was time to join her real family, replace Lolc Aon."

"I don't like the sound of that, Jinaari."

"Neither do I, but we can't solve the problem overnight. I'm getting some sleep. Talk to Caelynn without Thia hearing you, set up a watch with her. I'll take third." Jinaari rose from the chair and moved to a cot. Sitting down, he began to pull off his boots.

"Are you worried about our safety? We're in your chapterhouse," Adam said.

"My concern isn't for who's out there," he replied. "Rather, who might be in the room with us and we don't know." Pointing to the small table, he said, "Make sure whoever's on watch has the key in their pocket. We don't need Thia to go wandering." Pulling the blankets over him, he turned to one side. Thia's bed was within feet of his, still empty. Closing his eyes, he kept his ears open. *I need to know she gets to bed, that's all. Tomorrow, I teach Vadim a lesson. If I'm lucky, Jynth will attend. We can accept her fealty, get out of here before anyone else bothers us. That dream wasn't normal. If someone's trying to possess Thia, who? And why?*

Light steps came closer. He heard someone get into the bed next to his; blankets shifting against each other as they settled in. Opening his eyes briefly, he caught sight of the back of Thia's head. Closing them, he cleared his mind and fell asleep.

"Jinaari?"

His eyes flew open at the sound of Caelynn's worried voice. "What?" he asked.

She glanced to his left. Following her gaze, he saw Thia

sitting up; her feet flat on the floor. The Mark on her back glowed through the fabric, pulsing with each breath she took.

Pushing aside his blankets, he whispered, "When did this happen?"

"A minute or two ago. I tried to ask her what was wrong, but she won't answer me."

Jinaari kept his movements small. Walking around the end of the bed, he kept his gaze on Thia. Her eyes were closed; the muscles in her face twitched beneath the skin. Her lips moved slightly. Sitting across from her, he said, "Thia?" She didn't show any reaction to indicate she'd heard him. Reaching out, he put one hand on hers. It was cold to the touch. "Thia?"

Her eyes flew open and a cold smile crossed her face. Jinaari drew back in shock; her pale lilac eyes were rimmed with red. "*Is dochas aca mise,*" she said, the words laden with spite and hatred. "*Is dochas aca mise.*" She kept repeating the phrase.

"Thia, listen to my voice. I know you're in there. Find a way to fight back from whatever's happening." He grabbed her other hand, holding both tight. "I'm here. You can do this." Without breaking eye contact, he said, "Caelynn, grab something and write down what she's saying."

"Got it," the bard replied. He felt the mattress shift under her weight as she sat. "It's Olc, isn't it? Thia doesn't speak the language."

"I know," he said. "Someone else is saying it." He kept his voice even, "Thia, you know how to break out of this. I know you do. I believe in you, in your strength."

A snarl came from her throat as the light from the Mark flared bright. The redness left her eyes as the muscles in her face softened and warmth returned to her hands. "Jinaari?" she asked, her voice drifting off as her eyelids drooped.

"How are things with you?"

Without answering him, she pulled her hands from his

and laid back down, turning her back to him. The Mark no longer glowed.

He sat there, watching her breathing. Once he was certain she'd fallen back asleep, he gently placed the blanket across her body. "Get some sleep," he said to Caelynn. "I'll watch her for a while."

She held out the paper to him. "Do you know what it says?"

"No," he said, taking it from her, "but Thia will. I'll ask her later." *After the duel*, he thought.

"Okay," Caelynn said as she crawled into the cot he'd used. "Don't worry about the fight, Jinaari. I'll make sure she's there."

He didn't answer her. Instead, he watched Thia sleep. *Garret, I hope this isn't a sign that things got worse instead of better.*

NINETEEN

The pain pushed through the darkness, waking Thia up. Without much thought, she imagined the sigil and willed it away. It died down but didn't dissipate like she anticipated. Panic flared in her, and she tried again.

"Thia?" Caelynn's voice pierced her mind.

"I'm awake," she said. She kept her eyes closed, and felt her friend sit next to her. A gentle hand brushed some hair away from her face.

"What's wrong? You don't look good."

"I had a headache. That's all." The pain left at last. Opening her eyes, she looked at Caelynn.

The bard looked at her, worry etched in her face. "Thia, your skin's warm. Are you feeling feverish?"

"No," she said, sitting up. "It was just a headache. I probably drank too much mead at dinner." Glancing over, she noticed they were alone. "Where are the others?"

"Outside, getting ready for the duel."

Thia threw back the covers. "You should've woken me up." Reaching across the bed, she grabbed the gray dress from where she'd left it the night before. A wave of dizziness washed over her, making her slow down.

"I don't know that you're in any condition to go," Caelynn said.

With deliberate movements, she took the linen shift off. "I'm fine. Jinaari was right; if I'm not there, it says we're not united. I don't agree with why he's doing it, or even understand his reason for calling Vadim out, but I have to be there." Slipping the dress over her head, she fastened the three small buttons at the back of the neck as she spoke. "Can you grab me some clean socks?"

Caelynn rose and dug through the pack. "You've got to tell him you're sick, Thia. He'd understand." She held the socks out to her.

"I'm fine," she assured her friend. As she put one on, she said, "If it makes you feel better, I'll tell him about the headache after the fight. I promise." She stopped, looking at the one still in her hand. "I was horrible to him last night. Before anything else, I need to apologize to him. I can't let him go into this thinking I meant anything I said."

"I doubt he's still mad. Jinaari's pretty forgiving, even if it doesn't look that way. He and Adam have had some blistering arguments in the past, but they're still brothers. He also knows you've been sick. Back in Tanisal, you said things that weren't you. He won't see last night as any different."

"They were, though," she said as she finished putting on the socks and slipped her feet into her shoes. "Last night was all me. I got rid of whatever presence was in me after the nightmare." Caelynn's face shifted, and Thia's heart sank. "What happened?"

"You don't remember?"

She shook her head slowly, "No," she whispered. "Tell me."

The other woman sat, grabbing her hands, "Last night,

Jinaari asked me and Adam to keep watch. At one point, you woke up. Sat up on the side of your bed, but your eyes were closed. I asked you several times if you were okay, but you didn't answer. That's when I noticed the Mark on your back."

"What about it?"

"It was glowing. Bright enough I could see it through your shift. It pulsed in time with . . .. something. It could've been your heart, or your breathing. I can't be sure. That's when I woke Jinaari up. He came over, and your eyes opened. You kept repeating a phrase in Olc—."

"I don't speak Olc!" Thia said.

Caelynn nodded. "We know that, but that's what it was. Jinaari had me write it down."

"Show me."

"I don't have it. He took the paper from me, told me to get some sleep. I don't know what he did with it."

"Do you remember any of it?" Thia insisted, her voice edged with the panic she felt within.

"I'm sorry, I don't. It wasn't long, maybe four words?" Caelynn apologized.

Thia pushed down the fear. *Jinaari has the note. He'll tell me what I said.* Drawing in a steadying breath, she said, "It's fine. I'll ask him later, once we're done with all of this." Standing up, she walked to her pack. Tossing it onto the bed, she rummaged through it.

"What do you need?" Caelynn asked.

"I don't know why, but I'm certain the princess is going to be there. If not to watch the duel, she'll come after. I need visual proof that I'm the Scepter."

"You'll have it with you. Isn't that proof enough?"

"The way Jinaari was talking, no." Her fingers found the box she was looking for. Pulling it free, she caressed the small barrel lock that kept it closed. "Elizabeth gave this to me before we left Cirrain. I didn't understand why, but I do now."

Her fingers worked the lever and the box lid came loose. Inside, resting on a bed of blue velvet, was a coronet. Wire spiraled around the silver band, creating a delicate sculpture of leaves. In between, embedded on the band itself were eight different cabochon gemstones, four on each side. The center of the circlet had an enameled representation of the scepter rising above the leaves.

Thia pulled it out, tossing the box onto the bed. She heard Caelynn's gasp of amazement. As she put it on, she turned to her friend. "Is it straight?"

Caelynn's eyes were wide. "Hold on," she said. Thia saw her hands tremble slightly as she adjusted it on her head. "That's better."

"What's wrong? You look like you've never seen me before."

The other woman shook her head. "Not like this, I haven't. Why didn't you tell me you had that?"

Thia reached for her belt, her hands pulling at the knot that kept the scepter attached. "I didn't think I'd ever need to wear it. Jinaari has his circlet, and Elizabeth thought it best that I have one as well. They're both different from the crown itself." She threaded her right hand through the loop at the bottom of the scepter. Grasping the shaft, she cradled it with her left arm. "I hope it's not cold out there," she muttered. "I don't like it, but this city needs to know who I am. I can't hide beneath a cloak today." Taking a deep breath, she steadied herself before looking at Caelynn. "I take it you have the key? I've never known him to leave us without it."

She pulled it out. "Yes, it's here. Are you ready?"

"As ready as I'll ever be."

Caelynn walked toward the door, and Thia followed behind. Outside, the Commander stood with four other paladins. He turned his head toward her and bowed.

"Scepter," he said, "it would be our honor to escort you to the arena."

"Thank you," Thia said. Walking to his side, she put out her left hand and rested it on his. "Will the duel be happening in the courtyard? I hate to question your decision, but the ground was uneven. Both men will have difficulty fighting on it." Caelynn fell into step with them, just behind her. The paladins followed.

"We set up something outside the chapterhouse," Paul replied. "The Shield let me know yesterday that you needed Princess Jynth to swear fealty, and that it was best done publicly. As Vadim is known to be one of her favorites, I thought it best to do the duel in full view as well. The last thing any of us need is to have accusations of cheating flung about."

They descended the staircase and Thia saw the front gate stood open. A score of paladins, dressed in armor, formed a corridor for them to walk through. "Vadim and his friends are a minority among us, Scepter. Garret's Laws command that we treat all with respect and kindness, no matter their position or heritage. Rest assured that none of them will allow harm to come to you or your companions. If necessary, we shall make sure you leave the city unharmed."

"And what of the Shield? He's doing the fighting this morning, not me."

"I won't lie to you. Vadim is one of the best I've ever trained. I've heard stories of the Shield's talent with a blade. The fight may be a difficult one to watch, brutal even."

"I know my place, Commander," she said. "I will not interfere. Honor is a strange beast; one I don't understand fully. At least not the way your Order interprets it."

"You are the Daughter of Keroys. The bearer of the Scepter of Avoch. I've heard almost as many tales about your deeds as I have the Shield." He turned to look at her, a smile on his face, "I believe you have a greater understanding of honor than you think."

Trumpets blared as they walked out of the chapterhouse. Several hundred people turned to look their way. Thia held her head high, forcing down the nervousness, and focused on what was ahead of them.

The crowd parted, giving them space to walk. As they passed, she heard a mix of startled gasps and excited whispers as the people saw the Mark on her back. Ahead of them, a large arena had been cordoned off. Platforms had been erected on three sides, high enough to see the combat but stay clear of it. The one in the center and her left both had single chairs; on the right, there were two.

The platform to her left was occupied by a woman. Older than Thia, the woman was slender. Her white gown a stark contrast to the black hair that fell in a straight line down her back. A gold crown, sparking with multiple gemstones, sat on her head. Behind her, five women stood. Around her neck, a bright orange scarf moved in the light breeze.

Two men, dressed in armor, stood in the arena. Thia recognized Jinaari within seconds. He wasn't far from the platform to the right. His focus wasn't on her, though; he watched his opponent.

Paul stopped at the barrier. Adam stood on the other side. As paladins moved it aside, he said, "I need to leave you now. I cannot show partiality during the fight itself. Your friend will escort you the rest of the way."

"I understand." Thia replied, walking through the gate and taking Adam's arm.

The commander bowed, then walked briskly toward the center. "Let's get you seated," Adam said.

As they walked, she noticed the Princess rise. She walked to the barrier, summoning Vadim. With deliberate motions, she pulled her scarf off and tied it around the paladin's waist. "Why'd she do that?" she asked Adam.

"She's showing the crowd who she favors in the contest," he replied. "Giving him a token of hers to mark him as her Champion in this battle."

"Is that important?"

Adam nodded. "Yes. I'm not sure how to explain it, but it means a great deal to the fighter. It gives him a purpose, a sense of being justified in the win. It's not just his honor he's trying to protect; it's that of the one he fights for."

Thia looked at Jinaari; he stood alone, watching the activity across the arena. His face showed no emotion, but she saw his hand open and close across the hilt of his sword.

"Adam, wait a moment," she said as she stopped. "Don't let me fall."

"What are you doing, Thia?"

Using his arm for balance, she let the scepter fall free. Quickly, she slid her foot out of her left shoe and reached down, pulling her sock off. Shoving her foot back into the slipper, she repositioned the scepter while grasping the stocking. "Take me to Jinaari," she said. "I need to talk to him before I sit down."

"Okay," he said with a small laugh.

When they were ten feet away, Jinaari turned and looked at her. "I've got it, Adam," she whispered as she let go of his arm. Jinaari bowed as she came closer. "I owe you an apology. I was horrible to you last night. I don't understand this," she said, her eyes locked on his dark ones, "but that doesn't mean I should question your judgement in anything dealing with your Order."

"I don't know that it was all you last night, Thia."

She nodded. "Caelynn told me this morning that there was an incident. I want to know what I said, all of it. But after the fight." She pulled the sock free of her fist. Smiling at him, she said, "I can't let my Champion go into battle without a token, can I?"

He glanced at her hand, then raised his head. The smile reached his eyes. "A sock?"

"I had to improvise. Besides," she said, holding it out to him, "it seems wildly appropriate. It's dry, though. Try to keep it that way."

He took the sock, tucking it into his belt. "I'll do my best."

Thia glanced toward the Princess, then back to Jinaari. "Do what you need to do," she said, her tone serious, "then we deal with her. If what the Commander told you is true, she's going to try and come after you as much as the scepter."

"Won't work. My mother made a betrothal agreement with another family before I was born."

She blinked, shocked. "You've got a fiancée?"

He pulled the cloth cap out of his helmet and set it on his head. "Not sure. Mother said she was going to write to Elizabeth, get it nullified. I don't know if that ever happened."

"You were betrothed to one of my cousins?"

"The marriage was to be between me and the first-born daughter of the eldest Beckenburg son. Thing is, he disappeared and no one knew where he went or if he had any children." He picked up his shield, tightening the straps across his forearm.

Staring at him, she started to put the pieces together. "My father was the oldest son," she whispered.

Jinaari nodded, "I know that, Thia. I didn't know about the arrangement until we were at the encampment before we faced Drogon the second time." His eyes softened, "I don't hold to arrangements like this. A piece of paper doesn't matter if either party is against it, for whatever reason."

"Paladins! Come to me!" Paul's voice rang across the arena.

"Go," he told her. "I know you have questions, Thia. Lots

of them. I can see it in your face. I'll answer them all once I deal with Vadim."

Before she could stop herself, she kissed him. She felt his arm circle her waist, pulling her closer as his mouth met hers. From behind her, she heard Adam cough. Reluctantly, she pulled away. "Go be the arrogant prick I know you are," she said.

"You, my stubborn witch, are full of surprises." With a smile, he put his helm on and walked toward the center of the arena.

Turning around, she dared a glance at Jynth. The woman wasn't as good as hiding her emotions as she should be, and Thia saw jealousy play across her face briefly. Rejoining Adam, they walked toward the viewing platform. Thia settled into one of the two chairs, laying the scepter across her lap.

Jinaari and Vadim stood in the center of the ring, the commander between them. "A challenge was issued last night, in response to an insult given to a guest within the halls of Garret's Paladins. We here assembled are to bear witness to this challenge. The fight will continue until one of the combatants yields or is knocked unconscious. There will be no interference from anyone. Is this agreed on by both parties?"

Thia's hands gripped the arms of the chair as the commander spoke. *I can't show how nervous I am*, she thought. Jinaari turned to face her, raising his sword in salute. Glancing across, she saw Jynth rise and acknowledge Vadim's gesture. Quickly, she grabbed the scepter so it didn't fall from her lap and did the same.

"Lay on!" Paul called out, backing away from the two paladins.

They began to circle each other as Thia sat back down. "Don't worry, Thia," Adam said from behind her, "Jinaari knows what he's doing."

"I know," she said, her eyes never leaving the fight in front of her. The clang of sword meeting sword echoed in the morning air as Vadim charged Jinaari and he blocked the blow. They separated, but not for long. Vadim came at him with a flurry of blows, driving him back several feet. At the last second, he changed his swing and dropped low, sweeping Jinaari's feet out from under him.

Thia tightened her grip on the chair, forcing herself to stay seated as Jinaari raised his shield to ward off Vadim's attack. He kicked at his opponent's knee, knocking him back as he fought for balance. That gave Jinaari enough time to stand.

She noticed the change in his stance; Jinaari went on the offensive, his sword striking Vadim's armor several times as he was unable to parry as fast as Jinaari swung. Pressing his advantage, Jinaari kept driving him back. Vadim dropped to his knees; his sword tip embedded in the ground. Thia watched Jinaari step back, giving his brother paladin space. Before she could blink, Vadim slashed at Jinaari's legs. This time, though, he was ready. Jinaari sidestepped the blow. Spinning quickly, he drove the pommel of his sword into Vadim's helm. The man fell back and lay still; his hand no longer gripping his weapon.

Paul stepped back into the arena and walked toward the fallen paladin. He knelt at Vadim's side, blocking Thia's view. Rising, he said in a booming voice, "Victory, honor, and justice to Jinaari Althir, Shield of Avoch." Four paladins ran onto the field to carry the unconscious man away. Jinaari saluted Paul before sheathing his sword and walking toward Thia.

Gripping the scepter, she rose and walked down the steps to meet him. He took his helm off as he approached; sweat ran down his face. Kneeling in front of her, he pulled the sock out of his belt. "I believe this is yours."

Taking it from him, she smiled, "You kept it dry." Her tone turned serious. "Are you hurt?"

"No," he replied, rising. "Let me get some water, then we'll deal with Her Highness."

"I'm going to take care of her while you recover." She put one hand on his chest, her voice firm. "I did what you asked. I stayed out of your fight. Now you get to stay out of mine."

"Be nice," he said.

"Only if she is," Thia muttered. Walking past him, she focused her gaze on Jynth. She sat in the chair, trying to project a calm demeanor and failing miserably. The fight had not gone as she anticipated.

Stopping in the middle of the arena, Thia waited for the crowd to be silent. Tapping into her stores, she imagined the sigil needed to make her voice heard by everyone. "There are three symbols of rule in Avoch. The Crown is within the care of Elizabeth Beckenburg in Cirrain. The Shield is there," she pointed behind her at Jinaari. "You have seen for yourself today how well it defends and protects Avoch. This," she raised the scepter above her head, "is the Scepter. Which was created here, in Tavisholm. Artisans from two families, commissioned by the Gods themselves, created it. Not for glory or riches, but to help unite all the people into a single kingdom. To end generations of war, hatred, distrust, and death. I am Thia Bransdottir, the Daughter of Keroys. You can see the Mark he placed upon me. When the Shield defeated Lolc Aon, the Fallen died with her. They are now the Thahion and will rejoin the rest of us on the surface. In an effort to show their peaceful intent, they found the scepter in her lair and brought it back to Almair. I did not ask for it, yet it responded to my touch." She lowered her hand and stared at Jynth. "If you feel you are more deserving than I am, come and take this burden from me. If it accepts you, it is yours. Along with everything that goes with it. If it does not, you have a choice; swear fealty to us, as Scepter and Shield, or war. Make your decision."

Jynth rose, making her way down the stairs. Thia heard Jinaari walk up behind her, "Do you know what you're doing?" he whispered.

"Trust me," she whispered back, keeping her attention on the other woman.

Jynth walked closer, her attendants trailing behind. "You would give up your power that easily? There is little honor among the Fallen, or whatever you're calling yourselves these days. How can I trust your word?"

"I am half human," Thia said. "I was raised on the surface. My lineage is an accident of birth, same as you wearing the coronet that you have. My champion has defeated yours. That should be proof enough of my intent." Kneeling, she placed the scepter on the ground. Rising, she gestured at it. "Go ahead. If it welcomes your touch, then it is yours."

Jynth's blue eyes locked with Thia's. Slowly, she bent down and picked up the scepter. As she straightened, she smiled coldly. "I should probably thank you for bringing this home to us," she said, "but that doesn't atone for the theft. I —" Her voice stopped, and her face twisted in a grimace of pain.

Thia watched as the silver rod began to glow red beneath the other woman's hands. "I would let go, if I was you," she said, her voice quiet. "It's only going to get worse the longer you try to force your will onto it."

A startled gasp rose from the crowd as the smell of burning flesh began to drift across the arena. Screaming in pain, Jynth let go. Thia reached out, catching the scepter before it fell. The metal instantly returned to its normal color. Steam rose from the other woman's blistered palms. Without hesitation, Thia healed the burns but left white scars on her skin.

"You have a choice to make," she said.

The Princess knelt, lowering her head, and said, "I,

Princess Jynth of Tavisholm, do recognize the authority of Jinaari Althir and Thia Bransdottir as the Shield and Scepter. And, through them, the Crown. Tavisholm will answer any call for aid. Long may they lead Avoch."

"Grateful are we for the loyalty of Tavisholm," Jinaari said. "May the lands prosper beneath your watch."

Jynth rose, a guarded look in her eyes. "Will you join me for dinner tonight? I would love to hear news from the rest of Avoch." She looked at Jinaari, avoiding Thia's gaze.

"We have pressing matters to the south," he replied as he held out his arm. Thia took it, watching Jynth's face. "I know you would not wish to endanger the safety of Avoch."

Without another word, they walked toward the chapterhouse.

TWENTY

As soon as they reached the room, Thia kicked off her shoes. "Pack up," Jinaari ordered. "I want to be riding out of here within an hour."

Her pack lay open on the bed where she'd left it. Thia dropped the scepter and her sock onto the blanket. Removing the circlet, she placed it back into the box and locked it. "You really don't want to have dinner with Jynth, do you?"

"Not one bit. That woman made my skin crawl," Jinaari said from his cot.

Thia dug out some traveling clothes before starting to unbutton her dress. Throwing the tunic over her head, she tugged at the sleeves underneath as she said, "Is that the only reason?"

"Yes. Why?"

Lifting her legs from the dress as it pooled around her feet, she shoved her arms through the sleeves of the tunic. "I hear I was talking in my sleep last night." She looked at him as she grabbed for her pants.

"Later." His face grew serious. "If we're on the road, it's less likely we'll be overheard. I know you've got questions,

Thia. I plan to answer all of them. Just not while we're in the city."

"I understand," she said. Sitting down, she put her sock on while watching Caelynn and Adam direct Gnat to help with their gear. "How far is it?"

"Where?"

"To Helix."

Slinging his pack across his back, he looked at her. "A week, by horse. Longer if we walk or encounter something. Why? Are you feeling sick?"

Thia shoved her feet into her boots, stamping the ground to get her heel past the stiff leather near the ankle. "I'm not sure. I had a headache this morning, but I could've drunk too much mead at dinner. Caelynn thought I felt warm when I woke up." She raised her head, meeting his gaze. "Between that and suddenly speaking Olc in my sleep, I'd like to get there sooner over later."

Jinaari nodded. "Definitely. Adam can't transport the horses, though, and we might want them to get Gnat home. Grab your pack and let's go. I'm not wasting time you may not have."

Minutes later, she followed him down the stairs toward the stables. Gnat, Caelynn, and Adam were behind her. As they entered the courtyard, their horses were saddled and waiting for them. Paul stood at the bottom of the steps, watching.

"How's Vadim?" Jinaari asked as they approached.

"He's going to have a massive headache, but it was earned," the commander said. Thia stopped next to Jinaari while the others went past her. Adam came back, reaching for her pack, and she handed it to him. "You won more than just a duel today, Jinaari. You and the Scepter both put Jynth on notice that her antics won't go unpunished."

"We don't want war, Paul. None of us do. The purpose of

the relics was to unite Avoch, not tear her apart at the seams," Thia said.

"I understand. I think Jynth will, after a while. The rejection of the scepter was brilliant. Did you do that?"

Thia shook her head. "No. The scepter did. If it was meant for her, it would've allowed her to hold it. I needed to give her the opportunity, though. She wasn't going to let go of the dream otherwise."

"We need to get on the road," Jinaari said. His hand pressed against her back, and she walked over to her horse. "Send a letter to Drakkus. He's moved the Dragonspire chapterhouse to Cirrain, on Garret's orders. Tell him we were here, and what happened. The Crown trusts him. He'll be able to get what you need to reestablish trade routes with the rest of Avoch, provide for Tavisholm's citizens if it's needed. If we can, we'll stop by for a longer visit once our business is concluded."

Mounting up, she watched Jinaari shake the commander's hand before heading to his horse. Paul turned, his face calm. "Whatever mission you're on, may Garret guide your sword."

"May Garret bring you peace, Commander," Jinaari replied as he vaulted himself into the saddle. Grasping the reins, he nodded at her as he led them from the chapterhouse.

He set a quick pace, and Thia urged her horse to keep up with him. People stopped, bowing silently to them as they rode past. She felt them staring at her; some were openly hostile. *Old wounds are the hardest to heal*, she thought. "I feel horrible," she said.

"About what?" Jinaari said without looking at her.

"I'm not sure what, but I think I should've done more for them. Reached out to the sick, made sure they were in good hands. Something," she paused, "that showed I'm not just the Scepter. Not just here to rule over them."

"We have to come through on our way back to Almair. We

can spend a week or two, let you show them what you're really like. Though there's likely to be meetings with Jynth in the mix. I'm not going near her without one of you with me."

"You don't think I made her rethink her ambitions before the fight?"

She caught the slight upturn of his mouth before he answered. "No," he said as he brought his horse to a standstill.

Twenty feet in front of them, barring the path to the city gate, stood Jynth. She wore the same dress as she did at the arena. A small group of people, likely courtiers or bureaucrats, stood with her. "Your Highness," Thia said as they drew closer. "Here to see us on our way?"

Jynth glared at her, then switched her attention to Jinaari. "We are bereft to see you so anxious to leave our fair city. What possible threat to our lands calls you forth, that you ignore the demands of hospitality?"

"No threat," Jinaari replied. "Rather, one of duty. Our friend, Gnat, lives to the south. He was instrumental in many ways to recent events. Honor dictates that we reward his bravery by escorting him home."

A forced smile crossed Jynth's face. "If there's no threat, then allow us to celebrate Gnat's deeds with you." She raised her arms, gesturing to the crowd. "A festival, with dancing and feasting! Where bards can come and immortalize his bravery in song! We have long been without joy. The Scepter," her face darkened as she glanced at Thia, "is back on the surface where it belongs. To hear the stories, first hand, of how it came to happen would make amends in our hearts. Would you deny us the chance to celebrate with you?"

"Of course not," Thia said. *I have to be the one to respond, force her to deal with me.* "The Shield and I were just discussing the need to get to know the people of Tavisholm. However, a promise was made. We are, as he said, honor bound to see our companion safely reunited with his family. We will return, have no doubt."

"If there's no danger, why does Gnat require an escort? Could not your attendants go, allowing you the chance to remain? The road is not as comfortable a bed as one at an inn."

"I don't have the patience for this," Jinaari muttered. Squaring his shoulders, he looked at Jynth. "Gnat saved my life, the life of my sister, and that of my brother. I *will* see him reunited with his kin. It is said that the Shield protects the Scepter. I cannot do that if she is not with me. Stand aside and let us pass. As Thia said, we will return." Clicking his heels, his horse began a steady walk toward the group. Thia urged hers forward, keeping pace with his mount.

The dignitaries parted, leaving Jynth standing alone. Thia moved her horse to her right, making sure the scepter would be within reach as she passed. As they drew up next to the woman, she reached out and touched Jinaari's leg. "You deserve more than her."

"That's where you're wrong," he replied. "She deserves more than me." He put his heels to his horse, urging it to pick up the pace. Thia followed suit. By the time they went through the gate, they rode at a full gallop. She watched him turn toward the south, riding hard.

Staying on his heels, she waited until he slowed down to ride up next to him. "Do you still feel like staying there after we're done?" he asked.

"Not everyone in the city can be as ambitious as she is. There are good people in there, ones that we should talk to. We can't ignore them."

"That's why I told Paul to write to Drakkus. He's got Elizabeth's ear. I'm not saying things will improve before we get back there, but I doubt there's little we could learn that Paul already doesn't know." He paused. "He said she'd been informed of my betrothal in that her overtures to my mother were rejected. Her behavior suggests that she still thinks the door is open. Us staying there could become problematic."

"In what way?"

He glanced at her. "In that she'd demand to know who I was to marry. Finding out it was you may see us needing to define our relationship in a public way. Well," he smiled, "a more public way than you did in the arena."

Thia felt her cheeks grow hot. "I'm not sure exactly why I did that."

"I'm glad you did."

She coughed, blushing even more. "You think it would mean we'd have to either announce a formal engagement, or publicly refute the betrothal. Am I right?"

"Yes. What's between us is that, Thia. Between us. I never wanted the rest of the world to get involved, which is one reason I didn't mention it before. That, and Mother said she planned to force Elizabeth to nullify it."

"Is that what she said that made you rush us out of the camp? All you said was she wanted to have me arrested because I was part Fallen."

"She told me about the betrothal first, then said some rather unsavory things about you being unsuitable due to your bloodline. It bothered me that she couldn't see past your eyes, so I said I was done with all of it." He looked at her, his dark eyes holding her fast. "I knew any marriage I had would be arranged, that there was a high probability I wouldn't even meet them until the engagement was announced and a wedding date set. That it ended up being you, someone I know and care for, wasn't expected. Any decision about it would be yours, Thia."

Taking a few deep breaths, she turned her head forward. Ahead of them, the Taigh Forest stretched for miles. The evergreen trees ran up to the slopes of Mathaireil, disappearing into the snowy peak. "What did I say last night?" she asked, trying to change the conversation. Emotions ran through her, jumbled into a mass so tightly packed she feared to try to untangle them.

Reaching into his boot, he pulled out a piece of paper and handed it to her. "You tell me. I don't read Olc."

She grasped the reins of her horse in one hand, grabbing at the paper with the other. Unfolding it, she recognized Caelynn's neat handwriting. "*Is dochas aca mise*," she read with a sigh. "It means, 'I am their doom'." Pausing, Thia tried to steady her nerves. "I've said this before, haven't I?" she asked as she handed the paper back to him.

"You did, on our way into Tanisal." He slid it back into his boot. "The phrase is important, but I don't know why. I'm hoping Helix will."

"Important how?"

"When I spoke with Garret, that phrase caught his attention. He demanded I tell him your exact words. Once I did, he ordered that I stay by your side, let him know if there's anything else that makes me doubt you're you." He paused, then looked at her. "The phrase wasn't the only thing that happened, Thia."

"What did I do?" she asked, her voice cracking with worry.

"Your eyes changed. They were rimmed in red. Adam told me that he thought he'd seen them change when Caelynn was telling him what happened with Vadim."

A cold shiver ran through her body. "Valtikka had red eyes," she said. One hand went to the scepter that hung from her waist. The metal was smooth, but something felt off. "Do you feel anything from the shield?"

"What do you mean?"

"A presence, a sense that it's alive?" The words rushed out of her mouth. At the same time, she felt a knot of fear in her stomach.

"No," he said, "nothing. I'm used to fighting with it, knowing where it's weak or strong, but that's it. Why?"

"Ever since the first time I touched it, I've felt . . . something . . . from the scepter. Like it's alive in some way. At first, I stored it in my pack. When we got to the cave to look for you, it felt right to take it out." A wave of nausea hit her, and she pushed it aside. "The changes in my personality, the nightmare, it's got me thinking. What if Lolc Aon did something to the scepter after she took it?" Her stomach spasmed, and she bent over in pain.

"Thia!" Jinaari exclaimed. Reaching over, he grabbed the reins of her horse. "Adam!" he called over his shoulder.

"I'm okay," she lied.

She heard another horse approach. "What's wrong?" Adam asked.

"I'm not sure, but we have to find a place to camp. Take Caelynn and Gnat, find somewhere. I'll stay here with her."

"On it," the warlock said.

The pain subsided. "I'm fine, really," she said. "I probably just ate something that doesn't like me." Her throat felt dry; the words scraping against rocks. She looked at Jinaari; his face shifted into the mask he wore at court.

"I don't believe you," he said in a firm voice.

She drew in her breath, ready to argue with him, only to hear a stranger's voice come from her mouth, "You're smarter than you look, Althir."

Thia shivered from the cold that ran through her veins as the presence took over. "Who are you?" he demanded.

"Thia knows who I am, even if she won't admit it. I'm her. Or, rather, who she could be if she'd stop being so damn stubborn." Thia felt her head tilt to one side and her mouth curl upward. "How do you tolerate it, Althir? Honestly, I believe you think it's endearing."

"I don't know how you got inside her, but I will find a way

to get you out."

A dry, mirthless laugh tore from her throat. "Try. You don't know anything, Althir. Your God does, but Garret didn't trust you enough to tell you. I'm amazed at how much blind trust you have in others. I really am." Pain seared through her, forcing tears to drip down her face. "You want her to live, don't you? Then listen closely. Don't visit Helix. He can't do a damn thing to rid Thia of me. No one in Avoch can. The only one that could was the one who created me and you killed her with that pretty blade of yours."

"You're the Scepter, then." Jinaari's voice was calm.

"Not really, but I'm connected to it. And, now, to Thia. You can't just throw me aside, Althir. Now that I'm part of her, I can make her feel anything I want. If you even try to separate us, I'll kill her from within. Every single fear, anxiety, or terror she's known will be amplified. By the time I finish, there won't be a Thia Bransdottir any longer. I'll be whole, with all the power she possesses at my disposal, while she's nothing more than a broken sliver of a memory in my brain."

Thia saw him reach across his body and grasp the hilt of his sword. Forcing the other presence aside, she screamed, "Do it!" Within the recesses of her mind, the other voice laughed, relinquishing control of her body as it hid. She slumped forward, grasping at the saddle horn with both hands to keep from falling. Her stomach heaved. She felt Jinaari's hand grab her coat, steadying her as she vomited.

The spasms stopped. "Here," he said, his voice low.

Opening her eyes, she saw the waterskin. "Thank you," she whispered. Taking a drink, she spit out the liquid. She looked at him, "You should've killed me," she said as she raised the bag to her lips again.

"Not yet. We're going to find an answer. There's got to be a way to get rid of whoever that was."

"It was Valtikka."

"From your dream? You're certain?"

Thia nodded, handing the waterskin back to him. "I know her voice." She watched his face shift, grow concerned. "What is it?"

"I need you to trust me."

"I do. You know that."

Jinaari shook his head. "Not like this. I don't like keeping secrets from you, Thia. You know this. But I can't tell you what's next; where we're going, what will happen. Not as long as she's connected with you. That's the only way to make sure she doesn't know."

Taking a deep breath, she chose her words carefully. "I understand. There's a chance she'll glean some of it but the only way to keep her off balance is if I'm in the dark. You're an arrogant prick, Jinaari. But you're also my Champion. You've kept me safe thus far; I know whatever scheme you and Adam come up with will be the best one. It won't be without risk, but you've never deliberately put me in harm's way."

That's what you think. Valtikka said in Thia's mind.

"We found someplace," Adam's voice made her head look forward. His horse trotted toward them, deftly moving around the trees. "It's not far. Can you ride, Thia? Or should I transport you?" he asked as he came closer.

Jinaari said, "We ride."

The warlock nodded. "Everything okay?" he asked, his face concerned.

"I'll explain later," Jinaari replied, his tone short and curt. "When I know we're not being overheard." He handed the reins of her horse back to her. "Follow him," he instructed, "I'll be right behind you. Don't make me chase you down."

Wrapping her hands around the leather straps, Thia nodded. "If that happens, don't hesitate to do what you have to do."

"Not unless it's absolutely necessary."

TWENTY-ONE

"It's not much farther, from what I remember on the map. We should be there before nightfall." Adam's voice was low, and Jinaari knew why.

"Good," he replied. He resisted looking over his shoulder to where Caelynn rode next to Thia. "Some answers would be nice. Or hot food if it can be spared."

"He's a death mage, Jinaari, not a barbarian. If anything, we're about to have one of the most gracious welcomes we've ever had. It's doubtful people come here simply because they've wandered by. Anyone knocking on his door is going to be searching for him, wanting something. Helix knows this."

"It's a game, then?"

Adam shrugged. "Pretty much. He'll want to figure out what we need, how much we're willing to pay, before he offers anything. If it's not worth his time, he'll be honest. We will be fed, given warm beds, because we're new. He's a collector of lore – all mages are – and he'll want to hear our story. Don't worry," he paused, "I know what I'm doing. For once, let me take the lead."

"I need him to speak with us alone."

"I know. Caelynn and I talked about it. She's going to stay with Thia, keep her occupied somehow. We'll get in the door with Gnat, make sure he gets Nyfe back. After that, we're likely to be shown to our rooms, told when dinner will be. Once we get them settled, you and I will meet with Helix." He paused. "We're all worried about her, Jinaari. Any new issues? The more information I have, the more likely we'll get a real answer from him."

Jinaari shook his head, "Valtikka hasn't resurfaced that I know of. The only thing Thia's mentioned was her Mark was itchy."

"That's new. When did that start?"

"Two days ago, when she woke up with the fever." Jinaari sighed. "She's not saying much because she's scared to give Valtikka ammunition." The forest around them was quiet, too quiet for his liking. Birds and squirrels moved about, but there'd been no evidence of larger animals. "Wait here," he said as he turned his horse around and rode back toward the others.

Coming up alongside Thia, he said, "How are things with you?"

Thia nodded; her face composed. "Good. Don't say anything else," she said. "Just do what you need to do."

Reaching into his saddle bag, he pulled out a length of cloth he'd torn off one of his old tunics the night before. "Caelynn, you're going to guide her," he said as he wrapped the fabric around Thia's head. Small beads of sweat dotted her forehead; the fever hadn't abated, even with the healing he'd tried.

"Tie my hands to the saddle horn," Thia said. "Then I can't remove it."

He knotted the blindfold, securing it tight enough that it wouldn't slip. "Good idea." Working quickly, he made sure the rope wasn't going to cut into her hands. Glancing at

Caelynn, Gnat stared back at him. "She's going to be fine," he reassured the cobalus.

"Gnat hopes so. Gnat doesn't like to see Friend Thia sick."

"None of us do," Caelynn said as she wound the reins to Thia's horse around her hand.

The cobalus looked at Jinaari. "Gnat can ride with Friend Thia. Gnat will keep Friend Thia safe."

Jinaari nodded. "That's not a bad idea." Within moments, Gnat sat in front of Thia, his hands around the reins. "I don't expect you to fight anything, Gnat. Your job is to get her to safety if something comes after us. Understood?"

"Friend Jinaari doesn't have to worry. Gnat will take care of Friend Thia."

Wheeling his horse around, he nodded once to Caelynn. *She'll stay close enough to give them cover if they have to run.* Urging his mount forward, he rejoined Adam. "Let's get to Helix."

Shadows crept into the forest as the sun began to set. Through the trees, he saw several balls of light not far off the ground. The glow didn't flicker like torchlight, however.

"We're here," Adam announced, pulling his horse to a stop.

Jinaari came up next to him. Ahead of them was a clearing. A stone path, wide enough for them to ride side by side, was lined with glowing orbs. "What are those?" he asked, his voice low.

"I'm not certain. They're not magical, but I have no idea how they're powered." Adam pointed ahead of them. "We've been seen."

At the end of the path stood a group of five people. Beyond them, the imposing stone manor was larger than he expected. Not quite the palace at Dragonspire where he grew up, but nearly the same size. To the right sat a barn with a corral that rivaled the house in size. On the left, a small village of ten or twelve small stone homes. Each one had someone standing in the doorway, watching them. Some had young children with them. The distinctive ring of a hammer on metal came from an open enclosure. Jinaari could easily see the forge's fire glowing in the twilight. "I thought you said he stayed isolated, removed from the world. Helix has his own town."

"It's not what I expected, either. Come on. It's considered rude to keep our host waiting."

Jinaari glanced over his shoulder, making sure that the others followed. As they got closer, he began to make out the features of the woman who stood in the center of the group. "That's impossible," he muttered.

"Why? We haven't seen Ashynn since Alesso took her out of the tunnels under Tanisal. She looks good." Adam paused. "I'm surprised she's here, yes. But why do you think it's impossible?"

"When I was Samil's prisoner, Alesso told me she was dead."

"Are you sure it was him?"

He shook his head. "No. I'm not sure what was real from you leaving until Thia talked to me outside of Cirrain."

"I'll add it to things to ask Helix, later. Alesso may have been real, but her death an illusion."

Jinaari felt Adam's gaze on him. "I'm good," he said. "We need to focus on why we're here, not untangling the knot of my memories from that time." *I promised Thia I'd talk to her about what happened. She was right; I can't keep it locked up forever. It's starting to cloud my judgement. Once she's free of Valtikka, when she's safe, I'll find the time.*

They drew to a halt in front of the group. Four of them ran forward, taking the bridle of each horse so they could dismount. As he swung his leg around, he saw Caelynn untying Thia's hands. He walked back to them. "Caelynn," he said, his voice quiet, "go up with Adam. Take Gnat with you. I'll lead her." Putting his hands around Thia's waist, he continued, "Ashynn's here."

Her head tilted toward the sound of his voice. "I thought you said she was dead."

"I was Samil's prisoner. I can't believe anything that happened in those weeks was real." He took her hand and placed it on his belt. "Grab hold. I'm not taking the blindfold off yet."

"Good," Thia replied, her voice shaky. "The other one's off-balance."

"How are things with you?"

He felt her hand tremble as she grasped the leather. "I've been better. Maybe I'll be able to sleep some tonight."

"This is going to work." He put all his conviction into the words. "Trust me."

"Always," she said.

He took small steps, making sure he didn't rush her. The cobblestones were even; no rocks or debris she could trip over. Ahead of them, their horses were being led toward the barn while the other three spoke with Ashynn. Her head turned toward him as they approached.

"Greetings, Shield. I understand from your companions that the Daughter has fallen victim to an illness. Please, follow me. There's refreshment inside, and comfortable beds. Once she is resting, Helix will speak with you."

"Nyfe?" Gnat asked, his eyes wide.

Ashynn smiled. "Nyfe is inside, Gnat. He is safe and waiting for you. Once Thia's taken care of, you'll be reunited."

Gnat began to dance, hugging himself. Ashynn's grin widened, and she looked at the others. "Come," she said as she turned around, "night is falling and the temperature will drop. It's best that we don't stay outside long."

Waiting for the others to go in front of them, Jinaari

whispered, "We're moving again." He kept his stride slow, approaching the steps that led to the house with an even pace. "Five steps, going up. They're deep, look even." As he led her up to the door, he could hear her count the steps under her breath.

Walking through the entry, the warmth of the house amazed him. No fire burned that he could see, yet it was comfortable. "This way," Ashynn said, gesturing to her right.

"We're turning," he muttered as he led Thia into another room.

Several stuffed chairs were scattered around the small room. In the center was a circular table. A tray with a decanter and six glasses sat in the center. Ashynn walked toward it, pulling the stopper free, as she said, "Please, take a seat. It may be a few moments yet before your gear is in your room." She began to pour drinks into the goblets. "I saw your face, Shield. You were surprised to see me here. I'm curious as to why?" She held out one of the drinks to him.

Jinaari made sure Thia was seated before he responded. Taking the glass, he said, "I had been told you'd died." He raised the drink to his face, sniffing the contents. *Water.* Taking a sip, he set aside his suspicion. When Ashynn handed him another glass, he gave the one he had to Thia.

"Why would someone think I was dead?" Ashynn asked.

Shaking his head, he said, "It wasn't said at a time when I was surrounded by much truth." *I'm not going to tell her more.* Changing the subject, he said, "Have you heard from your mother? She's working for Thia in Almair."

The young woman shook her head. "No. Once she learned about what my brother and I did to gain her freedom, she refused to speak to either of us. That's how I ended up here. I traveled south, hoping to start a new life in Tavisholm. No one there knew who I was, or so I thought. I was mistaken. Within days, no one would take my coin or give me work. When I got a message, offering me a position, I didn't question who it came from." She paused. "It's not what I expected, but I'm treated well here. Please," she looked at him, and he saw the tears in her eyes, "let my mother know that I'm here and will respond if she chooses to write."

"I will," Thia said.

Jinaari glanced at her. Her face was calm beneath the blindfold. Turning back to Ashynn, he said, "We both will."

"Thank you." She put her glass down and began to collect the others. Once they were back on the tray, she said, "I'm certain your rooms are ready by now. Follow me."

Grasping Thia's hand, he helped her to her feet and made sure her hand held his belt before he followed Ashynn from the room. "Stairs," he said, "banister is on your left. Change hands if you need to."

"Any idea how many?" she whispered.

"No, but I'll give you warning when we're near the end." Placing his hand on the smooth wood, he made sure Thia could follow him easily. "Small landing, stairs again on your left," he whispered. Glancing up as he reached the landing, he counted the steps. "Seven steps, then we're in a hallway."

"Got it."

Ashynn stopped in front of a door. "Your bags are inside. There's a separate bedchamber for each of you. I told them to leave your belongings in the main room, rather than assume who would be in what room." She held out a key, "This is yours, as long as you stay here. Helix does not lock his guests in."

Adam took the key. "It's appreciated. Once we get the ladies settled, would it be possible to have a private word with our host?"

"He's usually in his study at this time. I'll let him know of your request. If he agrees to meet with you before dinner, you'll find your way easily." She smiled, then slipped past them and headed back down the stairs.

"Open it," Jinaari said. "Let's see where we're staying tonight."

The blonde man nodded, inserting the key into the lock. Swinging the door open, he stepped inside. Caelynn and Gnat followed.

"We're going in," Jinaari told Thia.

"Don't run me into any furniture, okay? I'd rather not have bruised shins."

"Not going to do that." He walked across the threshold. The room was large and warm. But there wasn't a fire or braziers. Sconces on the walls glowed with light, yet no flame flickered behind the glass. Several couches and chairs sat in the room. Five doors, all open, led off the main room. Caelynn came out of one. "What's in there?"

"A bedroom, with a private bath. The others are the same. No windows, or a servant's passage." She looked at Adam. "It reminds me a lot of our suite back at the Green Frog. I don't know if that's because you both trained at Helmshouse or to try and make us more comfortable."

"It could be both," Adam replied.

Jinaari felt Thia rest her head against his back. "What's wrong?" he asked, turning around to face her.

"I'm really tired," she said.

"Caelynn," he said, "lead her into one of the rooms. Adam and I can move the packs. Once you get her settled, I'll take him and Gnat downstairs. We'll locate Nyfe, meet Helix."

"Come on, Thia," Caelynn said as she walked over to them. Taking Thia's hand, she placed it on her shoulder. "I'm not going to run you into anything."

"Can't I take the blindfold off?" Thia asked. "It's not like I know how to get back to the front door."

"When you're asleep, Caelynn will take it off. Not before

then," Jinaari instructed. He watched as the pair disappeared into one of the rooms. Adam followed, carrying their packs.

"Gnat get Nyfe back now?"

Jinaari looked at him. "In a few more minutes, Gnat. Get your pack and toss it in a room." He grabbed his and walked over to the room between the exit and the one Caelynn took Thia into. The furniture was ornate, more than he personally liked, but the bed looked comfortable. *We're not going to be here long enough to unpack.* He tossed the pack onto a chair, then left the room.

Adam and Gnat were waiting for him. "Helix?" the warlock asked.

Nodding, he said, "Yeah. Let's do this. Gnat, as soon as you get Nyfe, I want you to return and help Caelynn keep an eye on Thia. We'll be back as soon as we can." Caelynn came out of the room. "You still have the key?"

She held it up. "Thia's asleep. I'll keep the room locked until you come back."

"Gnat bring Nyfe back to help guard Friend Thia!"

Caelynn smiled. "I'll unlock the door for you, Gnat. I'm excited to meet Nyfe!"

"Let's go," Jinaari ordered. He opened the door, waiting for Adam and Gnat to leave. Caelynn walked closer, key in hand.

"Don't worry so much, Jinaari," she whispered. "I finally have my family again. I'm not going to let anything happen to her." With a gentle shove, she pushed him into the hallway and closed the door behind him. The faint clicking of metal tumblers reached his ear.

At the end of the hallway, his friends waited. Adam's face was a stony mask. "Remember in my tower, when I told you about your vow of silence? Time to take it again. I know what we're asking for, old man. And what price may be needed to be paid."

"Don't agree to die, brother. Thia'd kill you first if you did."

"Despite their reputation, death mages rarely kill. They're patient and want you to live out your natural life span. Anything he asks for along that line won't come about by his hand."

"It's your choice. I get that. But I don't want to have to explain it to Thia," Jinaari said as they began to descend the stairs.

Adam nodded, "First things first. We take care of her problem. Once she's better, I'll explain it to her. It should go better than me telling her about the spider nest."

"Gnat is sorry. Gnat didn't know Spoone was sick," the cobalus said in a sad voice.

"It wasn't your doing, Gnat. I fixed Spoone, same as I did Forkke," Adam replied.

"Will Magic Friend fix Nyfe if he's broken like Spoone and Forkke were?"

The blonde man laughed. "Yes, Gnat. I'll fix Nyfe if I need to."

Jinaari held his tongue. The idea that a death mage had kept whatever this Nyfe was for this long didn't sit well in his soul. *Adam's right. There's a chance something's wrong with it. I'll have to ask him for details when we're alone.* He stopped as soon as the floor below them came into view.

The large foyer they'd entered was gone. Instead, a well-lit library opened in front of them. Thick fur rugs sat on the floor. Adam and Gnat stood at the base of the stairs. Jinaari came down to join them, taking in the rest of the room.

A few tables were decorated with odds and ends. One wall of shelves held thousands of bottles behind glass doors. In the center of the room, behind a massive mahogany desk, stood a man. He regarded them carefully; his eyes made Jinaari's blood run cold. Pale blue, with white irises.

"Gnat came back for Nyfe! Is Nyfe better now?"

Helix smiled. "Of course, Gnat. Nyfe didn't require much work. He's over there."

Jinaari watched as Gnat ran toward a table. "Nyfe! Gnat is so happy to see you again!" The cobalus picked up a warhammer with leather wrapped around the heads and hugged it close to his chest. "Why Nyfe have clothes on?"

"He's very sharp now, Gnat. I had the hoods made so you don't get hurt by accident. They come off easily."

Gnat yanked at a leather strap. The wrappings fell away, revealing two rows of spikes circling each end of the weapon. "Nyfe is perfect!" Gnat exclaimed, dancing around in happiness.

Jinaari felt Helix watching him and met the mage's gaze. "I need to speak with your companions alone, Gnat. And I believe you're supposed to go help the bard watch over your other friend while she sleeps."

"Gnat was so happy about Nyfe Gnat forgot promise he made Friend Jinaari!"

Picking up the leather, he secured the hood around the warhammer. He ran past Jinaari and Adam, disappearing up the stairs.

Jinaari watched as the staircase melted away and a wall full of books replaced it. His head snapped around, looking at their host.

Helix's demeanor changed. The congenial smile replaced by a stern expression. "Now we shall discuss why you felt it necessary to test my hospitality by bringing the evil above us into my home."

TWENTY-TWO

Adam coughed, but Helix's gaze remained on Jinaari. "Thia's not evil," he began to say.

Helix's hand flew up, silencing the warlock. "I wasn't talking to you. I will hear the request from the one who makes it, not his mouthpiece."

Jinaari said, "She's not evil."

"Are you so certain? You should've killed her when she told you to. Instead, you bring that creature into my home. Sit," the mage commanded, "and tell me why I shouldn't make sure she never wakes up."

Walking to a chair near the desk, Jinaari sat. Leaning back, he said, "You're the one who convinced the farmer near Solace to raise the spider. Why?"

"I was trying to prevent the very thing you let happen." The words came out as a hiss. "You gave her the scepter. That sealed her fate. She has to die or we're doomed. Every single one of us."

"I don't believe that," Jinaari said.

Adam cleared his throat. "We didn't give her the scepter, Helix. A delegation from Byd Cudd brought it to the surface, gave it to her in Almair. Jinaari and I were in Helmshouse at the time."

Helix leaned back, looking at Adam. "What happened when she touched it the first time? Do you know?"

"Caelynn told me it was covered in grime and filth but that it fell away at Thia's touch. If it didn't want her to wield it, it wouldn't have done that."

He turned back to Jinaari. "When did the symptoms start?"

"A month or two later. She had a cough, wasn't sleeping or eating much. She got injured during a fight in Tanisal and couldn't heal herself. Said a few things that didn't sound like her. I talked to Garret about it—"

"Let me guess? He did nothing but tell you to keep a close eye on her." Helix snarled. "Keep going."

"The nightmare was the next event. Someone overtook her mind when she slept. She set fire to a tent, bolted out of it like Lolc Aon herself was chasing her. I caught up to her, convinced her it was a dream. Once she was herself again, she told me someone named Val—"

"Stop," Helix said, "don't say it." He rose and walked to one of the bookshelves.

"You know the name?" Jinaari asked.

"Yes," he replied, his hand running across the spines of several leather-bound books. "Names have power, Shield. In this case, this person learned how to pick up on those who spoke her name. So much so that even writing it down could draw her attention." He pulled a tome free and came back to the desk.

"The person is Lolc Aon's first Daughter," Helix said as he sat. Opening the book, he began to thumb through the pages. "The Goddess gave her so much power that she felt she was invincible. Damn near was, too. Ah, here's the page," he turned the book around and tapped one of the pages. "Read this, but not out loud. Does this sound like the person from your friend's dream?"

Leaning forward, Jinaari read the page:

And the host of men, along with six of the Gods, descended on the plain. Their goal was to recover that which Lolc Aon had stolen: the Scepter of Avoch. They faced not an army of her followers, but a single woman. Her blonde hair framed blood-red eyes that made grown men shiver as if ice ran through their bones. Lightning poured from her fingertips. As the armies charged, she smiled. With a loud voice, she said, "I am their doom. A reckoning for the path they chose." Electricity flew from her hands, snaking through the advancing army. The Gods, seeing this, surrounded V-------. Only through their efforts was she subdued. When they were done, the woman still bore the Mark of Lolc Aon but had no stores of magic. The Gods had stripped her of the ability.

She ran into the hills, diving into the tunnels to escape. The Gods let her go, believing her to be a threat no longer. They buried their dead, healed the wounded, and began to lead them back home. She did not die right away. Stumbling in the dark, she was found by Lolc Aon. The Scorpion Queen saw what her family had done to her Daughter and vowed revenge. Grabbing the Scepter of Avoch, she cast the soul of V------- into it. "In here shall my beloved remain, until one of my blood can take it up. Sleep, and find your strength again. For when you awaken, you shall tear their children apart as they have torn mine."

His head snapped up, and he stared at Helix. "You mean the soul of Lolc Aon's Daughter is in the scepter?"

The mage nodded slowly. "She's had centuries to nurse her wounds, her hatred. And now she's gaining her strength. Thia's a direct descendant of Lolc Aon. She's her blood. And she's Marked, giving her access to as much magic as Lolc Aon's Daughter had." The cold gaze that Helix wore chilled Jinaari's soul. "Over time, Thia will shrink away under the onslaught of mental anguish she'll be put through. When she's weak enough, that's when the other will make their move. Your companion will be cast aside, become a prisoner in their own body. A spectator to the vengeance that will engulf Avoch by her own hand. I know you care for her, Shield. But this cannot come to pass. Your blade is touched by two Gods. If used to kill Thia, the other will die as well."

He shook his head. "There's got to be a way to sever the connection, get Thia free of her."

Helix leaned back, fingers drumming on the desk. "There's two that come to mind. One's impossible."

"Why?"

"You killed Lolc Aon, then Thia sent her soul to Nannan. You're never going to get a Goddess who no longer exists to reverse the spell."

Adam said, "What's the second way?"

Helix rose again, heading back to the bookcase. "The other six Gods banded together to cut her off from her power. You'd have to get all of them together, in one place, and agree to finish her off. They didn't, out of respect for their sister. Lolc Aon was misguided, but she was still family to them. The problem with that," he said as he pulled another book from the shelf, "is getting them all to answer your summons. And convincing them to do it." He flipped through the pages. "Ah, here it is." He handed the book to Jinaari. "You can read this aloud, if you like."

Glancing at Adam, he cleared his throat. "And deep within the mountain the seven went, bent on finding the monster the villagers spoke of. Coming into the grotto, they stared in awe. Lightning bounced around the crystal walls, bathing the area in light. Steps led down into a pool of water so clear they couldn't tell how deep it was. In the center, a single stone altar surrounded by seven pedestals. On the altar sat a woman. Her opalescent skin shimmered in the light. Brilliant blue eyes sat beneath the short, white hair. 'I am no monster,' she said, though her lips did not move. 'I am the last of my kind. If you spare my life, I can give to you the power necessary to guide your tribes, unite them into a people who will no longer fear each other'." He paused, looking at Helix. "You're talking about where the Gods were born?"

The mage nodded. "Yes. It's the only place you can go where they'll have to answer. They're bound to those pillars. If you get Thia onto that bier, all six will come." He sighed. "Whether or not they agree to your petition is another matter. As is getting her there without her guest preventing it. That blindfold was a good short-term solution. While she's here, it's not necessary. My wards will prevent her guest from understanding what we say, or what Thia sees. However, she's adapting, learning quickly. I doubt you'd be able to get close enough to Mathaireil to find the right path, let alone go into the mountain itself, without backlash."

"Thia's asleep now. I'm sure we can work something out," Jinaari said confidently.

"That arrogant belief that you can single-handedly save the world isn't going to keep her alive. Or her guest from doing whatever she can to take Thia over. The reason she's sleeping is I spiked the water Ashynn served you. I needed her to sleep so we could talk and not draw the attention of the other."

Leaping to his feet, he ignored Adam's effort to hold him back. "You drugged us?"

"Not all of you. It was specifically targeted at her. None of the rest of you would be affected, or you wouldn't be here now. It's not going to hurt her. She needed the rest, we had to talk without the chance of her passenger realizing it." Helix stared at him; his eyes narrowed in thought. "If I could kill her myself, I would. Your blade is the only thing that can. So, coddle her a few more days if you must but put your emotions aside and think about the rest of the world. Avoch would become a memory if Thia's overtaken. I'm not above sacrificing one soul to save thousands."

Adam stood, his arms coming between Jinaari and Helix. "I don't think any of us want to see that," he said, his voice even and calm. "How far is it from here to the grotto?"

Helix sat back down. "A week, maybe ten days. It depends on how long you take finding the right entrance. It's not exactly out in the open."

"Is there any way you know of to keep this spirit from controlling Thia while we're on the way there? I know you taught alchemy back at Helmshouse. Your textbooks are still referenced." Adam glanced at Jinaari, motioning for him to sit back down.

Jinaari did, forcing the anger down. "There has to be a way to suppress it."

"There is, but you won't like it," Helix snapped.

"There's nothing about this that I like, Helix. I'm her protector. I'm honor bound to do what I must to try and save her."

"Then take your sword and slit her throat before she wakes up."

"Not unless it's absolutely necessary. What else can we do?" Jinaari stared at Helix, trying to keep his anger in check. *I'm not killing her. She withstood Lolc Aon, defeated Drogon and Samil. She can withstand this one.*

Helix narrowed his eyes. "Fine. There's an elixir I can make. It'll suppress the other consciousness, keep it from influencing Thia. I'll know in the morning if it worked, then I'll send vials of it with you. You'll have to make sure she takes it daily, or it'll wear off. There's a risk, though."

"I'll make sure she takes it. That's not a problem."

Helix stared at him. "It could be. It's going to take a toll on her physically. You'll have to move fast if you expect to get to the grotto before Thia becomes too weak to walk. She won't be able to cast, either. All her stores will go toward keeping her body alive."

Adam's voice was low. "That sounds a lot like a poison, Helix."

The mage turned to him. "It is. One you have to give her every day, knowing it's killing her. It's slow acting at first. But it's the only way to keep her guest so numb to what's going on that she can't do anything. The more Thia takes, the faster the effect." Helix looked back at Jinaari. The stern expression softened into one more sympathetic. "If you do this, you must push hard. If she dies before reaching the grotto, or if you can't get the Gods to agree, the only option left will be putting your sword through her chest."

"How do you plan to give it to her? Or do you think poisoning all of us is an option?"

"I'm not going to tell you, Shield. I don't need you watching her, and me, so closely that she clues into what's happening. It will happen. She's the only one that'll get it. You need to stay alive in case this doesn't work. Because, if it doesn't, you're the only one that can stop her. Now," Helix continued, "I recommend you go back to your companions, Shield. I need to speak with Adam alone."

Jinaari glanced at his friend, catching the barely noticeable nod. *He'll tell me later. And I've got to decide what I should tell Thia.* He rose, looking back at their host. "If you think she should die, why share a meal with her?"

"I'm a realist, Shield. Not a barbarian. Her death serves a greater purpose; saving all Avoch. I hold no ill will toward her personally. It's only proper that I dine with those who take shelter under my roof." The mage pointed at the wall behind him. "She's waking up. I have no doubt she's got questions to ask you."

Bowing stiffly, he turned around. The staircase had reappeared. Taking the steps two at a time, he glanced back when he reached the landing. The entry hall was behind him. Shaking his head, he shoved aside his doubt. *Thia needs me to be certain, confident. The arrogant prick*, he thought. *I don't like the solution Helix gave me, but it's the only one we have right now.* His chest tightened at the thought of killing her. *She'd tell me to do it, wouldn't blame me. But I can't believe that's the best, and only, way to save her. I've got to find another way.*

Walking down the hallway, he stopped at the door. Pushing the worry aside, he raised his hand and knocked once. "It's me," he said.

The door swung open and Caelynn moved aside, giving him room to enter. Thia sat in a chair; the blindfold around her eyes. Gnat sat on a rug, cradling Nyfe like an infant.

"Where's Adam?" Caelynn asked as she closed the door.

"Our host needed to speak to him privately," Jinaari replied.

"You mean he stayed behind to negotiate a price for healing me," Thia said. "I don't need anyone dying because of me, Jinaari."

He closed the gap, grabbed a chair, and pulled it in front of her. As he sat, he reached for the blindfold. "Helix can't heal you, Thia. But he gave us a destination," he began to untie the knot.

Thia raised her hands, pulling his aside. "Leave it on," she said. The resignation in her voice tore at his heart. "I'd rather be led everywhere than give her anything she can use against you."

"I was told it was safe while we're here. He's got wards up that'll prevent your guest from being a problem." He watched her face as he spoke. The muscles relaxed, and she moved her hands from his. He started to work the blindfold free. Once it was away from her face, he tossed it aside. "You look better. How are you feeling?"

She shrugged. "Numb, I think. I'm so tired of dealing with Val—"

He put a finger to her lips, silencing her. "Don't say the name. Your guest has the ability to focus on things when her name is said. From now on, we don't say it. Got it?"

"Got it," she said with a sigh. "Did he know who they are?"

"You're not going to like it."

A small smile crept across her face. "What of this whole situation do you think I like, Jinaari? Who are they?"

"The spirit of Lolc Aon's first Daughter," he said, keeping his voice even. As he spoke, he watched her eyes closely.

Thia closed her eyes, swallowing hard. "That explains a lot," she said as she opened them again. Falling back in the chair, her hands rubbed at her face.

"Like what?"

Her head moved back and she stared at the ceiling. Jinaari could see the tears that threatened to spill from her eyes. "Like why she looked so much like me, said we were sisters. Family. Though the bit about Herasta being her mother was likely a lie." Her hands worked through her hair.

He kept silent, waiting for her to regain control over herself. He'd seen her do that motion so many times, usually when she needed to focus on something other than a problem she couldn't solve. When she dropped her hands, he said, "There's a place about a week or so from here. We'll take you there, appeal to the Gods to separate you from your guest. This is going to work, Thia."

She sat up straight and looked at him. "The grotto? Do you really believe it exists?"

Caelynn sat next to Thia. "I thought it was a myth. Some of the oldest songs and stories reference it, but never say where it was. The way is lost. The Gods made sure of that so they wouldn't have angry mobs of people summoning them all at the same time."

"I've been given directions."

Jinaari stood quickly at the sound of Adam's voice. The warlock was closing the door behind them. "Caelynn, did you lock the door?"

"I was given a second key," Adam held it up. "Our host thought it would be easier if there were two." Walking over, he put it in Jinaari's hand. "Either you or Caelynn will be with Thia at all times anyway. This way, there's always someone who can keep her safe until we leave." He sat in a chair.

"How far is it?" Jinaari asked.

"It'll be close to a week of riding to get to the base of the mountain. We can't go too fast because of the forest. We're looking for a specific rock formation, with a large amount of thornstalk nearby. That's the entrance. From there, it's about a two day walk to the grotto itself."

"We can't ride?" Caelynn asked.

Adam shook his head. "Not unless you can convince the horses to enter a cave." He glanced over at Gnat, then lowered his voice. "The biggest issue is Gnat. His village is in the opposite direction."

Damn it, Jinaari thought. *Thia doesn't have that much time to waste.* "I'll talk to him later, explain the delay. He wants Thia to get better, same as the rest of us. I don't think he'll be upset if it waits until after that's done."

He felt Thia's gaze on him and met it. "Why the rush? I feel fine. There's no reason we can't take him home first, like we promised. What aren't you telling me?"

Taking a deep breath, he chose his words carefully. "There's a good chance your guest is going to try and prevent us from reaching the grotto, Thia. The faster we move, the less painful it'll be for you." *Believe me*, he thought. *I'll tell you the rest later. Give you the choice to say no. But not until I know it actually works.*

Someone knocked on the door, and Jinaari's head snapped around at the sound. "I've got it," Adam said as he rose.

Jinaari stood, holding out his hand to help Thia up, as the warlock crossed the room. The door opened and Adam stepped aside so they could see Ashynn. "Helix requests your presence at dinner. Please, follow me."

"Gnat hungry!" The cobalus bolted past them.

Looking at Thia, Jinaari waited for her to react. "I've never met a death mage before," she whispered.

He threaded her arm through his. "He's blunt, to the point. Utterly convinced he's right about everything and everyone," he replied as they walked toward the door.

"In other words, he's an arrogant prick," she said, sarcasm dripping from her voice. "Something tells me you don't get along with him."

TWENTY-THREE

Thia walked with Jinaari, following Ashynn down the staircase. *He's not telling me everything,* she thought. *I know the look he had on his face. With the other one inside me, though, it makes sense. If he held something back, there's a reason.*

"Things will look different when we get downstairs," he whispered. "This house is a lot like our rooms back at the Green Frog, but more advanced."

"I was blindfolded before. I wouldn't know what was different," Thia said as they reached the landing. Her hand caressed the smooth wood of the banister. "This feels the same."

"We came into a foyer when we entered. When Adam and I brought Gnat down, though, the staircase led straight to Helix's study."

The polished wood floor ahead of them reflected light, but she couldn't see the source. "Is this the same room?" she asked him.

"No."

Thia picked up the irritation in his voice. "You really don't like this person, do you?"

"If I thought we could leave now without causing problems, I'd do it. Unfortunately, we need to stay the night."

She looked at him. "Why do we need to stay? There's plenty of times we left, not caring if we put someone's nose out of joint. Tavisholm, for example."

"Good evening." Thia's head turned toward the voice. A tall, lean man stood in front of an archway, bowing formally. His hair was shot with gray, reminding her of the markings on a cat. "I'm honored that you've agreed to dine with me tonight." He straightened, and her stomach lurched when she saw his eyes. Holding out an arm, he said, "My name is Helix. Allow me to escort you to your seat, Scepter."

Glancing at Jinaari, she removed her arm and moved to take Helix's. "Thank you," she said. "I'm sorry if I seem startled. I've never seen someone with eyes like yours."

"Not to worry. I've grown accustomed to the reaction. I daresay mine startle whereas yours cause anger. They're lovely, by the way. Many in the world cannot see beyond such trivial matters. Our character is what makes us who we are, not our appearance."

They walked into a large room. The table would seat the six of them comfortably. Close enough for conversation, but they wouldn't be on top of each other. Looking at the place settings, she asked, "Is Ashynn not dining with us?"

"No," Helix responded, pulling out a chair for her on one side. "She prefers to dine alone. I understand her mother now works for you, Scepter. I'm encouraging Ashynn to reconnect with her at some point. It's my hope you'd do the same on your end."

Sitting down, she waited as Jinaari sat opposite of her. Adam was at her left, while Caelynn sat across the table, next to Jinaari. Gnat went to the end opposite of their host. "I will, but the decision isn't mine to make. It's Abigail's."

"Of course. We all have the right to do as we feel best, after all." Helix responded as he sat. Someone reached out from behind her, filling her glass. "Don't stand on ceremony with me, Scepter. Feel free to eat and drink as much as you like."

"Please, call me Thia. I find it easier to talk to people as equals. Titles rarely make anyone a better person simply because they're used." Reaching out, she picked up the goblet and took a drink.

"Thank you, Thia. Indeed, we agree on this. Are you feeling better? Your companions let me know you weren't well."

A bowl of soup was put in front of her. Glancing up, she saw her friends being served. "Tired, that's all. The road isn't always a comfortable place to sleep." She picked up her spoon and began to eat.

Helix chuckled. "It's been several years since I did so, but I remember it well enough. There always seemed to be one rock that found the perfectly wrong place against my back, no matter how well I picked the ground clean before laying out my sleeping pad."

Returning his smile, she nodded. "There is that small problem."

"Jinaari," Helix gestured to him, "tells me you plan to take Gnat home. I'm well acquainted with his tribe. I took the liberty of sending them a message when you arrived. It was answered faster than I anticipated. They'll be here tomorrow morning, probably before you rise."

"Gnat's tribe comes here?" Gnat asked.

Thia looked at the cobalus. His eyes were wide with excitement.

"Yes, Gnat. You've become famous in your absence. Tales of what you might have done grow with each telling.

Everyone's excited to see which story is true. Sano is coming, as well."

Gnat's face softened, and his grin widened. "Mate Sano come here? No," he began to shake his head, "Bad idea. Mate Sano stay home, in Gnat's nice cave. Mate Sano needs to take care of Baby Gnat so Baby Gnat can come out of Mate Sano."

Helix rested his elbows on the table, folded his hands and looked at the cobalus. "Sano is fine, Gnat. She's bringing the baby with her."

"Mate Sano had Baby Gnat while Gnat was gone?"

Thia's heart broke at the pain in his voice.

"She did, and everything went as it should. You'll see for yourself, tomorrow morning."

Thia watched as different emotions played across Gnat's face. *I didn't know he had anyone. That he was going to be a father. We've always just taken his presence for granted without bothering to ask him anything about his life.* "I wish you'd told me about Sano, Gnat. I'd be honored if you would introduce her to me tomorrow."

"Friend Thia wants to meet Mate Sano?"

"Very much so. She's important in your life, and that makes her important in mine." She smiled at him, and he returned it.

"Caelynn," Helix's voice snapped Thia back to the rest of the table, "I've heard you play before, but it's been many years. Would it bother you to give me a small concert tonight? Not more than a couple songs, mind you. You need to rest as much as your companions."

"I would love to," Caelynn replied. "Do you have any favorites?"

Thia tuned out the conversation, concentrating on the food in front of her. Absently moving it around on the plate with her fork, she tried to decide if she was hungry. Someone tapped her foot under the table. Glancing up, she caught

Jinaari's gaze. With a sigh, she lifted a fork full of vegetables to her mouth.

Her mind wandered as Helix made sure to talk with everyone. His attempts to draw out Jinaari were met with short answers. "You'll have to excuse him," she said with a smile. "Jinaari's not known as a great conversationalist."

"That's quite fine," Helix responded. "I can spend weeks without speaking more than five sentences to anyone. When our minds are on weighty matters, as you know, other things tend to be forgotten that shouldn't be." He folded his napkin and placed it on the table as he rose. "Excuse me for a moment."

Thia watched him walk over to a long cabinet. On the top, a single decanter filled with wine, surrounded by goblets, sat on a tray. Helix picked up something else she couldn't quite see, then turned back. "I understand your birthday is today, Thia. I would be honored to return this to you, to mark the occasion." He held out a small, cloth wrapped bundle.

"Thia!" Caelynn exclaimed, "Why didn't you tell us it was your birthday?"

"I honestly forgot. I haven't kept track of the day for years," she stammered. Taking the gift from Helix, she said, "You really didn't have to do anything."

"Nonsense," he said, sitting back down. "It's been in my possession for some time now. I had thought of sending it to Cirrain after receiving news of your ascension to the throne, but then word came that you were no longer there. This saves me trying to track you down, and gives me the pleasure of seeing your face. Please, open it."

Thia glanced at Jinaari; his face was calm, and he nodded slightly. Pulling at the ribbon, she said, "It's been so long since anyone . . ." she paused, staring at what was within the cloth.

"I purchased that from your father before you were born.

I've done the work to free the mechanism from my touch. Go ahead and open it; it should be yours, as well as the contents."

Picking up the silver box, she scanned the filigree for the three acorns. Her fingers touched them, and the lid flew open. Nestled inside was a small bundle. The leather was singed on the edges, and the strap keeping it tied shut was worn. Lifting it out, her fingers trembled as she unfurled the cloth. An array of delicate tools lay within individual pockets. In the center rested two locks of hair bound by small gold rings. One was pale blonde; the other brown.

"Thia? What is it?" Jinaari asked.

Tears spilled from her eyes as her fingers brushed the contents lightly. "These are my father's tools. The ones he used to make my box." She looked at Helix. "How," she whispered, her voice cracking with emotion, "did you get this?"

He smiled at her. "Nothing nefarious, I promise you. I was in Almair and went to see a colleague. I'd purchased the box itself from his business partner about twenty years earlier, and hoped to get a second. He let me know that the artisan had sold off his interest and left suddenly. That's when he brought out the tool set. Let me know that someone from River Run had come into town, trying to sell it. He recognized the mark, knew who they'd belonged to originally. He purchased them and put them away. My friend was getting ready to retire, so I gave him a generous offer. Once I learned of your parentage, I put them in the box." He gestured to the hair, "I know he meant a great deal to you, Thia. It does my soul good to see it returned to you."

Swiping at the tears, she took a deep breath. "Thank you. It means more than you know." Carefully, she began to roll the leather. Once she secured the tie, she put it back into the box.

"I think this deserves a celebratory toast." Helix rose again, heading back to the sideboard.

"You've done so much already," Thia began to say.

He put the tray down, laughing. "Nonsense. That kit was yours. I merely kept it safe, and complete, until it could be returned to you." He began to pour the wine into the glasses, handing one around to each of them. "To you, Thia. May your life be full, your troubles few, and your companions always at your side."

Her friends rose, and Thia hastily joined them. Touching her glass to theirs, she said, "Thank you," before drinking the contents.

"I hate to cut our celebration short," Helix said, "but I do have other things to attend to this evening. If you'd permit Caelynn to stay for a few songs, I promise I won't keep her long."

Recognizing they were being dismissed, Thia paused. "Is there anything we should be concerned about?"

"Nothing at all. I've learned, over the years, that it's best to be prepared for any possible outcome of events. It's one reason I've lived as long as I have. Your journey is not over, Thia Bransdottir. I will rest better knowing you were able to avoid a rock in your back for at least one more night."

Jinaari came around the table as she picked up the box. "Thank you for this. I won't forget it," she said as she took his arm.

Turning the corner, the stairs were where she remembered them. Gnat darted up past them, followed by Adam. "I don't know why you said he was blunt, Jinaari," she whispered. "Helix was a perfect gentleman at dinner. He's even solved the problem of getting Gnat home for us."

"He wanted something from you, Thia. And I think he got it."

"What? I didn't say anything that isn't common knowledge."

"I don't know," he replied, "but the gift was too perfect." Jinaari glanced at her. "Is it really your birthday?"

Thia nodded. "Yes. I didn't even realize it. I haven't celebrated it in any way for years."

"I'd ask why, but I think I know your answer already." They reached the top of the stairs. Gnat and Adam waited at the door. "We can't change what your past was like, Thia. But you have a family that cares about you. Let us celebrate these things with you."

"One condition."

"What?"

"The three of you don't get to do anything for mine until you've told me when yours are."

Jinaari laughed. "I think we can do that." He unlocked the door and she walked inside.

"Do you think Caelynn will be long?"

Adam shook his head. "No. Only a few songs. And she's got the other key. We can go to bed if we want."

Thia looked at the warlock. "Was this a price for the information about the grotto? A private concert?"

"One of them, yes." He held up a hand, stopping her next question. "I paid the rest. I know you don't want us to have secrets, Thia. On this, however, I can't tell you the details. Not until we're back in Almair. It's important."

A rush of warmth flooded through her, and she felt her body sway. Jinaari's arm circled her waist, steadying her. "Thia? How are things with you?"

"Too much wine, I guess. Or the fever's back."

"Come on," he said, gently leading her toward one of the bedrooms. "Adam's right. Caelynn has a key and won't be long. You need to rest."

She didn't bother to protest.

CHAPTER
TWENTY-FOUR

Sitting on the edge of the bed, Thia held each box in one of her hands. The one Helix had given her was larger, but the design was nearly identical to hers. Placing the gold one next to her, she opened the silver one. Taking out the leather roll, she put the box down before taking a closer look at the tools.

The set looked like the one she'd found in her room in Cirrain. *Helix said something about them being marked, though,* she thought. Tugging at a thin bladed hook, she took a closer look. On the metal band that connected the instrument to the wood handle, she found it. Keroys's symbol, a set of balanced scales. Resting on each was the letter 'B.' *His initials. Not the surname I knew, but then he was an artisan before I was born.* A small wave of sadness washed over her. *I know you said back in Almair you were proud of me, Papa. That seems so long ago. I wish I knew if you still were.*

"Thia?"

She took a deep breath, then looked up at Jinaari. "I'm good." Replacing the tool, she rolled the case back up and secured it before placing it into the silver box. "Is it time?"

"The others are ready. We can get the horses saddled, leave as soon as Gnat's tribe arrives." His head tilted slightly. "How are you feeling?"

Rising, she put her box in the pouch on her belt. The other went into her pack. "Warm. Either the fever's back, or we've gone far enough south for me to get rid of my coat." She heard him walk closer. One hand gently touched her forehead.

"I'm thinking the former. Anything else feel off?"

Nodding, she said, "Yes, but it's hard to explain."

"Try."

"It's like part of me is numb. Not physically, but mentally. Emotionally. Almost as if there's some sort of barrier there."

"What about your guest?"

Thia shrugged. "I know she's there, but it's like she's asleep. It's been that way since we arrived. Why?" she asked him. "Is there something you're not telling me?"

"Yes," Jinaari said, "and I will tell you. Just not here. Tonight, when it's just the four of us and we've set up camp for the night. I promise."

"I can wait." She threaded her arm through the strap of her pack and hefted it onto her back. "Are you blindfolding me again? Tying my hands to the saddle? I doubt the other one will stay quiet all the way to the grotto."

"I will if I have to, but not right away. You do want to say goodbye to Gnat, right? If you'd rather sneak out like we did in Cirrain, I can arrange it."

"That didn't work too well, and you know it." She laughed. "Pan and Elizabeth came anyway. No," she said as she walked toward the door, "let's meet his tribe. It's going to make his status among them even more legendary than any story he tells will. Do you think we should give him some sort of honorary title? Elizabeth would back us on it, and he has done some good things. He kept you from becoming giant spider food, for example."

"You're not going to let me live that down, are you?" Jinaari grumbled at her.

"I'm simply making a point. We were told to bring him home, that there was a reason for it. It could've been that. I know I'm glad that the Shield is still alive. Shouldn't all Avoch be aware of his deeds?"

"You're starting to sound like Jynth," he said as he walked next to her.

Thia snorted. "You don't have to be mean."

Caelynn and Adam stood in the room, packs on their backs. "Thia," the bard asked, "it's early yet. Are you sure you don't need your coat?"

"I'm warm enough."

"Her fever's back," Jinaari added.

Thia watched concern flood their faces. "I'm fine. Right now, I'm in control. It's like the other one is sleeping or something. If Jinaari or either of you feel safer with me being blindfolded and tied to my saddle, I won't fight against it. The last thing I want is to hurt any of you." She glanced around. "Where's Gnat?"

"Ashynn collected him earlier. He said there was something he had to do before the tribe arrived. I didn't ask what. He seemed excitable this morning," Adam said.

"When is he not?" Thia asked.

"If he's downstairs already," Jinaari said, "then let's go. We're on a tight schedule as it is."

Thia glanced at his back as he headed for the door. *He didn't say anything about a schedule. Is that what he'll tell me later?*

She walked through the door. "We're on a schedule?" she asked, her voice low, as she stood next to him.

"Yes. I'll explain tonight. Trust me."

"Always." Following Adam, she headed down the stairs.

They ended in a small foyer; the door was open. As they walked outside, she blinked against the bright sunlight.

Their horses were saddled and waiting for them off to one side. Gnat stood in the center of the courtyard, watching the road they'd come down the night before. "Give me your pack," Caelynn whispered in her ear. "Adam and I said our goodbyes earlier. We'll be at the horses when you're done."

Thia shrugged the bag off her shoulder, handing it to the bard. At the end of the road, a small procession marched toward them. The steady beat of the drummer set the pace. Colorful banners fluttered in the light breeze as Gnat's tribe approached.

She stood next to Jinaari, behind Gnat. "Any idea what's about to happen?" she whispered.

"No, and that bothers me."

"Friend Thia and Friend Jinaari are safe. Tribe will not hurt Gnat's friends," Gnat said in a quiet voice. "Gnat is the one who left. Gnat is the one who will be in trouble."

"That's why we're here, Gnat. To help them understand," Jinaari's voice was firm, "that you did what was necessary."

The procession came closer. Behind the drummer, a cobalus with a red coat and staff stared at the three of them. He was followed by the rest. In the center of the formation was a female cobalus carrying something in her arms. *Sano?*

The drummer stopped and stepped aside. "Gnat came to Furry Man and not home. Why?" The leader demanded. "Gnat knows laws. Gnat left Sano alone. This was not good of Gnat."

"Gnat is sorry," he replied. "Gnat had to do something to help Pretty Lady. Special Man said Furry Man wouldn't give Nyfe back unless Gnat did it. Gnat not want to leave Mate Sano, but Gnat not have choice. Gnat can't protect Mate Sano and Baby Gnat without Nyfe."

"Gnat still protect Pretty Lady?"

"No, Pretty Lady is safe now. Then Gnat met Nice Brother who is now Friend Jinaari," he pointed to Jinaari, "and other Pretty Lady who is now Friend Thia. They brought Gnat home."

"Let Sano through!" a female voice, full of command, shouted.

Thia looked to the group in front of her. Several of them moved aside, letting her pass. A small arm stretched out from the bundle she carried.

"Mate Gnat has finished the quest?" Sano asked as she stopped in front of him.

"Gnat has, mostly. Is Mate Sano okay? Gnat is sorry he was not here for Mate Sano when Baby Gnat tasted life."

Sano held out the baby. "Sano hopes Mate Gnat will name Baby Gnat before Mate Gnat leaves to finish the quest."

Thia watched Gnat take the infant and push back the hood. The small cobalus looked at him with wide, green eyes. He belched, closed them again, and went to sleep with a sigh. "Gnat thinks baby look like Mate Sano. Very pretty. Gnat would like to call him Riku, if Mate Sano likes it."

"Sano likes the name."

Gnat handed the baby back to her, saying, "Gnat wants to stay with Mate Sano and Son Riku, but Friend Thia is sick. Gnat promised Friend Jinaari to keep Friend Thia safe."

Thia's heart broke at the tears in Gnat's voice. She glanced at Jinaari. "He should stay with them," she whispered.

Jinaari nodded, then stepped forward. "Gnat, I need to talk to you."

He turned around, standing next to Sano. "Has Gnat done something wrong?"

"No, you haven't," he said as he knelt. "You've shown me who you are, Gnat. You are honorable, brave, and loyal. I never worry about Thia when you're on watch. But Sano and Riku need you more than she does now. You should stay with them."

Gnat's head swiveled to look up at her, then back at Jinaari. "But Gnat made promise to Friend Jinaari and Friend Thia."

"I know you did. You've kept your promise. I'll keep Thia safe now. As safe as you kept me when the giant spider tried to eat me." He reached into his tunic and pulled off his paladin's medallion. "Do you know what this is?"

"That's the medal that says Friend Jinaari has lots of brothers. That Friend Jinaari is a warrior and can be trusted."

"Good. Because you are a warrior as well, Gnat. You can be trusted. And," he placed it over Gnat's head, "you're my brother as much as Adam or any other paladin."

Tears streamed down Gnat's face, and Thia realized she was crying, too. "Gnat now has Brother?"

Jinaari smiled. "Yes, Gnat. As your brother, you know I'll keep Thia safe, right? Because your job is to keep Sano safe, raise Riku to be an honorable warrior like you are. If you ever need me, take your family and the medallion into Tavisholm. Show it to the paladins there. They'll keep you safe and get word to us. We'll come as soon as we can." He rose and stepped back.

"We all will, Gnat," Thia promised him.

"Gnat ask favor of Friend Thia?"

"Of course. What can I do for you?"

Gnat pointed to Riku. "Friend Thia is special. Keroys said so. Would Friend Thia bless Son Riku? So that Mate Sano and Gnat know Friend Thia will take care of Son Riku if anything happens to Mate Sano and Gnat?"

"I would be honored, Gnat." Thia knelt in front of Sano. Reaching out, she touched the sleeping baby's forehead. "May your life know peace, your heart love, and your ears laughter, little Riku. May you never know hunger, hatred, or fear.

Within the love of family may you grow into the best you can be."

"We need to go," Jinaari whispered.

Thia looked at Gnat. "I'll miss you, Gnat. Same as I miss Pan. But you both have a place in my heart. I know you'll take care of Sano and Riku like you did me."

Gnat reached out and hugged her. "Gnat promises Friend Thia Gnat will remember!"

Standing up, she stepped back. Gnat wiped away the tears with the back of his hand, then put an arm around Sano. Together, they walked toward the tribe. The drummer began to beat again, leading them away.

Wiping away her tears, Thia took a deep breath. Gnat and Sano turned around once, waving at her. She waved back. Once they hit the trees, she turned and headed toward her horse.

"Daughter?" Ashynn said as she came alongside her.

"Yes?"

"Would you please give this to my mother when you see her?" She held out a sealed letter. "Helix promised he'd send it, but I would like it to come from you. I don't expect her to forgive me, but I wanted her to know I am sorry."

"Of course," Thia replied, taking the parchment. Tucking it into one of her saddle bags, she mounted her horse. Caelynn and Adam were ready, but Jinaari stood near Helix. The mage handed him a bag. Turning around, he slung it over his head and walked their way.

"Adam, you lead. You know where we're going," he said as he got settled into his saddle. "Caelynn, you've got the rear. I'll make sure Thia stays safe."

The warlock urged his horse forward, and she followed. They rode around the back side of the compound. The forest ahead was thick with trees. Adam led them toward a barely discernable path. "How are things with you?" she asked Jinaari.

"They're as good as they can be for now," he said.

"That's not much of an answer. Is something wrong?"

"Why are you asking?"

She looked at him. "I don't know much about your Order, Jinaari. But I know you wouldn't give up your medallion without reason."

"He earned it. He's as much family now as Pan is. But I knew he wouldn't accept that from me unless I gave him something to prove it." He paused. "Most paladins are only given one. The ceremony's done without spectators; only brothers and the commander are allowed to attend. On rare occasions, Garret himself shows up. Mother couldn't stand not being there, even tried to force her way in. Drakkus denied her entry into the chapterhouse. So, she had a second medallion created for me, and made a show of giving it to me at court. The one I gave him is that one. It has my name on it. No paladin will deny them care if he shows it to them." Reaching into a small pouch that hung from his saddle horn, he pulled out another one and put it on. "This one is the one Garret presented me with."

"He was there, when you took your vows?"

Jinaari looked at her, smiling. "Much like Keroys was there to accept yours. Our Gods saw something in us long before we saw it ourselves."

"What's in the bag?"

Jinaari's face darkened, and she saw the muscles in his jaw move. "I'll explain tonight, when we stop."

She ducked, avoiding a low hanging branch. "Why not now? It's not like we're being chased."

"I have my reasons," he replied. "I'm not trying to put you off. I will tell you. But I don't want to repeat myself. I'd rather make sure we're all settled, and I have everyone's attention."

She laughed nervously. "You make it sound like it's a matter of life or death."

"It is."

Her head snapped toward him. "What? Whose?"

His dark eyes held hers. "Yours."

TWENTY-FIVE

Jinaari kept his eyes open, scanning the forest around them. At the same time, he analyzed Thia's every word, each shift in her posture as they rode. *Helix said it'd worked. She told me she felt like part of her was numb, and it was keeping her guest at bay. That doesn't mean it won't change before we stop. Before I give her the choice.*

Adam's hand went up, and he pulled his horse to a stop. "It's getting dark," the warlock said. "Should we make camp or do you want me to make some light?"

Glancing at Thia, he saw her rub her hand against her arm. *She's getting cool, even with the fever.* "Find a good place. A traveling light is going to draw more attention than a fire will."

"There's a clearing up ahead. It should work." Adam urged his horse forward.

"Come on," he said to Thia. "Let's get the tents up, eat."

"Then I get to learn your secrets?"

He heard the irritation in her voice. "Yes. I have my reasons. You know that."

She sighed. "I do. It's just . . ." her voice trailed off.

"Just what?"

"I'm tired, that's all."

"Tired of what?"

"If I told you I was tired of chasing hope, would it make sense?"

Jinaari nodded. "It does. Don't give up, Thia. This is going to work. I know it will." *It has to!*

"It's hard to have hope when I don't know the whole story, Jinaari."

"You trust me, right?"

"You know I do," she said with a sigh. "It's just . . . I thought we all agreed to no more secrets? Yet here we are. You have one. Adam has one. And I'm following blindly, unsure of anything besides you being convinced my life's in danger. From what? My guest? There's no way to know if we'll find the grotto, or even that the Gods will help."

Reaching out, he put a hand on her arm. "I know it seems like we're keeping secrets, but we also told you when we'd tell you. Adam's waiting until we're back in Almair. It's possible that Helix put a *geas* on him. He may face a higher price than he already paid if he tells you earlier. As soon as the tents are up and a fire's going, I'll tell all of you mine. The others don't know this, not completely. I know you're frustrated, Thia. I've never risked your life needlessly. I'm not going to start now."

"Setting me up to release Corse wasn't risking my life needlessly?" Her tone was sharp, but not without reason.

"I can't defy Garret any more than you can Keroys."

She slumped in her saddle. "I know," she said. "And I wouldn't expect you to. Like I said, I'm tired." Her focus shifted and he saw her look ahead of them. "Let's get those tents set up. I'll grab my coat, warm up around the fire. That should help."

"You should eat something, too." Jinaari urged his horse forward, staying alongside Thia.

"I'm not hungry." The words barely reached his ears.

"She's still sleeping, but I can tell she's trying to fight back. You'll probably need to restrain me somehow while I sleep." She spurred her horse to a trot, moving far enough ahead of him that he wouldn't be able to talk to her.

Watching her back as they headed toward the clearing, his heart sank. *The choice is still hers. It has to be. This is different than the cage. I wasn't forbidden from telling her, giving her the choice. But which one will you choose, Thia? Gods, I hope it's not the wrong one.*

Riding out of the trees, he could see Adam at work on one of the tents. His blonde head looked up as Thia rode closer. Taking her reins, he held the horse as she dismounted. "I've almost got one tent up," the warlock said as Jinaari got closer.

"Thia, find your coat before you give him a hand. Caelynn's got the other one on her horse. I'll get the fire going, make sure we're not sitting on the ground."

"We know the drill, Jinaari," Caelynn said from behind him as he dismounted. "After all these years, you still forget we know what we're doing."

"Because he's an arrogant prick," Thia said as she threaded her arms through her coat. The sparks danced at the edges of her fingers; small dots of light in the encroaching night. "He needs to remind us he's in charge."

Jinaari bit back his response. *She's not herself. Arguing with her won't matter.* Without breaking stride, he walked over to a small circle in the grass. "Looks like someone's camped here before," he said as he began to clear away the stone circle. "I'll have a fire going soon."

The others got to work, and he did the same. Once the fire was going, he hung an iron pot from a tripod. There was enough dried beef and vegetables in his pack to make a warm dinner for all of them. If he'd learned anything over the years, it was not to overcook.

"Get your bedroll set up," Adam said as he came up behind him. "I'll finish this up."

"Thanks," Jinaari muttered. Straightening up, he watched Thia come out of one. He walked over to his horse and began to untie his pack and bedroll. Without hesitation, he took it into the one she'd exited.

Removing the bag Helix had given him, he tossed it on her bed before setting up his own. Once he was done, he grabbed it by the strap. Opening the flap, he saw the vials nestled in protective pockets. Eight doses of the poison that would keep Valtikka at bay while slowly killing Thia.

"There's not enough in here, Helix. You said it could take up to ten days to get to the grotto."

The mage nodded, "This is all I had time to create. You'll have to move fast, push her harder than you ever have. You know what's at stake, Shield. Will you honestly risk every person in Avoch for her? Would she even want you to?"

"Food's ready," Adam's voice pierced through the memory.

"I'm coming," Jinaari replied. He closed the bag and ducked out of the tent.

The rest were huddled around the fire. Above them, the cloudless sky had darkened enough to allow thousands of stars to shine. The moon, full and bright, was half hidden by Mathaireil. The mountain dominated the landscape. Maybe they were closer than he thought.

"It's impressive," Caelynn said. Her voice jerking him back to the fire. As he settled on an old log they'd found, she continued. "This is holy ground, you know. All the old stories and songs say so. We can hunt for food, but that's it. Nothing here should come for us, either. You probably won't need your armor."

"You should wear it anyway," Thia said as she pushed a

spoon around in the bowl she held. "Just in case the other one gets violent. I don't want to hurt any of you."

"You asked me earlier what was in this bag," Jinaari said, as he set it down on the ground between them. Caelynn handed him a bowl, and he waved it off. "Later. Right now, Thia needs to make a choice."

"Let's take a walk, Caelynn," Adam said as he started to rise.

"Stay," Jinaari said. "You two should hear this, too." He waited until they were settled again. "Thia's right about something. I've often told her to trust me but kept parts of the puzzle from her at the same time. When I was Samil's prisoner, I realized it was wrong. Thia," he turned toward her, "you've spent your life letting other people tell you what should happen. Allowing them to make decisions for you instead of raising your voice, making your own choices. I'm not talking only while you were in the cloister, either. Up until I was captured, until you were forced to take the lead, you've let us do the thinking. Yet you've proven to me, multiple times, that you have not only the intelligence but the right to make decisions about what you really want."

"You're better at tactics than I am," she began to say.

He held up one hand, silencing her. "You're right. I am. That doesn't mean you have no say in anything." He paused. "I can't make this decision for you. Not this time. I'm having trouble reconciling how much of what I saw, who I talked to, was real during my captivity. I've sworn oaths, more than one, to keep you safe. For me, that always meant alive." Pointing to the bag, he continued, "Helix gave you something last night. I don't know when or how, but he did. It's why your guest has been sleeping. There's eight vials of it in there. You'll need to take it every night if you want to keep her from preventing us from getting to the grotto. And we'll have to push hard.

There's a chance we'll run out of the potion before we arrive if we don't."

Thia looked at the bag. Reaching down, she opened the flap and pulled one out. "What else?" she asked as she looked at him.

"It's a poison, Thia. Taking it will keep your guest asleep, but it will kill you. The more you take, the faster it acts. Your magic will channel toward keeping you alive, and nothing else." He locked his gaze on her lilac eyes. "There were only two options to get you free of this. One was off the table, because we killed Lolc Aon. She can't reverse the spell she did to trap your guest. The other is the grotto. If we can't get the Gods to agree to help, we're out of options."

Trust filled her eyes, but a shadow of sadness passed over her face. "What happens if they won't? Or if I die from the poison before we get there?"

"The other one will take you over, have access to your stores and every sigil you've ever thought of. And she's spent a long time in the scepter, working on her revenge. Helix believes she'd burn Avoch down, turn it into a barren wasteland. There's only one way to stop her, but that would mean your death as well." He pulled his sword out, resting the blade across his lap. "Helix tried to get me to kill you as you slept, but I refused. I won't do that, not until there's no hope left."

Thia lowered her head, looking at the vial in her hands. "So, my choice is to take poison daily, and hope that we find the grotto and can convince the Gods to get rid of her. If I don't, then I could be taken over by her at any time. And you'll have to kill me to keep me from slaughtering everyone in Avoch. What happens if the Gods refuse or the poison kills me first?" She looked at him.

"Then I have to stop her from taking you over. And the only way to do that is drive my sword into your heart." He stared at her. "I don't want to do that, Thia. Please don't ask me to, not unless there's no hope left."

Swiftly, she uncorked the vial and raised it to her lips. Her face scrunched up at the taste. Adam handed her a waterskin. Taking it, she drank some before giving it back. Turning to Jinaari, she said, "Now there's seven vials. If I run out and we haven't found the grotto, I need you to promise me you'll end this before she can take control. I will not be responsible for the carnage she'd inflict. Make it swift, for both of our sakes."

His mind reeled from her words. The same ones he'd said to her outside of Cirrain. "If that is your decision, I will abide by it."

"No, we can't do that!" Caelynn interjected. "Thia, you can't give up. You're my sister. I've waited centuries for you to fill that void. Please, don't give up this easily."

"I'm not," she replied. "I'll take a dose every night, where each of you can see me do it. Jinaari can carry the bag. We push hard, ride as long as we can. When we get to the cave, we'll go inside. We'll talk to the Gods. But I can't let her take control of me, either. It'd be worse than anything Drogon would've done. It would make any new version of Lolc Aon I would've given birth to seem tame. This guest of mine has nursed a hatred against the other Gods for so long, Caelynn. Her vengeance would be . . . I can't describe it. It's that horrific. I know this. I've spent months now trying to convince the world that the Thahion aren't all evil. That there's more to them than what Lolc Aon forced them to act like. More than the surface world understands. How can I turn my back on that? How can I choose to let everyone die, knowing I could've saved them by Jinaari giving me a clean death?"

Adam cleared his throat. "What happens next, Jinaari?" His voice was subdued.

"We rest. I'll take third watch. Once the sun begins to rise, I'll wake the rest of you. We're going to push as hard as the horses can go. Thia," he looked at her, "let me know if you start feeling worse. The way Helix was talking, it'll take a few doses before things get bad. Once they do, though . . ." he began to say.

She nodded. "They're going to get worse fast. I understand." Rising, she looked at the three of them. "I'm going to bed." Without another word, she walked over to the tent and disappeared.

Reaching down, Jinaari picked up the bag and slung it across his chest. Adam grabbed the empty vial off the ground and handed it to him. "Might want to keep that," the warlock said. "I'd hate for there to be a residue in there that someone finds by accident."

Jinaari nodded and placed it in with the others. "You two can decide who gets what watch. No more than two hours each. The last thing we need right now is a lazy day."

"Agreed. Which means you'd best get some sleep too, old man."

He rose and walked to the tent. Ducking inside, he secured the flap. Thia was curled up on her bedroll. Her body shook as muffled sobs reached his ears.

Laying down next to her, he pulled a blanket off his pallet and threw it over the both of them. One arm circled her waist, and he held her close. "I don't understand," she muttered through her tears. "Why can't I be happy? Why is there always something or someone who demands more?"

"I don't know," he said. "I wish I did. You've met every challenge head on, though. Rose above them. You'll do the same with this one. You're too stubborn not to."

Her body shifted as she laughed slightly. "I'm tired of rising up, Jinaari. I really am. I thought I finally had a handle on everything. I could actually live a life, be with you and the others, and not worry about what will happen tomorrow. Except now tomorrow is coming fast. I don't want to die."

Her final words came out as a whisper, and his heart broke at the pain in her voice. "It's not happening. Not as long as I can prevent it. I'm not giving up hope yet, Thia. We take this one day at a time, same as we always have. We'll get up tomorrow, pack down camp, and ride as long as we dare. We keep doing this until we find the entrance."

"And then what do we do?"

"We go in. We find the grotto, and we convince the Gods to take care of you. Separate your guest from you for good."

"But what if they say no?"

"They won't." He kissed the back of her head. "Keroys Marked you. He won't let you die that easily. The others won't, either. They put forth the effort to tell us they didn't blame us for Lolc Aon's death, remember? And Volk said they all were on the verge to go looking for you if I hadn't found you, coaxed you out of the nightmare. The world is a better place with you in it, Thia. The Gods know this. I can't believe they'll allow your guest to take you over."

She rolled over and faced him. "You really believe that?"

"I do." He pushed aside a strand of hair. "I'm not giving up on you, not without a fight. I know how stubborn you can be. Tonight, yes. It feels like everything's closing in around us. Like every single bad thing in Avoch is determined to make us fail. But it's not in you to surrender to the pressure any more than it is in me."

She lowered her head, resting it on his chest. Holding her even tighter, he whispered, "Trust me. I'm not going to let you go without a fight."

CHAPTER
TWENTY-SIX

The first rays of light shone through the small opening of the tent. Thia sighed, giving up on sleep. Any minute now, Jinaari would come in and chastise her because she hadn't slept that night.

Or any since she started taking Helix's elixir.

Taking a deep breath, she cringed as her lungs spasmed in pain. "That's new," she muttered.

"What's new?" Jinaari asked.

Sitting up, she looked at him as he entered. "It hurts to breathe," she said as he knelt in front of her.

"You look horrible," he said, gently brushing aside some hair. "You haven't slept in days." His face changed. "I hate seeing you like this, Thia. Maybe you should skip a dose of the potion."

"No. I can't. If I do, she'll come back. I'm not risking your life, or theirs, to get a few hours of sleep." Wincing, she glanced at her chain shirt. It was in a ball on the ground, where she'd let it fall the night before. "I can't wear that anymore," she said in a whisper. "It's too heavy."

"I saw the bruises on your shoulder last night." His eyes

held her, and her heart broke at the pain she saw in them. "You've lost so much weight that your tunic's too big. I don't like this, Thia."

"I don't, either. But I'm not ready to give up and have you put your sword in me." She looked down, grasping his hands in hers. Meeting his eyes again, she said, "You know why I asked you to do it, right? I can't live with what she'd do if she controlled me. She'd make sure I saw everything, experienced the terror she'd inflict." Her voice broke. Ignoring the pain, she took a deep breath and continued, "I'd become something worse than I would've been if I'd given into Lolc Aon's demands. I can't live that way, be responsible for that much death."

"I understand." His deep voice was barely above a whisper. "I don't like it, but I understand it. More now than when Keroys asked me to do the same thing, because this is your choice."

"I've got to talk to Adam and Caelynn. I'm not sure they see it that way. I can't," she paused, "I can't die   "

"You're not going to die. Don't say that. We're finding the grotto, convincing the Gods."

Her spirit soared at his insistence. "I can't accept the potential outcome if things aren't right between the two of them and me. Not and be at peace with it."

He nodded. "When we get started, ride up with Adam for a while. Talk to him first. Of the two, Caelynn's the one likely to try and get you to change your mind." Smiling, he said, "I know better. You're too damn stubborn."

"I'm not the one who tried to do magic without the necessary stores for, what did you tell me, six months," she teased him.

"That was out of my arrogance, my drive to be the best." His face shifted, becoming serious. "I will do as you've asked me, Thia. I gave my word. But I will also do everything I can to prevent it from being necessary. I won't lose you without a fight. Trust me."

"Always," she said. "I'm not surrendering to her. I'll fight until my last breath. That's why I'll take a dose again tonight, even if it means I can barely walk tomorrow. That's my vow to you."

"Horses are saddled," Adam said from the doorway. "All that's left is what's in here, and the tent."

"Hold on," Jinaari said. Looking at her, he continued, "Go. We'll pack everything up."

Thia thought about arguing, but the pain made her rethink her words. Rising, she picked up her belt and began to wind it around her waist. Pulling it snug, she realized the loose end was significantly longer. *Jinaari's right. I have lost weight.* She adjusted how the pouch and scepter rested against her hips, trying to alleviate the pressure. There were bruises forming on more than just her shoulders.

"Thia?"

She looked up, meeting his gaze, "Yeah?"

"How are things with you?"

"Not good, but I've handled worse."

Jinaari pointed to the scepter. "Is it too heavy?"

"Not yet." She walked out of the tent, choosing her steps carefully. *He's worried enough*, she thought. *He doesn't need to know I'm dizzy. Him knowing won't change it.*

Adam stood near the entrance as she emerged, the same concern on his face as Jinaari wore. "I'll get you on your horse," he said, gently taking her arm. Caelynn held the reins, one hand caressing the mare's nose. "How are you feeling this morning?"

"I won't lie," she said, "I've felt better."

The warlock linked his hands, ready to boost her into her saddle. "You've looked better. I know Jinaari wants to push hard, but it's taking a toll on you."

Settling onto the seat, Thia moved the scepter so the weight was distributed evenly. "I agree with him, Adam. We don't have time to wait for me to feel better. It's not going to happen until we get to the grotto."

"I'll go help Jinaari," Caelynn said, her voice thick.

Thia watched her walk away. The bard hadn't looked at her directly when she'd gotten to her horse. In fact, she didn't look her way at all.

"She's scared," Adam said, his voice full of concern. "She's trying to hide it; not let you know. You've got enough to worry about and she doesn't want to add to it."

"I need to talk to her, Adam. When we're camped tonight. Can you make sure we have the time for that?"

"There's a cabin on the way, within walking distance of the entrance we're looking for. We'll be there before dark. It'll be a good place to rest. You'll have plenty of time to speak with her there."

"And you didn't tell us about this last night because?" Jinaari asked as he walked toward the horses. In his arms was the canvas for the tent. Caelynn followed behind with the poles. Thia's pack was slung across her back.

"Would you accept that I wasn't permitted to?"

Jinaari looked at him. "Helix?"

Adam nodded, "Helix. I couldn't say anything until we were within a day's ride. It's well stocked, secure, and comfortable. We'll be able to eat our fill, rest without needing a watch. There's a barn where we can leave the horses. You three can start to relax. I'll ride out, find the grotto's entrance. Once I know where it is, I'll come back. Tomorrow morning, we take our packs but leave the horses and I'll transport us to the spot." He glanced up at Thia, "The effects are likely to be worse for you, but it's the fastest way to get you there."

"I'll be fine," she replied. Smiling, she continued, "Just be ready to catch me in case I pass out."

"I thought you weren't some pampered noblewoman who would faint if she stubbed her toe," Jinaari said, a grin on his face, as he walked closer. "Don't worry," he put a hand on her knee. "I won't let you fall." Turning toward Adam, he continued, "She'll ride up with you for a while. I want to go over what to do when we find this cabin of yours with Caelynn."

"Can't I hear that?" Thia asked.

His dark eyes met hers. "Not as long as I'm in charge of your safety, no. You've said it yourself, more than once. I'm better at tactics than you are."

"Adam said we won't have problems tonight, though. That no watch is needed."

"It's not safe until I know it is, Thia. Besides," his voice dropped to a whisper, "this gives you time to talk to Adam."

"I've got everything secured," Caelynn said from her horse.

Thia watched Jinaari mount his horse. He nodded at her, and she urged her horse forward.

They rode in silence through the valley. The tall grass was covered in dew. The tiny droplets shimmered like small gems, evaporating into mist as the rays warmed the water. *There's so much beauty around us*, Thia thought, *that will go missing if she wins. We may be the only ones who ever see this, but it matters. Everything and everyone in Avoch, including those who think like Bryant do, matter. I don't want to die, Keroys. But I can't let her destroy the world either.*

She raised her head. Not far ahead of her, she saw Adam look back at her. Spurring her horse to move faster, she drew up alongside him. "How far will we be riding today?"

"The distance is going to be tricky," he said. "We're going to see the cabin hours before we reach it. The terrain's rocky, so we'll have to keep the horses to a walk."

"I understand," she said. "I trust you, Adam."

"Even after learning about my mission?"

Thia laughed. "I admit, it made me mad." She paused, then looked at him. "I said some things I shouldn't have said, that I regret. I hope you can forgive me for them."

"It wasn't all you, Thia. Samil's embedded spell amplified what you were feeling. And we didn't have Jinaari with us. You were off-balance before I said a word. I know you were mad," he flashed a grin at her, "but there's nothing you said that warrants an apology. I've had people," he pointed behind him where Jinaari and Caelynn rode, "say far worse to me."

"We're good, then? You and I?"

Adam looked at her, puzzled. "We always have been, Thia. Why would you ask that?"

"It's just," she paused, searching for the right words, "things have the potential of going bad for me. More than Jinaari wants to admit they could. I can't . . . go into what could lie ahead of me and not know things are right between me and my family."

"That's why you asked me to make sure you could talk to Caelynn tonight, isn't it?"

Thia nodded.

"I'll make sure it happens. I think it'll put her mind at ease, too. As to you and me, I'm going to tell you the same thing I told Jinaari when he learned about my mission. By the time I knew whose Mark you bore, you were family. I was ready to die before I let anyone hurt you. I still am. But," he said with a sigh, "I understand why you asked Jinaari to do it if it needs to happen. Same as I understood why you would if our gamble to free him didn't work. Does that help you?"

"It does."

"Good. Because that's not going to be easy to cross."

Thia looked ahead to where he pointed. The wide chasm was dotted by dead trees and jagged rocks. A narrow band of water snaked through the bleak landscape. At the end, a lone building stood.

"How do we even get down there?"

"Good question," Jinaari said as he rode up next to her. "Adam?"

"Over there." The warlock pointed to her right. A narrow trail had been cut into the rocky ground. Steep switchbacks wound down to the canyon's floor. Adam's warning earlier about it taking hours to get to the cabin made sense.

"Adam, you have the lead," Jinaari said. Looking at Thia, he continued, "How are things with you?"

"I can ride. There's no way we're taking that faster than a walk. I won't fall off."

He nodded. "Let me know if you need help. I'll be behind you, as close as the terrain lets me be. Adam?"

The blonde man turned his horse toward the path, and Thia followed.

The sun was high in the sky by the time they reached the bottom. Sweat ran down Thia's back. Raising the waterskin to her lips, she drank deeply while waiting for Caelynn to join them. "Can we refill our supply from the stream?" she asked Adam.

He looked at her, his blue eyes concerned. "There will be plenty waiting in the cabin. What's wrong? You're flushed."

"It's so hot down here," she muttered. She unbuttoned her coat and started to pull it off. The fabric of her tunic clung to her damp skin.

"Only it's not," Adam said. "Jinaari!"

Thia closed her eyes, trying to push away the wave of nausea that swept over her. "I can still ride," she said.

"The fever?"

She opened her eyes and met Jinaari's. "Yeah. It's worse."

"I can see that. You're sure you can ride?"

Nodding, she grasped the reins tighter. "Stay close, though."

"I will," he promised. "How much farther, Adam?"

"Another hour, two at the most. The terrain's too rocky to move the horses any faster, but we're through the hardest part."

"Go as fast as you dare," Jinaari ordered.

Thia looked at him as he moved his horse closer. "How many vials are left in the bag?" she asked.

"Two."

"How many days will we spend walking once we find the entrance?"

He locked his gaze on her. "I don't know."

He didn't say anything else, but he didn't need to. She understood what he meant. One dose tonight, one the next night if they don't find the grotto before they have to rest. After that, her time would be measured in hours and minutes. Blinking away tears, she focused on Adam's back as he led them through the canyon. *I don't want to die, Keroys. Not yet.*

Neither do I, Thia.

"Jinaari."

He grabbed at the bridle of her horse. "What's wrong?"

"She talked to me." Thia said. "She doesn't want to die, either." She drew a deep breath, cringing in pain. "She's gone now. She's scared, though. I know Adam said this place is safe. I don't think whoever built it considered the danger being within someone taking refuge."

"When we get there, Caelynn and you will stay outside. Adam will do what he needs to do while I check inside. That gives you time to talk to her. Get you settled inside, then we'll start taking care of the horses once Adam's back. One of us will stay with you at all times. If you need us to, we'll restrain you."

"I'll let you know. I promise." She looked around. "I wonder what killed off the trees."

"I'm sure you could ask a historian in Cirrain or Almair," Jinaari's tone was calm, "when we get back. Several would want to interview us. Few know of the grotto any more, let alone get there and come back."

"Are we all coming back, though?"

"Yes, Thia. We're all coming back."

The quiet assurance in his voice washed the fear within her aside. Touching her heels to her horse, she urged it to keep pace with Adam. The cabin was a benchmark; a place of rest, but the last one before things got even worse.

An hour later, they rode up to the front steps. Jinaari dismounted, then reached up to help her. "There's a bench on the porch," he said. "Once you're sitting down, I'll go inside. Caelynn?"

"I'll stay with her."

Adam turned his horse around. "I'll be back as soon as I can. The entrance isn't far." He set off at a trot.

Thia sank onto the bench. Caelynn leaned against the rail across from her while Jinaari disappeared inside. Looking up at the bard, she said, "There's room if you want to sit down."

Caelynn crossed her arms across her chest, her pink curls dancing as she shook her head. "I've been sitting for too long. Standing, and not moving, feels good."

"We need to talk," Thia said, keeping her voice soft.

"I know what you want to say," Caelynn replied, her voice thick. "I don't disagree with your decision, Thia. You're the only person I've ever met that was a match for Jinaari in doing the right thing, no matter the personal cost. Just because I understand it doesn't mean I like it. I hate it. And it's not that I hate you. It's that I hate that you're in this position, that the Gods finally gave me back the family they promised me centuries ago only to tear it apart. Again." She swiped at the tears that fell down her face.

"I don't want to die, Caelynn. I haven't waited as long as you have, but you three are my family. The only one I've had since Papa died. I spent the last seventeen years feeling like I couldn't breathe without asking permission first. Hiding who I was more than what I was, burying myself so deep that I didn't believe I could ever let my true self out without being hurt. As much as I complain about the Mark, the role of Scepter, I know they're part of who I am. Who I've always been. I wouldn't be who I am without you. The only reason I'm not curled up in a ball, crying my eyes out from fear, is because you've shown me I'm stronger than that. I need that more than ever now. So does Jinaari. If he has to do what I asked him to do, I'll feel better knowing you and Adam are there to help him after it's over. Same as you would've been there for me if things hadn't gone right outside of Cirrain."

Caelynn nodded. "I love both of you, Thia. Adam and I were apart for so long, but at least I knew he was still in Avoch, somewhere, and alive. Please don't give up. I can't bear . . ." her voice trailed off as her eyes grew wide.

"What's wrong?" Thia asked. Her body shuddered and heaved, making her fall off the bench.

Give me control! I won't let you kill us! Valtikka's voice screamed in Thia's head.

This threw her head back, screaming in pain, as she fought the other one for control of her body. "Never!"

Through the blinding agony, she heard Caelynn screaming for Jinaari.

I will win! And you'll watch as I tear your family apart, as the Gods did mine! You haven't known pain until your connection to your stores is severed!

"Drink, Thia," Jinaari's voice broke through the fog and she felt something press against her lips. As the bitter elixir entered her system, Valtikka screamed and retreated from her mind.

Thia opened her eyes. Jinaari knelt next to her, one arm supporting her back. "I'm good."

"Let's get you inside," he said as he slid his arms under her. "It's more comfortable than this is."

"We only have one vial left now, don't we?"

"That's all we'll need. Trust me."

"Always."

CHAPTER

TWENTY-SEVEN

"Adam," Jinaari said, keeping his eyes on the darkness ahead of them, "I need more light." The tunnel was pitch black, making it impossible to see beyond the first five feet.

"On it," his friend said. Moments later, the gauntlet's glow increased. "How's that? Need me to make it brighter?"

He shook his head. "No, that should be good." He saw farther into the tunnel now; no bends or offshoots. That would make it easier on Thia.

She leaned against him, and he knew it was only his arm that kept her from collapsing. She'd taken the last dose when they stopped the night before. The potion kept Valtikka at bay, but it had taken everything shred of strength from her as well. "Not much farther," he whispered.

"You said that yesterday," her voice cracked with exhaustion. How long had it been now since she'd slept? The fever raging through her body made it impossible to sleep. At least he'd been able to get her to eat something this morning, drink some water.

"Come on," he said as he began to walk her down the

tunnel. "Everything's coming together, Thia. This is the right place. I know it is. Trust me."

"Always." It came out as a sigh as her head lifted off his arm.

He set a slow pace, trying not to tax her strength. *We have to get her there, and it's close. I know it is!* Raising his glowing hand, he led them down the corridor.

"It's perfect," Caelynn said from behind them.

"What is?" Jinaari asked without turning around.

"The tunnel. It's smooth, not a single bump or divot. Same with the floor. It's not natural, or man-made."

"Good."

"Why's that?" she asked.

Jinaari forced his voice to sound optimistic, light. "It tells me we're on the right path. This isn't a normal place we're looking for."

"And here I thought Adam and I were supposed to do the thinking," Thia teased him. She made a sound that almost sounded like laughter before it descended into a coughing fit.

Jinaari stopped and waited for her to catch her breath. "Adam," he said, "help Thia."

The warlock walked up to him, his arms circling around Thia's emaciated body, and letting Jinaari get his arm free. "What's wrong?"

"Nothing," he said. "I want to scout ahead, make sure the path doesn't have any rocks she can trip over." He put a hand under Thia's chin and raised her head. "Look at me."

She did as he instructed; the spark hadn't left her pale lilac eyes. "Don't leave me," she whispered.

"I'm just looking ahead. Adam and Caelynn are here. They'll take care of you until I get back. I'll stay within shouting range." He stepped back, locking eyes with Adam. He was as worried about her as Jinaari was. They both were.

Turning around, he strode down the tunnel. It bent to the

left, and he noticed the light coming from the opening ten feet away from him. Staying in the shadows, he saw lightning bounce off thousands of embedded crystal shards. It illuminated the chamber. A tiled floor surrounded a pool, with what appeared to be a set of steps leading down into the water. In the center, rising from the depths, was a raised stone altar. Seven marble platforms, wide enough for someone to stand on, rested on the surface of the liquid. Each one was within arm's reach of the altar.

Relief flooded through him. They'd found it. He turned around and ran back to the others.

"It's there," he said as he approached. "Exactly as we were told." He eased Thia away from Adam. "We get inside, then you take her again while Caelynn helps me get my armor off. I'll take her out to the bier."

"Why can't you leave it on?" Caelynn asked.

Jinaari looked at her, "Lightning's bouncing off crystals to illuminate the chamber. The armor will attract it, and she can't absorb that kind of a hit."

"I'll be okay," Thia said.

He shook his head. "Don't argue. Not this time." He adjusted his hold, making sure he had her firmly but not where he'd hurt her. *She's nothing but skin and bones now. There's not much time left.* "Ready?"

He felt her head nod slightly. Glancing at the others, he began to walk her toward the grotto.

Guiding her to the right as they entered, he stopped and waited. "It's beautiful," she said.

"This is going to work, Thia," he said.

"If it doesn't . . ." her voice trailed off.

"Don't," he said. "It's going to work. Let Adam help you while I get rid of the armor." Jinaari waited until his friend had wrapped a supporting arm around her. Sliding his pack off his back, he let it drop to the ground. Caelynn began to unbuckle the shoulder pieces. "I'm not worried about it being banged up," he said as he tossed a gauntlet to one side. "Just get it off of me as fast as you can."

As he started to unbuckle one of his elbow guards, he glanced over at Adam and Thia. She seemed to have shrunk since they got into the mountain. Her blonde hair, damp with sweat from the fever, no longer curled. Instead, it hung in dark strands that reminded him how sick she'd become.

"What about your sword?" Caelynn asked.

"It stays." He looked toward the lake. If something was out there, ready to attack, he needed to have it. Or if he couldn't convince them to help her. *They're going to do this! I have to make them understand!*

"Thia!" Adam said, concern in his voice.

Jinaari looked their way. She'd slumped to the ground and Adam was trying to help her up. The last piece of armor came loose and he dashed over. "What happened?" he asked as he knelt in front of her. Her chest still rose, but it was shallow.

"She collapsed, slid right out of my arms."

"Thia?"

Her head moved, but her eyes stayed closed.

Reaching out, he put his arms under her back and legs, picking her up as he stood. He stared at Adam. "Stay with Caelynn," he instructed as he walked toward the pool.

He got to the first step and looked into the water. It was crystal clear. The lightning reflected off the iridescent white tile at the bottom, making it impossible to know how deep it was. Methodically, he stepped down into the pool. The water came halfway up his thighs; rushing over the tops of his boots. The ends of Thia's hair dragged across the surface. He shifted his arm, drawing her head to him until it rested against his chest. "Hang on," he whispered. "We're almost there."

"And then what?" she murmured.

"And then you get cured and I can get a pair of dry socks on." Glancing down, he saw a small smile form on her lips.

The altar's surface was even with his waist. Carefully, he lowered her onto the stone. For a moment, her eyes opened. The pale lilac orbs were filled with an intense pain that tore at his heart. "Don't forget your promise. Make it fast," she whispered.

"Only if there's no other option, Thia."

He pulled his arms out from under her. One of her hands grabbed his. "Don't leave me," she said.

"Not a chance."

The lightning began to shift, drawing his gaze. It formed into a single ball of light before branching out into six thick bolts. Each one leading to one of the seven marble disks resting on the surface. The light became blinding, and he leaned over Thia's body, shielding her.

"Why are you here, Althir?" six voices said in unison.

He straightened up, looking down at Thia first. Her face was flushed from the fever, and her breathing fast and shallow. She was running out of time. Raising his head, he looked around.

On six of the seven pillars that arched around the altar stood the Gods. To his left, Garret stood. Keroys was on his right. In the center stood Hauk. Ash, Silas, and Lexi were also present. A lone pillar, between Lexi and Hauk, was empty.

"She's dying, Keroys. Your Daughter needs your aid, and that of your brothers and sister, to continue her work—your work—in Avoch." He pointed to the scepter that hung on Thia's belt. "Lolc Aon not only stole the scepter but imprisoned the soul of her Daughter within it. Thia cannot continue to do what you need her to until you get rid of Valtikka, make her whole again."

Hauk raised a hand. "For what reason, Althir, would you have us do this?"

"The scepter is a symbol of power in Avoch. None of us would have any others who follow in her footsteps be subjected to this tainted soul as well."

Silas shook his head. "For what reason, Althir, would you have us do this?"

Jinaari turned to him. "Because Avoch needs her in order to help the Thahion rejoin the surface world."

"You aren't listening to my brothers, Althir." Lexi said. "Thia is special, yes. Keroys put his Mark on her. But that is not what we have asked you."

Ash coughed. "I know I'm the youngest here, but we are dealing with your paladin, Garret. Maybe you should explain things to him."

Jinaari faced his God. "She has done so much for Avoch already, why should that not continue?"

"I agree, Althir." Jinaari's head swiveled over to Keroys. "She has done much, more than I anticipated. It's led her to the Path that Nannan first saw for her. We will rid her of the other so she can embrace that destiny."

"What do you mean?" Jinaari asked. "What destiny?"

The heads of all six Gods looked at the empty pillar. "With Lolc Aon dead, Nannan would raise her up and join us. In this way, the Thahion would have a Goddess to look up to again, teach them that there's a better life than what they've known for generations."

Jinaari looked down at Thia. *Raise her up?* His chest tightened as what they were suggesting hit home. "Does she have a choice?"

"Does it matter?" Garret snapped. "She'll be a Goddess!"

"Yes, it does," he replied, looking at his God. "She's taken on every burden thrown at her. Without question or hesitation. But she is still her own person. She's not a pawn! She has a soul, one that is needed in the world. Heal her, let her decide for a damn change, instead of constantly moving the bar!" Anger rose in him, and he turned to Keroys. "You never asked her if she wanted to bear your Mark and put conditions on her to unlock her power. She did those because that's what was right. She's questioned herself a hundred times but relied on your faith in her in order to move forward. And now, instead of letting her have a life with people that care about her, you want to move that bar again? She's still not comfortable with the role she has, the way people see her, and you want to make that even worse? She's able to help the Thahion now, in life, far more than she could being worshipped by them! Right now, she's one of them. Something they can aspire to. Make her a Goddess and it'll kill her! If you love her at all, respect what she's done, understand that stubborn nature in her, you'd at least give her a choice instead of forcing it on her!"

"Althir!" Garret said, his voice commanding his attention. "I told you before, you cannot serve two masters. I ask you now; for what reason would *you* have us do this? What hold does she have over you that makes you throw away all the training I've given you? Would you surrender your sword in exchange for her soul?"

Jinaari kept his eyes locked with Garret's as his hands went to his belt. Deliberately, he unbuckled it and pulled it off his waist. Throwing it aside, the sound of the weapon hitting the tile floor echoed in the tense silence. "My sword was yours, yes. But she holds my soul in hers. I cannot wield it with honor if I won't fight for someone I love."

The room filled with light, and Jinaari threw up his arms to shield his eyes. When it faded, the pool was gone. Blinking, he looked around. They were in the common area of their home in The Green Frog. His armor, shield, sword, and all the packs were in a pile near the door to his room.

The Gods, and Thia, were gone.

Jinaari looked at Adam. He had wrapped Caelynn up in

his arms; the woman's shoulder's shook with grief. Walking over to Thia's door, he twisted the knob and opened it.

The room was empty. On the far wall, the illusionary sea washed onto the beach with small waves.

He turned around, not bothering to close the door behind him, and went toward his room.

"Is she there?" Caelynn stared at him, tears streaming down her face. "Please tell me she's there! They can't take my sister from me!"

Jinaari paused but didn't turn around. "I don't know where she is," he said, his voice quiet. "Or what she's going to be when we see her again. If we ever do."

"We have to go back!" Caelynn cried, running over to him. "We can't leave her there, Jinaari. She belongs here, with us."

Looking past her, Jinaari met his brother's eyes. The blue ones were filled with unshed tears. Adam pulled the bard away. "Come on," he whispered, "we'll figure something out. Right now, we all need some sleep."

Walking into his room, Jinaari slammed the door behind him. Closing his eyes, he let the pain wash over him. *They took her*, he thought, *with the idea that she'd become like they are. Join them. She'll be alive, in a way.*

But not the way she wants to be. Or I need her to be.

Crossing to the other side, his hand hit the worn patch on the wall. A panel slid aside, and he walked into the hidden room. The punching bag hung from the ceiling; designed by Adam to never fall apart, no matter how many rage-filled hits it took.

In his mind, he could see the last memory he had of Thia; lying on the bier, barely alive. She'd asked him to stay there, and he promised he would.

I broke my word.

His fist went flying, driving into the side of the bag. Followed quickly by the other one. Forcing his mind to go blank, he focused only on the sand-filled canvas dummy in front of him. Each punch was filled with rage, pain, and a sense of hopelessness he'd never admit to anyone else. Ignoring the blood that broke through the skin, he kept hitting it until, exhausted, he slumped against the wall.

He closed his eyes; his breath coming out in gasps as his lungs fought to regain normal function. Tears mingled with the sweat running down his face. *It doesn't matter.*

"Are you done?"

Jinaari didn't turn toward the voice. "I failed, Adam. I promised her I'd keep her safe and I didn't."

"She's with the Gods, brother. How could that not be safe? Keroys said they'd take care of her guest. Wasn't that the goal of taking her to the grotto?"

Shaking his head, he said, "What they'll do to her... that's not who she is, not who she should be. They didn't even give her a choice. And now," he paused, "I've lost her. Everything I did to help keep her safe was for nothing."

"So, we rest and get her back."

He opened his eyes, staring at the warlock. "How? That grotto's too far for you to transport in a single trip. By the time we can get back, she won't want us there. She'll be too busy with the Thahion, setting up her church or whatever she wants to call it, to bother with us."

"I don't believe that. Caelynn doesn't believe that. And I don't think you do, either." Adam leaned against the doorframe. "You need to sleep. I've already got Caelynn in bed. Tomorrow, when our heads are clear, we'll figure this out. We may not love her like you do, my brother, but that doesn't mean we don't love her as well."

Jinaari pushed himself up, grimacing in pain. Glancing down, he saw the bruised and bloodied knuckles of his hands. *They're as beaten and battered as my heart.*

"It's a wonder you didn't break anything," Adam said. "I'm going to heal those before you get in your bed."

"Don't bother," Jinaari grunted as he walked toward the warlock. "Either they stay this way, or she heals them." Brushing past Adam, he went to his bed and sat. Pulling off his boots, he threw them into a corner. He stared at his hands, knowing his friend watched him. "The last time she was alone with a Goddess, we almost lost her. I'm scared we won't get her back a second time." The words came out as a whisper.

"The first time was Lolc Aon, drugs and who knows what else was involved, and Thia was completely unprepared. This time is different. We'll get her back, or at least have her tell us she wants to be there."

Looking up, Jinaari stared at Adam. "How?"

"That's what we need to figure out. Get some sleep. You can't rescue her if you're falling over from exhaustion." He left the room, closing the door behind him.

Laying down, he stared at the meager light from the fireplace as it created shadows that danced on the ceiling. *Adam's right. You're stronger now, stronger than any of us. Hold on, Thia. Be true to who you are. Force them to let you have a voice in this.*

TWENTY-EIGHT

t doesn't hurt to breathe. The realization was enough to make Thia take a deep breath, reveling in the normalcy of it. *The fever's gone, too.* She put her hands under her, expecting the stone bier Jinaari had put her on. Instead, her hands sunk into a soft and pliable mattress.

"I know you're awake. None here will do you harm, Thia Bransdottir."

Something about the woman's voice pulled at a memory in her mind. Sitting up, Thia looked around.

It was a cave, but not large. In one wall, a door had been placed. There were no candles, no torches, no fire in a hearth, yet the room was well lit and a comfortable temperature. A woman sat at a table; an empty chair opposite of her. On the table sat some food and a decanter filled with an amber liquid. Thia's stomach growled, but she ignored it. The woman had her full attention.

Her short hair was white, as was the robe she wore. Her skin was iridescent, constantly shifting colors in the light. Cornflower blue eyes looked at her with a mix of both compassion and curiosity.

"Nannan?" Thia said, the word barely above a whisper.

The woman nodded once. "I thought this would be a form you'd be more comfortable with, Thia. Besides, this chamber," she raised one arm and gestured around her, "is not large enough to allow me entry otherwise." She smiled. "Come and sit with me. You need to regain your strength after your ordeal. We can speak while you eat."

Pushing the blanket aside, Thia looked at her waist. Her belt, along with her father's box and the scepter, were gone. Her heart began to beat rapidly. "The scepter . . . my box . . . where are they?"

Nannan pulled the stopper out of the decanter and poured some of the contents into a crystal goblet. "In the next room, with your family. Come, eat something."

"My family? Jinaari and the others are out there?" Thia rose, glancing at the door as she walked toward the table. *Maybe I heard things wrong when I was sick and on the bier. Maybe it was all a fever dream, another night terror.*

"You misheard me, Thia. I said your family, not your friends. They were sent home, to continue their lives. Keroys and the other Gods severed the link between you and the scepter. They're currently pulling Valtikka's soul from it. When they're done, and it's safe, everything but the scepter will be returned to you. That will be returned to Avoch and given to another worthy soul to assist the Crown and Shield."

Thia sat, stunned. A single tear escaped her eye, and she didn't try to stop its path down her face. "How long ago did they leave?"

"Time is irrelevant here, Thia. We move in our own ways. You will learn to control this. But, if it helps, they arrived in Almair a few hours ago. I have no doubt they're resting from their ordeal to accompany you here. A noble one that should be rewarded, but I leave that up to Garret and Lexi to determine."

"They're gone, then? I won't see them again?" The tears came faster.

"I'm sure you will, at some point. Though I caution against trying to convert them to worshipping you. It's considered bad form to poach followers that have ties to the other Gods." Nannan's tone was dismissive. "Eat something, that will help." She nudged the plate toward her.

"I'm not hungry," Thia whispered. Closing her eyes for a moment, she took a deep breath. "I don't want to appear ungrateful, as I'm not. I understand the honor you bestow on me. But I don't want this. Can it be undone?"

"You refuse what is offered? Thia, I have watched you for many years now. Guided Keroys into how best to encourage you to become what you are, with the idea that you would be the one to reunite the Thahion with the surface world. Garret's spent countless hours directing Althir's training so that he could defeat Lolc Aon, clearing the path for your ascension. I'm offering you everything you've ever wanted. The others are out there, ready to embrace you as their sister. You would have a family, a home. A chance to make a real difference in Avoch. Is that not enough for you?"

Raising her head, she looked at Nannan. "I have a family. One that I chose, and that I trust. People I care deeply for, and that care for me. I have a home wherever I go because of them. I don't want more power. I don't want what comes with being the Scepter most days. There's days I don't want what Keroys gave me. But my friends, my family, need me to accept those roles. They've always seen me for who I am, even if I didn't. I can't lose that."

"But Keroys and the rest would love you. Can you say the same for your friends?"

Thia smiled. "We may not say it with that word, but we tell each other all the time. It's there when Adam calls Jinaari old man, or Jinaari tells Adam he thinks too much. It's in the way Caelynn worries and fusses over all of us. It's me calling Jinaari an arrogant prick, or him calling me a stubborn witch. You can love someone and tell them in a thousand ways beyond a single word.

"I was happy with Papa. I didn't ask for Keroys to Mark me, but I accepted it when I found out. I learned what he meant by the conditions he put on that power and grew into it when I was ready to accept the responsibility. My friends, my chosen family, were there every step of the way. Lending me their own strength, showing me that I was capable of doing everything I doubted I could. If not for them, I'd still be hiding in the cloister in Almair, unaware of my Mark. Unsure of myself, waiting for the day that someone had enough of my presence and put a knife in my back. To take all they've given me, all they've sacrificed while I grew into who I really am and leave them now isn't fair. To them or me."

"Do not the Thahion deserve a new Goddess? One that can show them a better way than what Lolc Aon did? Think of the good you could do, Thia. You can make them walk a better path as their Goddess."

"I'm doing that now. I'm out there, changing one mind at a time. If I'm not mortal anymore, but a Goddess that's to be worshipped, all the progress that's been made will be lost." Thia leaned forward, pressing her case. "The new God or Goddess needs to be comfortable with the role, someone who is willing to guide the entire race. One that can strive for a balance I'll never possess. I barely tolerate being in court as the Scepter; it took me weeks to not run screaming from a room if someone asked to see the Daughter of Keroys. What I'm good at is showing people, one at a time, that not everyone is limited by their bloodline. Whoever replaces Lolc Aon needs to heal all their souls while I prove to Avoch that what matters is within us, not our eye color."

Nannan stared at her, and Thia sat back; the piercing blue

gaze was unsettling, but she held strong. *You didn't bring me here to give in, Jinaari. I'm going to be as stubborn as you always claim I am.*

"If not you, then who? You've proven that you can shoulder the burden, Thia. You took on Lolc Aon, her Son and Daughter, as well as the last Demon Lord. You've got more power at your fingertips than most can imagine, yet you never abused it. Is there anyone in Avoch that you can name that you believe in your heart would be better suited than yourself? To whom would you entrust the souls of the Thahion?"

Raising her hand, she held up two fingers. "I can think of two. One is called Laith Deos. He led the delegation out of Byd Cudd to Almair and brought the scepter back to the surface. The other is a monk of Silas named Mishar. He's apprenticed to the scribes at the monastery near Tanisal. Either one would be a better choice than me. I know this." Thia lowered her head, then looked back at Nannan. Putting everything she could into her words, she said, "I have done everything that has been asked of me to this point. All I ask now is to be with the family I chose, and that chose me in return. If it means the Scepter goes to another, or Keroys removes his Mark and all that it means, then I willingly surrender either or both. I would not be the person I am now, or will continue to be, if not for their strength and friendship."

Thia kept her gaze locked with Nannan's, waiting for some kind of response. After what seemed an eternity, the Mother of the Gods nodded once. "If this is truly your wish, Thia, I am willing to grant it. On one condition."

Sitting straight in the chair, she forced her anxiety aside. *Whatever it is, I must do it.* "I agree, whatever it is."

Nannan smiled, and Thia relaxed. "That you agree without asking what it is tells me more than anything else.

Your friends are truly fortunate to have you see them as family, Thia. What you must do is leave this room and explain your decision to the Gods. If they all give you their blessing, then I will allow you to take the scepter and leave. If even one dissents, insists you remain, then that is what will happen."

Thia rose. "Thank you for understanding." With measured steps, she walked across the room to the door. *Speak from my heart, and they will listen. I must make them listen!* Pulling the door open, she walked through the opening and closed it behind her.

The six deities stood around a marble topped table. On the end closest to her sat her belt; the pouch where she kept her box still attached. In the center, within reach of the Gods, rested the scepter.

"Hello, Thia. Are you feeling better?" Keroys asked, a small smile on his face.

"Yes, in no small part because of what you've all done. Thank you." She drew a deep, cleansing breath, letting it out slowly.

"We just finished," Keroys said. He pointed to a bottle resting in front of Garret. Inside the glass, an inky black substance swirled. "Ash, please take that into Mother. She needs to dispose of it once and for all."

The youngest God grabbed it and headed toward the door. He stopped next to Thia, grinning, "Don't start the party until I get back," and left the room.

Thia felt their eyes on her, a sense of expectation in the air. "You refused, didn't you?" Lexi said.

Looking at Keroys, she nodded. "My soul belongs to you, Keroys. It has since I was born, regardless of the Mark you placed on me. But my heart is with my friends. I can do more as your Daughter, as the Scepter, than I can by joining the rest of you."

"Wait," Ash said, coming up next to her. "What do you mean? Don't you love us?"

Thia smiled at him. "I am needed by my friends, and I need them. I will forever be guided by Keroys, but my path is not an immortal one. I made my choice; Nannan has granted it if you all agree. I'm asking for the freedom to continue to make mistakes, live a life of chasing monsters and changing minds. One where I am with those who make me happy, support me, and give me strength and hope when mine fails. It's not about not loving you, Ash. It's about loving myself and my chosen family more than power. If I remain, agree to what Nannan and the six of you want from me, I will become less and less the person I know I am. I will disappear back into the shell I was in the cloister; going through the motions of living a life of purpose and never being truly happy."

The six deities had sat as she spoke. Reading their faces, she saw disappointment in some. Others showed understanding. Keroys's face shone with pride, and he smiled at her. "Much has been put upon you in your life, my Daughter. Each time, you have risen to the challenge. At first, I thought it was to get you where you would join us at this table. I now see that it was to reject this Path, and finally put your feet on one you want to walk. I am proud of who you have become, Thia. While I will miss what it would've been to have you as my equal, I look forward to seeing where your life goes from here. You have my blessing, and love." He turned to Lexi, "What say you?"

"I was looking forward to having a sister, but I can wait. It would be rude of me to promise that to Caelynn and then take you from her. You have my blessing."

Silas coughed. "I heard a name given to Nannan. I will seek this person out, let her know my thoughts on them. You have my blessing."

The eldest God, Hauk, stared at her. "I am glad that my

brother can give his Daughter what I could not give mine; peace of mind. You have my blessing."

"Pan would kill me if I took you away from him!" Ash raised a tankard high. "Give your cousin my best. You have my blessing."

Thia looked at Garret, hope surging through her. He met her glance with a scowl. "Absolutely not," he declared. "I have put up with this nonsense long enough. Do as you are told, girl! Stop trying to reach for things you were never meant to have!"

The rest of the Gods began to shout, shocked at what he said. Thia stood straight, forcing the tears to stay hidden. "For what reason do you decline your permission? I am owed that much."

He leaned forward, scowling at her. "I don't trust you. I want you here," his finger pounded the table's surface, "where I can watch what you're doing. Know you're not distracting Althir from what I want him to do."

Stunned, Thia said, "In what way do you believe me to be a distraction?"

Garret stared at her. "I know what will happen. You'll tell him he can't go where I need him to be, insist that he remain with you while you dust some silly piece of pottery. You will let his skills rot away until he's nothing but a shell of the paladin I trained him to be. It's what all women do to strong men. He's meant for better than you."

Thia chose her words carefully. "If, indeed, I wished to do that I would understand your refusal. But that is not my intent. Jinaari is who he is because of his faith in you, Garret. He is the person I trust the most, outside of Keroys. I would never tell him not to go where you would send him. On the contrary, I would pack a bag and ride with him. I would be there, ready to heal his wounds or aid him in battle, whichever was necessary. Because we trust each other. Because we believe in each other." She drew a breath, feeling her cheeks flush as she spoke. "Yes, we've shared a bed. But that doesn't mean I want him to give up who he is to earn my favor. He earned my respect and admiration because of who he is, not in spite of it. To restrict him, restrain him in any way would lessen him. Me standing here, asking for this boon, is only because he taught me to believe in myself as much as he did. His strength is mine, and mine is his if he needs it. That makes us who we are more than a shield or scepter. More than a sword or Mark. You don't have to trust me. I'm asking you to trust him."

Garret stared at her, and she didn't flinch. The silence in the room became deafening, but she stood her ground.

"Garret, you're my brother and I love you," Keroys said, his voice quiet, "but sometimes you're an arrogant prick. For once, let someone else be happy."

Sitting back, he glared at Keroys. "And you're a soft-hearted bastard." Thia caught him glance at her, the smallest hint of a smile on his face. "You have my blessing."

A wave of relief flooded through her. "Thank you," she said.

Keroys rose. Picking up the scepter, he walked toward her, grabbing her belt as well. Holding both out, he said, "These are yours, Thia. Valtikka's soul is gone. The scepter is now as it was meant to be; a symbol to unite Avoch and nothing more."

Taking the belt, Thia wound it around her waist and secured it before reaching for the scepter. As her God placed it in her hands, she realized the sense of presence she'd felt since it first came to her was gone. "Was I always meant to wield this, Keroys? Or did it only come to me because of my lineage?"

"If it wasn't meant to be you, Thia," Garret said, "then it'd still be on this table."

Her hands closed around the silver shaft. Meeting Keroys's gaze, she smiled. "Thank you, for everything."

"Go find your family, Thia. They need you as much as you need them."

The room swirled around her and disappeared.

The colors solidified and Thia began to grin as soon as her vision cleared. She knew the bar against the wall, the tables scattered around the common room, the stage near the giant fireplace. It was late in the night; no patrons were in The Green Frog.

She walked over to the staircase; one hand caressing the wood that was worn smooth from use. *I'm home.* Tears filled her eyes. *Keroys sent me here for a reason. They should be here, too.* She ran up the stairs, taking them two at a time. When she reached the landing, she slammed her hand against the keyed panel. The passage to their suite opened and she ran inside.

The common room lit up as she entered. Looking around, she saw the gear piled in a heap in a corner near her room. The door was ajar. Thia began to walk toward it, dropping the scepter onto a couch, when she heard another door open.

"Thia?" Caelynn's voice was barely above a whisper. "Is it really you?"

Turning, she put her hands on the back of a chair. "Yeah, it's me."

The pink-haired woman ran at her, crying, and Thia welcomed her embrace. "We were so scared," Caelynn sobbed, "we didn't know what happened to you."

"Thia?" Adam said.

Looking past her friend, Thia smiled at him. "I'm back."

"Thank the Gods," he said as he came closer. Thia found herself sandwiched between them. Adam was the first to pull away. "How? What happened?" he asked. "Are you okay now? What about the other one?"

"I'm fine," Thia stepped back, swiping at the few happy tears that escaped her eyes. "The Gods removed Valtikka's soul. The scepter's as it was meant to be, as your parents made it." She looked at Adam. "Where's Jinaari?"

He nodded behind her, and she turned around. Jinaari leaned against the doorframe of his room, watching them. His hands were bloody and bruised. "How are things with you?" he asked.

From the corner of her eye, she saw Adam pull Caelynn back into his room and close the door. "They're good. How are things with you?" she asked him as she stood still. There was a guarded tone in his voice that she'd never heard him use around her.

Cocking his head to one side, he looked at her. "I'm not sure. It depends on if I'm talking with the woman I know or a Goddess."

"I see," she looked down, gathering her thoughts. "It was offered, but I declined the honor." She raised her head and saw the momentary shock that played across his face. Her heart raced as she looked at him. He scrutinized her and it hit her why. *He blames himself, and I'm the only one who can help him with that.* With measured steps, she walked toward him. "What happened to your hands?"

"I, uh, got overly enthusiastic with a punching bag when we were sent back here."

"Why didn't you heal them? Or ask Adam to?" she asked, puzzled.

He looked at her, and she could see the pain he felt in his dark eyes. "He wanted to, but I told him no. They were going to stay this way until they healed. Or you could do it." He walked toward her. "You defied Nannan? And the Gods? Why?"

She formed the sigil in her mind and released the magic, healing his hands. "I don't want power. I never did. I'm not entirely sure what to do with what I have. The Thahion need someone to lead them, yes. Guide them as they move away from the shadows they used to live under. But that person isn't me. I'm needed in other ways." She stopped, inches from him, and so did he.

He lowered his head, touching his forehead with hers. "I would agree with that."

"I heard what you said, when I was on the bier."

"I meant it."

"I know you did." She paused, "Jinaari, I've never felt like I belonged anywhere, not until I met you. And I've never had anyone fight for me to have a choice in my life. I've always done what I was told to do, what I 'had' to do, until you taught me to fight for what really matters. When I woke up and Nannan told me what she wanted me to agree to, I remembered what you'd said to Garret, to Keroys. The more I listened to her, the more I knew it wasn't right. I'd still be there, doing what was expected of me, if not for you."

"You've done so much already, Thia. I'm constantly amazed at how you adapted, took on the burdens that were shoved on you. I had doubts, yes, when I first met you. Now I sit back, smile, and wait for the world to realize who you really are. Because you are the most amazing person I've ever met. Nannan sees it too, or you wouldn't be here. I know your stubborn streak; she didn't stand a chance against you."

"Nannan was agreeable, but said I had to convince the other Gods." She hesitated, trying to keep her voice steady. "All but one gave me their blessing. Any guess who the holdout was?"

"Garret?" Jinaari asked, his voice tinged with shock.

Thia nodded. "He was certain I was going to keep you from answering any call he gave you, any mission to slay a monster or such. I pointed out that I was more likely to pack my bag and come with you than stay put, pouting. Keroys called him an 'arrogant prick,' said he needed to let people be happy for a change. That's when he relented."

Jinaari chuckled, raising his head and pulling her toward his chest. "Keroys actually said that?"

Melting into his embrace, she nodded. "He did. You have no idea how hard it was for me not to laugh, either."

She felt his cheek rest against the top of her head. "I have never been happier for you to be so damn stubborn."

Raising her head, she looked at him. "Back in the refuge," she said, "you told me something."

"Can you narrow it down a bit? There were lots of things I said there." His dark eyes sparkled with laughter.

Placing one palm against his chest, she stared at it. "You said you didn't know what this was between us, that you wanted to take some time and figure it out." Taking a deep breath, she looked up at him. "I don't know what this is, either. But I know that I trust you, care about you, and being here is the only place I've ever felt like was home. I don't mean The Green Frog. I mean with you, Adam, Caelynn...it doesn't matter if we're here or sleeping on the road. It doesn't even matter if we never keep each other warm again." She felt her cheeks grow red but kept talking. "What matters is that I know you have my back, no matter what. That you've shown me I can be who I want to be, who I really am, without hiding. Whatever comes next, I can handle it because you believe I can. Your faith in me, that arrogant assurance that I'm more than what people see with their eyes, gave me the strength to tell Nannan no. I don't need anything from you beyond that. Just be my friend, even when I mess up, and I'll be happy."

His hand caressed her cheek, and she leaned into the touch. "Are you done?"

She nodded.

"I meant what I said in the grotto," he said, his deep voice sending shivers down her spine. "I've never said that to anyone before. This is one of those choices you have to make for yourself, Thia. I can't see the future. I don't know where it will go. No matter what, we're family. I will always have your back, trust that you have mine. Nothing could change that."

"What if—" she started to say but stopped when he put his finger against her lips.

"That's not the road we're on, Thia. Unless you're cooking up one of your schemes, my stubborn witch, you need to stop trying to overthink everything."

She smiled, leaning against her chest again. "You're probably right."

"Of course I'm right," he said, wrapping his arms around her. "About time you admitted it."

"Arrogant prick," she teased him.

He laughed, and she reveled in the joy the sound brought to her soul.

ACKNOWLEDGMENTS

If you've followed me on social media, you know that I'm a big Dungeons & Dragons player. I've played the game since the late 1970's/early 1980's. It's been a constant source of inspiration for books, stories, and a way for me to explore the possibilities of life. Sometimes it takes playing a character who's strong for us to find that strength in ourselves.

Since 2015, I've been playing with one group of friends. We've kept characters around while players had to leave the table for months on end and found a way to stay connected during the pandemic. These people are my chosen family. We call ourselves The Murder Hobos.

I cannot let this book end without acknowledging the members. I think it's important to let the world know who they were, and which character they brought to life at the table. While the characters have changed and evolved between the game and the plot of the books, I tried to capture the core personality of each one.

Ed Brabant – Jinaari Althir
Dale Collins – Helix Yarnchaser
Joshua Collins – Pan Beckenburg
Jillian Morgan – Caelynn
Matt Morgan – Adam
Rob Rowland – Gnat
K.M. Warfield – Thia Bransdottir

ABOUT THE AUTHOR

Born in the late 1960's, K. M. has lived most of her live in the Pacific NW. While she's always been creative, she didn't turn towards writing until 2008. Writing under the pen name of KateMarie Collins, she released several titles. In 2019, the decision was made to forge a new path with her books. The Heroes of Avoch series, along with a new pen name, is the end result.

When she's not writing, she loves playing Dungeons & Dragons with friends, watching movies, and cuddling up with her cat. K. M. resides with her family in what she likes to refer to as 'Seattle Suburbia'.

www.ingramcontent.com/pod-product-compliance
Lightning Source LLC
Chambersburg PA
CBHW061636190726
48289CB00006B/1627